Donovan Roebert is a practitioner of Mahayana Buddhism for over a decade, he has also written several religious and philosophical articles on reconciling new physics and neuroscience with the subjective human religious experience. Donovan Roebert is also a painter whose works are sold internationally, from his home in South Africa. This is his third published book.

Lama Charlie's

BIG BANG AND WHIMPER

donovan roebert

Contact Publishing

London, United Kingdom

June 2010 © Donovan Roebert
Written by Donovan Roebert

British Library Cataloguing in Publication Data.

A CIP catalogue record of this book is available from the
British Library ISBN 978-0-9547020-8-3

Cover Design by Maria Rodriguez

Contact Publishing Ltd

www.contact-publishing.com

This is the way the world ends
This is the way the world ends
This is the way the world ends
Not with a bang but a whimper.

T. S. Eliot; *The Hollow Men*

'...All your efforts to escape from the noose of your perplexity only leave you more firmly caught than before. I know of only one remedy...since you're not satisfied by the answers of the wise, take counsel of some fool...You know how many princes, kings and republics have been saved, how many battles won, how many perplexities resolved, by the advice, counsel and predictions of fools.'

Rabelais, *Gargantua & Pantagruel*

CHAPTER 1

In Which The Inner Light Reveals
Its Tendency To Sputter

We now know with reasonable certainty that we don't stand a chance. Fifty to one hundred years and we'll all be frazzled, frozen, drowned or starved. Anticipating the end of life as we know it is a painful exercise and even the fact that it comes by our own folly doesn't make it altogether funny (although, hell, something in you wants to laugh).

The fraction of the space-time continuum which I occupy in this universe is very small. Infinitesimally so. But how large I always seem to myself. I really do loom. But that's because I'm the one experiencing myself. I'm the one who knows my *angst* in the world and the fear of death, my death. In comparison with which the death of the planet seems trivial. But then, the end of the world seems trivial even when compared with the loss of my income.

I am cooped up in my motorcar, dashing across town to the Buddhist temple where I'm expected at six. It's now five-thirty, or twenty-five per cent into rush hour. I'll probably be late again. I'll arrive to the quiet susurrations of the meditating group. When I enter the shrine-room on tiptoes in my socks most of them will exhale a sigh of exasperation.

Interrupted meditators don't blow their stacks as, for instance, interrupted copulators do. There are no wild gestures and embarrassed exclamations. Only a slight tremor in the breathing, a flaring of the nostrils and the beginnings of a set of nasty thoughts arising. Then one settles in among them.

I'm thinking, God, how exhausted I am! Then I realize again for the umpteenth time that for me there's unfortunately no God to whom I can address my complaints. I can't blame *him* for the difficult life I lead. I must endure without recourse. It isn't that there's no one at home. It's just that the number doesn't exist.

The city skies are dull with evening coming on, ashen and expiring. In contrast, the traffic lights seem to twinkle festively. I'm at home on these streets, among these drawn faces huddled over steering-wheels, doors locked and windows up against the prowling criminals. This is my own warlike, terrified tribe – the whole variegated mess of it. In it I sometimes sink, sometimes swim, and expect to drown at last.

Mona (Moaner) wouldn't come today. She hadn't much of an excuse to offer; the silence of meditation was too deep for her. 'Too deep', she said, 'is not very far from too shallow.' For my part I'd have preferred the blatant truth: 'It's a bore, Charlie. I like trouble and excitement.' Like the time left to the world, my time with Mona seems to be wearing itself out too.

And when I think about it, so many things are coming to an end. For one thing, the end of my youth is upon me. All that depends on youth for its sustenance will naturally go too. Energy, clarity, confidence, the roaring libidinal ego. I'll have crossed the divide between wit and wisdom, wary of one and lacking the other. So the upshot can only be confusion.

Business has been bad lately: bank account tottering from red to scarlet. The Buddhist that I call myself should stand detached from scary debits. This is Samsara with its tricky human systems to which the average person clings as to flypaper, or thinks he clings while he's actually glued to the poison. Clinging and wriggling and, of course, slowly dying.

How did I manage to land here, for God's sake? (There *he* is again.) It's obvious though. They put some sort of perfume on flypaper, or is it a pheromone? Moth to the flame, pole to the hole, hand outstretched to the jackpot.

And here's the result, the overworked techno-dependant, squeezed in tight in the fast lane choked with cars to a crawl.

My cellphone yawps at me. The jazzed up tune was once Bach, I think. I wrench it from my twisted pocket and flip it open in defiance of the traffic laws. It's Mona, after all. Who can tell what crisis has visited her since I left the apartment twenty minutes ago? A sudden nosebleed, six volumes of the Britannica fallen on the cat, the oven on fire? But these are unlikely to have occurred a second time.

'Hello Mona.'

'Have you arrived yet, Charlie?'

There's something ominously unroutine about this routine enquiry.

'If I had, I'd be in meditation, Mona. My phone would be off.'

'You shouldn't answer it while driving.'

'Well, goodbye then.'

'God, Charlie, you can be so fricking puerile. I mean, Jesus! You really are such a wanger! You're at the point –'

'Speaking of points, Mona, can you get to yours? Then I can get off the phone, which as you rightly point out –'

But Mona has cut me off.

The woman in the yellow car is wagging a finger at me, distressed at my having got away with a cellphone offence. My instinct tells me she's a man-hater. There's such a quantity of agonized distaste in the way her eyes take hold of me, as though I were her husband.

Now Mona's calling again. I know I shouldn't do it, I shouldn't give the man-hater any reason for a keener loathing, but the timing is so perfect.

'Hello again, Mona.'

The yellow car, enraged into frantic action, makes a sudden swerve at me, then pulls back into its own lane. Then it hoots rudely, twice. Now the finger is triumphantly up, the sawing middle-finger, not the wagging index. Why does she so detest me? I can feel her anger sliding like sickness into my gut. For all she knows, I might be dealing with a real emergency. Can't she see that, if I were, there'd be no place to pull over anyway?

Mona is furious, thrashing up and down the verbal scale. Her words strike my eardrum but miss the cortex. They are walloping sounds, meaningless, while the yellow car injects its venom into me. I'm coming to the boil. Then the lid comes off.

'Go fuck yourself!' I yell, carefully mouthing every syllable at the toxic eyes in the yellow car. They widen with disgust as Mona begins to yell back.

'Not you, Mona!'

But she's rung off again. Well then, two birds with one stone.

This isn't right. The distance in my case between knowledge and action is appalling. I'm acting out of the ignorance of anger, raging at the flypaper. The yellow car is a suffering consciousness whose misery I've just increased. Moaner, in her way, suffers while she inflicts her demented whims on me. Am I not the one seeking enlightenment? Through the practice of a wiser kindness?

Not just at the moment.

Right now there's another mind in the ascendant, pissed off in its cage. I am carrying it to the balm of the Buddha, if I ever get there. And I'm transporting it, even as I speak, to the run-down old edifice that serves as the temple. It's a desperate business. It is, in fact, an emergency.

The yellow car has somehow got ahead of me; a veteran, she. I will never have the opportunity to address her irritated unhappiness, to soothe it just a little. She'll remember me as the prick with the cellphone and the dirty mouth. A gambit to fling at her husband; a conversation piece for her club of androphobes.

About Mona I don't now wish to think. No matter how vividly *she* springs to mind, she must dangle for a while outside of me. I switch off the cellphone, knowing that I'll pay dearly for it. Whatever the current crisis, it will be ratcheted up beyond all the available notches.

The last few months (how many? eight? nine?) have been passed in the wilderness where, I've come to learn, you are better off alone. Every attempt at companionship is a distraction, not only from your problems, but also from the search for solutions. Advice, even friendly advice, is trite or misleading. A dollop of the glib too. As when Paulus, who calls himself a friend, would have me 'withdraw from the field, a tactical retreat.' As though I hadn't already been forced to retreat, as I say, to the bloody wilderness. Or as when Mona exhorted me, yet again, to 'be a man'.

Ecce homo. Or, rather, *ecce unde.*

'How did I get here?' asks the bum among the dogturds in the city park. What was the first *faux pas* and (the really relevant question) what was the subtle impulse that stung the mind to turn the foot and set it off in *that* direction?

Or was it only the crassest of motivators: the penis leading one on, going before like some hilarious figurehead? Was that the whole why and wherefore of my cheating on Mona? If so, how stupid – in retrospect and in retrospect only. Nothing stupid about it at the time. No siree! It felt not at all like catastrophe.

And there seem to have been no consequences. Mona knows nothing. Not even Paulus knows. But there's the rub, hey? That I know and must go on knowing alone. *The invisible worm; the dark secret life.* How dearly I'd like to come clean! But would it be a kindness to purge myself at her expense, and to the disappointment (or delight) of those who respect me?

Not even Precious Teacher knows.

To do myself justice, I broke off the liaison very quickly. Not above thrice did I dip my wick. But thrice was enough to earn the status of recidivist.

So now I am a hypocrite, treading my path with an unhealthy complexion on the cheeks of my once rosy wisdom. It must be showing in my eyes too, and in all my deflated prattle. Sooner or later someone will catch me out. I'll be saying, 'Get up and walk on' and they'll reply, 'You first, mate.'

Turn left into the Brixton slums: people of all ages and colours hanging out on the sidewalks, slumped over their verandahs, someone pissing on the lowgrade graffiti. I am surprised to see a boy and a girl holding hands; a throwback to the age of innocence. When was that? A mere thirty years ago? I find myself nodding as though I were an innocent too. Probably the smile is at the complex charm of the sight, shot through with an unsuspected sexuality.

I enter the temple parking lot. There's Ivan's car, Darryl's, Marta's Beetle. Together they look like something you'd find at a Woodstock revival. My Merc takes on an air of staidness and authority. It looks repressive.

Then, with a pang of discomfiture mingled with glee, I recognize the yellow car and park alongside it. Karma again, much too obvious to be written off as black serendipity.

The really big golden Buddha statue (made in Taiwan) is surrounded by candles and water offerings. He gazes serenely across the meditating group, some of whom have turned about from their waists to glimpse the latecomer. So much for their undistracted absorption. I remove my shoes and plod across to my cushion, eschewing the absurd struggle on tiptoe. Muffled thuds on the wooden floor. Precious Teacher looks up. He's the only one smiling.

Om Namo Bhagavate benza sarwa pramadane, tathagataya arhate samyak sambuddhaya …

The meditative posture is comfortable except that my bony ankles always grind into the hard wood below the cushion. Sinking into my own breathing, I try to let go of my discursive mind which seems to be in the same place as my aching ankles. Mona goes, comes back, goes again, comes back; the yellow car gives me the finger. *What the hell can she be doing here?*

Eventually a languid mental *carte blanche* settles in. Not meditation but narcosis. This is all right for now; an empty space for a few minutes' refuge. Beyond the blank haze, however, the finger is up at me and the banshee's visage glares at me. I take it as the object of my meditation, study it, imbibe it.

The bell tinkles, the fuddled heads rise. A pause. Then Precious Teacher speaks:

'This world is now in very big danger. It is getting very warm and the lives of all sentient beings can go out. Yes, and yours too can go out. Very soon will be nothing can be doing. This is – how you say? – the globble warming?'

He is teaching on the most important question of the day, the grilling of the planet. I am peeking and leering about to catch a glimpse of the man-hater. And a voice is crying out inside me, 'Get your cellphone out and call Mona!' I actually fish it from my pocket and twirl it about.

There's the man-hater! Right up front at Precious Teacher's feet, in a complete shambles of a lotus position. We'll meet over tea and biscuits after the talk, no doubt. My pulse sets off. She may be one of those crazy dames who shout you down no matter what the present company: 'So you're the gentleman who told me to go fuck myself!'

I can see Paulus falling to the ground with laughter while the others look on with cringing delight and Teacher looks about puzzledly. I have to prepare my rejoinder, something immensely unruffled. But a simple 'yes' is all that comes to mind.

Yes, that's me.

Sitting immoveably beneath the Bodhi Tree, the Lord attained his enlightenment. Seeing the truth of all existence, how all exists and does not exist, and is transient, suffering and not-self, he overcame the evil one.

It will pass, mate.

'Now we hava opportunity day by day to make a difference. What can we do? So many things we can do. But first to develop a warm heart. This is very important. There's nothing without compassion you can do.'

He radiates across us all, a beautiful Tibetan, full of age, suffering and selflessness. With a gently absent nod the talk is ended. The experienced meditators rise briskly; the others wobble up on semi-paralyzed legs, trembling with relief. I just sit, noticing that the Yellow Car wobbles with a determined dignity and that Precious Teacher is making much of her. Evidently she's not a mere casual visitor.

Paulus has loitered across, sits down on the cushion beside me, legs outstretched. He's experienced without having had to learn much. For him life is such a barrel of laughs that I wonder why he's a Buddhist at all. What does he make of the first noble truth, that all life is suffering? But of course he has answered me that question long ago: 'The third noble truth cancels out the first.'

'How are you, old chap?' (Pseudo-Oxonian from Durban.)

'Who's the woman in the yellow car?'

'Someone on shore-leave from the yellow submarine?'

There's something about his silliness, about the world-weary seriousness behind it all that always impels us to cackle and hoot at the slightest provocation. So the yellow submarine sends us over the brink.

Teacher nods approvingly and Yellow Car turns about, instantaneously recognizing me. The big temptation is to give her back the finger she gave me. That should get Paulus and me rolling on the floor. But I sober up when I realize that she might be thinking we're laughing at her.

I walk over into the conversation.

'This is Merry,' says Precious Teacher, meaning 'Mary.' 'And this is Chully.' Our hands go smartly out while our confused minds stumble along behind them. A cool handshake and then she says, 'Interesting to finally meet you. Rinpoche has been telling me a lot about your work here.'

'All in the last two minutes?'

'No. We've discussed you before.'

'I'm mystified. But it's interesting meeting you too. Not that we haven't already got to know each other a little.'

Marta is tugging gently at my sleeve, mouthing the words 'I need to speak to you.' I wonder what it'll be about this time. How the ordinary mind stands in relation to the wisdom-consciousness when the wisdom-consciousness is not aware of the ordinary mind? Or will it just be a question of how the Buddha Nature can be obscured by something as puny and thin as an endless stream of silly thoughts? I smile and nod. Of course I'll talk to you. There's a little queue behind her too. I nod at them all, and they trot off to the tea-lounge.

Precious Teacher is saying something about healing the world. Apparently Merry has an important role to play in the matter. I ponder, perhaps she'll shake it all together by giving it the finger.

But Teacher is giving me to understand that I have a part to play too. A part, moreover, that involves working with Merry.

'But we speak later,' he says, 'After your talk and interviews.'

Oh yes, I have to give a talk after tea. I'm the experienced Buddhist around here, teachers *ersatz* man. My subject: The four noble truths. Before all that, however, I need to get someplace private and have it out with Mona. Whatever she's up to, I have to nip it in the bud.

The post-meditation rush for the toilet is over. I sit myself down on the cold plastic seat and call her.

'So now you want to talk?'

'Mona, now is the first time since leaving home that I *can* talk. What's up?'

'I can hardly bring myself to say it, Charlie. It sticks in my fricking throat.'

'Just say it calmly.'

(I am anything but calm right now. She can usually bring herself to say anything at all.)

'I'm more afraid of what *you'll* say.'

'I'll say whatever is appropriate.'

'That's what frightens me.'

The voice is high-pitched with pain. I'm beginning to tremble. Something awfully awful is dawning on me.

'Please, just say it.'

'You've been cheating on me, Charlie. You've been screwing around.'

I am holding on to the toilet seat.

'It's true,' I moan, 'But it's over.'

'*Over*, is it? *Ohh-verr*, you say? You must be a bigger cretin than I ever imagined if you think it's *ohh-verr*. It's only just beginning, Charlie boy!'

'Please Mona –'

I visualize my skulking mental continuum slipping through the somatic element into the toilet bowl below me.

'You thought I didn't know, you sonofabitch.'

'I hoped so Mona.'

'Of course you did.' (This with menace thicker than my dried-out tongue.)

'Why didn't you –?'

'Because until now the time wasn't right to screw you over so completely that you won't ever doubt your karma again.'

The panic these portentous words evoke has got me by the bowels. Trousers off.

'I'll be home soon. We'll talk.'

'*Home soon? Hohhmme?* You think you still got a home?'

'What do you mean?'

'You'll see, Charlie boy! You'll see when you get *hohhmme!*'

'Mona ...'

But Mona's gone.

Disbelief to the depths. It's not that I can't believe what life has just thrown at me from Mona's side. It's somehow very clear to me now that she could never not have known. What baffles belief is that I have to speak on the noble truths almost as soon as I get my trousers back up. It's too exquisite. I writhe to my feet.

In the shrine-room everyone has settled in. They've had their tea and some have popped out for a fag. Now it's all ears, waiting to be tickled. I enter limply into the atmosphere of calm anticipation.

I begin: 'All life is suffering –'

At the back a delicate white hand goes up. Can it be possible that someone has not grasped my opening line? I nod at the pretty owner of the marble hand.

'I don't sink so.'

Why must there always be a German?

'You don't think so?'

'I don't sink so because ze suffering, it's not really a good translation from ze Sanskrit, I sink.'

Silence. But no, there is a bit of a titter from somewhere in the centre. *Carpe diem.* I invite her up to explain to everyone exactly how the Sanskrit should be understood. This means a break for me, a few moments to gather up my intestines and shove them back into the hollow space they've recently vacated. There isn't much I can do about the palpitations, except adjust my breathing. But I can hardly breathe anyway.

'I sink ze good translation is ze unsatisfactoriness. There is never ze satisfaction in this life. Nobody can get this satisfaction.'

The tittering is now on the rise. But it is Paulus who brings the house down with an impromptu 'I can't get no satisfaction.' To my horror someone actually takes up the chorus 'An' I try, an' I try, an' I try, an' I try!'

'Exaktly,' says the German girl.

Somehow I manage to get through it in under half an hour. For all her absurdity, the German girl has saved my sizzling bacon. Between her efforts and the legacy of the Rolling Stones the whole idea of suffering and its remedy have been adequately conveyed. Precious Teacher looks satisfied. There is genuine happiness in the air. A good joke has been perpetrated. And in the midst of it all is terrified me.

The group begins disbanding, most of them making ready to leave. Marta and a few others are waiting to speak to me. The German girl is among them. But Teacher is indicating that he wants to see Merry and me in private. For the life of me I can't guess what's on his mind. Bright-eyed Merry evidently shares in my confusion, but for different reasons. She gives me a brisk once-over before we enter Teacher's office. 'Can't imagine what possible use anyone might have for you' her trembling nostrils seem to say.

Teacher has a problem. He's been invited to attend the Conference of World Religions on Planetary Issues. All very academic, with expansive lectures by a variety of eggheads from various parts of the dying globe. Discussion sessions, action proposals, and all the other unproductive conference activities. Sounds like a vacation in Hypothesis-Nirvana, only more obscure. No wonder Precious Teacher wants to hand it over to someone unqualified.

'His Holiness Dalai Lama teaching in Canada. I must going there same time.'

He'd rather attend His Holiness' teachings in Vancouver. I'm not surprised. But for the second time this evening I'm being bowled over by karma. Here is my chance to get away from Mona without having to brew up an escape strategy. I must have done something right. No. Probably just something less wrong.

'Where's the conference being held, Rinpoche?'

'*Perrk.*'

'Perrk?'

'Prague,' says Merry, 'In the Czech Republic.'

'Well, thank God it isn't *Perrk*.'

'Very good,' says Teacher.

'Merry knows Perrk,' says Teacher cheerfully. 'Very experienced journalist.'

'Ah, a journalist!' (That explains *everything*.)

'Ecology generally,' she clarifies, 'Gaia in particular.'

'Well now! That would explain why –' (Gad, what am I saying?)

Something in the way she lifts her eyebrows compels me to go on:

'– why you don't like people.'

How shall I describe the smile she flashes at me in response? Is it the smile of the Great White suddenly discerning your nutritional value? Or are these the twisted lips of the archetypal spouse who sees right through you to the most unappetizing parts? I am quite unnerved.

'What's my role in all this, Rinpoche?'

Merry nods in vigorous agreement.

'You will know what to do. And, you will help Merry. Chully is very helpful and very useful. Also very intelligence. He will bring back valuable report. So, you will going Chully?'

'When, exactly?'

'After two weeks.'

I bow my head to Precious Teacher.

'And Merry, she is not a Buddhist. But you will hava good understanding.'

I smile back at the Great White non-Buddhist journalist. Teacher is nodding gently at her, a sign that she is to leave us two alone. I can tell that he sees through her too, right down to the upraised middle-finger. She flashes again, an understanding smile. Can't say she ain't beautiful.

'You hava problems Chully.'

'Everyone has problems, Rinpoche.'

'But your problems very difficult right now.'

'You want me to tell you my problems, Rinpoche?'

'No. I'm not asking. I'm knowing already, Chully. I'm knowing everything.'

'Everything?'

'Mona, she told me.'

The insidious viper. Crazy cow. Dirty sodding hang out your washing in public.

'That is why you need to going this conference Chully.'

I don't pretend to see the logic. But I trust him completely.

'I'm so sorry, Rinpoche.'

'Sorry is good, but not very important. Important is to find your path, Chully.'

I love you from the depths beyond the silly places, Precious Teacher. What a pity it cannot be said. Only proven by conduct.

And into this thought drift the images of Mona, Clara and Jessica. And then the world in general.

Now for the penultimate ordeal. The one before I go errant to slay the dragon in the apartment which, I am reminded, is no longer my home. Marta is waiting with the little group. The girl who didn't sink so is lingering too. I dawdle gauchely across the threshold of the interview room. A big photo of the Dalai Lama looks down at me, scarved in a brilliant white Tibetan *kata*. Prayer-flags are nailed to the wall, defeating their purpose of flapping in the mountain breezes to scatter plaints to the Buddhas of the ten directions.

Marta follows me in and joins me on the sofa. I'm desperate for a smoke but am forced to settle for a peppermint. I look at her. She seems to be squirming and squinting a little. She enjoys a very complicated spiritual life, probably the result of a Calvinist upbringing. She has difficulty understanding predestination in terms of karmic preparation. She can't really understand why Buddhists are not generous enough to make some room for the old testament God. It takes the spice out of sinning and leaves a void where the perfume of forgiveness should waft.

'Is there something on your mind, Marta?'

'Yes Charlie. But it isn't something. Or, actually it *is* something.'

I lean forward, implying: 'Ye-e-es?'

'It's something Mona told me.'

I am now leaning so far forward that my head is almost in my lap. Swooning, I think, perhaps Mona has only plied her with some bizarre doctrinal point, knowing it would eventually land up on my plate.

'I can understand why you did it, Charlie. I really can. Mona's not an easy person. I've thought for a long time that you needed someone who'd know how to show you warmth, plain friendship, as well as all the rest. But you could have come to me. I would have known exactly what to give.'

No doubt about it. I'm being seduced beneath the picture of the Dalai Lama.

'And I wouldn't have told anyone. That's for sure.'

This is where I have to make my stand:

'Marta, get this: whatever's happened, I still love Mona. She's the only woman who will ever be able to know exactly what I need.'

It comes out with such conviction that I am forced to pause. Does my heart have reasons that my reason cannot comprehend?

No, by God, I've had it with Moaner. And I've had it with Merry. And with seductive Marta too.

'That,' I tell her very formally, 'is your answer.'

Next … next … next. Finally it's the German girl's turn. By this time I've regressed to being little more than a shallowly breathing pre-cortical hominid. My eyeballs have dried out. Henry V never yearned more deeply for the privilege of sleep.

'You are Charlie, yes? I am Ulla.'

'The Martians' war-cry.'

'No. It is short for Ulrika.'

'Of course. What can I do for you, Ulla?'

'I sink your talk is good but too much simplistic.'

'I have to consider others, Ulla.'

'I have studied Buddhism in ze Cherman university. I can help.'

'That's wonderful. I'll talk to Rinpoche about it.'

It is wonderful indeed. Here before me stands the one who will keep them on their toes while both Teacher and I are elsewhere. It is wonderful, too, that I shall at that time be absent. And wonderful that all the others will be present. Why must there always be a German? For just such a situation as this.

Goodnight, Rinpoche. Goodnight, Miss Merry. Goodnight, Ulla. We'll meet next week to talk it all over.

It is finished.

Driving *home*, I'm torn between fear and the certain knowledge that there will be a respite. Whatever is waiting for me at the apartment will soon be followed by a sojourn in *Perrk*.

Unless Mona actually kills me, that is.

CHAPTER 2

In Which The Infallible Dogma of Karma Demonstrates That Its Bite Is Commensurate With Its Bark

Roads are much quieter now. A smear of lights. I can't decide whether they're cosy or cold. Stars obliterated by light-pollution. If you could see them they'd be smog-veiled anyway. It's really an interior cityscape, innit? The black highway beneath my wheels is carrying me home, a road paved of yore with good intentions.

Home is in the upper-middle-class burbs. How I made it even this far is a tale of too many drags, spurts and hiatuses to recall with any sense of gratification. A tale of being processed by the system Jack built.

I ascend the stairs (*with a bald spot in the middle of my hair*). My bowels by now are creeping up somewhere between my lungs. I'm a condemned man. Why did she choose tonight of all possible nights to come out with it? Why had she said, 'Too deep is not very far from too shallow'? Well that's obvious now, innit? That's me in a nutshell. Too deep to relish life's superficial offerings. Too shallow not to be tempted by some of them though.

Loathing harmfulness, yet far from incapable of it. Those three delightful shags, nakedly viewed (so to speak), were three acts of betrayal. But betrayal of what? Of the emasculated love between Mona and me? Of a crumbling trust already broken in a thousand words and deeds?

No. It's hope that I've betrayed; the kind of hope that exists between two survivors in a shattered boat out on the big big blue. That the stronger will not toss the weaker overboard when the food runs low. Or will not, as has sometimes happened, slay and eat her.

I ought to have been content to suffer alongside her, waiting in hope that the lacerations would eventually heal. My hope, however, has swung round to its obverse face, the snarling face of fear. Fear, not hatred, being the opposite of love.

While Mona has been hoping and fighting headlong down the rushing corrida of endless marriage, I've switched to the easier option: the mouldering resentment that refuses any longer to be mauled. That has stooped to seeking comfort between a different pair of willing tits and thighs. Tits that know nothing of your failures. Thighs that embrace you regardless.

Too deep is never very far from too shallow. Yeah. My profound self-rejection, engendered, naturally, by Moaner, now looks to her like rejection of herself. A sweet little irony of retribution, that.

Yeah, that's it. All too reasonable, even to me. Wrung from the wily wisdom of the unconscious no doubt. It's the one explanation I can give her that doesn't leave me looking like the lone defendant in the dock, and should provide at least a hint that there was never any question of my rejecting *her*.

If you look deeply enough, Mona, you'll see that it's been your fault all along.

Anyway, she's not at home. The angles of the apartment ramify quietly in the unlit gloom. A feeling of complete abandonment seizes me about the heart. Lights on. The search for a note. No note. This isn't the nineteenth century. If there's a note it will be on your cellphone. But it hasn't alerted me to any messages.

In the kitchen I examine the slips of paper collected under the fridge magnet. Grocery slips. A reminder to visit the rip-off beautician.

(Always the striving against the multiple forces of ageing. Hold back the free radicals that will get you in the end. Above all, be sexy. Bottom line: you have this crevice between your legs into which the admiration of the universe must be drawn. Therefore, increase the field of attraction as far out from the centre as possible, creating the vortex that sucks towards the animal centre of love.)

I put the kettle on. Sitting at the fruit-laden table I weep. What the hell am I blubbing about? But must there be a reason even for this? Well then, am I weeping because she has left or because she may return? Both possibilities are equally frightening.

'*Perfect love casteth out all fear.*' Thus St. John. And the Buddha: '*May I not be ruled by anxiety and dread.*' Yes, those are noble thoughts; seeds to be planted in noble minds. So, in the nature of things, they leave me not only unaided but actually unaddressed.

Let's have a nice cuppa tea instead.

I am tremulously sipping and smoking when the front door is flung open with destructive intent. My cup trembles and clatters in

the saucer. But hang on mate, she ain't alone. The other tread is
heavy, masculine.

Fee fi fo fum. I get up in anticipation of whatever vengeful surprise she has prepared for me. She starts yelling very raucously.
Mustn't leave the neighbours, especially the very correct couple in
22, uninformed.

'Charles! Cha-a-arles! Come back *hohhme*, have you!?'

Gatto, uninvolved and unimpressed, is purring and rubbing
against my leg.

Into the kitchen she stalks, her countenance a terrible confusion
of barely controlled fury and agony. Behind her, self-righteous as
the devil, hulks her older brother, Mauro (Mauron). They smell of
red wine and basil pesto.

Yes indeed I married an Hightalian and here is *fratello* come to
save *sorella* from the pernicious *Inglese*. I can't help remembering
the cro-magnon warning (we were twentysomething then), unsuc-
cessfully mitigated by winey billows of laughter: 'Charlie, I love
you, but I love my sister more. That's natural. You ever hurt her, I
won't love you anymore. That's natural too.'

Now I know why she picked exactly that moment when the yellow car swerved out at me. Because at *that moment* Mauron had
arrived from the family farm, had filled two glasses with sticky red
wine and nodded at her. Karmic conjunctions. Unfathomable.

'Is it true, Charlie?' asks the Italian force of nature, glowering.

'It's not as simple as *is it true*.' (It isn't, man, it *isn't*.)

'I knew this crazy Buddhist shit would bring you down eventually. Everything's so complicated you can't make head or arse of it.
Is it true, Charlie?'

No trace of the old fraternal cameraderie in his black eyes now.
He shoves at my chest. I can feel my fists balling as my nausea at
his violent intention rises. He punches me in the guts and I crumple
up, wheezing.

'If you won't tell me, I'll just have to take Mona's word for it.'

Bent double with pain I somehow have a sense of real detachment, of the ultimate stageyness of Samsara. It's all summed up
in this here soapie episode from adulterous bonk to hooligan
brawl. *All phenomena are transient, suffering and void of self.*
Then Mauron takes another swing at me.

'Don't hit him in the face!' wails Mona. 'He has to attend a
conference!'

In the midst of her bitterest disgust she's exhibiting this concern for my dignity, wants to spare my face, the clearest expression of me. In spite of myself I am touched. This is real love.

How come she knows about the conference? There's only one possible answer. Teacher has told her. Why? *Mental note: ask Teacher why.* Also, how long have you known about my misdemeanours, Mona? And how did you find out? And why have you kept it to yourself for who knows how long? Am I only thinking these things or can I be asking them out loud? To what semiconscious realm have I been translated by Mauron's hairy fist?

'Give me your phone, Charles,' she demands.

'Why?' (An easy word to get out under any circumstances).

'Just give me the goddamn phone.'

Still crumpled, I fish it out and hand it to her. She gets busy on it, then passes it back to me. And there it is, *her* number. Moreover, it is on call-back mode. She snatches it away from me.

Found out by an electronic device with a readable memory. What an age is this! When everything you do is traceable right down to the date and time you did it, unless you are a meticulous deleter. Which clearly I am not. Before my fuddled mind's eye there is suddenly *a vision of karma such as I have never seen.*

'No darling,' Mona is saying, having pressed the call-back button, 'this isn't darling Charlie boy. This is darling Charlie boy's wife. You fricking animal …'

Her trailing voice tells me that the fricking animal, affrighted, has rung off, or just dropped her phone and run like hell. A pang of aching disgust sweeps through my inmost being.

'It was an all-too-human shag,' I protest. 'She's not an ani mal, you're not an animal, I'm not an animal. As for Mauro, however –'

'No one gives a damn what you think!' roars the animal, coming at me again.

'Keep your big stupid fists out of it, Mauro!' shouts his sister.

'How long have you known?'

'Since the day you took my phone by mistake, and left yours behind.'

What would Jung make of this? That unconsciously this over-sight, so pregnant with disastrous negligence, was a deliberate act? A compulsion to confess? An urge developed during all those years of desperate Catholicism? That I loved Mona too much to want to keep her in the dark?

And to conclude that, whatever else I may have become, I have remained honest?

'So you've known for two weeks.'

'No, Charlie boy. I've known for much longer than that. But for two weeks I've had the goddamn proof.'

'You spoke to her?'

'No. I waited. Just in case you might find the balls to own up. Now I have other plans. Big and bold plans.'

'What are your plans, Mona?'

Big Mauro looks on, his impatience running out, transforming itself into something murderous. But I have to know, even at further cost to my physical wellbeing.

'To methodically screw you out of everything. So meditate on that while you guru around on your little conference trip, banging anything that falls at your lotus feet.'

'That's not fair. I ended it eight months ago.'

'Well now you can start it up again, Charles. You're a free man now.'

A free man. A castaway is what she means. Freedom, out on the big big blue, in the derelict little boat called *me myself*. I don't want this freedom. No really, I don't.

'But I still love you, Mona.'

'Far cough, Charles.'

'Yah. Far cue, Charlie!'

'Well I didn't say I love *you*.'

He just flicks his fat finger across my extremely prominent nose. Hurts like hell. Then Mona leads him away to the bedroom. In a minute they are lugging suitcases down the passage, Mauron carrying with the effortless ease of a porter, born and bred. I sit down at the table again, nursing my lukewarm tea, and my resentment.

It's time for the great and terrible goodbye. The sense of melodrama is again upon me. How is it I am so caught up in it? Why does it feign reality so well?

'So you're off to save the world, Charlie.'

I am too forlorn to take up this gambit.

'Can't even save his screwed-up marriage, but he's off to save the universe!'

Mauro shakes his head in dismal disbelief, as though I were a failed lasagne.

'I won't be saving anything. It's only a conference.'

'I'll be doing some conferring too.'

But there is a tremendous sadness in her eyes. I only hope she can read the reciprocal echo of agony in mine.

'Have you told the girls?'

She nods. This is a responsibility we still share.

'Those poor kids,' Mauro moans, his bruiser's head wagging again.

'What does Charles care?' Her head is wagging too. 'He's off to save the world.'

They shuffle indignantly towards the door. After some fussing with the baggage the latch clicks quietly to, in keeping with the air of a dismally ordinary tragedy. Then they are gone, and my nose is still stinging.

I slowly suffocate my way through a fag, contemplating my next move. The sense of a *fatum* embraces my brain like an iron hoop round a mouldy barrel. Whatever I do now, it had better be both right and skilful. This is one Titanic that musn't go down.

(Or is it already torn in two and sinking? *No, only the ordinary mind mistakes appearances for truth.*)

I phone Clara, the lovely, the angelic:

'Hello sweetie.'

'Thanks a lot, dad. Thanks a hellofalot!'

'I can't explain it all now. But I love you –'

'I don't want to speak to you.'

'– and I'm sorry.'

'I have an exam tomorrow. I don't want to speak to you now.'

'All right.'

Her turning away is like the slam of a door in my broken face.

I phone Jessica, the precocious, the sage:

'Hello Jessie.'

'Oh, the other asshole. Did you know I've got four assholes? One in my pants, one for a husband and two for parents?'

'What do you mean, an asshole for a husband?'

Not him too, surely.

'Not as big an asshole as you, daddy.' (Thank God.) 'At least he doesn't pretend to be anything else.'

'Is he giving you a hard time?'

'Nothing like the time you're giving mom.' (Thank God.)

'I'm sorry.'

'You two assholes just get your shit together!'

She has my way with words, Jessica does. I know she will not be as badly affected as Clara. Like her asshole daddy she never loses sight of the light at the end of the tunnel. Like him too, she understands the cyclic nature of every pattern. Beyond the soul-sucking grip of hope and fear, she makes do with the way it is. If only she did not have to make do with the way Adam (Madam) is. An effeminate fellow, a *prima donna* in his bashfully arrogant way.

Pfui. Whaddya want? He's a musician after all. 'Buddhism,' he once told me, 'is like Schoenberg. It only makes sense if you aren't expecting music.' (I thought he might be referring to Tibetan chant, but he denied this. What then? Oh, just music, a harmony beyond mere elegant analyses, something more in tune with one's emotional life, less of a denial that the emotions have anything to teach us.)

'I'll do my best. But I'm going away soon. Conference in Prague.'

'That's good.'

'Why good?'

'You don't think it's good?'

'No, I –'

'All right then, it's good.'

'I love you, Jessie.'

'I'm suspending all love at this time.'

I phone Precious Teacher, the unconditioned:

'Hello.'

'Hello Chully. You hava some suffering tonight, eh?'

'Yes.'

'That is good, very good.'

'Why did you tell Mona about the conference, Rinpoche?'

'She is your wife, Chully.'

'Is there anything else you've discussed with her?'

'Many things.'

'Anything I should know?'

'If you should knowing, I would hava telling you, Chully. That is very for certain.'

'Indeed.'

'I'm very tired now, Chully. Long day; old man. We shall speak on Wednesday.'

'Goodnight, Rinpoche.'

'I'm glad you suffering, Chully. It means your mind is not yet dull. If there is suffering, there is still a chance for happiness. Goodnight.'

Now I am really weeping. I understand him perfectly. It's the tragi-comedy of myself I cannot comprehend. The formula, after all, is so bloody easy. Be rid of fear and all the spacious skies of love will radiate from you, and in that roominess is joy. But fear and awareness are the inseparable horns of this sentient dilemma labelled Charlie Fincham.

Revert to dull normality. Employ your reason. Where's Gatto? I find him dozing on my pillow, wake him and lead him to the kitchen for a snack. Companionship. Feline trust, hard-won.

A hot shower washes away the tear-stained weariness and soothes my bruised abdominal muscles. The large proboscis is still red on one side. What a palooka, that Mauron! If anything, I feel humiliated on his primitive Itey behalf. Too many mafia movies keeping alive this myth of violent Italian honour. How they do dwell in it though. The upkeep of style: smart clothes, smart cars, smart food and wine. Behind the stylish façade lurks the brute, behind the cordial *famiglia* the endless watching for vengeance. Mona not at all exempt. That's what really irks me. And yet it's so damned true to life itself.

The doorbell rings; a playful rhythm that can only be an improvisation by Paulus. I don't know whether I'm relieved or inconvenienced. Plumb in the middle actually. I want to know what he knows and does not know, and what he isn't letting on.

He's toting a carton of books and a bottle of champagne. If it weren't Paulus it would seem a trifle odd. But Paulus has been known to cross the city to pay me a visit in his pyjamas. One of the many reasons why Mona never could take to him. Among the others were his wasteful intelligence, fake Oxford snottiness, sloppy forthrightness, slight regard for convention and intrusive friendliness. Too many bad qualities to be credible. Ergo, the man must be a phoney.

'Hello, old chap,' looking about him. 'Where's Mona?'

'You really don't know?'

'Really don't know what?'

'She's left me.'

'That's probably not good. But what do I know? What I *do know* is that you're off to Prague. Conference or some such gathering of bores. Religion and the end of the world. Not with a quiring bang but a prayerful whimper, eh? Would've done better sending me instead. Help them see the serious side.'

'And the books?'

'For you, Charlie. Everything you need to know about the end of the good old days or simply about the end – *period*.'

'I don't think I'm up to this right now.'

'Of course you aren't. Mona's just left you. Emotional wreckage. But being up to it or not is hardly the point. There are bigger things at stake. It's a grave matter, this destruction of the only known live-able planet in Samsara. Your own cares are trifling by comparison. Luring Mona back should be a piece of cake compared with coaxing the rich to sacrifice a fraction of their billions for the sake of *terra firma*. Still, the question of Mona's desertion does intrigue me.'

'I had a brief shagfest some months ago. She found out.'

'Not surprised, Charlie, on either score. You've been in dire need of cheering up for some time now and a roll in the hay will certainly accomplish that. That's why no one can put a stop to it. Hence, gross overpopulation. You'll find it all in these books. Naturally you got found out. You're a Buddhist. Can't keep ahead of your karma as Christians seem always able to do. They've got forgiveness instead, you see.'

'Where'd you get hold of all those bloody tomes?'

'Compliments of Rinpoche. Instructed me to deliver them *tonight*.'

'Aha.'

'But the champagne was my own idea. *Bon voyage*, or some such excuse.'

I fetch two tumblers. Can't be bothered with champagne glasses. A born-again teetotaller. But I won't dishonour Paulus' gesture. Sip. Sip.

'Problem's quite simple, of course,' he drawls.

'Which problem?'

'Well, not the universal problem, meaning of life and all that. I'm referring only to the domestic one.'

'Yes?'

'Ohhh! No, no! Unintended, old chap! I mean the problem of the end of our own local world! Naturally that could be seen as a universal problem too. I mean, no living beings, no material universe, possibly. Anyway, *our* problem is simple. Too many people. Obliterate two thirds of our *pernicious race of odious little vermin* – perhaps a fraction more – bingo! Planetary recovery!'

'You think I should propose that at the conference?'

'Someone should admit it at least.'

'It's a conference on religion and –'

'I know. I know. But take the Mahayana, the story of the passenger who intends to kill all the others on board. What does the compassionate Bodhisattva do? Kills the killer. Takes the karma on himself. One life has to go to save the many.'

'I always thought that story had a Christian ring to it.'

'No problem for Christians. Wiping out the two thirds, I mean. Starting with the Muslims. Started already, actually.'

'That isn't what I meant.'

'All the same, occurs to one.'

'Your simple solution isn't all that simple. Who do we select for extermination? The greedy, the violent, the powerhungry?'

'On no! That would include you and me. Besides, they don't make up two thirds. No, just a random swipe. Everyone has a fair chance.'

And so on until I feel almost normal again. I am sorry to see him leave. I want to cling to his uncontaminated bachelor's *unbearable lightness of being*. So far he has made no further reference to Mona. But, rising to leave, he says: 'Simple solution to *your* problem too, old chap.'

'What? Kill Mona?'

But he's serious now.

'Pay heed to what you really feel for her. The rest will follow.'

After a last cup of tea I go to bed. With Gatto at my side I pay heed to what I really feel for Mona. Like a riddle wrapped up in a mystery wrapped up in an enigma, I am conscious of an undeniable love enveloped in a complex ache.

'Trust me,' it seems to whisper.

Sleep.

CHAPTER 3

In Which Deviousness And Disaster Are
Partly Averted By A Superior Being

Tuesday ninefortyfive ayem. The warehouse is hanging about quietly, hoping for a revived interest in Tibetan artifacts. We have *tangkhas, rupas, katas,* carpets, jackets, incense, jewelry, inlaid tables. Or rather, they have *us*, tied up in an overdraft which we should be able to pay off in the next two or three lifetimes. Except there is no longer any *we*.

Only an I.

The office is my other home. I haven't spared myself any comforts. A blotchy desk crowned with a crabby computer, a telephone hosting irate callers, a fax machine that churns out reams of creditors' impolite statements and invoices. A beautiful Tibetan rug (delivered with the damaged warp skilfully hidden) under the feet of all who venture in.

A sofa for guests and honoured clients. Minifridge, automatic kettle, tea things. On the wall above my chair a blown-up poster of His Holiness about to break out into the national form of laughter at anything self-important, insulting, conflated or confused, or just anything at all. How often I have imagined him laughing down at me.

Harvey (Halfie) is at the door. He's one of the very few people I know who can look me straight in the eye when they are standing and I'm seated. When we're both on our feet I tend to turn my back on him. It seems more dignified.

Seeing him waiting, I quickly sit down.

'Morning Harvey. Come in please.'

'It's not just morning, Charlie. It's *good* morning.'

'That may be so.'

'It's good morning because ...'

He hands me a sheaf of printed bills with large amounts in the grand total lines, to which my practised eyes are immediately drawn before they travel upwards to the letterhead. I'm aghast with agitation for the duration of the short upward journey. Then I whoop like a John Ford Redskin.

They are orders for my beloved goods. Halfie chuckles and puts the kettle on. I'm flipping through the pages, skimming along their bottom lines, calculating roughly. Then I instinctively turn about to check on the Dalai Lama's smile.

'Can we deliver?'

Harvey doesn't deem the question intelligent enough to merit a response.

'I mean *everything*?'

'Just about everything.'

'No, I mean *do we have everything they require*?'

'As I say, we'll have some things left over.'

Hurrah!

The cortical machinery is running at high speed now, approaching the Singularity almost. I might have to plan a trip to India, to replenish my stocks. That will want yet more time away from the current crisis. I'm jubilant, but anxious too. What have I done to deserve this sudden upturn? Isn't it more likely to be a cosmic trick, a karmic mirage sent forth to repay me for my deception of Mona?

In the silent inward parts I'm disturbed and disappointed at my wavering reactions. Why am I so trapped in this ridiculous circus of illusion? This money-cycle beckoning like plankton to a whale. In at the one end and out at the other, where the creditors drift, only their fins above water. Should money ever strum the strings of my delicate emotions? Isn't that the cause of all the trouble? I am sometimes a creditor too.

I can feel His Holiness behind me.

Still, I'm so excited that I've stood up without turning my back on Halfie. I am beaming down on him like the sun. He's reading the inscription on my tee shirt.

'What's it say, Harvey?'

'Can't make it out. Seems to be in some foreign language. Could be Russian. Oh no, wait a sec, you've got your shirt on inside out.'

Right side out it says *Free Tibet*.

After drinking our chai we get to work, he to pack the orders and I, having reversed my shirt, to call the bank. Today I can assume an upbeat tone with my nominal bank manager (nominal because,

look where you will, every aspect of actual management is handled
by a computer.) That's probably the main reason why we're on first
name terms. Like me myself, he has no authority at all.

His position in today's world resembles God's. You can't put
your faith in him because he can't do anything for you. The automated system has shortened his arms. You can't get angry at
him because, at least as a real manager of affairs, he simply
doesn't exist.

So I just call him Wally.

'Standardized Bank, good morning.'

'Good morning. Wally Walters, please.'

'Who's calling please?'

'Charles Fincham.'

'One moment please.'

Click. Then a less-than-mediocre performance of Haydn or
Dittersdorf.

It goes on and on, augmented by an *ennui* of variations, until I
put the phone down, and ring again. The phone is picked up and
the line dropped. I ring again.

'Standardized Bank, good morning.'

'You said one moment for Wally.'

'Oh. One moment please.'

'Shouldn't that be one moment *more*?'

Haydn Dittersdorf continues until the stampede of strings and
brass is reigned in somewhere near the start of the cadenza.

'Sorry, sir. He's busy on the other line. Would you like to hold?'

'For a bit.'

Now it's the London Philharmonic playing the Beatles. *All you
need is love.* This might be a direct message from Brahma. But it is
cut short as the line goes dead again. I give up. Let the mountain
come to Mohammed.

Next call on my list, the computer service agency:

'Good day. This is Prime Line Computer Services. For account
enquiries press one, for internet support press two, for new
contracts press three, for technical assistance press four …'

That's me. *Four.*

'Good day. You have reached Prime Line Computer Services
Technical Assistance. For hardware problems press one, for software
problems press two, to speak to a technician press three …'

Three.

'Good day. You have reached Prime Line Computer Services Technical Department. All our technicians are currently busy. Please hold. Your call is important to us – (hi-tech music undulating like a roll of silk) – Please hold. Your call is important to us – (music) – If you hang up you will be placed at the back of the automated queue – (music) – Please hold. Your call is important to us ...'

I'm trying to work out whether it's all the same voice. The 'back of the automated queue' sounds more threatening, the other has an assuring lilt.

What has happened to us? That we have become crass enough to communicate with one another by means of a disembodied voice? A voice with which we can't joke, plead or remonstrate? An arrangement that wears us out with the sheer effrontery of its cheapness. Why have we stooped to accepting this treatment?

Because we have no choice.

By now the refrain has taken hold inside my head: 'Please hold. Your call is important to us. Please hold. Your call is important to us. Please hold ...'

I hang up. Well, that's two calls dealt with.

Perhaps the monotonous refrain has hypnotized me. I suddenly see the immensity of the intricate system at whose feet I grovel, whose arse I am being forced to kiss from morning to night, day in day out, from the cradle to the grave.

All worked out in daily, weekly and monthly cycles, enmeshing me in a routine that holds me back from almost every meaningful pursuit. What's the point even trying? The ongoing beat has made *itself* into the meaningful pursuit. It is meaningful to perform the myriad obeisances that keep me solvent because solvency is *life itself*.

Not to love money is to perish.

It's an ancient plaint, to be sure, but the ancients had the wit and means to wriggle out into one bizarre alternative or another. Now there are too many worms on the one sticky apple.

Whether you join in the frenzy or never lift a finger to partake, the system will scoop you up anyway. It's not only obtruding itself into your conscious activity. It shadows about in your drowses, your depressions and your dreams.

'If you hang up you will be placed at the back of the automated queue.'

This is the grind that keeps yer eyes fixed on the flickering troglodyte shadowplay while the real world has so far eluded yer attention that it's likely to be annihilated in consequence of yer sheer inability to notice its rapid diminishment and rise up off yer arse to do something about it.

Yer fricking home is burning down around yer ears while ya mope in the study working out yer traffic fines, taxes, electricity bills, municipal fees, detailed telephone accounts, cellphone debit orders, bank fees, insurance premiums, medical aid, service provider's fees, satellite TV fees, bond repayments and what's left over for food, clothing and fags.

Man who is born free (though not free of charge) is everywhere a link in a computerized chain. A very clever way to work it out, to take the chains off our limbs and reposition them around our brains. So now we are free in a free market where everything is up for sale with the guarantee that planned obsolescence will have ensured an inbuilt flaw.

Harvey steps into my reverie.

'By the way, Charlie, they asked me to ask you to call them back.'

'Who asked you to ask me?'

'In fact they told me to tell you.'

'In that case, thanks for telling me.'

'Do you know who told me to tell you?'

'Do *you* know, Harvey?'

'Not exactly.'

'More or less?'

'Whoever sent the order.'

'Thank you again, Harvey.'

The phone rings before I reach for it. It's Clara. She's changed her mind. She wants to speak to me now and she wants to do it face to face. I explain that I'm tied up (yes) with a very large order. She wants me to explain how this can be more important than *everything else*. I explain that it isn't, generally speaking, more important. But right now it is. She's crying and my heart floods with her tears.

Sensitive Harvey doesn't move, his eyes fixed on *Free Tibet*. I know that he aspires with the zeal of a drooling gastronome for titbits and drippings from my personal life. I have to ask Clara to hold while I deal with him.

'It's not Mr McNamara on the phone then?'

'Who's Mr McNamara?'

'The one who told me to tell you. No, his name wasn't McNamara.'

'It's my daughter. It's personal.'

'Oh yes. I see. It's about Mona leaving you.'

I'm flabbergasted squared. The abiding ache of love for Mona flips over like some cuddly furry creature with an unexpectedly vile underside.

'Get the ffffout of my office, Harvey!'

'Right ho, Your Lamaship.'

The silly honorific he has invented for me doesn't derive only from his younger than puerile wit. Twenty-four-or-five years ago I *was* a monk, one of those early dreamers who put their hopes in the first lamas to visit the West. In those years the Tibetan teachers had not yet learned how capricious our hippie-formed minds really were. We, on the other hand, couldn't yet imagine how many of them were mere shorn frauds in maroon dresses. Most of us disrobed after a year or two.

I cast aside my robes for Mona. They still hang, neatly ironed, in the unused corner of my wardrobe, two sets of burgundy and yellow. Now and again I touch them briefly with a subtle sense of failure.

And in their turn they touch my sardonic thoughts with the reminder that, in the last five years, excepting my triple adventure, I've returned to the celibate life.

I resume with Clara, explain why I can't spend an hour driving to her campus right now, but will surely do so this afternoon. Late this afternoon.

'I'll take you out to dinner.'

She further disturbs my detached tranquillity with a threat she's never made before:

'You'd better hope you find me alive.'

I don't want to swallow this one.

'I do hope so, Clara. I hate dining alone.'

She's too upset to manage a riposte.

'I love you, Clara. I'll be there as soon as I can.'

'Actually it's worth staying alive just to hear what you have to say for yourself.'

That's my girl. (Or Mona's.)

I scramble to call back The Exotique, to reach whomever (McNamara?) has told Halfwit to tell me to return their call. Have they decided to cancel after all, confirming my sense of a tricky karma? Or might they want even more of my precious stocks? This sort of thing is usually handled by my secretary, who also doubles as my wife.

'Good day. You have reached The Exotique, home of the finest décor items and *objets d'art* from around the world. All our operators (*they only have one; I have physically verified this*) are currently busy. Please hold. Your call will be attended to shortly.'

In this case the music ain't half bad.

'All our operators are currently busy. Please – *Good day, The Exotique. How may I help you?*'

A live one!

'Put me through to your buying department please.'

'Which buying department, sir?'

'What do you mean?'

'Local, international, soft goods, décor, furnishings?'

Am I local? I work in the same town. International? I deal in Tibetan artifacts. I have soft goods, décor and furnishings.

'I don't know. Mr McNamara?'

'Mr McNamara isn't in the buying department. He's in goods receiving.'

'All right then. Let's go for McNamara.'

'Going through.'

Music.

What proportion of my telephone bill represents time spent speaking only to the people I wanted to reach in the first place? Twenty per cent? Less than that? Mental note: set up an experiment (timer required) to measure this.

Especially: what proportion of my bill goes to endless reaches of unsolicited music? How many hours of such music in a month, a year, a decade? How much productive time is lost, globally, while the music plays on to perspiring callers waiting for ... I suppose for Godot, really.

Since in this case I absolutely must speak to McNamara, I ponder the question in rather more depth while I wait.

What, then, is the essential function of this energy-sapping music? Well, it fills up the span of time that would otherwise be spent listening to nothing at all. It does away with *waiting in silence*. No doubt it's meant to soften the humiliating blow of being kept hanging about on the outside of a shut door. Gives the illusion, too, that life is still going on elsewhere while you wait and wait.

Yet I feel there is something even more radically symbolic in this insertion of sound and fury into the silent interstices of mere existence. *Could it be an isomorphic expression of what palpable life really is? This brief, irritating blast of sound?*

Abrupt cessation of music.

'Morning, John McNamara speaking.'

'Good morning, Fincham from *The Roof Of The World*. I was told by my assistant that you told him to tell me to call you back.'

'Is Mona out then?'

'Er, yes, I'm afraid she is.'

'Well, tell her that our packaging slips and delivery notes must be completed using the CRAB formula from now on. This is important. Suppliers who don't use the CRAB formula won't be paid. Got that? Only the CRAB formula interfaces with the new accounts program. Got that? C-R-A-B.'

'Do the letters stand for anything in particular?'

'They stand for quick payment, pal. You just tell Mona, you hear?'

'Okay. I hear.'

'Good. Give Mona my best, you hear?'

'Did Mona negotiate this order?'

'Don't know, pal. Probably. Wide awake, that girl! What a girl!'

'I'll tell her.'

'Right. Bye.'

Dismissed.

Shite. The *crab* formula? I summon Halfwit.

'Do you know about the CRAB formula, Harvey?'

'Mona mentioned it before she left. It stands for connected something or other. No, it's not connected – *collected* – sorry.'

'Please call Mona and find out what to do. It's important for delivery purposes.' (Not to say, payment).

'Now?'

'Yes, now.'

'Right ho, Your Lamaship.'

I leave the office, wander over to the packing department where the boys are already at it. I saunter through, trying to muster a glimmer of interest in the work going on. There's a sort of dumb acknowledgement of my directorial presence. Not a word is spoken. I'm alienated and redundant. Mona has run the show for years. Other than my buying trips to India and my prescribed conversations with Wally, my value to the enterprise has declined to that of constitutional monarch. Which would suit me just fine if Mona were still at her desk.

I'm feeling very uncomfortable. If Harvey knows, they all know too. I wonder how much they know and how much of what they know is accurate information.

Then, all at once, on a wave of insight into the absurdity of the thing, I stop caring. Whatever they all know really amounts to knowing nothing.

Back in the office Harvey is waiting, his face writhing between dejection and glee.

'Well, what's CRAB?'

'I don't know.'

'You spoke to Mona?'

'Yes.'

'And?'

'She says fax the orders to her. She'll do the documents on her computer, on the farm. Says it'll save you the trouble and confusion.

(This means that she can redirect payment into her own account. See?)

'No.'

'You're the boss,' he affirms (superfluously, of course). He goes on to mutter something about *Mona's permission*, an aspersion which, for the sake of my own nervous condition, I decide to ignore.

A frenetic drive through the rotten core of the city to the offices of The Exotique, there to learn all the mysteries of CRAB. I am directed to John McNamara who would, it is clear, mightily prefer to see Mona.

'Mona's away, Mr McNamara. And I am in fact the owner of the enterprise where Mona works as my secretary.'

Pausing to take it in.

'But she asked me to send copies of the orders to her office on the farm.'

'Have you sent them?'

'Why shouldn't I have?' Defensively.

Gotta think fast.

'Well that's fine then. If she's prepared to work on them down there, saves me the hassle. As you say, John, she's a fine girl. All the same, I'd like the dope on CRAB. She's obviously taken her files along with her.'

'No problem.'

It's a twenty-pager.

Back in my car I call Mona.

'Harvey says you'll do the delivery notes on the farm. The CRAB thing.'

'So?'

'So thank you. I'm seeing Clara tonight.'

'Try not to screw that up too.'

'Why don't you just come back? Let's just pick up the pieces what?'

'Jesus, you really have no idea, Charlie boy.'

'Okay. I have no idea. I'm sorry. Please have the documents ready by Friday. I need three days to pack the order.'

'They'll be ready.'

'Okay.'

'Okay.'

On my way back across town to the office I'm thinking at the speed of light.

'You ever heard of overtime, Harvey?'

'I've heard rumours, Your Lamaship.'

'I want these orders delivered tomorrow morning.'

He is gazing at *Free Tibet*.

'Which means that you and the team will have to work through the night.'

'Sudden big demand for Tibetan stuff?'

'Why doesn't matter.' (I'm damned sure he knows exactly why.)

He is almost sulking.

'It's double pay of course. No excuses.'

He sighs, 'Sure.'

'Just one more thing.'

I am frowning down at him like Zeus Pater.

'There's more?'

'Just the one wee thing, and *boy do I really mean it*.'

Getting serious now.

'Sure.'

'You contact Mona about this or anything else, you'll be much more than just fired. Don't mess with me on this one, Harvey. Your Lamaship and all that aside, *you're fucking with the wrong Buddhist now*.'

I can hear Precious Teacher instructing my other mind: '*Anger is not either good or it is not either bad if you in charge of it. Only use it as an instrument, skilfully, and without the energy of violence. If your motivation is pure, everything is pure.'*

I am not inflammably angry at Halfie, and my motivation is pure: *pure anxiety.* Who can blame him (of all people) for being in love with Mona? Can't help blaming her, though, for working on him. He's in a tight spot now, and I have to drive my point home earnestly enough to nullify the romantic delight he probably feels at being bamboozled into nestling in the palm of her pretty (but tough, *tough*) hand.

'Believe me, Harvey. I know what's potting here. Your and Mona's game.'

He's blushing, the little shit.

'In a little while Mona and I will be back together again. That's guaranteed, Harvey. We've painstakingly built up a life that's just too big and overbearing to throw away over a minor peccadillo. If you go along with her emotional craziness now, she'll be the one demanding that *you* leave. I'm sure you can see it.'

'You don't like me, Charlie.'

'That's never been a reason to harm you.'

He blinks. Regretful twinge on my part. Too late.

When I've put the ship in order it's time to scramble off to my dinner date. I go by the eerie apartment first, for a wash and a change of clothes. Might as well make a mature impression, put Clara under the illusion that she's in the company of an adult, however much the facts refute the grown-up appearance.

It's all illusion, man. Even the older guy I see in the mirror still thinks of himself as a kid.

But how much easier it was when I was a kid. *And not only because I was a kid.* The world really was different then, in the minimalist sixties mouthing out into the tempest-struck oceans of the stroboscopic seventies, the last decade of innocence. After which the death-rattle of the heroic ideal, of the authentic search for truth, of the side-burned and serious individual. Then the inauguration of the age of the triumphant system, the war against the establishment having been lost by us, the drug-befuddled anarchists, bolsheviks, beatniks.

Who says Orwell got the year wrong?

I've told Halfwit that I'll be back later to go on with him through the night. This arrangement will keep him honest. Before evicting him from my thoughts I send him a single pulsing quantum of compassion. One to Mona too. After that the steady stream is poured out on Clara.

I call her and ask her to pick a restaurant.

When I arrive she's seated at a table on the terrace, lovely as a Modigliani girl. Although she has inherited something of my snout, the Italian influence has Romanized it. Her grey-green eyes are steady shields, keeping all intruders out. But the mouth and chin are still all child. Her auburn hair flickers in the breeze.

Of course I can't do the gung-ho routine. It's up to her to set the tone.

'You even look like a fraud,' she winces.

'Too well-dressed?'

'I'm alluding to the sanctimonious expression on your face.'

I clear my throat, feel it constricting, clear it again.

'How can I … what can I say to help you understand?'

'There's nothing you can say. *What* can you say, dad? You're supposed to be a Buddhist, a person who knows what to do. Where was the Buddhist while you were doing *it*? I mean, *where was your mind*? Or are there *two of you*?'

This is not the time to theorize about the multifaceted mental continuum which, in the absence of a central gravitational force, will shatter outwards into anything that will receive it or, if fortune favour you, slam its particles of desire into an inert mass.

Where was the Buddhist? Where the hell is the Buddhist now, for that matter? Where, so help me God (the unknown Idea), has it ever been, come to think of it? I don't know.

'There is no Buddhist. There's only this. The Buddhist has only ever been an inescapable intention, something that won't go away even though you can't ever find it when you look for it.'

'Then it was *you*.'

'Yes.'

The *Vajracchedika Sutra*: 'No person will ever be brought to enlightenment.' Because the person himself is a fallacious construct. How much more unreal the Buddhist, the fallacy laid upon the fallacious construct.

'It was *me*.'

'Then who are you now, dad?'

'I could say, *here I am, the same person, the guilty one*, and that would be true. I could also say, *that was someone else, not this me*, and that would be true as well. Or I could say, *that was the real me*, *and this is someone else.* All of it true and all of it untrue. It's not simple.'

'I need something simple and true, you know, *the simple truth*? Or else I'll never know who you are and who it is I can love or despise.'

If something is not simple, it is not simple, Chully. And no one can make it simple. Therefore we not always able to telling the whole truth. And even Lord Buddha has told many different truths to many different people. Depends what they can understand.

'I did it, Clara. It was me. I did it and I deeply regret it. I'm so sorry for the harm I've caused.'

'Why? Can you just tell me *why*?'

'Because I was a fool who felt that he wasn't getting the attention he deserved. Or the love. Or the respect.' (Can't mention what else I wasn't getting, eh?)

'The attention, love, respect? That you *deserved*?'

'The appreciation.' (The hokey-pokey, slap-n-tickle, ya know. *Everyone* deserves a bit of that, surely?)

'One big ego trip.'

'Yes.' (There isn't only an ego up here in the head.)

'And to what extent is your big ego trip going to further mess up my life?'

'Ego trip's over, Clara.'

'But the mess is just starting.'

'I'll fix it. I promise.'

'Do you know how hard it is for me right now, at this very moment.'

'I might have some idea. I'm not sure.'

'It's very, very hard. My one safe place is gone.'

'I'll fix it.'

'It'll never be the same.'

And this is the suffering of change. Everything is always changing, Chully. That is why you should not holding on, grasping, grasping. It will always change. That is very for certain. Letting go is all you can do.

'Perhaps it will be better. I hope so.'

'I hope so too because I need a safe place in this *fucked up world*.'

'Yes.'

'This world without a future. The one your famous generation had the chance to change, but *fucked up even more instead*.'

'We tried. I can't remember why we gave up. Maybe we failed to realize how self-destructive and stupid people actually are. God knows why. Because we'd put a man on the moon, perhaps. Then we got older and busier, got married, had babies, forgot.'

'Babies! No point making any more of those. Forty years from now there'll be no more planet to baby around on. I'll still be alive then. You'll be dead and buried.'

'Cremated.'

It's disturbing, this ceaseless pre-occupation with the steep decline of quality of life on earth. The worst part is that it isn't a melodramatic student gripe. It's as real as the changing weather patterns, wars being declared everywhere, the sense of universal anxiety.

How did we manage to bring it to this?

'There's still time to put it right.'

'That's *bullshit*. Nobody's going to wake up in time.'

This shakes me.

'What do you and your friends intend to do about it?'

'We speak about that a lot. By the time we're in a position to do anything it will all be too far gone. We'll be able to save only some bits and pieces. The time for action is *now*. But *now* is the period of rule by the worst of the worst.'

'That's seldom not been the case.'

'Exactly. It's hopeless.'

'Who knows what people will pull out of the hat?'

'I don't think they can prevent this anymore than they can prevent their own deaths.'

'Why? It's not inevitable in the same way.'

'So much of the damage has already been done.'

'That's true. But things change. So can people, so can minds.'

'Yes, everything can change. Anyway, we've already decided that, when things get so bad we can't live like human beings anymore, we'll kill ourselves.'

Here is my child, almost a woman, on the threshold of youthful venturesomeness, of all that knowledge, experience and love might offer. And she's envisaging, while the vegetarian platter is being served, a foreshortened life. It's not a stupid plan, her plan. Horrifying, yes. But if things come to that.

My God, to see it so clearly and she so young!

There is no God to prevent it, or to restore it once it's gone. The end of a *kalpa*. It's so hard to accept that I've been born to partake of this phase of the cycle, the beginning of the end, or that the finale will be brought on by *mere people*.

Everything's contaminated by the greasy human fingerprint that points to our undeniable guilt. The vegetables on this plate are probably genetically modified, the waitress modified by smart anti-depressants.

'You obviously know I'm going to this conference.'

'The way mom put it, you're off to save the world.'

'That's why you're telling me all these things?'

'Reminding you. I've told you so many times before.'

'Not about the suicide pact.'

She sees what's in my eyes.

'Don't worry prematurely, dad. It won't be for some time yet.'

I leave at nine, not at all sure that I've been forgiven. Anyway, what does forgiveness mean? Only that you haven't written off a particular relationship yet? In that case there's still hope.

'You're precious to me, Clara.'

She just nods a little shyly, a little challengingly.

'Stay in your trousers at the conference.'

'For heaven's sake!'

I get back to the office after ten, to find that Halfwit has taken me seriously. We don't have overmuch to say to each other. He supervises the packing while I prepare the reams of CRAB packaging slips, delivery notes and, with even greater attention to detail, the cash invoices, less five per cent.

By sunrise the boxes are stacked in orderly rows, the first load already on the delivery van. The packers are grabbing some shut-eye in the dark, incense-charged corners of the warehouse. Halfie's in the office now, helping me sort out the documentation.

'How many trips are needed to deliver the lot?'

'Three, Your Lamaship.'

'Should be done by eleven then.'

'If the van holds out.'

'It'll hold out.'

'And then?'

'And then you can all go home and rest up at company expense.'

'I didn't really know what to do, Charlie. Mona told me things –'

'That's all right, Harvey. *I* knew what to do.'

'And I don't really like *you* either, but I don't think you're a bad person. It's just the way you act, as though you're superior.'

'I *am* superior.'

'Well that's that then.'

By ten-thirty all the deliveries have been made and the invoices are on the accounts desk of The Exotique. Mr McNamara is again baffled with surprise. Mona has let him know that the goods will be delivered on Friday.

'You're certainly on the ball, Mr Fincham.'

'That I am, Mr McNamara. You be sure to tell Mona now, you hear?'

Devious bastard.

Having locked up the warehouse, I drive straight home to rest for two hours before the meeting with Precious Teacher and Merry. My mind is full of Clara's truncated future. When we were kids it was only the bomb, and we couldn't even rid the world of that single menace. By the time Chernobyl came apart we were already inured to living and dying with it.

Thank you, Nobel laureate scientists, you experimenting brats. We might have been impressed by your heartfelt warnings, Lordgod Einstein et al., but did you really have to delay your protests until *after Hiroshima and Nagasaki were sent into the ether*?

Never thought I'd see the day when I, a virtual-reality-Buddhist at least, would find myself as appalled by the so-called spiritual as by the so-called unspiritual mind. Both equally driven by their One True Greed to suck dry the terrestrial innards before blowing the whole blistered body to bits.

O Boodle! O Lolly! O lots of it!

I unplug the land line, switch off the cellphone. Unreachable for these two hours, I flatten myself against the cool sheets. Vertigo. I teeter at the edge for several minutes, swayed like seaweed, before being swept into the dreamy maelstrom.

O Buddhas of the ten directions, help me now!

CHAPTER 4

In Which Wisdom Is Seen To Float Upon Laughter, And Laughter Upon Tears

Teacher is just finishing his umpteenth cup of tea when I arrive. The Tibetan capacity for this civilising hallucinogen isn't even remotely rivalled by the collectively addicted English. I greet him, palms together at my chest, before being invited to sit down.

'The journalist is late.'

'No. Merry is not late. But first we meditate awhile, and some talking.'

He gets up with an unconscious flourish, a gracious *mudra* of motion, and leads the way to his shrine-room. We remove our shoes, make our prostrations before the luminous shrine and sit down on the golden-yellow cushions. It's quiet in here without being merely noiseless. There's a *presence of quietness*.

It's all maroon and yellow, white, blue and gold. The brass *rupa* of the Shakyamuni Buddha shines warmly among the flickering tongues of flame from the light-offering candles. In seven bowls are the seven water offerings symbolizing drinking water, washing water, flowers, incense, light, perfume, food. Beside them stands a miniature Tibetan horn, the offering of sound. Here is authentic devotion to whatever truth may prove itself to be.

'You hava good night?'

'Yes, Rinpoche.'

'I'm not agree, Chully.'

(Suddenly we are laughing as though the essence of life, its own *raison d'etre*, were an outrageous farce.)

'I don't agree either, Rinpoche.' (ha ha ha ha).

'Ho ho ho ho hooo.'

'Hah hah hah ha ha haha.'

'Heh heh heh … heh heh … heh … now we meditate.'

It's as though the world has suddenly burst asunder at the centre of my heart. I'm crying like a man at the end of days. Every sense, expectation, memory is burning, disintegrating, swallowing up all life itself. My sorrow can't find the real measure of its expression, even in this cloudburst. It is *my life* going lost, dragging all other life down into darkness along with itself.

It seems to go on for hours before it's finally spent.

'You see, Chully?'

'Yes. I'm a failure.'

'So true, so true. How long you hava been a Buddhist?'

'You know it, Rinpoche. Twenty-nine years, almost four of them in robes.'

'Too long time. Very much too long. It must stopping now.'

'I don't understand.'

'You laughing and you crying, Chully.'

'Yes.'

'When your essence mind laughing, your Buddhist mind starting to cry.'

'Say more, Rinpoche.'

'Let it go.'

'Let the Buddhist mind go?'

'If that time has come, you should go beyond the religion.'

'Beyond it to what instead?'

'There is no instead. There is only freedom. When you laughing, always laughing, you will be free. And you will share that freedom with others. Then it is easy, so easy, to giving and to loving.'

'Have *you* let go of your Buddhist mind?'

'No need for me letting go, Chully. I'm a *tulku*. Many times reborn. Everything let go already. Only not this human life. But, in its time, it also will go.'

'Everything will go.'

'Yes. Even if you not letting it go. But then must waiting very much longer. No need to wait. You can let it go.'

'Why worry about the destruction of the earth then. Why go to this conference?'

'To letting go is not same as to destroying. If you can only letting go by destroying, then better to holding on.'

'Perhaps I am destroying my Buddhist mind. Maybe that is why I cry.'

'Nobody can destroying a mental creation, Chully. But it can take you only so far. Then, when can seeing your own heart, no need looking with a religion mind.'

'But it's looking at my own heart that makes me weep.'

'Then, very for certain, you can letting Buddhist mind go. Come. Merry is here now. Very nice not-Buddhist girl.'

The very nice not-Buddhist girl is waiting in Teacher's parlour. Dressed in a yellow skirt and top, she is well camouflaged amid the décor of maroon, yellow and gold. Against the back of an old fashioned wingback chair, re-covered in maroon, her blonde hair and milky skin put me in mind of nothing so much as a repressed angel in full but dour control of all her assets. Her frosty blue eyes overlay this impression with a sense of peril. They were designed to put one in one's place. Because of them she need not swagger about in the termagant's masculine attire. They convey something more as well: that she has seen and survived some bitter things.

Breaking the ice, I decide to make her closer acquaintance without preamble:

'Do you always use your middle finger on people you disapprove of?'

'When more polite gestures don't penetrate, yes.' (Unimpressed.)

'It's a very ugly gesture. Doesn't suit you somehow.' (All that milk, blonde and blue.)

'On the other hand, I didn't think my lip-reading abilities misread the man behind *your* reaction. Seemed to suit *you* very well.'

'Ah well, then at least you have me pegged too.'

'Perhaps we can proceed, Rinpoche?'

'So … yes.' (Teacher is never instructed to proceed.) 'Now we hava some tea.'

It's all been prearranged. From the kitchen Marta enters with the tray, very demurely serves Teacher, then Merry with deliberate deference. With me she is decidedly warm, not neglecting to brush against my shoulder in the act of placing the cup on the table beside me. I feel misread again, diabolically, deservedly.

Teacher sips and nods, sips and nods, waiting for the skilful word to arise. If he is at all present to us, he's not letting on. He smiles at Marta. She understands and leaves the room. He plucks at some folds in his robe, then pats them neatly into place.

'Where your parents coming from, Merry?'

'They're English, Rinpoche.'

'Ah … ah … and, living here in Africa?'

'No, in England.'

'Mmm … You are alone here?'

'Yes, for now. But I travel a lot.'

'Ah. Little bit difficult. Your father, what is he doing?'

'Retired.'

'And *before*?'

'He was a policeman.'

'So, very important job. And your mother?'

'Policeman's wife.'

'Also very important, but not easy, I think.'

Merry shows no sign of thawing. I don't believe she's meant to yet.

'Now, Chully's father, he is dead. He was, how you say? A scoundrel?' turning to me for confirmation.

'To put it mildly, Rinpoche.'

'But a very good teacher. He making Chully see so many things, so many important things. This is also good, I think.'

Now addressing Merry: 'Maybe your father, if he hava meeting Chully's father, he would hava arresting him. Heh heh heh … heh heh heh heh.'

'Ha ha ha … hah.'

'Hee hee hee hee hee hee hee hee.'

'Ho ho ho ho … hoh hoh hoh.'

'Hee hee hee hee hee hee heeeeeh.'

'Heh … heh … So, now you hava been properly introduced.'

'Hee hee hee hee …' She keeps peeking guiltily at me but can't help herself. It's too delightfully true not to evoke the unstoppable assent of laughter. I can just see it too, her copper father arresting my crooked old dad, and we two children, rigidly disciplined girl and hooligan boy, left behind facing each other in Teacher's parlour.

'I'm sorry, Charlie.'

'No need, Mary. Just look at what I've managed to become in spite of all that.'

'And me.'

'So, now we talk about the conference. Please, Merry, you first.'

'Quite straightforward. I'm going as a representative for a number of media to report on the contribution by religious institutions from Africa. But unofficially I have a special interest in the Buddhist angle.'

'Chully's angle.'

'Which originally would have been yours, Rinpoche,' raising her perfect eyebrows, conveying her disappointment. 'But yes, I'll take keen note of Charlie's contribution, among others.'

'Very good. Chully hava twenty-nine year Buddhist mind.'

'Interesting.'

'And, Chully?'

'I'm going to make a Buddhist contribution to saving the planet.'

'And all sentient beings as well.'

'Of course.'

'Paulus hava giving you all those very large books?'

'He has.'

'I not hava time to reading them. But Paulus was thinking they hava very good information, very useful.'

'I'll study them.'

'If you aren't sufficiently informed on Gaia, I can help,' says frosty blues.

'Thanks. I'll let you know.'

This is not the time to be seen consorting, even academically, with any blonde.

She removes some folders from her efficient-looking briefcase and hands one to me. It's the conference agenda, list of delegates and other relevant documents, including my airtickets. She's been very busy reworking Teacher's arrangements for his *ersatz* man. I awake to the ludicrous impression that she has somehow been put in charge of me.

I scan the list of delegates from South Africa. My name has been inserted directly above that of Popo Mbana (chequered Popo: as junior lecturer indicted for accepting students' bribes – duly promoted to senior lecturer – found guilty of sexual harassment – duly promoted to rector).

'I see Paw Paw Banana's on the list.'

'Professor Mbana's representing traditional African religions.'

'I hope he won't be slaughtering any goats for our instruction.'

'That's a bit facile, Charles.'

'I think thinking it facile's a bit facile.'

'To slaughtering a goat is not good,' Teacher opines.

'Especially for the goat.'

Merry moves the agenda forward. I'm given advice on obtaining a Czech visa, what weather to prepare for, how to confirm my hotel booking by email. It's all there in Times New Roman font, but she insists on talking me through it anyway. The aboriginal older sister. But I can't help succumbing. Ludicrous, yes; but it's really rather nice to be considered somewhat helpless, and may actually work to my advantage.

As soon as she's done she has to rush off to another meeting, and then an interview with the CEO of a misbehaving mining house. She suggests I read all about it on Sunday. (Mental note: Don't miss this opportunity to get a closer look.) Then she's gone.

'Very much working,' says Teacher.

'Well, she is a policeman's daughter.'

'Heh heh. You very nervous, Chully.'

'I suppose I am.'

'But, she is more nervous than you.'

After a last cup of tea I'm on my way home.

Back at the apartment I plug in the landline jack and switch on my cellphone. It immediately lets me know by means of an odd sci-fi sound effect, which puts me in mind of 'Forbidden Planet', that Mona has called about fifteen times. So she must be more than usually enraged by now. I decide to wait rather than call back.

I don't have to expect it for very long before the jazzy Bach ring-tone shakes up my scurrying neurons.

'Hello Mona.'

'I suppose you think you've pulled a very clever stunt.'

'Not clever. *Necessary.*'

'Necessary for what? You think I'm going to sit around and let you siphon off all the fricking money from a business that belongs to both of us? I've already made an appointment with Papa's attorney.'

'There's really no need to waste money on that.'

'No need from your jerkoff point of view, I'm sure.'

'I intend to pay all this money over into your account anyway. That's what it's all about. We're not savages trying to get at the dinosaur steaks by making cunning grabs behind each other's backs.'

'So it's all about Mr Immorality making a fricking moral point.'

'It's all about demonstrating that we can proceed with trust.'

'Well, I won't trust you until I see the fricking money transferred. All of it, I mean. And, Charlie, don't you count on trusting me. I want to see you pay and pay and pay.'

'I'll transfer the money first thing tomorrow.'

'Well you'd better.'

'I love you, Mona.'

'We'll see about that. We'll see how much you love me when I'm fricking well done with you.'

I sit and sit. When dusk touches the windowpanes, touches me too with a sense of inner fading and loneliness, I turn on the television. Skipping from one inanity to the next and the next, I finally settle on CNN.

War and rumours of war. A transparent attempt to mollify the daily horrors of Iraq, in the best American tradition, by a laughable resort to sentimentality. The little Iraqi boy so badly burnt that he'll need seven very dollar-consuming surgical procedures. The good Yankee doctors working gratis day and night to patch him up.

Sob.

A switch to the big big story. Iranian Prime Minister (and fanatical dictator) about to make a speech at Columbia University. The whole of New York's Jewry in a flap, like spoilt-silly children protesting a visit by an outcast cousin who presumes the right to share their candy, their toys and, God forbid, their bedrooms too.

'This is a guy who calls the holocaust a myth, who says the State of Israel has no right to exist. It's an insult to New York and a travesty of what Columbia University stands for. How can they invite this Hitler to speak here?'

Yarmulkes everywhere. Israeli flags with their air of blue innocence flapping in the breeze. Hatred. Fear. Tribalism. Religion.

Inside the hall the Iranian leader looks weedily dignified. The university president begins the proceedings by courageously ridding himself of an insulting diatribe: 'You, sir, are a petty tyrant ...' The tyrant is unmoved. He knows the rector has to keep his job. He knows, too, that the rector will be slowly disembowelled in the foreordained paradise when Jihad has its day.

When the academic heckling, booing and catcalling subsides and he is finally allowed to speak, he seems to be the only one making some sort of sense. At least he's not biting back. He's calling for a way to peace, bowing almost humbly to the pressures of the Pax Americana. Please America, don't come bomb my people into the dust. We're rather nice in our own way, though a little eccentric (if wanting our very own bomb is eccentric), if you'd only take the time to get to know us.

What will the Great Satan do? Whatever it wants, of course. And not because it is the Great Satan (what the hell *is* that anyway?), but the Great Human Being, absolutely corrupted by absolute power. Quote Abe Lincoln unquote.

It has free rein in the over-governed world. It stirs up technology to new heights of destruction and self-defeating gain. Where technology is insufficient, it hands over to the Little Human Being, who stirs the minds of religious malcontents to use what is at hand; rocks, petrol-bombs, passenger aircraft, with the promise of a paradise that might be said, albeit politely and with all due respect etc., to tend a wee bit to the ludicrous.

The Great and the Little Satan. Hard to choose between 'em.

I am astride that same old nightmare again. There is fire on the mountains. It's not the brush and trees that are burning. The earth itself is ablaze, blackened, rippling and gaping. Like distressed insects the people run up and down, helpless to save one another, fearful beyond all courage. If only I could understand what they are shouting into the flaming air, each in his own incomprehensible dialect. They don't even see, far less hear one another. Perhaps, if they would only pause from panic, they might decipher the babel of speech. But terror has shut down all that is held in common between them.

I struggle out into paralyzed wakefulness. CNN blahs on. Turn off the telly.

'I go for refuge, until I am enlightened, to the Buddha, the Dharma and the Sangha. By the virtuous merit that I create through the practise of generosity and the other perfections, may I attain the state of a Buddha in order to benefit all sentient beings.'

But none of this any longer provides sufficient cover. I go for refuge to the human being I ought to be, which, in my sober moments, I also want to be. And which, in the soberest moments, I know I never will be.

The parody of Bach. It's Mona. I'm a refugeless refugee.

'Yes.'

'Yes.'

'Yes, Mona?'

'Yes, Charlie?'

'Well, goodnight Mona.'

'You alone, Charlie?'

'Yes.'

'Well, goodnight.'

It's hard to break the habit of caring for the part (or whole) of yourself that in the course of a chronic relationship has become so stubbornly lodged in the other. Until you do you won't know love. Not the love that never faileth.

CHAPTER 5

In Which Painstaking Research Is Found To Be Unavailing Before The Stern Face Of The Inevitable

I'm surrounded by the weighty clutter of Teacher's very large tomes. Time to explore the apocalyptic literature of science. When, why and how will we humans perish, and what will we leave behind, if anything? And to ponder the question, *what can religion do about it?* and, more darkly, *how has religion contributed to this coming holocaust that will not be recorded by historians?*

Right.

By 2050 our experience of life on earth will be much more unpleasant than it is even by today's tacky standards, and we will have been the sole culprits. Even the most orthodox Buddhist will question the Buddha's opinion that, of all possible births in the six realms of Samsara, human birth is the most auspicious.

What, according to the expert literature spread out across my desk, can we expect?

Disastrous changes in global climate.

Instead of being the unwearied object of daily complaints, the weather, changed by our insistent interference into a raging fascist, will simply kill off millions upon millions of would-be complainers. Burning, freezing, hurled about like plastic cups in a whirlwind, they won't bother with the usual inanities. 'Lovely weather today, Bertie,' will no longer do as the conversational opener. We'll be too occupied in fervently praying for it. 'Crappy weather today, Joey,' will mark the speaker as a madman. All kinds of weather will become the objects of our daily deepest hopes and fears. There will be a half-hour weather forecast followed by two minutes of the daily global news. Weather permitting, of course.

There will be war on weather and defeats suffered at the hands of weather. The human-made system will be flooded out, washed away, blown apart, charred. Every living thing, except the most mutable, the most adaptable (nay, the virus and bacteria), will be made to kneel at the stern altar of the elements.

Clara will be forty years old, give or take, Jessica forty-one. I might still be alive to experience again what people haven't experienced for millennia: inescapable planetary cataclysm. Where will we be? In our living rooms, kitchens or bedrooms? In underground bunkers? Huddled together in the mountains?

Suddenly seeing it for the first time?

'Mr Fincham, what is the charge against the defendants?'

'That they have irrevocably buggered up the weather, Your Honour.'

'Buggered it up to what effect?'

'To the effect that the planet is virtually unliveable, Your Honour.'

'I see. And what do you propose I do about it?'

'Well, I suggest you devise a punishment proportionate to the crime.'

'What punishment could possibly be proportionate to such a crime?'

'None that I can think of.'

'Very well then, case dismissed.'

Drought, with rivers and waterways drying up.

No water. The prime vital commodity. Weather-resistant desalination plants for the richer nations. And the rest? And all other living beings? And agriculture? And the whole of nature in general?

A great business opportunity though. Humanity supplying water by the tricks of technology will sell water by the tricks of commerce. The rich will pay and drink their fill. The remainder will thirst, scramble, scuffle, deal on the black market, and kill.

For water, matey; for *pani*, you dig?

An ongoing fight, desperately carried forward, driven by something far more compelling than politics. By simple physical thirst, to wit.

Yet others will languish. Would I languish rather than struggle to survive in such a place among such fellows? Most will not languish on principle but because they have no means to fight effectively for their share. The rest will rely on *criminality*, a weird epithet for what must be done in such an unimaginable exigency. You will be dragged before the law, charged with the theft of a litre of water and a gee-em turnip.

'What say you, Your Honour? Theft of a litre of water and a gee-em Turnip?'

'Under the present dire circumstances this court has no option but to make an example of the offenders. Sentenced to life imprisonment on both counts, the sentences to be served concurrently.'

'But have you paused to consider, Your Honour, how much water will be drunk in the course of two life sentences, even if they are served concurrently?'

'Indeed, I have not. But now you mention it, it is clear that the death sentence is the more appropriate in this case.'

Destruction of marine life.

Good bye to all that, the faerie kingdom. Good bye, jewels, animal and vegetable and mineral, in *chambers of the sea.* You have been *woken by human voices after all.*

'Fish and chips, Bertie?'
'Yeh. Weren't those the good old days!'

But every fish, oyster, crab and crayfish seems to me a work of art, the marine iconoclast the destruction of another universe entire. Only dead water left, leviathan gone. The loss, not only of something so magical it may as well have been a myth, but of the myth that reposed so naturally beneath the real. Gone, our terrene window into the unreal.

I, Charlie Fincham, stood upon the shores before dawn to be dazzled by the chill sun rising. I saw Aton ascend from the western rim of the deep. And in the deep the life of the deep, endless. *Shine on us, Aton, for thou art our sustenance.*

What will the shark eat?

Mass famine in ill-organized countries.

What does he mean by *ill-organized* countries? Countries that are lazy and therefore poor? Yep. *Countries made lazy and poor by alien intrusion and exploitation. Countries whose natural traditions of survivalist productivity were displaced by a foreign landlord.*

Now the poor buggers have to jump to it, get themselves reorganized before the day of reckoning. Problem is, the day of reckoning has already arrived for most of them. It's too late to rally the few fully human survivors among them. Most of those have fled to the wealthy lands anyway.

Charlie can't take care of them, so who will?

Or will they just be left to starve? (What's that? Already starving, eh?)

'I contend that they're already being criminally left to starve, Your Honour.'

'There is no law compelling generosity, Mr Fincham.'

'That seems remiss in the face of mass-starvation.'

'Nonsense. If you introduced such a law, you'd have to criminalize greed.'

Pandemics of new diseases.

Hang on. Is this a bad thing? Not by Paulus' theory. One could argue on pragmatic grounds against this being added to the list of impending catastrophes. An unstoppably ravenous killer pandemic versus an unstoppable mindset of greed. Might do the trick.

The problem is that only the greediest, most destructive types will have the money and power to protect themselves. Those who pose the least danger will be carried off. Even so, less of any sort will no doubt be better.

And if Clara and Jessie are carried off? And Mona? And Teacher, Paulus, Madam, Halfwit, Merry, Marta, Ulla? And, er, Mauron? And Charlie too?

A tricky question, this one. An easy problem for the abstract mind of the scientific ideologue. An insoluble riddle for the *human mind*, and at least as ancient as thinking itself: What to do in cases where allowing or inflicting suffering turn out to be the only radical remedies for suffering?

And the even more ancient question: Why is death viewed as a problematic evil when it is so inarguably the only final answer to every possible problem?

'Well, why *is* that, Your Honour?'

'Better the devil you know than the devil you don't.'

'I suppose so. But can we move on to the really pertinent question: why is it that we insist on saving the lives of people whose excessive numbers are a threat to the stability of the earth? This seems so much in illogical contrast to the fact that we send soldiers off to kill members of much smaller populations if those populations pose a risk to the limited population of another nation.'

'It does indeed seem illogical, but for that you must blame the Hippocratic Oath.'

'But does that oath imply that you must save even those who, by the sole fact of their existence, decrease the chances of survival of the whole?'

'I suppose it does.'

'Then, Your Honour, it seems a self-defeating oath, because it purports to uphold the principle of compassion with the left hand while completely negating it with the right.'

'Your suggestion being, I take it, that the withholding of compassion is in some circumstances the appropriate compassionate act.'

'Well, *yes.*'

'And is that, in your opinion, compatible with the Buddhist view?'

'Yes, *in extremis.*'

'Even *in extremis*, it seems rather hard-hearted.'

'But irrefutable by logic. I would submit that it is more hard-hearted to invite a thousand people to a meal that can adequately feed only a hundred. Such an illogical act would mean the starvation of them all.'

'Your point is taken. But whom should we allow to live and whom to die?'

'That, in terms of this argument, is nature's prerogative.'

I wonder, will this be half as easy as turning away from the beggars I encounter in the city streets every day? Oi, sir, can yer spare uz yer loose change fer a bite and a drink? Nah, just look atcher, ya lazy shiftless bum.

That's the problem with the starving, innit? Just too damned lazy to work.

Poor nations becoming increasingly destitute.

Disposed of as unsaleable remnants. Left to starve or to be killed off by an unstoppable pandemic of new (and old) infectious diseases.

Even if a modicum of compassion survives in the human mind under the severe stresses predicted for us, what can compassion accomplish without resources: without food, water, medicines? The job of compassion will consist in helping people to accept death and to go with silent dignity *into that good night.*

Economic progress must take the blame for this.

Blame the game.

And Charlie, the player, too.

Worldwide mass migrations of refugees.

When the flood of starving refugees becomes very much bigger in size and more devious in tactics than the measures taken to prevent its influx into the lands of plenty, the world will become everybody's rotten oyster.

Global nomadism and the banditry of nomadism. The return of the hunter-gatherer in conflict with his local competition, while the settled society wages sophisticated war on him as well. The critical point reached, why not opt for the final control mechanism?

Keep out the migrants, nomads, hunter-gatherers, *parasitic vagrants.* Will we again make use of the lessons of inhuman efficiency, learned over the centuries from the Assyrians through the Romans through the Germans through the Russians through the Americans through the Israelis and even through the Europeans as a single dehumanized leftist bureaucracy bent on destroying what is not politically correct?

It's only an innocent question.

God help those politically incorrect parasitic vagrants.

Cheap and easy access to weapons of mass destruction.

Everything becomes cheaper when it's mass produced and has a mass market. Mass produced mass destruction for the masses. Masses of money for the weapons industry (and the weapons black market which is the legitimate industry's most treasured client after governments, bad, worse and worst.)

'Hand me down that phial of smallpox virus, Bertie. I got a score to settle next door.'

Bandit regimes with biological weapons and nuclear warheads. Or banana dictators with antisocial tendencies. A lunatic with a racist gripe, or a lunatic simply.

I am trying to form a cinematic picture of all this in my head. It already seems like a tragic epic too large even for Hollywood to conceptualize. But no, they *have* conceptualized it in *Star Wars*, where an unacceptably nasty little planet is blown to smithereens every fortnight.

Growth of squatter cities with crime, poverty and violence.

A paradox. Amidst the extreme violence and poverty these shantysprawls continue to grow. Violence and poverty don't outgun the subversive activity of spermatazoa and ovum, nor discourage bumpkin newcomers from increasing the size of the community.

Too many people. Too many poor. Too many getting poorer. Too little wherewithal. The city is a gamble. It's not 'if you can make it there, you can make it anywhere' but 'if you can't make it there, there's nowhere else you can.'

For all its pretended globalism, globalization ignores the hick towns.

Huge increases in suicide terrorism.

Mental query: Shouldn't those nice old bearded paternal types make this a sin against the Only God. Why haven't they done so yet? Something fundamentally fishy here. On the other hand, for what gain would *you* be willing to give your life at the expense of the lives of others'? To blast your way to the source of food and water kept out of your family's reach beyond the moats of a wealthy fortress nation?

Kamikaze may not be cricket, but not everyone sees cricket as the only valid standard of warfare. The cricketing soldier is one who goes to war *not intending* to die. He certainly goes, however, intending to kill. And, is the hero who rushes the enemy position, grenade in hand, knowing that he must perish in this act of courage, fundamentally different from the young bomb-wielding Arab in the midst of his enemies? Those who will not let him get on with life on his own turf and terms?

Meritorious or not, the young Arab will be visiting your city soon, and in increasing numbers. When you see him, get off the plane, train or bus. Cross over to the other side of the street. Eventually, I suppose, when every young Arab is a suicide bomber, you'll be entitled to shoot him on sight, with inevitable mistaken shootings of young Arab-looking non-suicide non-bombers.

'Why did you shoot your stepfather, sonny?'
'Mistook him for a young Arab, Your Honour.'
'I see. Case dismissed.'

Nuclear / biological terrorism.

'How did the enriched uranium and smallpox virus pass from the saintly hands of the scientists who cooked up these horrors, for the noble purposes of increasing human knowledge and safeguarding civilization, to the diabolical talons of the laymen who will put them to this awful use?'

'By a specific principle of inevitability, Your Honour, which the scientists don't seem to have discovered yet.'

'Pray, what principle is that?'

'That nothing has ever been made that was not capable of being stolen.'

'I believe we in the legal game would have to agree with that. But why were the scientists, for all their alleged brilliance, unable to anticipate it?'

'By a specific principle of blindness, Your Honour, which afflicts us all.'

'I see. But, pray, what principle is that?'

'The Faustian one.'

*Ach Gott, die Not ist gross: Die ich rief, die Geister, komm'
ich nun nicht los!*

Religious war between Muslims and Christians.

Would ya believe that the most informed among us predict such a thing? A religious war in the 21st Century?

'Mr President, do you predict such a thing?'
'Shore I do. We cain't leave all that oil in the hands of the wrong God, now cain we? Besides that holy consideration, we cain't let Jesus be seen as a waikling, cain we? No sir, the Lord shore ain't no waikling.'
'But he recommended turning the other cheek. Meek, not weak. The meek shall inherit the earth.'
'Yeah, all six feet of it, boyo!'

'And you, O Grand Mufti and All-Supreme Leader?'
'The Great Satan must be destroyed. The one true religion must be everywhere established.'
'Isn't that view a trifle primitive considering the times we live in? I mean, live and let live and all that?'
'Is that a hypothetical question or a blasphemous opinion in disguise?'
'A humble, stupid and misguided question, Your Eminent Peerless Holiness. In fact, I don't remember ever asking it. I believe I've been maliciously misquoted by myself.'
'Then you shall not have your tongue cut out, your hands chopped off, your legs thrice broken at the knees and your head crushed between volumes one and two of *How To Win Friends And Influence Them To Blow Themselves Up*. But do not ask it again.'

Global warfare with nuclear and biological weapons.

Though you place a fool in a mortar and grind him with a pestle, yet will his folly not depart from him. (To quote Solomon, who married a thousand wives.)

'In this regard, Mr President, do you believe that the politico-military establishment is largely an assembly of immoral fools?'
'The military mebbe, but not the politicos.'
'Thank you, that is very reassuring.'

'And you, General Schickelgruber? Do you believe that the politico-military establishment is largely an assembly of immoral

fools?'
'Not the military, son.'
'Thank you, that is very reassuring.'

'Why, Your Honour, are nuclear and biological weapons stock-piles maintained if no country ever intends to use them in any future war?'
'Deterrent purposes, I am told.'
'But how can they act as a deterrent if they are never to be used?'
'By Jove, I see your point! Perhaps they are being kept for some other purpose known only to the men at the top?'
'What other purpose can they serve if their use must inevitably mean the eventual destruction of the planet?'
'It is most mystifying.'
'But – but – isn't it obvious that the only practical purpose in view must be to obliterate us all in some ultimate showdown?'
'Well, *that* should be something of a deterrent.'
'Not, I respectfully submit, to the Ultimate Suicide Bomber.'
'Now there's a thought.'

Dangers posed by extreme science – for instance, genetically modified pathogens.

Or, simply, genetically modified anything at all.
And what, really, is extreme science? Is it not *any science that makes extreme science possible*? That places in human hands the remotest possibility of bringing about universal destruction?

'How say you, Jury? Guilty or not guilty?'
'Guilty, Milord.'
'But have you taken into account the question of *intention?*'
'We have, Milord.'
'And?'
'We find that the intention was *not to avoid* scientific experimen-tation that put the planet and all who live on her at risk.'
'But that is hardly the same as the intention to destroy the whole bang-shoot.'
'Correct, Milord. That is why we find these scientists guilty only on the lesser charge; terracide, faunacide, floracide and genocide in

the *2ⁿᵈ degree*.'

'And you have not found anyone who can reasonably be charged in the *1ˢᵗ degree*?'

'No, Milord. It is our considered opinion that *that* can only be established once the planet has actually been blown up.'

'Quite right.'

'And so, Mr Fincham, what are your conclusions at this stage?'

'Your Honour, it is my firm belief that human nature is the culprit. It is furthermore my contention that religion has traditionally had the reponsibility for rehabilitating the said human nature, but has manifestly failed in its task.'

'Do you have any opinion on why it has failed?'

'Yes. Human nature has created religion. How then can the creator be transformed by its own creation? Will it not tend rather to modify, embellish, twist, elaborate, mangle and maul its religious beliefs to suit its current self-view?'

'What then may the remedy then be, if any?'

'To go beyond religion to truth.'

'But, if I may quote, *"Quid est veritas?"* '

'In my opinion only this, *that all harmful behaviour results in self-destruction*. That's the only truth that matters now.'

'And how shall we proceed to achieve the compliance of human nature with this truth? Religion cannot do it, apparently. The law, too, has failed. Your own failure in this regard, Mr Fincham, has also been noted.'

'In the final sense, human nature may only learn its lessons by one last big experience. A bit of a Catch 22. We can only know what it's like not have a planet once we no longer have one. It's a problem, this sort of learning curve.'

'What will you say at the conference, Mr Fincham?'

'I honestly don't know.'

I get up from my desk, worn out with useless thinking. The rows of bookcases stand about dumbly, seeming to ponder helplessly their own superabundant stocks of knowledge. But would they be able to give answers even if they could find expression?

Petrified frustration.

I am pulled back down into my chair.

'*Chully.*'

'*Yes, Rinpoche.*'

'*You really not knowing the answer?*'

'*Apparently not.*'

'*But you hava mentioning the human nature, and it should not harming.*'

'*Well, not if it doesn't want to destroy itself.*'

'*But, Chully, it wanting very much to destroying itself.*'

'*No point advising it to avoid harmful behaviour then.*'

'*No. And this you already know very for certain. Before you have actually doing unfaithful relations with that woman, you have knowing that this was a harmful action, no?*'

'*No doubt about it.*'

'*And that it would destroying your world.*'

'*Only if I was found out.*'

'*Heh heh. Nobody not found out. I mean, deeply. Karma is like that.*'

'*Yes, ain't it though!*'

'*So, why you doing this harmful thing? Must be to wanting to destroying your human nature and the nature of your world.*'

'*My God ...*' (There he is again.)

'*The human nature it is a self-hating nature, Chully, and also it hate this world which has been created by it.*'

From the centre of his forehead and his heart, streams of light penetrate my worn-out mind, shimmering brightly among the sparsely distributed brain-cells.

'*This world which people have created; it is not separable from their own nature and their own minds. That is why they are its slaves. It is inside their heads, not outside in their hands. And it causes very big suffering because their minds are inside this world which is also inside their minds. Therefore, it is their prison. Prison of their minds.*'

'*Then there's no escape.*'

'*Nowadays is very much difficult because middle-way has been abandoned and, when middle-way is abandoned, very hard finding your way back to it.*'

'*As simple as that, Rinpoche?*'

'*No, it is not simple. Only sounding simple.*'

'*Where have we left our middle-way then?*'
'*When your way of life is poor and empty, that is not the middle-way. When you making it good, you have found your middle-way. But people never satisfied; they always wanting make it better. Then, making it better and better, they losing again their middle-way. When it is good, you can making little bit better. But too much better, that is not middle-way. Too much better is same as too much bad.*'

Too deep is not very far from too shallow.
O Mona! O Moaner!

'*When people having everything they needing, that is good. Then, when making better and better and better, that is only greed. Today our world is too much better. Getting our needs is always simple, but our greeds are always complicated. The open path is always simple, very simple, Chully, but ... heh heh heh ... the prison is very much complicated, no? It must have so many rules, gates, locks, passages ... heh heh.*'

How simple it was on the open path with Mona before we began consciously planning and constructing our lives, fear becoming our guiding lamp, lighting our way towards a better future.
    And here it is, that future.
    'Have you understood anything of what Teacher has said, Mr Fincham.'
    'I believe it is slowly seeping inwards, Your Honour.'
    'What will you say at the conference?'
    'I honestly don't know.'

Madam and Jessica are at the door. The farewell Sunday lunch has been baking in a single oven pan while I've been considering the end of days. I have done my best with what's available: a potato-and-desultory-vegetable bake. I haven't done my best keeping an eye on it baking.
    It's unsatisfying leaving my friends and mentors behind in the study. We haven't yet reached those tidy conclusions on whose terms an approach to the conference can be formulated. This sort of unfinished business always leaves me depressed. I fear that we may not be able to reach any conclusions at all.

'Hello, dad.'

'My darling Jessie.'

'Hello, Charles.'

'Adam.'

Why do certain imbeciles revert, when naming their firstborn sons, to the idea of the prototype mudman? Don't they realize that these boys' wives will unfailingly and evermore be associated with apple-pie Eve?

Jessie takes over from me, so that we are soon seated around the overbaked bake. Fortunately, she's brought a hefty salad and some Italian bread. I set the example by chewing through the first potato-wedge while Adam watches with that irksome air of *comprendre tout*. Then he too pops one in and chews, rather more pensively, with an air of distant critique in his eyes.

'Have you spoken to mom recently.'

'Yes, last night.'

'How is she?'

'She's always enjoyed visiting the farm.'

'I think what Jessica means –'

'I know what Jessie means, Adam. Mom's holding up. She has a strong personality.'

'You mean she's a strong person.'

'No, I don't think I mean that.'

'So, you're off to save the world, I hear,' Adam interposes.

'Yes, if you like.'

'Seems a nutty idea, this sort of conference.'

'Does it?'

'Well, *yes*. Religion's *irrelevant* to all the important issues.'

'I hope you're right. In that case my contribution won't matter and I needn't break my head over it.'

'So you'll be making a contribution?' (Still pensively chewing, chewing.)

'Yes, an irrelevant one, of course. The Buddhist angle on saving the world.'

'Buddhism's not detached in that regard?'

'For heaven's sake, Adam, Buddhists are people too.'

'Thank you, Jessie.'

All through lunch I am thinking how nice it would have been if Jessie and I were alone. I want to communicate my love for her, a love that has much of its basis in the recognition of the traits we share. I see so much of myself in her, but it's myself in a much more successful guise, myself without the burdens of my particular history. Or myself minus about eighty per cent of myself.

I also want her to understand that I am not an adulterer at heart. Mine is the unconscious, blundering flit of the flight-crazed fruit bat, not the treacherous dive of the wasp. I slam into those scandalous occasions that come out looking like premeditated crimes but are really the thoughtless misadventures of a mouse with ill-fitted, badly designed wings, not to mention poor eyesight.

I doubt that I will ever be as grown up as she already is.

For all his gauche one-upmanship, Madam is not entirely unlovable. For one thing, he bears with the me in Jessica which, although present in a far less neurotic form, is nevertheless no easy companion. Naturally, when it comes to his treatment of the me in myself, I consider him an impertinent twit. But that's only because he's enjoyed such a cosy upbringing, cosseted to the extent that suffering is for him not much more than an abstract concept. This makes him facile. Having known nothing but love and admiration all his young life, he must insist on the risibility of the search, the *religious* search, for the sense of belonging in the world. So, as I know only too well, he can't help laughing at me.

I'm very glad that he is Jessie's husband.

Just before they leave he slips me a CD. It's Bach's keyboard concertos done by Gould, with whose embellished interpretations Adam doesn't agree, and which he finds disagreeable, and which don't agree with him.

'I'll never understand why you think them so *original*,' he insists, handing it over.

'That's very kind of you, Adam.'

'Bach's the *original* one of the two, you know.'

'Thanks all the same.'

'Enjoy Prague, dad, and don't worry too much. Adam and I will be visiting mom while you're away. It'll be okay.'

'God, I'm such a bloody idiot!' I blurt out.

'We know that,' says Adam. 'You think Gould's a great interpreter.'

Jessica delivers an understated peck to my flushing cheek and Adam limply swings my hand about. I suppose, in spite of myself, I love them as an incongruous and perplexing duet; say, Domingo and Marianne Faithful.

'*Bon voyage.*'

I return to the study, not expecting to make much further progress. Once I've made myself drowsily comfortable in the wordy jumble of books, I notice that a new face, solemn and supercilious, has been added to my group of interlocutors.

It's Mr Griffith-Jones, counsel for the prosecution. (You know Mr Griffith-Jones, eh? The twit who led the prosecution against Penguin Books in the case of *Lady Chatterley*?) It seems I am being charged with ignorance.

'I put it to you, Mr Fincham, that you still have no idea who is to blame for our planetary crisis, nor what role religion has played in the matter, nor what religion may or may not be able to do about it.'

'If it please the court, I can only say that I now believe it all has something to do with the abandonment of that balanced simplicity associated with the *golden mean*, the same golden mean which Precious Teacher has termed the *middle-way*. As to who is to blame, I have made it clear that *human nature* is the culprit, and that religion has failed in its task of leading people to a moderating, not to say *a transcending*, of that fatally flawed nature.'

'You contend, then, that all humanity shares in the blame since all partake of the same fundamental nature?'

'Yes.'

'And that religion is the proper institution for correcting that nature.'

'By its own claims, yes.'

'And that it has failed to effect such a correction?'

'Yup.'

'Thereby allowing humanity to develop, or regress, beyond the golden mean?'

'Yup again.'

'In what, then, does the crucial failure of religion consist?'

'In its strong resemblance to the old human nature which human nature desires religion to rid human nature of.'

I have slipped away into a doze. All the people in the world are on their knees confessing their collective human nature. Their numbers stretch away across the mountains and along the plains to the horizon. Behind those kneeling in the West the sun is sinking, shedding drops of liquid light the colour of blood. I am looking about desperately for angels, devas or other spirit-beings that might be arriving to rescue them, or even to listen to their forlorn confessions, but there are none.

The onus is on me, apparently.

Griffith-Jones, seeming to have lost his mind, is prancing wigless among the crowds, announcing in a sing-sing voice, 'It's up to Mr Fincham, the ignorant Mr Fincham; can't save his rocky marriage but he's off to save the world.'

This all seems very unfair.

When I come round, the study is stuck, frame-frozen in the stillness of mid-afternoon. My intellectual researches have left me stymied. It's to the dreams and nightmares beyond reason that I must turn for answers because, if they can be found at all, it is there, *in those dimly lit chambers where all people concoct their unreasonable motives*, that the crazy solutions might be stumbled upon.

In the early evening, having meditated for an hour, I ring Precious Teacher.

'I think you should wearing your robes again in Prague,' he says casually.

'Am I to become a Buddhist monk again, Rinpoche?'

'You know that robes not making a Buddhist, Chully.'

'Then what's the purpose?'

I can sense the clarity of his mind as he ponders this question to which he has an ultimately uncommunicable answer.

'Is there any specific reason?' I insist.

'I do not know specifically.'

'You have no reasons?'

'To hava no reasons is good because then no reasons you can arguing against.'

'I'll have to trust you.'

'I am your teacher, Chully.'

CHAPTER 6

In Which Several Instances Of Airborne Human Behaviour Are Followed By A Bumpy Landing

In the check-in queue with Merry, I am still able to feel dimly the old sense of the traveller's excitement, until I notice that Paw Paw Banana is on the same flight. Paw Paw is known to me not only through misinformation contrived by the malicious lies of the white-controlled press, but also at a more personal level, as a rotter and a soak.

I have dealt with him at close range on two occasions. The first was a homely diplomatic soiree at the office of Tibet, which Banana attended by invitation as a representative of the new post-apartheid academia. What impressed me most on that occasion was his relentless partiality for Tibetan mutton momos and expensive Scotch. I was also very intrigued to hear him loudly argue the view that the Chinese oppression of Tibet was as nothing compared with the treatment of Blacks at the hands of Whites in the apartheid days, and that the only way forward for the Tibetan cause was the way of the terrorist.

The Tibetan officials, unnerved yet polite, explained that the Dalai Lama was not likely ever to contemplate such an approach. Paw Paw refused to admit this consideration as an obstacle: 'You should vote him out.' Neither could he be persuaded by the argument, put forward with awkward delicacy, that His Holiness was a living Buddha who could not be voted out: 'If he izi a living god, he should have powah to put some sort of spell on the Chinese. Otherwise he cannot be a god.'

The bewildered officials roared with laughter.

The second occasion was a conference on racism which I attended together with the Tibetan delegation. Here again Banana was to be seen mainly at the bar, playing the role of the intellectual wild man. Having recently been raised to the rector's chair, he took a particularly learned view of the racist question in the world. If the Americans and the Europeans had indeed abandoned their racist inclinations, he wanted to know, *why was Africa still so impoverished?* The Tibetans again roared with laughter, and so did everyone else.

And here is Professor Banana shifting up along the queue to make small talk with Merry. He is draped in stereotypical Nigerian garb, his pan-African statement, I suppose. His boozy eyes and smile are subtly terrifying. One feels rather at a loss, as in the presence of a notably unpredictable beast.

'Miss Grimes!'

'Professor Mbana.'

'It's not always a good idea to have a janalist around.'

'I think it's always a very good idea. This is Mr Fincham.'

'Pleased to meet you, Mr Fincham.'

'And you, Mr Mbanana.'

I leave them to their cordial chitchat, hoping mightily that neither will want to sit beside me once aboard because, to judge from their apologetic chumminess, you definitely can't have one without the other.

Having checked-in, I lose myself for a while in the airport hubbub while Merry goes looward and Paw Paw ambles over to the bar. Here, all around me, I can't but recognize the microcosm of Precious Teacher's 'better and better and better'. Nor can I escape the press of Paulus' too many people.

Too many people fussing at the business of ceaseless self-involvement. There is a half-formed vision here, an hallucination of the *passionlessly intertwined writhing of a brood of vipers*, that has me bolting for the door.

It's damp outside; perfect weather for a cosy smoke. I'm already missing not the presence but the proximity of Clara, Jessica, Mona, Halfwit. In the next few days and weeks I shall have to make the acquaintance of other, unfamiliar madnesses. And I am thinking with Strindbergh, 'I do not hate man, I fear him.'

'Excuse me, may I bother you for a light!?'

For a crazy moment, still confused by my spontaneous identification with the Swedish dramatist, and looking inwards at the sparse light flickering there, I have the impression that some suffering being is importuning me for the light of insight.

The man is spare and angular, a composite, blurred geometry of ovals, triangles, lines, a cubist portrait come to life. There's something about the arrangement that seems inclined to fall apart, and you wonder what internal force is struggling to hold it together.

'Of course.'

'Thank you. That's a Buddhist rosary you have on your wrist!'

'They're called *mala*. Tibetan.'

'We carry ours in our pockets or hang them from our motorcar mirrors!'

'Catholic.'

'Yes indeed. I'm Charles!'

'No.'

'Yes!'

' I'm Charlie.'

'How delightful! I noticed your rosary in the check-in line and wondered whether you might be taking part in a conference which! –'

'I am.'

'Well, there you are! I'm going as an observer for the White Fathers! Heard of us!? The Spiritans! Founded by Francis Libermann, a Jew who converted and became a great saint! At least, *we* think he should be canonized! We Spiritans were the first into the remotest regions of Africa!'

'And your angle at the conference is?'

'The catholic one, naturally! But that doesn't mean we don't see the bigger picture, if that's not a contradiction in terms! Ha! It's very big indeed! How does one begin to assess the problem!? Not to speak of trying to solve it by religious or, for that matter, any other means!'

'I have a simple view on that.'

'You do, do you!? Fix the ozone layer! Stop CO_2 and methane emissions! End pollution! Eradicate poverty! Deal with the population explosion! Effect an escape from global consumerism! Find clean energy! Stop the wholesale destruction of nature! Practise clean politics! Put an end to war and terrorism! Deal with new diseases! Cope with runaway science and immoral technologies! Avoid direct interference in evolution! Hold back the Frankensteins from manufacturing enhanced human beings! Establish a new and universally responsible civilization! Rescue the earth from becoming a virtually lifeless rock! All to be accomplished in the next twenty years! That's all the time we have! You have a simple view on all that, do you!?'

'I'm afraid so.'

'Well, God bless you!!'

I wander off to the relative quiet of the car park. Hundreds of exhaust pipes poke out at me, each with its own insidious history of sun-obscuring carbon emissions. The cars keep coming and going in an unbroken flow. Every two minutes or so an aircraft lands or rises dirtily and magnificently into the sky.

I feel too small to care.

It's drizzling now, with black clouds massing over the lit-up urban sprawl. The freeways are crammed with slow-moving vehicles crossing my line of sight like weary but persistent thoughts. You couldn't count them if you had nothing else to do.

Evening is rolling over into early night. Everywhere new lights are coming on. Millions of jittery people are calling it a day, wedged in traffic jams, shuffling into lifts, crawling into pubs, stepping across one or another threshold. The nightshift is about to commence. Silence, cessation, is an unimaginable idea.

As the plane ascends, the bowl of multicoloured lights spreads out below us. There is no end to them until we climb above the clouds. Suddenly the sense of being part of the hyperactive world is entirely gone. Up here, in this temporary lifeboat, a small, fractured quiet envelopes the passengers, a spontaneous tribute to the dreamy experience of flight.

When the drinks come round the agitated buzz starts up again. We are packed in so closely that the word 'economy' takes on new and unexpected connotations, having nothing to do with its etymon. Alcohol and various pills are used to create the illusion of space.

'Are you sure you're not mistaken?' I ask the flight attendant who is inviting me to go forward into business class.

'You are Meester Charles Fincham?' she insists with businesslike sultriness.

'Yes.'

'Pleez folleu me zen.'

It's Merry's doing. Whatever her credentials are, Air France are aware of them. As I am ushered in beside her, she slips me a tolerant smile with the slightest hint of smugness, and then a burst of barefaced *noblesse oblige*.

'Very kind of you.'

'So many untaken seats in here, it seems a shame to waste them.'

'Will you be handing one down to Paw Paw Banana?'

'Now that *would* be a waste. Besides, I'd be pushing my luck.'

'This is very nice of you, Mary. Keeping Paw Paw out is also nice.'

'I'm sure he'd prefer it this way too.'

'Oh? I had the impression that you two were quite friendly.'

'Call it professional regard. I've written some articles about him.'

'Really?'

'You could say I was responsible for some of his promotions.'

'That was *your* work? The sexual harassment thing?'

'Yes, and the other thing too.'

'I read your interview with the mining CEO. You're obviously taken seriously, to say the least. I was impressed by your diatribe on their dirty little ventures with the Chinese regime in Tibet.'

'I believe in what I do, Charlie.'

'I wish I did.'

'Rinpoche was at pains to assure me that you are a very sincere person.'

'I suppose I'm a sincere *satyagrahi*. When my truth changes, I change with it. It's been changing rather rapidly lately.'

'What new truth are you bringing to the conference then?'

'Whichever occurs to me *in situ*.'

A familiar voice is being raised from a few rows behind us, while the meals are being distributed.

'I'll have the ragout! And some more wine, thank you!'

(An unheard reply.)

'Well then, take the ragout off somebody else! You haven't run out of wine too, I hope!? I really can't have the fish!'

'Sounds like my namesake.'

'Oh, you've met him?'

'Only as Charles the Catholic.'

'He's something more than that. He's Bishop Charles Bell, former head of the international interfaith committee. He holds several doctorates, not only in the religious disciplines. The bishop's also something of a scientist. He's written some highly regarded papers in the fields of paleontology and ethology, and has published popular works on cultural evolution. I suppose with that kind of brain he's bound to turn out to be something of an eccentric. These days he's parked in an out of the way parish in Transkei. Apparently he's done some controversial things there, too; social experiments that work well for the poor but antagonize the tribal leaders.'

'You know a lot of people.'

'I know about a lot of people. There's no helping it in my job.'

'You're just the slightest bit more accomplished than I've been giving you credit for. Can't say it surprises me, though. You look the part.'

'Let's just say that in my freelance work for the Associated Press, the Sunday Times is only one job among many. I have to add, in my turn, Charlie, that I suspect there may be more to you as well.'

'There's more, of course. But it hasn't earned me any renown or influence. It's what you might call the normal sort of more. The more that becomes less as you grow older. Or matters less – or perhaps matters more – because it's diminished by time.'

'What matters is that you take a stand.'

'Like your stand on people using cellphones behind the wheel?'

'Why not? It's not a stand for the rules. My father was a policeman. I know all about rules and how they can be bent. It's about mindfulness. I get angry when I see people senselessly splitting their concentration, endangering others by their carelessness.'

'It makes sense, even universal sense.'

'Yes, Charlie. Everyone's chatting on their cellphones while the planet gets raped.'

Our meals are being served with suave apologies for the ragout having run out. It's been an unexpectedly popular choice. I'm surprised to gather that someone has reserved a vegetarian meal for me. Mary confirms my suspicions by saying nothing, and she has a vegetarian dish too.

It's not long after supper when I am recognized by the perambulating Bishop Charles Bell, who stops by for a visit. Now that he's removed his scarf I can see the collar and the tarnished silver crucifix. He pretends, avuncularly, to introduce me to Merry.

'This is Charlie! He has a simple view on world affairs!'

'And this is Bishop Charles Bell,' I tell Merry, taking the cleric by surprise. 'A complicated Roman Catholic.'

'Simple *and* well-informed, eh!'

'I've been told you're quite famous, Monsignor.'

'Monsignor nothing! Just plain Charles! Famous, eh!? Infamous, I'd say! A prophet has no honour in his hometown or among the members of his own household! I've been warning them for decades that it would come to this! Nobody listened! Wouldn't be distracted from the saying of mass, the hearing of confessions, the rites of baptism, confirmation, marriage, ordination, last rites! Keeps them busy no end! Fiddling while Rome burns! Or is it Rome doing the fiddling? Not a far-fetched analogy! They've had other warnings too! Eliot, Lawrence, Hesse, Sartre, Becket, Monod, Teilhard, you could go on and on! Every kind of warning about the dehumanization of the human creature! No one could hear the meaning; too dazzled by the words! Great literature, great minds, great teachers! Their students kept too busy by their greatness to bother about what they had to say! Then suddenly even their greatness was passé! Now the scientists have the floor! Great theories, great minds, great breadth! What to do now, eh!? Now that these devastating difficulties are being presented in their rawest form to an already dehumanized race!? As if human nature weren't mischievous enough without its being dehumanized! I tell you, if anyone literate enough were to survive to record it in the long run, the 20th century would go down in history as the century of dehumanization! Now what will they do, eh!? Try to put things right by manipulating our genes!? Mad scheme! What's been taken away from us wasn't in our genes in the first place! It was outside of us entirely! In the natural world! In our awe before it! Who stands in awe of nature now!? No one! Why should anyone stand in awe of a force that lays itself down to be exploited by every passer-by with a pick and shovel!? Now it's about to hit back, eh!? Hit back hard!! But people have been plundering it with impunity for so long that they no longer believe it capable of defending itself, especially not of defending itself by *simply dying*! Taking all of us to perdition along with it, like Samson!'

No one in business class is paying any attention to the movie now. They have Savonarola instead. The flight attendants are keeping their heads low. This is more than a clamorous passenger; it's an inspirited bishop. It's not an annoyance; it's quaint prophetic entertainment.

'I can hardly wait for you to reveal your simple view, Charlie!'

'You'll have to be patient.'

'Well, God bless you!!'

The blessing falls loudly, like a blow. Merry hasn't moved throughout the harangue. The bishop nods curtly and balances his trim stature back down the aisle.

'God bless all of you!' we hear him calling from amidships and, when he has finally seated himself, 'You'll certainly need it!'

Merry is smiling very privately, and with a touch of strain. I am almost moved to pat her arm but it doesn't seem appropriate. She glances at me as though sensing the half-formed intention. I laugh out loud, hoping to impart at least a semblance of psychological strength.

We sit amid the rustle and murmur of our fellow voyagers. Whatever we are silently sharing has nothing to do with mutual attraction, or with any energy of personality. It is a sudden and keen detachment from all these accidents of personal existence.

Gradually my thoughts drift homewards to Mona and the girls. Clara so full of the beauty of virginal delicacy, of the pliable and fluid resilience of grace. Her sister so different again: her dark eyes warm with the straightforwardness, and frowardness, of the plain girl's wisdom. So fully known to me, yet often so surprising.

I deliberately breathe in Mona's pain, the pain that I have shared with her from the first, from the day I put aside my gorgeous robes of red and yellow, choosing for this karma. Ours was a very physical love. We joked that she brought out the Italian in me. But we both knew that one vow had been broken in favour of another.

Now that other vow has been trodden into the soft flesh of illicit sensuality and her sorrow must be at least as wearying as mine was then, feeling that I had come down off a mountaintop to be with her in the lower plains of happiness. I know now that it was only a romantic conceit of oblivious youth. There are no higher or lower plains of happiness.

The laying aside a *shemdap* robe wasn't, after all, what *this* was, a singularly disgraceful act: the thoughtless discarding of a tattered but very human love, and only because it had been worn to shreds.

Merry taps me on the shoulder. Bishop Bell is making the rounds again. I can see his tidy, polygonal face, mobile as an algebraic equation, bearing down on me. His demoniac blue eyes seem to skewer mine as he leans forward deftly to shout:

'Now take the Americans, Charlie! They have a simple view! That sinister Uncle Sam, that hybrid of Disraeli and Mephistopheles, *he* knows how to keep it simple! Drop a bomb! If that doesn't do the trick, drop ten, twenty, twenty-thousand, eh!? Blow your problems out of the water; never mind if those problems are other people! Know what the Americans call enemy soldiers, Charlie!? *Organic defences*! God bless us all! No problem dishing it out to the organic defences!'

'Keep it to yourself, old guy,' hisses an American businessman, pale and severe as a freshly resurrected corpse, rising from his seat.

The audience, mostly French, are trembling with sardonic delight.
'Yeh. Belt oop!' shouts a seated Brit.

'Now what could be more typical!? The Americans say "Shut
up" and the British yell "Belt oop" in chorus! Why do you suppose
that is!? Some sort of unconscious imperative still lingering on as a
result of the beating they had in the War of Independence!? And I
ask myself: are the Americans modelling their global policies with
reference to old-style British imperialism, or is it the other way
round!? Are the British attempting to revive the empire vicariously,
through the imperialist Americans!?'

'Zee ozzer way round!' shouts a Frenchman in the row
immediately behind us.

'I mean, just look at this infamous business in Iraq! How can any
decent human being countenance the bald deception, the medieval
bloodlust, the blatant hypocrisy and thievery that went into that
war of connivance between angry Uncle Sam and deferential John
Bull, and which was unnecessarily *the first war of this millennium*!
How can anyone with any sort of conscience be expected to *keep
that to themselves*!?'

'Look, you lunatic in a dog-collar, there was an incident we call
9/11 started that *first war of the millennium*! You recall that much?
Or does world news only reach you via the confessional?'

'Oi think you'd be wise to belt oop, mate,' the Brit advises hotly,
leaping up. 'It were them bluddy Arabs started all the trooble. Even
tried to do the pope in, didn't they? But then, what does the bleeding 'Oly Farver do? Gets himself all cosy like with Yasser bluddy
Arab Arafat!'

'Bloody Arab who what!!' shrieks a young Muslim, racing up the
aisle to confront the Brit. His pink shirt and white slacks absurdly
belie the highly-strung and lethal danger so very tightly encased in
them. There is something canine about his snarling lips, about the
way his whole body springs into aggressive motion at the merest
treading on his tail.

Spurred by an initial pang of dismay, my pulse speeds up. I am in
the presence of the unreasoning mind defending a divine territory.

A small party of Hassidic Jews are rising like startled crows to
the left of me. They seem concerned in a surrealistically calm man-
ner. They huddle together. It looks as though they're about to go
into communal prayer. But the phalanx is solid, held back in taut
rigidity for whatever-may-yet-come.

The young Muslim is spittle-shouting close to the Englishman's face: 'What bloody Arab who what!? You bloody bloody Amerrca Brrits go home! Bloody Satan bloody Zion Amerrca Brrits bloody shit!'

The freshly risen American corpse in the impressive suit dashes forward to shove the Muslim aside. He speaks with an executive authority proper to his position on the board, 'Now that's enough, d'ya hear? You get back to your seat asap!'

'No bluddy Arab wants to be called a bluddy Arab. Wonder why that is? Call him an Arab and he wants to reach for mummy's homemade tiffin bomb!' The Brit is clutching at the young man's lapel, shouting back into his rage-bruised face.

From a few rows behind me, to starboard, another young Muslim has risen from his seat. 'You think we need bombs!?' he screams. 'I show you something! I can kill you all now without any bombs!'

I turn about to see him smashing at the porthole, using his heavy camera as a bludgeon. He strikes twice at the glass before I am on my feet and bounding towards him. The women who have been occupying the seats where he's now concentratedly at his work are scrambling towards the economy class doorway. I spring across the aisle, crooking his neck in my bent elbow and tearing him away from the glass in one instinctive act of force. Then I pin him to the floor.

Almost everyone in the cabin is now on their feet. Commotion, shouts, curses. The cabin crew are at their mysterious phones. I can hear one of the Jews muttering, 'Kill the schmuck. Ice the schlemiel.' Merry is all around me, working her cellphone camera. The ruddy Brit and the other Muslim are locked in an upright wrestling match. The American is standing over me, exuding superpower authority. Some women are shrieking in French, their children frozen with bewilderment.

One of the flight attendants (delicately mustachioed) hurries towards us with a sombre, muscular Frenchman in tow. He tries to drag me off the young man, but I am pressing down with all the strength of the threatened survivalist. Suddenly the Muslim goes limp, his fury surrendered to futility. I am gazing into his beautiful dark eyes. It is as though my pent-up grief has moved down to the pit of my stomach, where it pounds and aches.

The French air marshal, so sombre he seems almost bored, gently pulls me away. I sense rather than see the bulge of the holstered pistol beneath his armpit. I roll away and sit down, shaking, on the carpet. The young man is put in handcuffs.

There is a flutter of absurd applause.

The air marshal moves over to the Brit, who is still hanging on to the other Arab. The flight attendant speaks in low tones, and the air marshal shoves the Brit away with forceful contempt. The other Arab is cuffed as well.

Four seats near the rear are cleared. The American, the Brit and the two Muslims are firmly ushered into them. At what seems like insistence on the part of the flight attendant the Brit, now frightened and indignant, is handcuffed too. A finger pointed severely into the executive American's protesting face indicates to him that he too should stay seated.

Merry is still taking photographs. The captain, endlessly unruffled, emerges from the cockpit to assess the situation. He speaks for some time to the air marshal and the flight attendant. At one point during the interchange he turns to look at me. I have recovered, and am standing at a loss in the centre of the aisle. Merry takes another shot of me.

When the captain has satisfied himself that order has been restored, he comes across to me and lays a hand on my shoulder. 'Thank you,' is all he says. He turns to look at the air marshal, who nods at him and then at me.

I'm the hero of the flight. One hell of a round of applause now breaks out. Merry, going beyond all bounds, kisses me on the lips. At this the applause intensifies. The kids start rushing me. Their parents remonstrate a little, but seem to feel that I have set a good example. They beam at me. Some press up and shake my hand.

I'm vaguely aware that I'm grinning helplessly, like an idiot put under pressure of praise. But the grin floats atop an abyss of sorrow and confusion, like that of the Cheshire cat. The part of me that matters (because its expression is authentic) is somewhere else. It's whirling about in the fire of human hatred into which I've just been dipped. And all this congratulatory smiling, coming at me from the ten directions, is not separable from those flames.

Bishop Beelzebub hasn't quite finished. He begins a philosophical summary: 'You see how near to us the instinct to warfare is!! A few *words* are all that's needed!.. .'

He isn't permitted to develop his argument. The air marshal gets up, wags his finger meaningly and commands, 'Silence! *Seelahns!*'

The bishop shakes his head. The problem has been neither solved nor elegantly summed up. He resumes his seat, mute and frustrated now.

The ensuing hours to Paris pass in the atmosphere of a glum, ruminative anticlimax. Everyone is constantly aware of the four unfortunates confined to their seats by the marshal. It spoils the air of being lifted above the mundane afflictions.

'Well done, Charlie,' Merry tells me when we are again seated.

'Yes, I suppose it looks that way.'

'It was very brave of you.'

'Yes. Thank you.'

'I've taken some good pictures of the fracas, and you feature very prominently.'

'I'll be in the newspapers.'

'You will be, Charlie. It's my job.'

'Under the circumstances I don't mind at all.'

I'm thinking of Mona and the girls and, with a chord of delight, of Mauron. There will have to be some revision of his assessment of Charlie as a flopped pastrami. Mona's love for me will be vindicated, however much she might stubbornly deny that it even exists. The girls will not, of course, rush to reveal my heroics to their friends. They're far more likely to wait to be asked whether Charlie Fincham, the guy on the Air France flight, is in any way related to them. But in the meantime, privately, they'll have to come to terms with this unsuspected other person lurking in their humdrum dad (so recently requalified by his humdrum misdemeanours.)

At Charles de Gaulle Airport we are led away to a stylish but spartan interrogation chamber. The cold American seems inconvenienced but controlled. The Brit has sobered up somewhat and, belatedly conscious of the gravity of what he's helped let loose, is now much quieter. The Arabs look about sheepishly, but with flashes of wolfish defiance in their eyes. Bishop Bell sits bent at an acute angle, ready to shout out a theorem. Merry is avid for any information that will fill out her story. Charlie wants to get it over with and move on to Prague, that ancient city of infinite charm.

The thing goes on and on. It's clear that we'll miss our connecting flight. I don't much look forward to unnecessary hours spent wandering, Jonah-like, through these vast whale-belly terminals.

'The bishop,' I'm explaining, 'was conveying several well-known facts about the war in Iraq. Unfortunately he coloured them with some opinions which upset the American and the Brit. I didn't think they were particularly insulting. They were rather funny in their way. I thought it unwise that he spoke so loudly.'

'Good God!' cries the bishop, 'My hearing aid! I forgot to reset it!'

'I can't agree that his remarks were not *particularly insulting*,' the American protests with cadaverous iciness.

'Ze Iraqi situation is perhaps not a very appropriate topique to discuss on board an aeroplane at zis time?' suggests an official with a world-weary stoop.

'Not so the whole cabin can overhear your one-sided opinions,' interjects the suit.

'My hearing aid!' insists the bishop, cringing with apparent regret.

'The Englishman was extremely rude and provocative,' I offer callously. 'Although I don't know the status of *his* hearing aid.'

'Mmm. *Les Anglaises* ...' another official muses, looking at his feet.

At this the Brit abandons his mild repentance. 'Like everyone else, including His bluddy Grace here, Oi was offering me own opinions.'

'You should have settled it with the bishop,' I tell him. 'You had no business flying into the Muslim character.'

'I suppose that's fair,' says the American.

'Oh you do, do you?' wails the faltering Brit, sensing the noose. 'Bluddy fair of you, that is.'

The French officials confer for some minutes. They have the whole story by now. It's time to decide what to do. It transpires that they intend to hang on to the Brit and the Muslims. The rest of us are free to go. Merry is asked to download her photographs onto their computer. When that's done we move towards the door together. The frigid American saunters away as though from a tedious financial negotiation.

Bishop Bell has the last word: 'How appropriately symbolic! The only way to avoid conflict is to speak the truth with your hearing aid properly adjusted! Otherwise those who need to hear it most will want to kill one another!'

The air marshal shakes his head at this, looking down at Monsignor Bell across the fullest possible range of his large French nose. The bishop, his *amour propre* not at all challenged by this grand disdain, disappears into the vaults of the airport like a fast-moving calculation. I know I have not seen, or heard, the last of him.

I see the Brit and the two Arab youths being taken away in a more confining direction. The marshal and another official come up to pump my hand. Merry gets the treatment too. She's been quietly helpful and is very pretty too.

It turns out that we're stuck in the terminal for another four hours. Merry divides this time up between her laptop and her cellphone. A multifaceted story is being filed. She works at some distance from me, her back turned on any curiosity I might display.

But I'm not curious. I'm flabbergasted after the fact, looking for clues that might help me understand what really happened on the plane. The image I have is of one of those mysterious and terrifying episodes of tooth-ripping fury that break out spontaneously among the members of vicious little animal packs.

I am thinking of the wolf, the hyena, the dingo, and also of the lugubrious primates. Among any of these images that of human nature is not out of place.

But soft! There he is, that insidious bit of assembled geometry with a paper cup of coffee at his elliptical mouth beneath the uplifted triangular nose. The eyes, attracting and repelling like zero in all its dreadful meanings, are fixed on me, drawing him in my direction by the shortest distance between two points.

'I hope you've reset your hearing aid, Monsignor.'

'Hearing aid nothing! I don't use a hearing aid!!'

'If you were a bishop in my church I'd have fired you or demoted you to monastery toilet attendant. In another epoch I'd have had trouble not having you wracked. Or burned.'

'Those aren't very Buddhist notions, Charlie!'

'I'd have been willing to bear the karma.'

'Whatever else may have occurred, it brought out the best in *you*!'

'You're not suggesting I give you credit for that?'

'Not at all. But I give *you* credit for it! You behaved like a human being, unlike those dehumanized versions that forced you to act as you did! As for my part in it, what of it!? As you can imagine, I've often been attacked myself, directly and bitterly, more times than I care to remember! It never drove *me* to a violent retaliation, or even to thoughts of violence! Why should we proceed in constant anxiety of stepping on such long toes that we can't help mangling them even when we don't intend to!? I spoke the truth as I see it!

The proper response would have been a reasonable arguing of the point!! *That's human!*'

He sits down beside me and fetches a book out from an inner pocket. It's a dog-eared Roy Campbell's St John of the Cross, a Penguin survival from the sixties. I'm surprised at the devotional nature of his reading matter.

He reads out the English with his own emphatic gloss:

'The farther that I climbed the height!
The *less!* I seemed to understand!
The cloud so *tenebrous* and grand!
That there illuminates the night!
For he who understands that sight!
Remains for aye, though knowing *naught!*
Transcending! *Knowledge!* with his thought!'

'Do you understand what he means?' I ask.
'Fully! Better than he understood it himself, I think!'
'I see. Well, that's progress for you.'
'Oh yes! Don't forget how constrained he must have been in his interpretation of his own spiritual experience, the church pressing down hard on every heterodox *thought!* Never mind expression! Nowadays one can look at his experiences with so much more, I won't say *complete*, freedom from institutional interference! What, then, do I find in John's poems!? Why, the creed of a man who has been driven beyond childish faith in God! An atheist who believes only because he insists on believing! In love with a divinity that is his own transcendent yearning, nothing more! A divinity whom he has *chosen into existence*. Thus, the God of us all, I'm afraid! There's no other I can think of!'
'It's an impressive view, but not the orthodox one.'
'Orthodoxy must be stretched to satisfy even the dullest among us, or leave them out altogether! We can't leave them outside the gates of heaven, Charlie! But you'd be surprised how many of us see it as John of the Cross did!!'
'And you're content to offer a lie to the rest?'
'Not a lie! A symbol isn't the same as the thing it symbolises! But that doesn't make it a lie! If something admits of many interpretations, which one of them is the lie!? Only the one you force yourself to accept, even when you can no longer believe in it!?'

'Well said, bishop. We're in the same spot of bother, you and I.'

'Yes! It *is* a bother, isn't it!?'

'At least we know that no God will reach down to save the planet.'

'Well, that's a bother, too, of course!'

'Yes. It's up to us.'

'Yet more bother!'

'And I don't see us succeeding.'

'Now that's the real bother!'

On the short flight from Paris to Prague I am again in business class, this time on my own merits as a skyborne hero. I can't help noticing the whispered exchanges between the passengers and crew, and the heads turning to catch a glimpse of the big-nosed man with the deepset eyes who doesn't seem the type at all.

Merry has already warned me of things to come. She's spread the word across the perishing globe. Probably the thing will be worked up into a full-blown hijacking attempt with the nondescript (nose aside) Joe who exemplifies what the ordinary man, under severe circumstances, is capable of. It won't be the biggest story, but it'll certainly be used as the ubiquitous filler.

I'll be everywhere at once.

I'm feeling hijacked myself now but not unhappily so. Here is a definite *bardo* of sorts, a mystical and mythical window of opportunity.

The airplane banks and circles, dropping deliciously by soft stages.

We bump down at Prague.

CHAPTER 7

The First Day In Prague, On Which Several Great
Intellects Descend Upon Matters Of Planetary
Significance, Sundry Plots Are Almost Hatched, And
The Buddhas Prevent An Utterly Honest Intimacy

I like the Best Hotel for its air of misguided optimism. Here is a forward-looking establishment, twenty years on from the days of soviet socialism, poking fun at the American sense of grand style, and with the clear aim to outdo it in every particular.

Checking in was at first delightful and then very bitter.

The girls at the front desk were sweetly beautiful and sourly charming, but without their efficiency being in the least confused by these conflicting qualities. You felt yourself tossed about in a sea of golden blond. Their native dourness was pleasant to experience again. It spoke of an independence of mind which would make no sacrifices to friendliness for the sake of the hospitality industry. Admirable, I felt. It left me feeling assured that they were *natural* blondes, too. Why else would they bother to be blonde at all?

My wide-eyed fascination evaporated when I was brusquely told that my conference roommate was a fellow South African, name of Banana. I tried for a while to argue the point. I was growing livid. The unsmiling blonde was joined by a very dry youth who drily insisted that the Best Hotel could not interfere with arrangements made by the conference organizers.

I turned to tranquil Merry who was checking in beside me. What influence might she wield, even here? But the most she could offer was a nervous smile of glee. I saw then that there was an experimental side to her. She'd like to know what happened when you mixed two such volatile chemicals. It struck me, too, that my heroic deed, now noted and filed, would purchase no further admiration from her.

I tried to battle it out alone:

'I *cannot*, you see, *cannot* share with Mr Banana.'

'Why is that, sirr?'

'Well, It's just that I really don't like him ... *at all.*'

'Could be he does not like you too, sirr.'

'But that's just my point. Why make us both suffer?'

'But the Professorr Mm ... Mmib ... Mmab ...'

'Banana.'

(At this the dry face grew considerably drier.)

'The Professorr has not asked not to share with you.'

'Perhaps he's a better man than I am. Perhaps that's why I dislike him so.'

'Perhaps. But I am sorry, sirr. I have not authority to change this booking.'

I was up against a show of blank bureaucracy empowered by its own impotence.

'Well, God bless you!' was all I could say, taking my cue from Beelzebub.

'And God blast you too, sirr!'

Merry laughed very loudly, and even the dour girl tittered. I felt completely estranged. I was unburdening myself honestly, after all, and none of these human natures were willing to take me seriously. They were incapable of seeing with the eyes of empathy how badly I *dreaded* sharing a spatiotemporal environment with Paw Paw. They were laughing at me, even as I was being ushered through the gates of personality-conflict hell. I felt the tip of my nose redden and twitch.

'Since you don't have the authority to change the reservation, please get me someone who does, the conference manager or whomever.'

'*Zhuty prazti werecksci,*' said the dry one, or something like it, turning to the dour blonde, who then got on the phone.

With visible restraint I was asked to stand aside while the matter was attended to. Merry, having coolly sailed through her own reservation, came to wait beside me. Her face was very readable: tickled curiosity as to what would happen next.

I wasn't being difficult, I felt. It wasn't my ego playing up. I just wanted inner peace in a sober environment for the duration of my stay. If I had to share a room, I wanted to share it with someone I could befriend.

With Merry, for instance.

'Chully, it is your enemies who are making your best teachers. Your friends always doing things to making you happy.

Therefore they are not making the very good teachers. Now you trying to avoiding this very excellence enemy teacher. This is not good.'

'I'm not up to this enemy teacher, Rinpoche. I simply can't.'

'If you not able to facing this teacher, then that is very more good reason to doing it anyway.'

'Well, I won't.'

'Maybe it is not for you to deciding.'

I didn't want to hear this. The admonitory vibrations at the end of my nose wouldn't subside. I glared at Merry, the laughing lunatic. How would she like to share a room with Paw Paw? She wasn't saying.

Help arrived in the form of something startling. Owing to the bloated, drooping cheeks, and the puckered orifice serving for mouth and lips, the bespectacled face peering into mine resembled a pair of sagging buttocks with eyes and nose protruding. I recognized at once that the whole was attached, above the dog-collar, to the front of an English clerics head. The eyes, the mind behind them, seemed as remote as God's. The rectum smiled bizarrely.

'What seems to be the problem?'

'My name is Charlie Fincham –'

'Father Peter Forbes. How do you do?'

'– and I don't want to share a room with Professor Paw Paw Banana.'

'Is there a Banana on the list?'

'Popo Mbana,' said helpful Merry.

'Oh, in*deed*! Why ever not, Mr Fincham?'

'I don't get on well with the type.'

'That hardly seems a good enough reason at a conference of this nature.'

'Still, it is my reason.'

'Would you mind elaborating?'

'Would it help if I said that I think he has a dark mind?'

'In*deed*. I hope this hasn't anything to do with your being South African?'

He mumbled something that sounded like 'er – eh – acism – that kind of thing?'

Merry intervened self-protectively: 'Charlie's not a racist. At least I hope not. There's a history of sharp disagreements.'

I gave her a look. *At least I hope not?*

'In*deed*. I'd like to think that even sharp disagreements might be put aside at a conference of this nature.'

'Perhaps I can plead religious reasons. I'm a Buddhist. He slaughters goats.'

'I'm terribly sorry.'

'About the goats?'

'Well, no, actually.'

'You won't change my room then? Even for reasons involving the slaughter of goats? At a conference of this nature?'

'Not to put too fine a point on it.'

'But you're the conference manager.'

'In*deed*. However, besides the logistical difficulties, which are one thing, *there is a principle involved here*.'

French Peter.

By the involvement of this unspecified principle I found myself, worn out by sheer tedium, still obliged to share with Paw Paw. Again I had to hand it to Precious Teacher who, if he ever got it wrong, always did so when I wasn't looking.

I went up to the room. Paw Paw didn't get in until very much later, smelling like an old beer can. I pretended to be asleep while he hauled himself, grunting and puffing, into his bed a mere metre away from mine.

I wake up to find that he's already left for breakfast. My grief over Mona returns with such a keen edge that I can hardly spare him a thought. It's like an oil fire that I must douse stage by stage before I can even take in my surroundings. Then a light-bulb flickers on in my memory files. I remember that I'm a hero, a man of courage and fearless honesty. I can win back her respect and affection if I can only hold to my course.

It isn't, I now see, that I need her to love me. But I need to love her, carefully, skilfully and thoroughly, as though she were a composite embodiment of all the universe's sentient beings, because that is exactly what she is.

'*And also very exactly what Professor Paw Paw is, Chully.*'

I get up quickly, splash, brush, shower, comb, and flee the room.

According to the list there are one hundred and fifty-two delegates. I enter the dining hall to find them all at breakfast. It's a bewildering and fantastical experience. There are robes, wraps, stoles and garments of every religio-sartorial whim. From the point of view of the unconditioned mind this can only be a carnival, a pageant of aliens, or a piece of surrealist theatre.

Breakfast is set out buffet-style and presided over by a selection of signs indicating *vegetarian, vegan, kosher, halal*. It's a little daft, considering that one of the questions on the agenda is that of impending global famine. Who will be picky enough to refuse any fodder (including goats) on whatever religious grounds then?

I choose a bit of this and that and make my way to a table with an open chair or two. I'm deliberately not taking refuge in Merry's familiar company. The Eastern Orthodox priests look me over and smile perfunctorily. Then Paw Paw Banana drifts along and joins us.

'Good morning, Mr Fincham.'

'Mr Banana.'

'Mba-na. *Mbana. Professor,*' he corrects me.

'Right.'

'I *wazi* told that you asked for me to be removed from *yowa* room.'

'No. I asked to be removed from *your* room.'

'May one ask why?'

'Your informant didn't tell you, Professor?'

'He did. I hope he *wazi* wrong. He said you did not like me.'

'He was right.'

'You have reasons for not liking me?'

'Your record of public conduct.'

'You are the judge of me?'

'Only of your public conduct.'

'Big white judge, heh?'

'White has nothing to do with it.'

'No, no, you see, white has everything to do with it. The big white conscience is truly a pain in the reah end, even though that *izi* where it belongs.'

'If you feel that way, perhaps *you'll* try asking for another room. Someone of your status will probably have more luck than I did.'

'No. We will wait and see what happens.'

Paw Paw laughs at me too, and tucks in with a jolly appetite. I nibble rodent-like, my infernal nose twitching uncontrollably. From time to time I look up at the Orthodox priests. They don't notice me, apparently. Their suspicious eyes are on mock-Nigerian Banana.

After breakfast I return to the room and get out my shaving tackle and hair scissors. It's going to be awkward shaving myself bald again; haven't done it for two decades. At all costs I must avoid a lacerated pate. Bit by bit, easy does it. And on the other hand; he who hesitates is lost.

In comes Paw Paw, just when I've trimmed the hair back to shaveable length and am applying the Old Spice foam. He whisks off his Nigerian *fila* hat to reveal his own clean-shaven ebony billiard ball. *Of course, he'll know how!*

'Sit down here, Mr Fincham. Heya!'

Gad! He's at my head with a brand new razor blade. He shaves, rubs, tweaks, laughs. Not once does he bother to ask why I want to be bald. I watch his concentrating face in the bathroom mirror. I watch my own too, glum and nervy. He breaks off to fetch himself a Scotch from the mini-bar. I hope it's his first.

'So you don't like my public record, heh?' (carefully shaving, shaving.)

I resist the impulse to nod, wiggle my eyebrows instead.

'Which part?'

'The part where you get promoted every time you do something particularly nasty.'

'*Maye*! You don't care what you say.'

'I have to speak honestly.'

'I'm a big sinnah, Mr Fincham, but I have powah, a lot of powah.'

'If you have power, you should use it responsibly.'

'But I'm a big sinnah. A sinnah with powah.'

'For God's sake!'

'But actually, I want to educate you. You seem a confused person. But you talk very straight. I should talk straight with you too.'

'Yes, straight is best.'

'You are just another arrogant white shit. You know why I call you an arrogant white shit?'

'Because you're an arrogant black shit?'

'No, not at all. I call you arrogant because you are judging me for doing what you whites have been doing since Noah left the ark. The only difference izi that you white boys are so bloody good at hiding it. You think my white predecessah was any bettah than me? I know all about him. And he was doing the same things as me, but nevah once caught out. Yes. Surrounded by whites who looked after him. And you talk about powah and responsibility! *Heye!* You whites taught us everything about the misuse of powah. You support the capitalist free market, but it izi actually a legitimate system of theft. But you whites know how to hide away from that fact. Now we bleks are doing the same things, exercising powah and making money whichever way we can, just like you. But we are not as experienced at subtle deceptions as you clevah white boys, so you usually catch us out. But, actually, no white has achieved wealth or powah in any other way. Study us bleks, Mr Fincham, so that you can discover everything that izi corrupt and evil about yourselves. We are only imitating *you*.'

I am by now both semi-bald and disgruntled. However much one part of my mind resents what Paw Paw's been saying, another part is unwillingly applauding him. He's making some sense in spite of himself, or *myself*. If the real difference is only that between the blatant fraud and the fraudster so subtle that he can't see what his own left hand is embezzling, corrupting, stealing or seducing, while his right acknowledges the public acclaim, then it *is from the blatantly corrupt that we must learn what the essential mechanism of our system truly is.*

It's a thought.

'*Nyet.* Nice try, Professor, but it's just too easy. It's true that our system invites corruption, but it doesn't tolerate it.'

'You can call me Popo.'

'Thanks, Paw Paw. I'm Charlie.'

'You're wrong, Chahli. Your system, it not only invites corruption. Corruption izi its foundation. The only thing it does not tolerate izi being caught out.'

'Your case excepted.'

'All cases with powah excepted. And also all cases with big money. And I tell you now, Chahli, there izi no other system to replace it.'

He's done. I look into my dark blue eyes, black-rimmed with intensity, recessed on either side of my wizard's snout. Above them the new white dome gleams fresh as a new-boiled egg. It'll have to do, this gauche assembly.

'Thank you, Paw Paw.'

'I hope you will stick around in this room, Chahli.'

He pours himself a second bracer while I unpack my robes and spread them out on the bed. Not a very remarkable outfit, considering its remarkable impact: long maroon *shemdap* skirt, sleeveless yellow *dhonka* jerkin, long maroon *zen* shawl to wrap around the waist and cast over the right shoulder, red socks and a pair of sandals.

I worm myself into these while Paw Paw looks on with passive amazement. When I'm done, he says, 'Buddhist.' And, slowly taking in the overall effect, he adds, 'It changes yowa emanation; now you look like a wise person.' He laughs out loud at the thought. Then, vaguely recalling, 'Mmm ... Dalai Lama.' He's piecing it together gradually.

I'm ready in time for the first session of the working group on global warming to which I've been assigned. Around thirty delegates are seated about a semi-circular table with a natty coordinator standing in the halfmoon no-man's-land. Among those seated I recognize only the preposterous prelate, Beelzebub.

The coordinator gets the thing underway: 'Good morning – contentious issue – numerous scientific theories – figures and facts – warming – melting ice caps, warm currents – cold – Ice-age – documented – Al Gore – but for all that – bzaw warzl wheedle whittle sawzle fiddle – twaddle dawdle – verble dribble ...'

I propel my mind lightly into calm meditation without withdrawing completely. I take in the string of faces threaded along the table, some in profile, some frontal; variously alert, keen, bored, bowed, excited. There's a thoroughly representative body of religionists, selected by the design, no doubt, of the managing churchman, French Peter Forbes.

There are several women, but none in burkas. In one or two cases (I can't resist the thought) this is a pity. In particular, there is a mother *ultrasuperior* whom the devil himself would disown for sheer terror. She has the demeanour of a bulldozer waiting patiently to solve a structural problem.

Near the centre there's a beaming androgynous-looking Buddhist nun in Thai robes, beside her a sisterly missionary, a wooden cross (Protestant, Christless) dangling near her ample bosom. The ladies are attentive. Mother Superior devours it all, open-mouthed, waiting to pounce.

A Hindu swami seems too mentally rarefied to care very much; this greenish moribund globe's only a small detail in the broader cosmic waste. Two imams, straight out of Burton, nod fiercely in tandem at every point at which the Hindu seems especially blasé. An American pastor, his Bible open before him, has an uncontrollable nevous tic which causes him to mutter, 'Praise you Jayziss', whenever the imams nod.

A corpulent rabbi shifts his yarmulke in a little circular movement, half rising as he dials, then settles down again. It's as though he'd be overjoyed to flee the occasion upon the least excuse, like someone in desperate need of the WC, or a fag. An Orthodox priest just sits, a frozen lump of Byzantine bigotry. Perhaps he's wondering what the hell he's doing here among all these idolators, heretics, schismatics and apostates of the demystified modern world.

'Therefore – no longer afford to wait – answers – technology – open the floor to responses – thank you for your patience – fizzle.'

The bigger of the two imams rises: 'In the Name of Allah the Merciful the Compassionate, I will say immediately that all our answers, all answers in these dire times, can only be sought at the feet of Allah and those of his Prophet peace-be-upon-him. He who is and always has been our guide –'

Good BBC accent, interrupted by the American's mutter: 'Praise you Jayziss.'

'– The provider even for those who do not know his Great Compassionate Name.'

'Good point,' the coordinator cuts him short. 'We should continuously seek the counsel of the divine.'

'The divine nothing!!' the Vitruvian Bishop interjects. 'Use your logic. If *he's* always been our guide, *he* must have guided us into this predicament!!'

'Thank you Jayziss,' mutters the Holy Roller.

Hubbub. The multiple faces swing about, wag, nod, shake, grimace, chuckle and perspire, like excited cartoons. Babel. From up here it looks much the same as an unruly session in the Parliament of Fowles.

The coordinator tries to insist on order. The melancholy rabbi lumbers towards the door. If anything's changed, the Hindu hasn't noticed. It's all Christian and Muslim now, a game of crusades. Eventually, cooling down by the dynamics of heat exchange, each makes a more or less inoffensive suggestion about involving the undefined divine. This crucial point with its intricate convolutions is duly noted, as if the undefined divine would otherwise not be disposed to involve himself-herself-itself.

The coordinator, mentally groping for an easier tack, has noticed that the Buddhists haven't yet contributed their piece. Ladies first, androgynity notwithstanding. The nun, bald as myself, very pale and delicate, offers this: 'We should less talking, less praying, less meeting, more just doing. Not making many large conferences, just being each person a working conference, thinking, walking, working, doing. Then something may change, I think. Yes. Let each person be his own conference, his own conference all the time.'

Like the absently swaying Hindu, I think.

The coordinator shifts his smiling gaze to me, the other Buddhist in the room. I can feel red-robed Charlie lifting himself to his feet, fixing his eyes on the wall opposite, shaking into place the *mala* on his wrist, and then I descend into him.

'The job of religion today is to prepare all living beings, and especially human beings, for the catastrophe that is about to descend on them all –'

'By God, it's *you*!!' expostulates Beelzebub. 'Yes, that *is* a simple view!'

'– because there is no way to prevent it.'

A tentative silence shifts its many buttocks on the chairs. The rabbi stops short at the door, twirling his yarmulke like a knob whose function it is to operate a servo, which turns his heavy body around. Having twirled himself to the desired orientation he just stands there. The Hindu comes shockingly alive.

'Yes. That is how it would appear.'

'But zat is totally absurd!' yells Mother. 'Und hopelessly pessimistic. How can we bring motivation und effort into zis world mit such ein despairing message?'

'Well I think it's spot on!! Truth before peace and effort, Mother!!'

'It's a thought that God himself might be thinking these days,' muses the melancholy rabbi, 'in a pessimistic moment.'

'It's all in *your* hands, bless ya Jayziss'

'Oh shut the hell up,' mumbles a sour, bearded American in jeans and T-shirt.

Mother's on her feet: 'Mit apologees to our Buddhist speaker, such an suggestion is totally misguided. Please remember zat we are dealink mit ze question of global warmink. So ze primary focus of our discussion must be on ze carbon und methane emissions. Ze question is what we can do to degrease zese deadly emissions. Und how can we educate ze people about zis problem. For zis we need to inculcate ein sense of cooperative effort. Zat is our job here, not zis apocryphal nonsense about preparing ze people for ze end. Zat is extremely irresponsible.'

'Educate the people!? Which people!? The people in here, the people out there!? *There are no people left*! This world's *peopled* by automata! Just look at them! Scurrying about like libidinous rats! Their minds are already saturated with the problems involved in surviving *one day at a time*, hand to mouth! What room is left for taking in the complex details about saving the world, never mind actually doing something!? Leave that to the experts who already know all about it and can do nothing! I think Charlie's right! Whatever people, especially those awful people in control of things, do, will be done too late! And God bless them!'

The Holy Roller rises like Elijah.

'Praise you Jayziss! Now I think the good Lord has it all worked out. It ain't up to us to be sayin' what the outcome will be. Jayziss predicted all of it way back when. The sun will turn to blood and the moon won't give her light. Flee to the hills, take nothin' along withya. Great and terrible is the day of the Lord. And then, after those days, behold! A noo heaven and a noo earth, the lion will lay down with the lamb ...'

'Jayziss, Woody, cain't ya shut the hell up?' The bearded T-shirt cranes his neck in lieu of getting to his feet. 'Folks, you have to excuse my Christian brother here; he's been waitin' for the end since nineteen sevenny niner. And, believe me, he *wants* it to come, and real soon too! Now I used to feel the same way, until I began to see it comin', I tellya. I see it comin' and I know it ain't no work of God, no sir! Ain't no work of the devil neither. It's just us, yeah, *ers*! Now we ain't gonna get it together, that's fer sure. And Jayziss ain't got nothin' to do with it.'

He's a hippie-Rasputin throwback to the Vietnam-protest days. The name card on his T-shirt reads *Tyrone C. Mather*. He's red-faced with outrage, black-eyed with meanness. He's a critter on the verge.

'The lady nun is quite right,' the big imam puts in, looking across at Mother. 'With the help of Allah the Merciful the Compassionate, we should decide means for forbidding the infidel practices that are exacerbating these global climate changes.'

'Forbidding!' screams Beelzebub. 'Yahaha! You think the whole world's congregated around an oil well in the desert, waiting to bow to the next clerical decree!?'

The imam exudes a patient cut-throat dignity: 'Well, to put it in your terms, dear bishop, we should devise means to pressure governments for appropriate legislation. And then, congregated around a casino in the desert, sustained by hamburger huts and bordellos, your people will have to obey those laws.'

I am beginning to wonder whether there might be a bomb scare.

Up jumps Tyrone, his elongated neck lending a touch of added intensity to his straining physique: 'S'pose we get the carbon and methane thing together, so what? If global warming don't take us out, we'll go find another way, a global war or a global virus or a nookeler accident. I tellya, if Jayziss is comin', as my Christian brother here insists he is, I hope he'll find some ferkin' way to git here before it's all gone.'

'I must caution you on your language, Dr Mather,' the coordinator interrupts him, resenting the distant insult to his professional coordinatorship.

'My language ain't your affair, buddy. Fer all you know I might be suffering from Tourette's. Now you wanna throw me outta here, you go right ahead. I believe this is all a waste o' my ferkin' time ennaway.'

'Praise you Jayziss!' he's clutching at the table leg, battling his burden of *angst*.

'Have it your way then. For this session, at least, you're thrown out!' the coordinator gayly takes his stand, his ego now the driving force. Two frantic rosettes surface near his dimples. With trembling fingers he flings back a rebellious wisp of hair. His foot taps the carpet.

'Doctor Mather is the only expert on envrronmental resstance tactics in this room,' the swami unexpectedly remarks. 'Please, please, let's not be troubled by irrvelances. Language is only a matter of words. With all due rrspect I submit that your harsh rrsponse is equally rrprehensible.'

'I'll accept your comments on your personal merits, Professor Koomaraswami. But I must insist that Dr Mather's language is highly inappropriate. If any of you disagree, we can put the matter to the vote by a show of hands.'

'No need for zese hands or feet or whatever,' booms Mother Virago, 'If ze American doctor cannot restrain his tongue, I can help him manage it.' With the barest glance she invites Dr Mather to test her on this.

'Praise you Jayziss,' Woody whispers. (I notice that his Special Edition Billy Graham Bible is open at Revelations.)

'Ja, und now we proceed. I suggest zat we use our churches und other places of worship for regularly spreading ze message about global warmink ...'

I ascend the gentle slope of self-involved non-involvement again. For me, this session is over. I've said all I have to say and there's nothing else on my mind.

The lunch break is eventually announced. We all trot, lumber and swagger across to the dining hall. Germinal little cliques have already been formed. Only Mutter Superior plods along alone. And Charlie-the-bald.

Birds of a feather are peckishly roosting around tables: here the black-clad, crowing Catholics, upright as penguins and slippery as eels; there the turbaned Muslims with a lean and hungry look; Protestants loudly protesting; Orthodox repressing their unorthodox repressions; capricious Hindus, exploring the seventy-thousand meanings of the seven thousand and seven deities; forlorn Judaists, eternally asking why-o-why of the Big Why in the Sky; sedately confused Buddhists hoping to catch a glimpse of the nothing that is really something (or is it the something that is actually nothing?), and so forth.

I notice Merry moving from table to table among all these febrile minds and quivering physiques, among the rows of feeding faces and shifty hands. It calls to mind a hell-scene from Hieronymus Bosch. I am sweating with shame and misery, posing in my rubine robes among these other outlandish garments. Yet I know it as well as I know myself: there's no help for this itchy human nature but it must scratch itself, and keep on scratching till it bleeds.

Spotting the table of Buddhist monks, she stops meandering and strides across directly. Her eyes catch mine and light up with perplexity. She laughs and laughs, at her own dumbfoundedness this time. It's contagious; the whole Buddhist *sangha* cackles in unison.

'I've been looking for *you*, Charlie.'

'I thought it best to adopt a camouflage.'

'This is going to be quite a surprise for everyone.'

She hustles me from the fodder-trough to one of the smaller function rooms of the Best Hotel. Cameras start flashing as I enter in tow. It seems I'm about to be interviewed on the subject of my thoughtless act of minor heroism aboard Air France Flight 732. For some unknown reason, owing perhaps to a dearth of very bad news, my deed has impressed the world at large for longer than the customary fifteen minutes.

I'm on all the television channels, I'm told, and in all the newspapers, especially back home. She shows me a few headlines: *South African Passenger Pacifies Air Rage Aggressor, Middle-Aged Man Manhandles Mid-Flight Madman*, and one or two other editorial tongue-twisters. Each article displays an unflattering mugshot (taken by experimental Merry) of a very-confused-seeming me.

The cameras stop flashing. The journalists gawp. Who's this bloke in the robes?

'This *is* Mr Charles Fincham,' Merry assures them, 'apparently a Buddhist monk, as it now turns out.'

She plants me behind the central table. The cameramen resume their contortions, shooting the lama from every angle. To my dismay there are a number of video cameras too. I want to rub my twitching tooter.

The questions begin. Merry goes first:

'What made *you* do it, Charlie?'

'Do what, Mary?' (You never know with journalists.)

'What made *you* tackle the Moroccan?'

'Was he Moroccan? Well, he was trying to smash out the aircraft window.'

'But none of the other passengers made any attempt to stop him.'

'Yes. That's why I felt it was up to me.'

'Vott vas the reason for the Moroccan's violent erektion?' a blonde Czech reporter asks, pencil poised.

'The Englishman's anti-Arab remarks obviously got his blood up.'

'Yah. Misterr Oomfreez of London.'

'Yes, well, Mr Humphries was a bit under the weather.'

'Onderr the vetherr?'

'*Brzamanski fernzni.*'

'Ah.'

It goes on in this vein until someone remembers my Buddhist garb and moon-white egg-bald cranium.

'Was your action in any way motivated by your religious beliefs?'

'Yes.' (Why not?)

'Might that have been a reason why it was you, rather than anyone else, who pounced on the Moroccan gentleman?'

'Possibly. You see, I pounced on the Moroccan gentleman because I felt he might be the cause of some very harmful consequences, and Buddhism is against harmfulness in any form.'

'Although you did cause the gentleman some harm.'

'Did I?'

'You broke his arm.'

Huh?

'I wasn't aware of that. Still, Buddhism would see my action as justified if my breaking his arm meant preventing a planeload of people from being sucked out of an exploding aircraft in mid-flight.'

Their attention now wanders to my role at the conference.

'You are participating in this konferenz?'

'Yes, I am.'

'As a Buddhist?'

'*Soforzka nya Buddhisti, shatt!*'

'Ah.'

'Vott is your views on this kurrent global krisis?'

'I'm of the opinion that people will simply allow matters to deteriorate to the point of global annihilation.'

'And this is part of yourr religious views?'

'Yes and no.'

'*Vzat broznye stravonzi?*'

'*Da, znotla, nyet, zbirsti.*'

'Ah. Yass ant … no?'

'All religions prophesy the end of the aeon. Why are they all agreed on that? Because they understand what people are.'

'What advice have you to give us then, Mr Fincham? I mean, of course, in your capacity as a Buddhist monk, and a religious delegate to this conference.'

'I believe it is the duty of all religious institutions to prepare people, and all other living creatures, for eventual cataclysm, and for the catastrophic suffering which awaits them in this century as we move steadily towards self-destruction.'

'Would you understand what I mean when I say that *that* comes across very oddly indeed?' asks the sardonic Times man.

'Of course. The catastrophe is some fifty to one hundred years away. I'm sure you've read the literature. So, right now, it would probably sound as stupid as Noah's prophetic warnings did. You may recall that he was forecasting a cataclysmic flood in a time of severe drought. There is this difference between Noah and myself, though: he was a mythical prophet; I'm only going by what the scientists are telling us.'

'But aren't they also telling us that we can effect timely changes to prevent eventual disaster?'

'Yes. They're telling us that ordinary people with little insight and no immediate motivation can undo the damage which science and technology, pandering to governments and industry, have helped bring about. It seems an unlikely solution.'

'But perhaps religion can help them to understand these problems and tell them how to be part of the solutions.'

'But I've just told you that the religions foresee cataclysm, and not solutions.'

'So in your view as a Buddhist, people should not be given any reason to hope.'

'In my view as a human being, people are not giving themselves any reason to hope, and it's not for the religions to lie to them. That's up to politics, business and science.'

'Yah! Yah!' cries the (blonde) Czech reporter.

When it's over I leave with Merry. 'Is this really going to be your line, Charlie?' she asks, misgivings scribbled in her chiding frown. I take her by the arm and stare straight into her. For several seconds she searches for the joker. But he's nowhere to be found.

I excuse myself and go across to the computer centre. The hum and crackle of information in transit (*where's the knowledge lost in?*) is almost as unsettling as standing in the middle of a busy freeway. I remind myself that I'm here to do something very simple: write a cover email and send it off to Mona, Clara, Jessie, Teacher and everyone else, including detestable-loveable-loathsome Halfwit.

At the ninth attempt I manage to set up a temporary online address and relay my deliberately reticent news: 'Arrived safely. The conference is a lot of fun. I hope you are all keeping very well. I love and miss you. You too, Harvey.'

That done, I head for a hidden corner of the hotel lounge where I can smoke a fag in privacy and peace. I have an hour before the next workshop: *The Religious Attitude to the Global Crisis*. At least I don't have to prepare any notes. That's one of the advantages of keeping it simple.

The chairs and carpets are deep red like myself and I can blend in like a ritzy red chameleon. This is my first smoke today. Suck and relish, suck and relish. *Crikey, did I really break his arm?*

The silent respite I am seeking is cleft by *that* voice, *that* tone, *that* volume:

'Sniffed you out, eh!? Literally, eh!? Charlie, I liked what you said in there!! You have to be a priest for some decades and a prel-ate for six years to know what, truly, man is and is not! You may be a monk, or a part-time monk, of the Buddhist persuasion, but I'll bet you don't hear confessions! To know people you have to shrive them! You shrive them once, twice; by the seventy-seventh time you know that you're dealing with a completely mad thing!! A thing that never learns!!'

'And that applies to all?'

'Every last one of us! I'll let you in on a secret, Charlie! Hush hush! I'm the worst of the lot! It's that knowledge that's driven me round the bend! Yes, I'm telling you, *clinically insane*! Why d'you think I've been tucked away among the hills and huts of Bongo-bongoland!? Because I'm an embarrassment to dear old Mother Church! I've gone crackers! Brilliant mind, oh yes, oh yes! But it's hit a snag some-where, Charlie, and no one, least of all the psychiatrists, have any idea what it is! It hasn't got out of hand for quite some time now, which is why I've been given a *dispensation* to attend this show! I've some pills that help me maintain a semblance of balance, but in my *spirit* I know that it's the *unbalanced* side that's the true one, the one that sees the real meaning of it all! What do you say to that!?'

'I'd have to know what you mean by balanced and unbalanced.'

'By balanced I mean just like everyone else! By unbalanced I mean *not in the slightest like anyone else*! By unbalanced I mean *sick to death of the lies that are fundamental to our sanity*! Can you see it, Charlie!?'

'Yes.'

'I know you can!'

He seats himself and shuts down, lighting up. We smoke and smoke in silence. A hundred non-linear problems write themselves

across the slate of his Braquesque countenance. Why has he chosen
to confess this to me? There's only one possible answer: he believes
I'm as dotty as he is.

A couple of cigarettes later he gets up and leaves without a word.
I order a coke from a blonde waitress. It's served all razzmatazzed
up with a twist of lemon and a swizzle stick. The glass has been
iced and the rim dipped in sugar. The straw is topped by its wrap-
per, which is coiled upwards in a zany helix. It has the look of a
hi-tech gizmo. It's what Bishop Beelzebub might call a balanced
drink. It's so cocked up I can hardly get to it.

The same goons are present at the second workshop.

The touchy coordinator has re-assumed his confident exterior,
every hair back in place above the professionally smiling face: 'During
our first session we considered a variety of practical approaches –
suggestions – In this session – formulate – attitude of religion in a
general sense – global warming – serious – *appropriate gravity*.'

'*gravis est dolor*,' croons Dr Mather.

'Excuse me?'

'*gravis est dolor nunc extinguitur mundi et astrorum lumen nunc
concipitur mali hominis crimen*.'

'St Augustine?'

'Cat Stevens, man. You never heard o' Cat Stevens? Well, he was
Cat back then, but now he's turned into Yusuf somethin' or other,
gone made himself a Moozlim. Back then he was a Boodist or a
Hairy Krishner or whatever. Ennaway, that's his song.'

'Ja, und ze point is?'

'You don't understand no Latin, Mother? I had you pegged as a
Catholic. The point is *nunc concipitur mali hominis crimen*, meaning, more or less, that now's the time for evil mankind to take the
blame. That's *ers*, we're the evil ones. So, Mother, the point is that
the only ride religious attitude is to put the blame where it belongs.
On *ers*. Let religion give it to us straight.'

'The Patriarrch Barrtholomew considerrs contrributing to global
warrming a morrtal sin,' the Orthodox priest informs us, coming
darkly to a shrouded semblance of vitality, like Lazarus rising.
'Perrhaps the Rroman churrch should do the same.'

'Why pick on ze Roman Church? We are considering ze attitude
of religions *in cheneral*. Zis is not ein dispute between Rome und
Constantinople.'

'Therr should neverr have been disputes between Rrom and Konstantinopolis, if only Rrom had rremained trrue to the ancient churrch trraditions.'

'Mein Gott, *sind Sie ganz bei sich*? How many times has ze Holy Fuzzer reached out to ze Orthodox Church? Und who is refusink zis reconciliation?'

'Rrom doesn't want rreconciliation. Rrom wants to rrule.'

'Of course Rome wants to rule! Who should rule!? Istanbul!?' Beelzebub interjects, rising as he rose on board the plane.

'What a rrotten thing to say!' The orthodox beard uncurls itself with loathing. 'It was Rrom who let us down when the Muslims took ourr city!'

'Please allow me to correct you,' says the big imam urbanely, his black eyes glistening with an even blacker delight. 'If anyone was to blame for seizing Constantinople, it must surely have been Mohammed the Great.'

'I'll tell you this much,' the coordinator, staring down at the crimson carpet, unburdens himself usward, 'I thank God I'm a born-again agnostic!'

'Hallelujah, brother! I'm a born-again Baptist!'

'Anything from the Buddhists?'

The Thai nun obliges: 'Too much thinking about attitudes, I think – why so much thinking? Better just looking, analysing, deciding – different situations – not only one attitude – all the time looking, looking, analysing …'

The coordinator, *Cunliffe* on the name-tag, seems to go into orbit around this soporific flux of verbs. His foot again taps the crimson pile, his arms fold themselves into a self-protective knot, his smiling lips hang down his frantically roving face. He looks to me for rescue.

'Yes,' I decide, 'We should indeed be looking, looking, not thinking too much, just walking, seeing, taking it all in, until we finally decide that religion is entitled only to one attitude, that of shame and remorse. And out of that attitude it should, while continuing to look and look, without thinking too much, prepare humanity for the end of the world.'

'Goddamn it son, you got that ride!' shouts Mather.

The Thai nun nods sweetly. It sounds right. Mother fixes me with a look of disbelief. Haven't I heard a word she's said? Pastor Woody rides a wave of perplexity: well, yes, but no. What has this

Boodist guy actually proposed? Is it right to agree with those weirdo Boodists under any circumstances at all?

The Orthodox beard fingers his beads; the Buddhists don't count. The imams are laughing out loud at the joke they think I've made. It seems to have been at the Christians' expense. Rabbi Tannenbaum regards me very gravely, tapping his yarmulke as he thinks and thinks.

'So it would appear,' concludes Professor Koomaraswami, pinching sagely at his raptor's beak, almost as superaquiline as mine.

The vote, when it finally comes after two more hours of nerve-jangling debate, decides that religion *in general* should work to oppose, *by non-violent means*, the *fait accompli* of global warming.

'How do you oppose a *fait accompli*!?' the bishop demands.

'You just oppose it,' Mother tells him. 'Zat's how.'

'But what happens when the unstoppable force of human folly meets the immoveable *fait accompli* of natural imbalance!?' Beelzebub insists.

'Perhaps zey just make him ein bischop,' says Mother.

Cunliffe sighs, filing his papers.

I realize, as I enter the dining hall for supper, that I'm the object of a good deal of furtive attention. Heads turn coyly, lips pout into recipient ears; there's a furore disguised as a buzz. Beelzebub bustles up at a tangent, inviting me to join the group at his table. Why not, after all? For all sorts of excellent reasons. But I go along anyway.

Tyrone C. Mather, Sooklal Koomaraswami, Yitzak Tannenbaum and Paw Paw Banana await us. They seem to have adopted a deferential attitude which disturbs my bullshit detectors. What do they want from me?

'We are all in aggrrment with your view,' Koomaraswami blurts out.

'That's ride boy. We're all with ya, Charlie.'

'In what sense?' I enquire, really shaken. This isn't right.

'In the *simple sense*! What else!?'

'The simple truth about the end of the world,' grunts Tannenbaum. 'I can feel it in my bones. I'd almost given up. But you've made me realize that there's still a job of work to do: put them wise to the final holocaust.'

'How do you fit in Paw Paw? You haven't even been at any of the workshops.'

'Chahli, I want to see where you are going.'

'I'm going nowhere, Paw Paw.'

'I don't agree. You seem too much mad to be going noweh. You going sumweh.'

'You think I'm mad, and that's your reason for supporting me?'

'Yes, Chahli. You mad enough to open yowa mouth, no matter what some sane somebody might stick into it. I want to see the results.'

'In that case, why not latch onto Bishop Bell?'

'Me!? Oh no! I lack your charisma, Lama! No, it has to be you!'

'Charisma? Me? What … exactly?'

'We wanna git your idea up on the conference agenda. We wanna agitate, see?'

'Othrrwise it will simply be ignored.'

'The end of the world izi nigh. I like it. Strongly original thesis.'

I've been elected head of the dissenters. When I ask for more considered reasons why they've lit on me, they grope their way through several responses, but all make the same gesture in the end: their hands point at my person, run over me from sandals to pate, taking in my robes. So that's it: I look the part.

'It ain't just yer git-up, Charlie. Sure, you have the presence, wise old buzzard in Boodist robes. That's neat, boy. But ferk it boy, yer a hero too!'

They all concur in the course of an extended nodding routine.

'Yeah, that's ride. It's all over the noos,' Tyrone concludes, chin stuck out, black eyes rolling with fierce finality. I get the feeling he wants a fall guy for some illicit Alabama-distilled purpose of his own.

But Merry's sniffed me out meanwhile, or sniffed out the smoke of conspiracy around this table. She joins us briskly, exuding a whiff of perfume and a staggering load of milky sensuality. At first I wonder what's changed. Where's the cool copper's daughter I've come to know and suspect? Then I smell the gin.

She searches my face with a slow-sly smile: 'In conference?'

'So it would appear,' the swami replies on my behalf, one eye running up and down her body, a number of brain-cells panting along behind it.

'He's our man!' Beelzebub tells her.

'*Your* man?'

'As I was just sayin', Charlie here's a hero. All sortsa people gonna listen to him. Now, if he tells them the truth about the state o' this burned out planet, they gonna listen, see? He ain't about hyper-involved theories and such; jest the plain truth, see? Tell them this world's days are numbered, and that it's *ers* ta blame.'

'The cancerr's alrrdy crrpling the patient's body. Nothing to do but telling him to prrpare himself for dying. Then watch how he scrambles to do all the healthy things he was suppsd to do before he got ill.' (The swami's words almost fondle her.)

'And that's the plan?' she asks.

'It might be the swami's idea of global therapy,' I reply, losing my dark blues in her azures, 'But I don't see any place for therapy at all. This world's done for, no matter how much they scramble for remedies. It's too late. That's a truth for which no plan is needed.'

'I feel it in my bones,' Tannenbaum reiterates. 'No, actually it's right down in my marrow.'

'Say li'l lady, would you like to join us fer a drink after supper?' Mather tries it on, 'Could be I could convince you to join our li'l conspiracy o' truth.'

'I uncover conspiracies,' Merry retorts, 'I don't join them.'

'Well I sure could help you uncover thissun.'

'It's too insignificant for my talents.'

Sooklal Koomaraswami flushes purple.

I say nothing more. They ask me to meet with them later in the evening. They want to discuss a strategy for forcing my simple view on the conference agenda.

I refuse.

On the way out I ask Merry to find out more about them. 'I'll see what's on the net', she says, 'Most people nowadays, especially the freakier types, have some sort of record in cyberspace. Yes, you're there too. I checked.'

The net, indeed. The web, yah. I trudge away to my hideout in the dimly lit corner of the lounge. For a while I sit mulling over the insightful proceedings of the first two workshops. My despair deepens. Just when I'm about to be overwhelmed by darkness Merry joins me, a mysterious grin, half malicious, twinkling all over her comely face.

While I light up another fag she orders a pink gin. Remembering the junk-sculpture coke I play it safe and order a cup of tea. (No one would do that to a cuppa, surely?)

'Not even a glass of wine, Charlie?' she pleads. 'I don't want to drink alone.'

'No. Tea's my drink.'

'Rinpoche was right about you.'

'It occurs to me that *that* may be the one thing Rinpoche isn't right about.'

'You're a stubborn, upstanding sort of man.' (*Eh? What's this?*)

'I'm the downfalling sort like everyone else. Just take it from me.'

An angel passes for several minutes. I contemplate the rising wraiths of smoke. Cities are burning, people are leaping silently from the thirtieth and fortieth storeys. The panicked motorcars are so thick in the streets that none can move. Millions of feet flee along the highways, not turning back for those who fall.

The tea comes with a chocolate biscuit, but the Czech brew's as weak as Charlie's faltering will. The pink gin is elaborated into a Guggenheimisch abstract. Merry plucks away the mechanical debris and applies her voluptuous lips to the rim. With an inner scream of hilarity I monitor the insidious animal beneath my robes and skin.

'Do you grasp what's really happening here, Charlie?'

'*Here?*'

'Well, *here* is a different matter altogether. I mean here, at this conference.'

'If I said yes I'd probably be wrong. So, no, I don't. Enlighten me.'

'Have you noticed that you seem to have landed among the misfits, the small, ineffectual people who don't really count?'

'Yes, now that you point it out.'

'They've all got here more or less on their own steam. They aren't part of the premeditated scheme of what's really going on. They're unimportant; they'll be kept busy debating and feeling useful, but they mean nothing.'

'Right. That's obviously the one thing in their favour.'

'But there are some very important people here too, Charlie. This conference is all about what *they* decide and how *they* sell it to the public. Your lot's just here to add some local colour, like extras on the set of *The Ten Commandments*.'

'*The Ten Commandments?* I thought it was a Monty Python thing. Doesn't bother me, though, one way or t'other. Even the VIP's can't change the facts.'

'No, but they can twist them and present the twisted version to an already complacent audience.'

'Why would the world's religions want to twist the facts?'

'Is that a serious question, Charlie? If it is, you must be a very nice sort of man.' (*What's that, Merry? Me? Nice?*)

'Well, let's suppose I'm just plain naïve.'

'Have you studied the list of delegates?'

'Not really. I'm the proxy chap here, Mary. I'm covering for Rinpoche, then I go home to patch up my marriage and forget all about the conference.' (*Did I just mention patching up something?*)

'I hope you don't mean that.'

'You've heard my contribution. I've said it and I believe it. What more is there for me to do? Head up the conspiracy of crazies?'

'Do you realize that the outcome of this conference has already been determined?'

'So what? Why not? It can only be a gesture at best.'

'Yes. The wrong kind of gesture.' (Pause. Perplexed misery in her lovely eyes.)

'All right. What's going on?'

'In addition to the influential religious leaders in this hotel, there are six politicians with clear agendas, eight bent scientists who belong to the status quo, and two befuddled Nobel Peace laureates resting on their laurels. What's happening here is that religion is being convinced, without needing much convincing, to go along with the big money in the world. The people who'll come out on top will be those who are dressing up gene technology, dirty energy, just wars, environmental poisoning, and all the rest of it, to look smart.'

'The religions will simply play along?'

'They'll come out sitting on the fence, saying things like: GM foods might be the best solution for an increasingly starving world, gene therapy may signal the end of heritable disease, departure from carbon based fuels might cause massive poverty, especially in the poorest countries, wars are wrong, but sometimes unavoidable. They won't oppose a single bloody one of those vested interests.'

'I'm sorry, Mary, but what's new? When has religion lifted a finger to really revolutionize the way the world is run? It's always been part of the problem, even acted to exacerbate it. I'm sure you know your history, even recent history. Did the Vatican advise Catholics to stand up against the invasion of Iraq? Did the Dalai Lama criticize it? Oh, of course, the Muslims were dead against it.'

'This is an important conference, Charlie. Perhaps you're too wrapped up in those sexy robes to read the papers or watch the news on television. I suggest you start doing so. You're a special man. No, no, I see it in you. I told you that Gaia is my subject. It's also my passion. I love this world, and I'm sorrowing over it. It's the only well of life, and it's being poisoned. And none of these very important personas are going to do anything effective about that. I'm asking *you* to do something for *me*.'

She takes me in piece by piece. *Gad, Mather's right. I must look like a buzzard with my bald dome, scavenger's beak and tall monk's stoop.* But she seems pleasantly impressed and she's oozing that ooky chemistry of scents and subtle excrescences, and that girlishly cuddly glow. It's glowing somewhere in the depths of my belly as well, and all along my spine. Can't be ascribed entirely to the tea. She's suddenly very, very luscious.

Sexy robes, did she say?

'Any suggestions then?'

'Yes. Don't just tell the truth, shout it out. Make a noise. I'll bring it to the public notice. In fact, I already am.'

'If, as you say, I've been stuck in among the misfits, I can shout as loud as I want and no one will take the slightest notice.'

'Of course you're right, you can't work within the conference gameplan. It's outcome's already been decided. You have to go outside it.'

'Outside it where?'

'Meet me at breakfast and I'll lead you to the place.'

What's she on about? Is she pissed? Pissed enough to mistake me for an habitual hero? Or is she putting her faith in these sexy robes which, as Paw Paw has intimated, lend to my tired presence a deceptive air of authority and effective wisdom?

What's under them is a confused stream of consciousness, a mass of biochemical reactions seething in their cauldron of toil and trouble. What is it she thinks she sees in me, that makes me a *special*

man? Is it that *something hard and true*? The thing that won't be
denied even while I fail to understand it or why it abides within me
and how it got inside me in the first place? The thing that, before I
let it go (through laziness or cowardice or both) shows itself in my
reddening, twitching hornet's spike?

The thing that usually gets me into all kinds of trouble?

'All right. I'll go along with you.'

'I'll go along with you too, Charlie.'

'Why on earth would you do that?'

'I lead a very lonely life. It comes with the job. I have magnificent
depressions.'

'I can well imagine.'

'Sometimes, in out-of-the-way places, something can happen, if
only briefly, between two people. That can be very sustaining.'

'Or very destructive. As you know, besides being a monk for a
few days I'm also a married man, and I've already had my something brief in an out-of-the-way place, and it did me no sort of good.
You've got my insides churning, Mary, but I must respectfully
decline.'

'You *are* special.'

'No to that too.'

Body and soul seem to be coming apart.

Pause and broil.

'Can't we just get back to business? Who are these nutters, Bell,
Koomaraswami, Tannenbaum and Dr Tyrone C. Mather? Could
you find out anything about them on the Googly or whatever?'

She almost blushes. Behind the insistent internal arousal, I detect
the flow of compassion from a deeper source in my quaking mind.
I don't (God knows I don't) want to turn aside from the precious
fling of pleasure and relief she's offering me. There's even the sense
that I'm unworthy of rejecting her suddenly vulnerable kindness. I
cast my eyes down, the battered victim. She smiles her little smile.

'Yes. They're there all right. Mather's an ex-Christian fundamen-
talist turned frenetic transcendentalist. He started out as a Baptist
pastor with a respectable doctorate in theology but seems to have got
himself defrocked for being too controversial about Christian social
attitudes. There's a book called *Why Did God Put The Devil In
Eden?* Why indeed! He's also got some obscure American
degree in environmental studies. Looks like he's taken to playing the
role of a sort of dark side of Emerson and Thoreau. *Darth Vader*,

perhaps. Given half a chance he could eventually turn into an environmental terrorist. He's chained himself to a few pieces of large anti-green industrial machinery, led some pretty disruptive demonstrations, said a number of obnoxious things on the smaller American TV channels, and even been arrested once or twice. But he's so crass, nobody pays him much attention. He makes the greens look bad.'

I nod. Yah. That much seems certain.

'And the swami?' (Holding to my course, gripping the shaky joystick.)

'Small-time academic, lectures in Vedic philosophy. He's run some minor but efficient programs, planting trees, cleaning up polluted streams, that kind of thing. There's a fascinating side to him too: he's written several papers on those marvellous erotic carvings (*another sly grin*) that adorn some temple gates and walls in India. In my opinion, he's probably capable of extending the Kama Sutra by a good many chapters.' (*Know what I mean, Charlie?*)

'I had the same feeling. An orgiastic mystic. What about the rabbi?'

'Sad story with a holocaust theme. He was involved in bringing some of those old Nazis to justice, the ones who tried to hide themselves in Argentina and other dark corners of the world. Immigrant American. He seems to travel a lot. I find him popping up at the oddest events. A dark horse.' (*Like myself, Charlie.*)

'And Bell?'

(*Oh God help me!*)

'Genius bordering on psychotic. But you already know that. Several random suicide attempts. Episodes of strange behaviour. You saw his act on the aeroplane.'

'I wonder, as they're all so fascinating, was I right in refusing to join in their insignificant conspiracy? I'm not completely uninteresting myself.'

'No. But you're another sad case. It's as though you want to hide your abilities, or hide away from them. You're very kind, so you act abrasively. You hide your intelligence by deliberately bumbling about. Right now you're hiding behind your robes and your marriage from what you need most, Charlie.'

'What do I need most, Mary?'

'Utterly honest intimacy.'

I can see the view of paradise stretched out far below me. I can feel the onset of vertigo as I sway towards the edge. My palms are damp. The only dry thing about me is my mouth. I am losing myself in her mischievous eyes.

But the protective *dharmapalas* are on their beat in the persons of Mather and Koomaraswami, who swagger and sidle up respectively, conveying a strong impression of something Pathan, insidious yet comical, and boyishly Kiplingesque.

Wheresoever there be an imminent need or a sudden peril, there the Buddhas appear.

'Y'all lookin' mighty cosy,' says Mather Buddha, 'Mind if we join ya?'

'We are smmwhat at a loss or prrhaps its only a loose end,' the swami explains.

'Yes, please sit down,' says Merry, 'We're just leaving.'

'I think I'll have another tea,' I whimper, smiling at her, ruining it all.

'Goodnight then, Charlie. Remember, after breakfast.'

I don't order. My karmic protectors giggle and guffaw by turns, trying to draw me into their witless conversation. I'm too exhausted even to feign politeness. In them I see again the truth that man is too pathetic to claim evil as the corruptor of his nature. And women, too, of course. By the third volley of helpless laughter, following on one of Mather's raucous environmentalist anecdotes, I excuse myself.

'I know you ain't gonna let us down,' the green redneck more or less instructs me.

'Don't worry. As a Buddhist he knows his univerrsl responssblity.'

'What was that about after breakfast?'

'I haven't been told yet.'

'I've been told after breakfast's *thee* best time, boy.'

'Goodnight,' I say, leaving Koomaraswami to writhe in doubtful mirth.

Paw Paw's not in the room, for which I heartily thank the *Nada*. I disrobe and stare for a long moment in the full-length mirror at my celibate nakedness, the aggregate of features and instruments that Moaner hasn't wanted to see or negotiate for years.

Oh Merry.

The shower's lukewarm, the minute cake of hotel soap keeps slipping from my trembling hands. Growing frustrated, then angry, then really pissed off, I give myself a full flagellation of ice cold rain.

Not at all drawn towards meditation now, at least not towards the wholesome kind. In the dark I shiver a little under the covers, draw them closer about this martyred knot of flesh. I've brought the fire down from heaven and the vultures are at my liver now. Up here my brain is swimming among images and sensations, predatorily painful, that have to do with utterly honest intimacy. I let the vultures get on with it down there. *The sharks take care of the carrion at this end.*

At last I'm able to seize on a stormy passage from Brahms. I turn up the volume in the part of the cortex that deals with classical music (romantic category, section B). The thundering strings ascend, then crash downwards again to where the growling piano waits to take hold of them, to refashion their voices into an extension of its own, until they become little more than servants of its dominant activity. It leads them in the dance of power until, the brass protesting indignantly, the entire orchestra is overwhelmed and subjugated.

For me it's the post-Beethovian battle: man against nature. The proud departure from the Goethean vision. So, lying still in the dark, I reconstruct the prophetic cries of Brahms. In unison with his groping mind I suffer the transition from the peaceful natural homestead to the anti-natural battleground.

The dog starved at his master's gate. The robin redbreast in a cage. The horse misused upon the road ...

Plump chickens fattened for the table in wire cells so small there's no room to scratch their feathered necks. (They chop their beaks off and tie up their legs these days. Keeps them healthier, I'm told.) Cows whose udders are so artificially inflated, they cannot drag themselves across a foot of field. Bullocks by the millions yawing with bovine terror in the clinical abattoirs, waiting not only to die but also to be eaten.

Der Tod, nicht die Arbeid, macht frei.

The coda comes unexpectedly: *fin de l'age.*

CHAPTER 8

The Second Day In Prague, On Which Several
Categories Of Personality Tamper With The Free
Flux Of Karma, Causing A Lama To Leap Into The
Dangerous World And Sulk Upon His Mother's Breast

Iawake to the hum in my ears and nose of sleeping Paw Paw
Banana. One cocoa-coloured foot dangles over the edge of the
mattress, the gleaming ebony head rests heavy and motionless
on the crushed white pillows. He's passed out rather than asleep,
lifeless as the burnished wooden effigy that he resembles.

He certainly won't be disturbed by the telly. There's an hour
before breakfast to see for myself what the BBC has made of Charlie
Fincham, prating pseudo-monk and minor man of action.

The lulling signature music sweeps me to the update of commodity prices: oil's up, gold's down, platinum's holding firm. The
Footsie's fractionally down, London's infected by some run or
other, the Dax looks boring; it's bullish here, bearish there.

I feel much better informed.

Baghdad. Jerusalem. Jericho. Tehran. An upbeat general, a
downbeat soldier, a flattened civilian. The American El Presidente,
cross-eyed with zeal, gives it to us straight: 'The French are like an
ageing actress still trying to dine out on her looks.' A coiffured
intellectual, raked up for the purpose of filling in the blanks (and a
three-minute slot), waffles out an analysis of this profound comment and its international implications. It seems the French don't
think much of it.

Conference of World Religions on Planetary Issues. A certain
Cardinal Giovanni Batista, well-fed and luxuriant-looking, talks
his head off: 'Extremely complicated anda importante – working
verre hard to finda consensus – difficulte – separate facts fromma
speculazione – considerina also the problem of global poverte –'

'Meanwhile, an interesting development: the man who probably
prevented disaster on Air France Flight 732 turns out to be a

Buddhist monk – presented some rather challenging views – religion should stop lying to the people – more useful to prepare them for inevitable cataclysm – Charles Fincham, a South African ...'

There's a mini cellphone video clip (Merry's work? some other passenger's?) showing Charlie leaping at the Moroccan gentleman and pinioning him to the floor. Running simultaneously beside it is the red-robed buzzard drawling, with a deep tinge of sarcasm, 'Well, he was trying to smash out the aircraft window.'

'So far there have been no official reactions from leading delegates to Mr Fincham's statements. Conference organiser, Father Peter Forbes has, however, declared himself opposed to what he called "such an obviously absurd view." On the other hand, popular reaction has been favourable on the whole, with many environmental NGO's calling to declare their support for Fincham's stance. Here's a response from one young man interviewed in the old city square in Prague ...'

Cut to old city square, Prague.

The camera has been set up to take in the whacky astronomical clock and the vampirical steeples of Our Lady of Tyn. 'So, is time ticking out for our world, as Lama Fincham insists it is? We asked several passersby, and here's what one of them had to say ...'

Enter a handsome young Czech with Tartar features (the reporter's a heavily made up frump): 'Of course this lama is telling the troot. Definitely he is not a person who is afraid. This is demonstrated on the heroplane, no? He is bravely telling the troot, and I am sure this conference will soon be perrsekutt him for this.'

He's briskly hustled out of the picture. '*To be or not to be,*' concludes the witty reporter, timing it perfectly. The clock strikes eleven, freeing from its bowels the ornate procession of clockwork apostles, 'At our world's *eleventh* hour, *that is the question.*'

The tip of my nose is twirling itself in an anti-clockwise circular motion. Leaving the BBC to get on with it, I take refuge on the toilet. There are only two choices now: shut the hell up and hide myself in some undiscoverable nook of the Best Hotel, or take hold of this double-edged karmic glaive and swing it about.

(Plop.)

Swing it about, of course. Why else have I donned these robes with their aura of authority, insight, credibility and power? Why else the self-effacing numinosity of my hairless scalp? Batman in Gotham, Superman in Smallville, Lamaman in Prague. Where would any superhero be without his magical mask and intimidating costume, and without the unfathomable karma that propels him thus to masquerade?

On the bidet I ponder Merry's role. She's in the process of fashioning my public story and persona, piecing them together move by move and word by word. That she's motivated by her own ends I have no doubt. 'I'm asking *you* to do something for *me*,' she said, with the blatant transactional undertaking, 'And *I'll* do something for *you*.' (Given sufficient quantities of pink gin.)

I shudder to think how close I came to the deadly spiral orbit of her flame. It's easier to see things dispassionately on a cold Czech morning with Paw Paw (my direct link to South Africa, Mona and my beloved kids) sprawled out like a sarcophagus in his bed, and an icy jet of water spritzing up my anus. If Merry's agenda and my cataclysmic truth coincide in the nature of things, that's good enough and simple enough for me. No further transactions are needed. (*However much, from my side, they may be desired, and however much, from hers, they may be more than a cynical means to an end.*)

From the big nobs' table at breakfast, as I enter the dining hall, there's a hush so audible it may as well have been preceded by a gasp. It's not so much antagonism I sense, it's rather that I've become the object of dire misgivings. Many pairs of eyes blatantly follow me to my table of choice.

It's not the round table of crazies with its vacant chair, nor Merry's threesome at the table set for four, although I see her waving to me. I join the sedate Buddhist monks pecking at their fruit and nuts. They greet me with bobbing nods and very broad smiles. Really, they're about to lose their heads completely. As I greet them each in turn with solid eye-contact, they fold up with screeches of laughter. One, overweight and wheezy, chokes on a hazelnut and mops his brow. Then it all subsides and we chew, suck, nibble and munch in the companionable silence of a settled sobriety. The weather is mentioned: it's not like that of India, it's not like that of Tibet, nor that of Burma nor of Sri Lanka. Neither is the food. The people least of all.

'I tinking dey very much cross with you,' the Tibetan Geshe murmurs. All the others agree, nodding vigorously again. 'Not liking your speaking.' Nods and smiles. 'Might be not liking even your toughts.' Smiles extend, lips tremble, nostrils flare. 'Or not liking maybe your heart as well.' Teeth and tongues appear, hands fidget. 'Not very much liking the all of you, I tink.' Peals of laughter echo down into the fruitbowls.

The Sri Lankan monk gestures with eyes and brows. We all turn to behold the approach of French Peter who leans down to place his placid buttocks close to my face, while the rectum once again manages a tight, official smile. The eyes are mild with fury as he invites me in a discreet tone to accompany him to a small meeting directly after the meal. It's an order.

'I already have a meeting to attend directly after breakfast,' I tell him.

'In*deed*? Perhaps this meeting will render the other redundant.'

'In that case I'd better not attend.'

'I must insist, Mr Fincham. It's important to all of us here at this conference.'

'But the other meeting is important enough to me not to risk its being rendered redundant. I'm sure you see the problem.'

'I do in*deed*. Perhaps we shall do best to try to find a compromise.'

'I'll just go find it now.'

I shuffle across to Merry's table of media mugs.

Merry smiles disdainfully up at me. The other journalists around the table grin openly, as at a dupe. I may be the story of the moment but they're controlling its progress. When I tell her what French Peter's up to the open contempt is replaced by excited concern. Then I see that the assumed *hauteur* is only that of the fury of which hell hath none like.

'Don't let them keep you for longer than half an hour,' she warns me sharply.

'Got it.'

'Oh, well at least that's articulate enough for you.'

'You're the one who's not getting it, Mary.'

'No, *you're the one who's not getting it.*'

(Oh, I know, I know.)

'Half an hour it is.'

'Then meet me in the lobby.'

The self-composed bum, perched jauntily above its clerical collar, awaits me at the door. It leads me to the lift and up two floors to a very posh boardroom. It bows itself humbly to those present, arousing, to my astonishment, not so much as a titter. Perhaps I'm the only one who sees it. Or perhaps it's considered just too tragic to be laughed at.

Oh yah. These are definitely some of the really big kahunas Merry's told me about. Some rise politely, most don't bother. Their facial expressions uniformly convey bored irritation, as if by prior arrangement. Yet there is one that seems delighted. Torquemada, maybe.

'Good morning, Mr Fincham,' drones the biggest kahuna, the delighted one (name-tagged Archbishop Francis Manners). 'Is that the right form of address? Please have a seat.'

'The right form of address is *Lama*.'

'Well then, *Lama*, please do have a seat.'

'Thank you. What is the right form of address in your case?'

'In my case it's *Your Grace*.'

'Thank you, *Your Grace*.'

'Firstly, um, *Lama*, we'd like to express our admiration for your courageous action on board that aircraft. Unfortunately we can't do so outside of this room. We wouldn't want to risk injuring the feelings of our Muslim colleagues.'

'You're all Christians in here? I thought this was a conference of world religions.'

'It certainly is that, but it has been arranged and convened by the Christian churches.'

'The *Western* Christian churches?'

'Well, that is neither here nor there, *Lama*. It has nothing to do with this meeting.'

'Of course not. I'm the reason for this meeting.'

'Very perceptive of you. As I say, we truly admire your courage, but other aspects of your behaviour are causing us some distress, particularly your views on *inevitable global cataclysm*. Is that a Buddhist view, *Lama*?'

'Actually, *Your Grace*, I feel sure that *Your Grace* is aware that inevitable global cataclysm is a key article of *Your Grace's* own religion.'

'It's not that we mind your holding such a view, Mr Fincham. After all, it is a possibility we all have to face. But we consider it unwise of you to disseminate that view from the platform provided by this conference.'

'It's not a view this conference might consider adopting, Mr Manners?'

'Most certainly not.'

'But the conference is still in conference. Who's to say what view will prevail when the conferring's done? In the meantime everyone is surely entitled to state their own opinion?'

'Unfortunately *your* opinion is enjoying a great deal of publicity, owing to your very courageous action in the air.'

'*Your Grace*, I can only hope that my actions *on air* will be as courageous.'

'I'd hoped you might be convinced to see the matter from our point of view. If you persist in going your own way, we shall be forced to reconsider your privileges as a delegate. Not that we want to, of course.'

'Please excuse me while you reconsider those. I have another appointment in ten minutes.'

'Perhaps we shall have to speak with the Dalai Lama himself.'

'I can't vouch for His Holiness sharing my views.'

Suddenly there's another voice, braying forth from the donkey's lips of a Yankee scientist dressed in a shocking combination of flagrant checks and stripes:

'You're behaving like an ass, Fincham. You don't know what you're getting yourself into. You don't know the trouble you're causing.'

'I'm here as a Buddhist monk. My first duty is to the truth as I see it.'

'No one gives a damn about your truth. Keep it to yourself if it's your own. You think you're some kind of goddamn post-modernist prophet?'

'No, but to quote your own Teacher, you can be sure that my own truth will make no headway if it doesn't find resonance with the truths of others.'

'Some people will believe any bunkum you put in their heads.'

'Including whatever bunkum you lot may serve up.'

'Look, pal, all I need stress is that you'd better keep your opinions to yourself and away from the media. Or face the consequences. Am I coming through loud and clear, *Mister* Fincham?'

'Please, Dr Hancock, that's hardly necessary,' His Grace admonishes.

'I think its exactly what's necessary here,' Dr Bogart Hancock retorts. 'Some people just won't listen to reason.'

'I'm sure the Lama *is* a reasonable man. He is a Buddhist monk, after all. I'm sure he'll prove me right in that regard.'

'I'm as reasonable as any of you,' I say, proving him wrong.

'Then you'll … *retract?*'

It's too perfectly inquisitorial. I burst with laughter like a deluge.

I leave the buttocks aghast with indignation, the archbishop vindictively stricken, Hancock outraged and on his feet, and the other assorted prelates in various postures of displeased solidarity. The earth does not revolve around the sun, *but it does*.

Merry's in the lobby, jumping with impatience. I try to explain to her what's just happened in the interrogation chamber but she's not interested in that right now. 'Come on, Charlie!' she yells, grabbing my arm, 'Let's get out there!'

Om mani padme hum.

There must be hundreds of them pressed together in the parking lot of the Best Hotel, and spilling over into the adjacent streets. More are arriving in buses, skodas and beat up ladas. Some are cycling up; some are on motorcycles.

They're holding up banners and placards, most of them with Czech slogans which I don't understand. But there are also several in English and German and even one or two in Russian. I can only assume that they all agree more or less with the English ones: *Tell Us The Truth; Tell Us No Lies; Tell Us No Half-Truths.*

I spot one with the old-fashioned announcement: *Religion is the Opiate of the People.* Then, with my hands dropping limply to my knees while the rhythm of my heartbeat goes awry, I notice a number of bright red and yellow placards with the appalling legend: *Listen to the Lama.*

Beelzebub, Mather and Koomaraswami stand amazed just outside the glass doors of the lobby. Only their heads are in constant motion as they look this way and that and turn to grin or yell at one another. Mather's neck seems to have grown by several centimetres, his wiry body's twitching with energy. He raises the revolutionary fist. His beard blows in the wind. He's Che Guevara in Prague. (No sign of the rabbi. His bulk's still feeding itself, I imagine, or resting heavily on a sagging bed.)

I step past them towards the gathering crowd. Some metres into the parking lot I just stop and stare. The wind swirls my robes about my legs. It's cold. I wrap the maroon shawl around my shoulders. My head's freezing, nostrils blown wide open, ears stinging. I stand looking out at a thousand smiling faces. They're all I can see, all that my mind can take in. I look. They smile. The wind blows.

Two men come up to me; one places a soft woollen coat over my shoulders and lifts the lined hood onto my head. They greet me with palms pressed together at their chests. They must be Buddhists. Yes, one has *mala* beads coiled around his wrist. They seem elated, looking intently, *even lovingly*, into my shocked eyes.

Recovering my sense of place, I again survey the larger scene: people of every age, oldsters, youngsters, children; motley, dappled, vibrant. There are several groups of journalists, filming, photographing, holding microphones aloft. As I look about, the two Buddhists beside me raise their hands. The crowd huddles together and gradually falls silent. I stoop in the wind, holding the coat shut at my breast. In the distance, across the river, the St Vitus Cathedral and castle buildings raise themselves on the Mala Strana hilltop above the thickets of grand architecture.

'For God's sake say something, Charlie!' shouts Beelzebub.

'Please to address these peepols, Lama,' urges one of the Buddhists, gently holding my elbow. The other one fusses with the hood, as though I were a precious child. Beneath the windswept robes my legs seem to have detached themselves from the rest of me. I am floating like a Buddha.

Silence. From somewhere in the assembly comes the tinkling of a prayer-bell, irregularly rung by the insistent draught. Must be more Buddhists in the crowd. I ask the man at my elbow. Crisp, open features, fluffy chicken beard.

'Yes. Every Buddhists in whole city of Praha. But also many others, not Buddhists. Most not Buddhists, I tink.'

'What do they want me to say?'

'What they want Lama to say? Whatever Lama want to say.'

'How do they know about me? And *what* do they know about me?'

'Television. They knows everytink, I tink.'

Everything?

The silence seems never-ending. And they want me to do something with it. Bogart Hancock's warning stings my dumb awareness: 'You don't know what you're getting yourself into – the trouble you're causing.' His self-willed anger prods at my rebellious side. But I pause to listen before I speak.

'*Hava peaceful mind, Chully. Whenever you speaking, always you are only speaking to yourself. There is only that simple truth*

*which your own mind is able to believing. Then you never can lying
to others.'*

I take in all these beautiful faces. They are all variants of the face
I call my own.

'If you are here to be ...' The wind blows my words away. How
many of them understand English anyway? Little frowns of mild
perplexity cross several brows. There's some bustling. A woman,
plump and dark, comes forward with a megaphone. I'm given to
understand that she'll translate. Smiling, nodding, a handshake, a
little bow. I bow back.

'If you're here to be encouraged by anything I have to say, I'm
afraid I'll have to disappoint you. I don't believe that we'll find the
wisdom and resolve to save our world. (Translation, grim faces.) In
many ways it's already too late. Much that we love about our world
today will be gone tomorrow, in ten or twenty years, or fifty. We
don't have the insight to see that tomorrow is that close. We are
concentrated only on today because today is the place in which the
system keeps us trapped. People can't move to save our world
because the system has their minds held tightly in its myriad tentacles. (Tentacles? *Octopus*, I wiggle my tentacling fingers. Right.)
It's myriad tentacles keep us busy day in, day out, and no one's free,
no world leader, no international thinker, no global technologist,
no universal saint even, can think or act outside their grasp. Service
to the system is the first priority, then come our own immediate
interests, our immediate instincts to survive *today*.'

'Yahoo, brother!' screams Mather, 'Yer comin' through loud and
cle-e-a-r!'

(What's he so enthused about? Is he hearing what I'm saying?)

'If what I'm saying isn't true, the next hundred years will prove
me wrong, and of course I hope they do. But I don't think they will
because, if you investigate carefully, you'll find that the sickness has
already gone too deep. I feel it's too late, even for partial remedies.
This is an unbearable truth. If it's not unbearable to you, you
haven't understood it. And most people haven't understood it.
They're like drunks who have burned down their own homes and
are still too drunk to realize what they've done. They'll realize it
tomorrow, and it will be unbearable.'

Around the lobby doors at my back there is a small commotion.
I turn my head and see French Peter surrounded by the hotel security personnel. Their militia-style uniforms, drab dark grey with

splashes of red, recall the fashions of the Stalinist era. It's intimidating. I should finish very quickly.

'Will the system let go of our physical lives? Of course not. And we won't free ourselves because outside of the system there's very little to keep body and soul together. Nor will we be able to overthrow the system. It's been in place for too long and the time at our disposal, before our home burns down, is far too short. So far as that goes we're – well – we're buggered. (*Buggered*? I can't find the translatable word. The crowd waits. '*Bagghard*,' the translator puts it to them megaphonically. They look about, chewing it over.)

'At a loss!' Beelzebub hollers, 'Stymied, powerless, paralyzed, stuffed!!!'

From the sound of it the translator settles for the idea of paralysis. A wave of comprehension passes across the assembled faces. Frenchy and the KGB seem immobilised for the moment. Still in conference, I suppose.

'The only freedom we can strive for is freedom of the mind; freedom from the drunkenness that has brought this tragedy about, freedom from the pangs of dread and loss, and *freedom in our minds from the system that made us drunk in the first place*. The only task of religion is to help us gain that freedom. That has always been its task, a task at which it has failed since it first taught men to paint their survivalist needs on the walls of caves. Religion is there to help us free our minds so that, when we perish, as we certainly will, we might perish with the dignity of our liberated minds. So what I have to say is mainly this: get freedom for your minds, not for the sake of the dying world, but for the sake of your own dignity as you die with it.'

I stand there in silence. The crowd politely applauds. I'm mildly bewildered too. They should be grieving. Perhaps they aren't yet able to take it all in. The thought occurs: *they can't see the overweening tyranny of the system*. I decide to allow myself an allusive demonstration.

'There's a conference of world religions going on in there. (I throw my head back towards the Best Hotel.) What do you think they'll be telling you? I can assure you they won't be agreeing with me. They'll lull you with compromise; there's still hope, they'll tell you; this can be done, and that, to keep the system running and controlling the world order, the industrial order, the scientific order, the dirty political order, the inane religious order –'

Frenchy and his cronies encircle me. My two Buddhist companions take hold of an arm each. They're not letting me go. The crowd sees what's happening. There are murmurs and mutters, and some tough guys, including not a few tough-guy females, step forward slightly.

'You're beyond belief, Fincham,' Frenchy hisses, 'No, I believe you're quite mad.'

'I'm done.'

'Bloody right you are.'

The apparatniks attempt to manhandle me back towards the hotel lobby, but the Buddhists won't let them. It gets rough. The comrade with the pencil moustache clamps a heavy paw down on my shoulder, forcing me under with such force that I fall to the ground. His muscleman henchmen see their chance, seizing me by the arms.

At this the crowd goes beserk. One of my two Buddhist bodyguards completely abandons the *ahimsa* principle. He shoves and slaps the pencil moustache backwards. A robust woman, perhaps an ex-customs officer from the pre-velvet revolution days, puts her face very close to the fading arrogance in the second guard's features. French Peter, alas, doesn't escape with his churchman's controlled contempt intact. He's on the ground beside me.

My bodyguards lift me gently by the arms and dust me off while the crowd hold back the security apparatus. At the door I can see Manners and Hancock. They seem to be deeply involved in a remote discussion.

I'm led to an ancient lada, powder-blue with rust spots. The rear door is opened and I'm carefully placed inside. My buddhyguards take their seats on either side of me. In the front are a man and a woman who turn to look at me. He nods vigorously as he smiles and then frowns with concern. She pats my hand. We drive off in the direction of the old city.

Deciding that it's the proper first step, I ask to be introduced. The fluffbeard on my left is Tomas; the sallow belligerent with the bright, happy black eyes is Libor; Pavel's at the wheel; Radka's still smiling back at me with an innocent devotion that is very troubling to both my conscience and my common sense.

'I'm Charlie.'

'Lama Charrli, very welcome,' says Libor. 'I to protect yourself.'

'Do I need protection?'

'Yes, of course. Most peepols hate the troot.'

'I won't be doing anything illegal,' I state, ask and implore in one multi-tasking confluence of tone.

'Anything can be illegal sometimes. Also the troot can be illegal,' he laughs.

'But you will tell the troot today, Lama,' says Radka devotedly.

Tomas is on the cellphone. '*Vaclavske namesti*,' I hear him say, and, '*Karluv Most, Nerudova*.' So that's the protest route: Wenceslas Square, the Charles Bridge, Nerudova Street which winds up to the castle (which doubles, I realize with a stab of distress, as the presidential palace.) Am I to tell the *troot* before the gates of a castle, one of whose tourist attractions is a wall built entirely of human skulls? And before the gates of which stand two palace guards presided over by two classical bronzes depicting muscular titans in the act of dealing the death-blow to two recumbent unfortunates?

My two bodyguards keep looking back. A mercedes-benz taxi is close on our tail. It's sticking to our rear so aggressively that I can make out the occupant in the passenger seat; it's Merry. Above the line of the rear window four heads rock and bump along, one of them brown and gleaming.

'Journalist,' I tell them, 'And some other friends.'

'Your friends, Lama?'

'Well, yes – I suppose.'

'Good friends always follow close behind,' tough Libor aphorises.

'You have many good friends, Lama,' Tomas assures me, as I sink to a new and wracking level of blank anxiety.

'You will tell the troot about the global warming and the destroyink of our planet,' Radka smiles as at a saviour, 'This troot must be told in Czechia in this times. All Czech peepols must hear it. Also all the world.'

– Oh God if by any chance there is a God please forgive my unbelief and reach down to save me now and I'll never not believe again and I'll revert to Catholicism and give up smoking too.

– Good-day. You have reached the Bureau of The Divine. Please hold. All our operators are currently busy. We value your call. Please hold. All our operators are currently busy. Thank you for your patience. If you hang up you will be placed at the back of the automated queue. Please hold …

A cold light *creeps by the snowhills* of my mind. What are saviours for if they can't be used against the devils? For a while now the green magazines and websites have been full of the blockhead assertions of the current Czech president who believes that global warming is a *new religious myth, an ideology which has replaced communism.* Thank you Mr President, that is very reassuring.

It's obvious. They want me to speak against him, at the castle gates, a few hundred metres further up the Nerudova Street from the Museum of Torture with its black display of hand-forged medieval instruments, and right beside the overweening cathedral. Why else do they want to take me across the bridge and up there?

I fucking well won't, *will not*, do it.

Hancock's hysteria and the archbishop's quiet frustration suddenly take on a distinctly sensible aspect. The desperation on French Peter's bumface (with its tickling invitation to a jovial slap) now seems much less ridiculous. Not for nothing has this conference been brought to Prague where the confrontational tension between green science and grey politics is being played out in a perfectly patterned microcosm at the fringes of the European Union.

In the faint light of the mental snowhills there's a sudden searing flash of lightning. It's a lashing of illumination that almost shines out through my eyes: *This is what Merry has been counting on all along.*

Then, finally, it does spill through.

'*How could you do this to me, Rinpoche?*'

'*You hava very courage mind, Chully. And you not completely without wisdom. You hava wanting to go beyond being a Buddhist, beyond some meditation, some mindfulness, some nice Buddhist mantra. You hava wanting to see your strength, to stand up for your truth. But, in the past you hava often failing. Now you hava this opportunity to stand, and for standing not completely without wisdom in very difficult situation. This is not an ordinary opportunity; you cannot doing it with your ordinary mind alone.*'

'You knew what I would say at the conference?'

'*I'm not knowing for sure, Chully, but I know what you hava many times said to me, and that is your own truth. So, I want to giving you this chance. I am your teacher, I must giving it to you. And I am standing with you or falling with you, because I hava given you these robes to wear.*'

It's true. Whatever I say here today, I say as the monk he has ordained and sent to say it. But am I saying what he wants me to say? Is my vision his vision? But that is not the point. The point is that he is trusting to something in this mental continuum that is a vision of truth belonging to neither of us, and yet inherent in us all.

We park in a street some blocks down from Wenceslas Square. The taxi pulls up alongside us and debouches its organic contents. Merry's beaming with excitement, her eyes wide and fixed on me as she strides up with a possessive air. Paw Paw stumbles out, still a little dazed, then Mather, wildly stretching his sinewy limbs, as though about to attack, and the swami lithe as a snake charmer and swaying like the snake. After a moment Beelzebub unfolds himself onto the pavement too, gathers his assortment of shapes into a single physique and stands there like a recently auctioned Picasso, staring out at all of us.

'We need to speak privately,' I whine at Merry, too limp to growl. 'Now.'

'Of course, Charlie.' She points to a coffee shop.

'I'm very much in the mood for disappointing you.'

'Whatever you do, Charlie, don't disappoint the whole world, or yourself.'

'What kind of crap talk is that?'

'The true kind.'

I explain to Tomas and Libor that I must have a private chat with the journalist. They don't mind at all and conduct me to the coffee shop, one on either side. When we find a table they take their seats in the same order. Merry, looking very satisfied, hops into a chair across from us and summons the waiter. Three coffees, one tea.

'Well, Charlie?' she coaxes, sweet and all-knowing.

'What are your plans for today? Your devious plans for me, I mean.'

'Devious plans? Only you know the plans, Charlie. You're at the head of things today. Why ask me? With you one never knows what will happen next. And, I have to say, it's wonderful to see!'

'You know about the President's views on global warming, of course.'

'I do.'

'And you know what these protesters are protesting about?'

'Yes. About his views.'

'And now I'm at the head of things? How the hell did that happen?'

'It seems the protesters adopted you.'

'You think I'm a sot? That I don't see your hand in this? And, let me tell you, Rinpoche's hand as well?'

'Let me get this straight: you suspect that Rinpoche and I conspired to set all this up? That you're some kind of lama-pawn in our game?'

'Suspect? Gad, woman, it's clear as … as …'

'As the conspiracy to get you to jump the Moroccan on the plane, so that you'd be all over the news, so that your views on the conference would fortuitously be included in the interview about the Air France incident, and so on?'

'My views were *fortuitously included*? I don't think so.'

'Well perhaps not fortuitously. Perhaps it's your karma.'

'*You're* lecturing *me* on karma now?'

'Yes, and you working so skilfully, so *wonderfully*, along with it, Lama.'

'Wonderfool,' Tomas agrees, touching my shoulder lightly.

'Do you know, at least, what happens next?'

But she's dreamily contemplating my anxious face, reaches across the table to slide the woollen hood from my head. Her hands smell of soap and, subtly, of themselves. They are lively, expressive and capable. I almost take hold of them.

'Your two companions know. Let's ask them.'

'Well then, Tomas, Libor? Do you know what my karma has in store for me?'

'Prepare for march on Vaclavske Namesti. After that we march to palass.'

So it's not been completely contrived, eh? Only purposefully developed by a small interference in the ceaseless sequence of action and decision, and uncertain motive. They are not as uninvolved, she and Rinpoche, as she pretends. They have acted too, blending their motives and choices with mine. And, intertwined in this triad moving towards the next moment, we are linked, as well, with these thousands in Prague, with our enemies at the Best Hotel, with Paw Paw, Koomaraswami, Beelzebub and Mather, and with the world at large, not only on millions of television screens but in the interdependent nature of everything.

I sip my insipid tea. This is not a storm in a teacup. The truth about the end of our world is also the truth about the end of our truth. What might or might not come after our collective extinction is all in the realm of myth, suspicion, intuition.

But we should not scurry like scattering rats to meet our violent end, nor turn away from it like children at play in the nursery, intent on denying the horror in the living room. I can't turn aside now.

'I suppose I can't turn aside now.'

'You won't, Charlie.'

'Please to have some more tea, Lama?'

Why can't most people see it? Why have they missed the one blip that has put everything on this new and catastrophic footing? We saw it back then, vaguely, stoned as we were, when *they* would not turn aside and couldn't bring themselves to say, 'This thing can kill us all. We'll have to lay it down.'

In our bell-bottomed blue jeans and floral shirts and headbands, making love on the grass, and high on grass, using our guitars as weapons, we knew that it must come to this. And then we grew up and forgot.

Human power corrupts human wisdom, frail and feeble as it is. That's a given, old as the hills. Ultimate power in our human hands must blow up in our faces, the more so as we refuse to let it go, demonstrating by our stubbornness the demise of our survivalist intelligence.

Proving even Darwin wrong.

'*Pull down thy vanity*,' is it? Mr Pound?

CHAPTER 9

In Which The Castle Is Attacked And A Prelate Makes A Kierkegaardian Leap Of Faith

We walk together to Wenceslas Square. The driver, Pavel, hulks along silently, sucking at a hand-rolled smoke. I need a smoke too and get one off Tomas, who chuckles at the incongruity of the wheezily puffing monk. Libor wants to crack a joke about tobacco being a vegetarian thing, but I'm smoking in earnest, like a condemned man. Radka's reciting her *mala* mantra.

The four goons hang back. I can't imagine what they're scheming or hoping for, especially Paw Paw. What's brought him along at all is impossible to say. Beelzebub, though sticking with them, is not one of them. He's always alone in his psychotic transcendence. *He knows why he's here.*

Merry has elbowed Libor out. She's at my right side, walking close enough to me to brush my arm from time to time, saying nothing. It's warming up and the wind has dropped. I stop to take off the coat. She peels it from me, hands it to Tomas and straightens the folds of my jerkin and shawl, avoiding my eyes.

We pass along streets crammed with Viennese architecture, neo-classical archways rolling unobrusively into art nouveau, not one façade missing a beat, all of them newly painted in the urgency to resuscitate beauty after decades of social impoverishment. It's like wandering through a movie set. A horse-drawn carriage clops and rumbles by, ferrying tourists to the new town.

Emerging into the square from behind the museum, I look on a numberless assembly, of which the few in the hotel parking lot must have been only a satellite emissary. I look across at Tomas; he's concentrated, nodding gravely at me. Libor again takes a careful but firm hold of my elbow.

'I have to get to the media gang,' says Merry. 'You're in my heart, Lama.'

'Look at all those people.'

'Just flow with them.'

I take her hand for a brief moment and let her go. It's a gesture of awakened friendship, a wordless communication that we both grasp. She's turned out to be dangerously loveable and Charlie may have fallen, but Charlie's nowhere to be seen.

There being no Charlie, there's no Mona, no Clara, no Jessica. There's no past defined by struggling relationships, futile labour, the pressing semi-conscious search for joy; the weeping, the fear and failure. There's only an urgent karma flowing in the present and a nameless mind swimming gracefully in its flux.

'*So, you hava no good reasons for wearing these robes? All these people, they are making the good reasons for you. The highest wisdom, it always seems to coming from nowhere but that same nowhere is the energy of interdependence. It is very much funny, no? To hava no feeling of importance in yourself while everybody else thinking how very much important you are – heh heh heh – like the person who does not know that he has the only sex organ which is still working – heh heh heh – in the whole world – heh heh.*'

'The penis beyond price – hah haha haa!'

'*Especially if it belonging to a monk – heh heh – heheeh.*'

Libor and Tomas don't know why, but they start laughing too. We are standing halfway down the grand staircase that flows from the commanding museum to the statue of St Wenceslas and the memorial to those who perished in the numb but efficient embraces of the unfriendliest comrades of all.

I can see, from a corner of my mind, the four goons standing behind us a few steps higher up. Below us the swirling river of the assembled masses undulates to a distance in the square far beyond the elegant beacon of the grand old Europa Hotel.

Pavel and Radka go down into the crowd, informing, shaking hands, directing. I can pick out the police presence at strategic intervals along the fringes of the rippling mass. There are police vehicles, what looks like a black maria, and an ambulance. The media, too, are spread throughout the square; in the centre, by the statue, on the sidewalks. Directly below us at the foot of the stairway is a concentrated crew of reporters and cameramen, Merry among them. I laugh and wave down at her.

Then I see why we've been waiting here. Pavel's coming back with a woman dressed all in white except for the flat red walking shoes. She's approaching with unforced energy, head erect, shoulders back, a woman at home in herself. As she nears us there is a tumult of applause. No doubt about it; she's their number one. Middle-aged, clear pale skin, shocking green eyes; the impression is of nobility, elegance and clarity of purpose.

'Helena Pikardt,' Pavel bows, 'Lama Charrli.'

'You came to us at the right time, Lama,' she says in a voice mellow with confidence and in easily recognizable English, 'Like a certain kind of gift.'

'This march was planned some time ago.'

'Oh yes, to coincide with the conference, of course.'

'It's a certain kind of gift as well.'

'Yes, and so many people giving it.'

'What am I to do?'

'Will you walk with us?'

I give her an affirmative look, a small nod. She takes my hand and lifts it high in hers, a token of solidarity. The people applaud and shout. She's extremely graceful, intriguingly at ease. One feels she could turn this flood of humanity about with the lightest of gestures, like a *deva* or, indeed, a *diva*.

We descend the stairs and walk down the central aisle of the elongated square. As we pass among them the people cheer. Those nearest us reach out their hands to shake ours. Many greet me with palms together. I'm laughing and everyone whose eye I catch or hand I touch is infected with my hilarity.

The goons still follow at a small distance. But it seems to me now that they're not merely stumbling in the wake of Charlie's swelling karma; each is marching to his own inner drummer, moving determinedly towards a personal destination. This is their karma too. It's *Eines in Einem*, make no mistake.

But where's the rabbi? I seem to sense him somewhere in the crowd, an intimation, as though I've glimpsed his twirling yarmulke somewhere among the thousands of bobbing faces.

My own situation among these multitudes remains baffling. Are they really buying what I'm telling them? And if so, *why? How hard it is in some cases to be believed, and how impossible in others*. I am presenting them with the ultimately incredible, the sort of news that ordinarily would have one checking the calendar to make sure it isn't April 1st. So why aren't they laughing at me, at least up their sleeves?

Because they want to test the feeling of this terrifying piece of fiction. They want to explore how they would cope with such a truth. If it were truly truth for them, as it truly is for me, they'd be murdering the messenger. I'm their pied piper, not their prophet. I'm a different kind of entertainment.

It's the child testing the unreal hypothesis of death.

Yet there may be one or two who see it coming and perhaps, after today, there'll be a few more true believers, seeing it clearly and steadily because it's written on the ancient tablets of their own stony hearts. Then, at long bloody last, those stones might evolve towards the dignity of something alive and free and growing as they grieve, facing the guilty end.

'*What say you, Your Honour?*'

'*A tad melodramatic for my taste.*'

'*See what I mean?*'

Among the four only Mather's enjoying the party. He's a fine old rebel and this is a fine old cause. I just know there's a confederate flag hanging rebelliously on his porch at home way down in Ole Alabammy. 'Boy, if this ain't the way ta go though,' I hear him crowing.

The others walk on in silence. Koomaraswami in his *dhoti*, and swathed in reams of Indian cotton, has turned himself into a *sadhu*, interiorly focussed and distant. You'd never know now that some lesser gateways of his mind are tooled with wondrous intaglio erotica. Right now, in this heaving ocean of life, he's the elevated man who's made it safely inside the temple. He is himself unobscured.

Paw Paw Banana's more wooden than ever. Inscrutable in his Nigerian get up, he plods along like some suspect African statesman. He definitely sticks out like a sore brown thumb in this broadly whitewashed throng. When he sees me turning to look at him as I shake a random hand, he lifts his head, acknowledging not me, but himself. He's been fooled one too many times by the passing caucasian show.

The bishop marches grimly, absently, his cubist proportions hanging together as though by an immense act of will. His meaning and motives are locked inside themselves, holding back their essential secret. He's alarmingly quiet.

Where's the rabbi?

Still at Helena Pikardt's side, I emerge at the head of the army of demonstrators, at the lower end of the square. Ahead of us lies the route past the opera house, along the banks of the Vltava and across the bridge up to the castle. Although I'm part of the vanguard, my strongest impression is of being led. The mass behind us doesn't at all coerce our forward momentum. They're being led too.

The river flows light and dappled, the impersonal symbol of us all. There are colourful boats on the water, plying their riverine business in remote separation from ours. The crowd has taken up an anthem. From the rear a rhythmic chant goes up. Banners are flying, placards are lifted high in the air, their slogans seeming, as they always do, to distort, by pithiness and vulgarity, the anger or pain or fear that are really on the minds of the marchers.

It's a sloganized plea for the world's survival. It's a small but urgent light that wants to dispel the ignorant fog of the universal bureaucrat but, of course, it can't hope to penetrate that far. Its impotence is evident in its being tolerated by the buffoons against which it is crying out. It's undangerous. Otherwise it would be crushed. Even the placards which announce *Fuck the American Dream* are part of the provisional freedom in which that reptilian dream coils and uncoils itself to be devoured by its self-involved ouroboros urge.

There is no placard bearing the truth that the avaricious dream has mortally wounded us. Or that against politics and subservient science we should be wailing with Mercutio: *A plague on both your houses; they have made worms' meat of me!*

Worms' meat. That's the thing they're missing. If they saw *that* they could not harbour sufficient frivolity to carry brightly coloured messages of festive chiding. This march would be what it ought to be, a *danse macabre. (Enlivened even then by a natural tendency on such occasions to a merrily ghoulish tomfoolery.)*

Even the cops are relaxed. Hell, it's a pleasant outing in one of the prettiest cities in the world. If it comes to having to clobber some loudmouthed kid or struggle ferociously to get a slippery grip on the tits of an hysterical girl, so much the better. Will they lay hands on the leaders if things get out of hand? What's Merry hoping for, despite herself?

The legions squeeze themselves through the arches of the ancient towers leading onto the bridge. This would be the appropriate place to ambush us all if the establishment felt threatened enough. But the functionary uniforms are sauntering along beside us up to the palace where the governing suits are fortifying themselves with strong coffee or a splash or two of exquisitely aged brandy.

'What's in your mind, Miz Pikardt?'

'In my mind is the thought that we are doing all we can do *today*.'

'And what, do you think, we'll gain by this?'

'Time, Lama. Perhaps we'll gain some time.'

'The last resort of the terminally ill?'

'Yes, perhaps. But who can say what treatments we may discover, given time.'

'You ... still hope?'

'I am a doer. I see the crisis and I must act, even if is too late.'

'Then you have nothing to learn from me.'

'Oh no, you have taught me something very important: to do even more.'

The walk up the Nerudova Street is demanding. It's a steep ascent and the overdone grandeur of the Mala Strana district strains the churning mind. Restaurants, postcard shopfronts, galleries, the torture museum; white, blue, rose, buttercup yellows. A last draining tramp and we're in the huge courtyard before the cathedral. Here we regroup and catch our breath. Below us the archaic city, the unlikely survivor of both Hitler and Stalin (might even these delinquents have said, 'No. We can't destroy *this*.'?) tumbles down the hillside and spreads out beyond the river: scores of spires lifted above the many-tinted watercolours.

Helena collects several scrolls of petitions from her lieutenants. Tomas and Libor adhere to me; it's obviously their brief. The goons step up.

'Hangin' in there, Lama?' Mather enquires. 'Jayziss, whadda climb!'

'Charlie's fine,' says Beelzebub, 'It's his day.' (What's cured him of the yells?)

The swami, looking me over minutely, seems to scoop me up into his eyes. He nods vaguely, compresses his big mouth approvingly. All real wisdom comes from India, and deep down inside me he sees an Indian.

And, yaar! He's right.

'The yoga of love,' he says mysteriously.

'Are we up to it, Swamiji?' I ask.

'Let me tell you, we nevrr love fully untll we're forced to. Suffring oppns our hearts. You're promising suffring to all these people. I hope they're abll to accept it.'

'Thanks for sticking by me,' I tell them.

'You're the star today, Chahli,' says Paw Paw. 'Tomorrow it might be me.'

'What's a star, Paw Paw?'

'The one who izi walking in front, of course,' he guffaws. 'No, Chahli. The star izi the one who izi shining.'

'No star shines forever, eh?' Beelzebub muses sadly, 'White giant, red dwarf, pulsar, black hole. Gather ye rosebuds ...'

'Prrhps it's better to scatter them while you may,' the newly-awakened swami sighs.

Helena is flanked by four scroll bearers now. These signed pleas on paper reams will be handed to whomever emerges from the castle gates to accept them on behalf of the dullard president. He'll fiddle with them and finagle them, these minor embarrassments in the daily routine. But how will they influence a mind so calloused by workaday thinking that it can't begin to imagine that the working day will soon be permanently halted by a final order of redundancy?

The procession pythons its way round to the grandiose presidential palace.

The two toy sentries stand at silly attention by the gates. It's no wonder people feel that mischievous compulsion to tweak their noses. Their silly posturing stirs the brain to silly thoughts. If things go awry, I suppose they'll have no choice but to step forward and bayonet someone. If they're mad enough to stand erect in that cuckoo clock hut, who can say what other orders they're mad enough to obey?

They look on with drilled disinterest as the crowd calls out for the president. The demonstration itself has been rubber-stamped several months ago. A lanky old gentleman with sparse strings of plastered-down hair appears at the palace doors after a suitably humiliating wait. He saunters calmy to the gates, waves at the cameras and accepts the petitions from Helena Pikardt. He lingers a moment to smile and listen with a practised official courtesy.

It's the moment that Mather chooses to launch himself into the public notice. Bounding forward with a limber acrobatic salto, he places himself between Helena and the suddenly alarmed spokesman. (Now furiously plastering the grizzled strands and checking to see if the sentries are where they should be.)

'Straight into the garbage can, ride? I tellya, I seen it all before. We shouldn't be handin' over rolls o' paper to y'all. Cain't read the signs o' the times, how the ferk yer gonna read this document? By Jayziss, we should be stormin' these here ferkin' gates, I tellya!'

He has his finger almost up the nostril of the official's classy crooked nose. Looking down at wiry Mather, the eldery diplomat is clearly at a loss, but he's working out an appropriate response for the unforgiving media. Mather upsets his cautious diplomacy by running at the gates.

'Let's go!' he's screaming at the immobile herd, 'Let's git inside where we can tell em to their faces, or burn their whole ferkin' barnyard down!'

The toy sentries devolve into real live soldiers, manhandling Mather from the gates. He's fuming and foaming like an epileptic: 'Ferk y'all! Goddamn stablishment bums!' He kicks and lunges wildly, a self-forgetful animal in the frantic thrall of his own instinctive rage. The crowd watches with distaste. This reflects poorly on their corporate quality of courteous outrage. Only an American could.

'Think yer ferkin'soldiers, do ya? Pair o' piss ant greenhorns! If you had any brains you'd be soldiering for *ers*! It's *ers* on the ride side, godalmidy! It's *them* ferkers in there you oughtta be arresting!'

By now the drooling cops have sped up to the bundle of shrieking sinews jitterbugging between the adolescent guards. A really big dick, swift with experience, grabs hold of Mather's straggling beard and wallops at his head with a truncheon. The demoniac goes limp, but he's still yelling.

'Please, please, is this really nessrry?' the swami fusses around them, 'Oh please stop this, please stop this, oh my gawd.' I can see that he's about to be bludgeoned too. The cops are poised before a fine trip-wire; a hairsbreadth of annoyance is all that's needed. They're waiting for it with relish.

Through her limpid green eyes, with quiet assurance, Helena looks to me. I can sense the cracking of my bald white eggshell under those thwacking truncheons. The front ranks have seen where she's directing her voiceless appeal. Hundreds of eyes are taking me in, summing me up. Libor holds my elbow, gently pulls it back. These are not the hotel security lightweights.

I break free and walk across to where Mather's about to have his cranium remodelled. He's spitting with frustration, 'I seen Iraq, you sons o' bitches! Yeah, I been there! Violence begets violence, and you bastards begot me!'

'You be quiet!' I yell into his face, 'Now!'

I yank him up to his feet and shake him by his shirtfront.

'Whaddya know?' he moans at me.

It seems no one wants to bring a truncheon down on my vulnerable rooftop, but my unthatched scalp's crawling nonetheless. I shake him again, hold his dark round monkey eyes in mine. The policemen pause to reconsider.

'Will you pipe down?' I insist.

'Whaddya know?'

'I know that you want to be the wildcard of this piece,' I tell him while I straighten his collar and sleeves, 'But I won't allow it. No individual reputations will be made today. Today's about telling the collective truth.'

'Yeah. *You're* the hero in thissun. Ain't no room for nobody else.'

I can't help laughing very loudly in his petulant face. He breaks into a broken smile, confused. What the hell is this idiot Boodist laughing at?

'Must arrest,' the big dick bellows, removing a pair of handcuffs from his belt. I stick out my arms. He shakes his head and looks pointedly at Mather. The crowd murmurs. Still holding out my arms to him, I say, 'Don't give him what he wants.' I look across at the buzzing crowd. 'Don't give him that gift,' I repeat, pointing at the cuffs. I look round at the palace official. He's grimly holding onto the petitions. He shakes his head subtly. The big dick comprehends.

Paw Paw steps up, a disgusted severity whittled into his face. He takes firm hold of Mather and leads him off, still woozy. 'Damn white fool,' I hear him mutter, 'You cannot attack at the head of a few thousand bloody white sheep. It's black sheep you need for that kind of thing.'

Koomaraswami puts a hand on my shoulder, relief touching tentatively his anxious eyes. 'We can't tollrate violence in any shape or size. It won't do. We've all seen enough of it oliver the place. It doesn't work. It's old hat. Time to throw it out.'

'Thanks for intervening.'

'We must oppose it, even at the risk of ...' his hand moves involuntarily to his head: 'A most unpleassnt thought, whether on the giving or the ressving end.'

The bishop preserves a strained silence, his blue eyes fierce as an angel's. He doesn't pay Mather the sympathy of a single glance. His thoughts seem taken up by other matters altogether. When I catch his eye he only nods once, stiffly.

The ruction over, Helena stands serenely, facing the flock. She delivers her speech in Czech interspersed with English passages for the benefit of the foreign media. She presses the point that this is no time for run of the mill political leadership; what's needed are governments of extraordinary imagination, minds that are able to take in the fact that the planet must now be their first concern. In some ways it's the oldest speech in the world, and the most ignored. Politicians putting anything, including planet earth, before their own immediate ambitions?

When she's done and has had her applause she lifts an arm to me. Probably because I'm perceived as a man of action, rescuing airplanes and saving American yahoos from themselves, I'm treated to an ovation. But it's wasted on me. More than that, it's repugnant, because it's wasted on any human being.

I launch out into the racket. The translator hurries forward. Charlie Fincham scampers off as the red-robed lama steps up:

'You've handed over your petition, but a petition doesn't change a mind, even if it may influence some decisions and actions. I don't know if it will accomplish even that. But to change minds something much more urgent is needed; the simple truth is needed. The simple truth today is that the foundations of our world are cracked beyond repair. From now on we'll be living out our future in a collapsing house. Cracks will appear in the walls. The doors won't fit properly anymore, the roof will sag, chunks of plaster will drop to the floor. We'll try to prop it up, but fresh cracks will appear while we plaster over yesterday's. Finally we might be able to say with Mr Eliot, "*Dust inbreathed was a house; the wall, the wainscot and the mouse,*" but, of course, there won't be anyone left alive to remember those lines.'

Beelzebub approves with another curt bob of the head. He's a literary man, after all. But there's something amiss. He should be shouting out an offensive platitude.

'I needn't carry on and on. You can all imagine what I'm sketching here. The only goal we can strive for now is to meet our end with dignity, with minds freed from slavery to the system. We can make hell into paradise if we refuse any longer to play by the rules of hell. Paradise is hidden in our minds. If we can make the necessary effort to find it there, and if we do indeed find it, we need go out neither with a bang nor with a whimper, but with peace. We need true peace to meet the coming struggle, to get through it, and to perish in it ... and then, even though it is too late to make amends, we might be able to forgive ourselves. All that's left us now is to face up to what we are, and to what we should be, and then to be what we should be. If we fail at that, the end itself will have been futile and meaningless. Our collective end is not fundamentally different from our individual ends. Remember that.'

They want more but there is no more. They'd like me to be less foolish, more compromising, more rhetorical; to pull the rabbit out of the hat and say, 'Hah! Had you fooled there, didn't I? Now you understand what may happen, don't you? So take care, take care!'

(*There are lightning like gods and hailstones like hammers falling on the hills, and floods like oceans in the valleys. I must drown, fry or be crushed. My mind cannot take in the dimensions of what has arrived to destroy me. It is far beyond the capacity of my most overwrought nightmares. I will die not knowing.*)

I'm standing in front of them, palms together. It's over. Helena thanks them. They begin to disperse, turning down Nerudova Street back towards the Karluv Most. There's chatter, laughter, and a few desultory shouts go up. A large group gathers by the cathedral, beginning some second phase of their demonstration. Many want to come forward to speak to me. Helena prevents them. I'm important enough to be unreachable. Only Tomas and Libor linger.

Merry emerges from the snarl of journalists among the crowd like solid ground rising from the churning ocean. We look at each other awhile. The goons hang about. Helena thanks me, extends an invitation to a press lunch which I turn down, offers to arrange a ride back to the Best Hotel. I decline and shake her hand. Then, over their friendly protests, I say goodbye to Tomas and Libor. They tell me they'll see me later. Really? *Oh yes.* I don't argue, as long as it's later. Right now I need a respite from the lama.

'Lama Charrli, you not need bodyguards. You is a bodyguard yourself.'

'Goodbye, Lama,' says Tomas.

They walk away together. At the bend in the street they turn to wave. Helena smiles a deft *ciao* at me. Her car is waiting. She's satisfied. She's done something today.

Some journalists try me out. They bounce me around: a tricky question followed by a trick question followed by an even trickier one. I stick to what I've already said. When they realize that I am a man of only one idea they give up. There are only so many ways to elicit the same response.

'Tea?' I suggest.

'Yes,' says Merry, laughing. She's happy and numinous.

'Did someone say tea?' the swami agrees.

We find a cafe and sit out on the sidewalk. After we order there's a pleasantly sustained silence all round. Then, suddenly, like a bat out of hell, Merry's back in her yellow car, swerving out at Mather, her face a tangle of disdain and superciliousness.

'Your impressive attack had historic overtones, Dr Mather. It put me in mind of a certain American general whom many misguidedly admire.'

'Is that ride? Which general d'ya have in mind?'

'General Custer.'

'Yeah well, General Custer warn't abandoned by his troops.'

'And much good it did them.' She slowly shakes her head at him. 'Can you help me understand just what you thought you were doing?'

'Please,' the swami intervenes, raising his hands as if to frame her face, 'It's not so very awfully complicated. It's only anger. Dr Mather has good reasons for experiencing a certain large quantity of uncontrllable anger. Why don't you tell them, please? Much bettrr for you if they understand.'

'Well, I have no trouble understanding uncontrollable anger,' says the bishop in a tone so subdued it chills me, 'and even lunacy, but stupidity's always baffled me. Did you really think you'd inspire that ruminative cohort to take a run at the palace?'

'Please, please tell them.'

'Those heads-up-their-asses sons o' bitches killin' off the whole damn world, those stablishment bums,' he stares at his cup. 'I done my share o' protestin' and revolutionisin'. Yeah, hell, I confronted a few stablishment bums in my time, got locked up, made a noise, but, *sheeyit man*, I never hurt nobody. Now I wanna hurt them real bad. Ferk, I wanna hurt this whole ferkin world till it wakes up screamin' fer peace ...'

Then it comes out, the entrapment, abuse, disillusionment, rage. A kid brother blown to smithereens in downtown Baghdad, a bereft wife and children, grieving parents; the deceit of it all, the needlessness and the futility. Ho Hum. Heard it all before. But here is the real live case study, blubbing snot-and-tears. It's heart-rending. A disgrace. A crying bloody shame.

The tension goes out of him as he breaks down. Koomaraswami tries to console him with a number of fastidious pats and rubs. But Mather's not with us. He's honking and sighing in the solitary confinement of his hopeless grief.

Beelzebub takes over from the swami, easily and graciously resuming his priestly burden. He makes the sign of the cross over the huddled weeping figure. His lips are moving in whispered supplication to the God he no longer credits: '*qui tollit peccata mundi, miserere nobis, donna nobis pacem.*'

I look on admiringly. Merry's stumped. Paw Paw's grave.

'There's no need, no need for all this verbal violence. It nevrr verks,' Koomaraswami admonishes, 'No need to prod the person until he dubbles up.'

'Yes,' says Merry, 'I understand.'

CHAPTER 10

In Which Several Modes Of Reactionary Heroism Are Brought to Bear On Large Established Problems

It seems the bishop had one last quantum of spiritual power to impart. Mather, after howling forever like an infant into the prelate's shoulder, came back to us somehow reborn. He said nothing more, but he smiled at each of us in turn like an abandoned child whose absentee family have suddenly turned up out of the blue. I, for one, saw the exchange of peace for agony occur ring as the bishop held him tightly. I saw Beelzebub giving everything away.

We decided to walk back across the Charles Bridge to the new town where we'd take a taxi back to the Best Hotel. We strolled down the Golden Street, past the little blue house where Kafka once lived. But we didn't speak about any of it. Below us the red tiled roofs of Prague formed crooked stairways down the hillside. Mist was rising off the lazy river. The air was soft and damp. We walked together alone.

As we passed through the tower onto the bridge Beelzebub broke the silence. He said, 'John of Nepomuk.' I felt very uncomfortable hearing this weird utterance with its unfamiliar syllables sliding so randomly from his lips. I didn't like the sound of 'Nepomuk.' It might have been a mad neologism, or a word spoken backwards like an evil spell. But 'Kumopen' sounded even worse.

Then, just when he'd said, 'John of Nepomuk,' the bishop scrambled up the low wall of the bridge and, without another word, jumped off. I saw him flailing down towards the misty water, silently, deliberately.

I began tearing off my restricting monk's skirt but Paw Paw took hold of both my arms and shook his head in my face. Throwing down his Nigerian cap, he took the wall at a bound. But he did not go over quietly. He screeched like a gull until he hit the water. Then he was all efficiency, diving under, resurfacing, swimming, diving again in search of John of Nepomuk.

The swami hopped about: 'Oh gawd, oh my gawd,' then collapsed to his knees and began to recite a mantra.

Merry stood shivering at my side. Then, having dawdled with his thoughts for several moments, Mather found himself. It was thrilling to watch. He slid up on the wall, sat himself down with his legs dangling over on the water's side, turned to smile at us briefly, *impishly*, and slipped over. After he hit the water, a very long way down, we watched him work with Paw Paw in the mist.

The swami, his curiosity overpowering his panic, got up to look.

After some minutes the captain of a little white and green boat, seeing the hubbub in the river, hauled his vessel up in the area and began letting out a lifeline. We could hear him shouting a number of instructions in Czech. Two crewmen appeared with lifejackets. They jumped in too. Then Paw Paw fished out a bedraggled body dressed in inky black and swam with it towards the boat, Mather helping to draw it along in the water.

Taking hold of the lifeline, they were dragged on board, and I saw Paw Paw roll the bishop over and squeeze the water out of his lungs. But the bishop looked as clumsily helpless as a discarded plastic mannequin.

I had to hold Merry very tightly to ease her silent but hysterical quaking. It surprised me that she hadn't reached for her camera. From her unprofessional reaction I could only conclude that she no longer felt only a storyteller's detached curiosity about our little band of misfits. Our karma had reached out for her too.

I waved at the boat and Paw Paw waved back. I lifted my hands in a gesture of enquiry and he shook his head. Our communications were cut short at that point because the boat was gathering speed.

We left the bridge on which a number of onlookers had now arrived to take in the show. I could see that Merry was done for. I put her in a taxi to the hotel together with Koomaraswami and made my way to the docks, the police station, the hospital. In all these places I was smiled at by some people while others went into whispers or were whispered at. But I was floating among them, disembodied. None of them could take hold of me or prevent me from moving effortlessly about my business.

By late afternoon I found Mather and Paw Paw at the hospital, filling out forms with two cops at their backs. Paw Paw seemed quite charred with distress; his red eyes bulged out at me as I walked in. Mather worked his pen patiently, sighed and with a shake of his head signed the document. I could tell from the way his hand swept into the air that the signature was bold and excessively curlicued.

'He died,' Paw Paw said.

'I know.'

'But he gave me this,' he removed the tarnished crucifix from his pocket.

'Did he say anything? Anything about why?'

'He did say something. He said, "*Beji lokuta*." Then he gave me this, and died.'

'Yeah,' said Mather, 'That's ride. He said "*Bayjee locuta*", ya know, least that's what it sounded like.'

'I wanted to save him, Chahli.'

'I know.'

'He didn't want to be saved.'

'That's ride,' Mather added, 'He didn't need no savin'.'

Bayjee locuta?

While the cops finished up with Mather and Banana (they didn't need *another* statement from me, they said), a Czech bishop strode in with two priests in tow. He spoke very rapidly in small staccato bursts, reminding me of a yipping lapdog with a fuzzy muzzle and sharp teeth. He was addressing the two dicks who now became quite servile.

Then he yelped something at me while angrily tossing his fuzzy head about. The dicks seemed ready to pounce at the first barked instruction to lay hands on me, but the enraged snapping tailed off into a howl of dismay and then a sorrowful whine. From this I could tell that he knew all about me, had probably been in contact with the archbishop at the conference, and was sure I was somehow to blame.

When they were all done shaking their heads at me we were free to leave. Beelzebub was in their hands now, but that no longer mattered.

In the taxi none of us had anything to say. The driver, however, proved a delightful conversationalist, speaking his mind in untortured English. He'd been a teacher and, he insisted, an *intellectual*, before the communist regime drove him to drink. Still, he hadn't lost his mind completely; he knew I belonged to a religious sect which believed that the world was on its last legs. That was the trouble with religion: it always had to cook up some daft idea which no one could prove or falsify, but which was calculated to scare the hell out of anyone who took it seriously. He wasn't like that. He took nothing seriously.

He let go of the steering-wheel to demonstrate how unserious he could be. I reached over and grabbed hold of it. He asked why I gave a damn about dying in his taxi if the world was about to end? That's religion for you, he said; daft on the one hand, inconsistent on the other.

We all agreed with him.

Evening was bringing on the city lights when we arrived back at the hotel. The group of demonstrators from this morning had either stayed and grown in size or returned to the parking lot in greater force. Some had photographs of my red-robed self pasted onto their placards. I saw with a start how technology could turn anyone into anything anyone wanted them to be. I had put on these garments only yesterday and they had travelled to TV screens and internet sites and now to these posters within twenty four hours. I sat awed in the taxi for several minutes, assessing what the photographs said and what the people holding onto them might be thinking and believing about me.

The western lama on the posters (in full colour) seemed purposeful and austere. His natural stoop made him appear habitually humble, as though he were bowing himself before the world in general. He was tall and skinny, someone unaccustomed to much eating and drinking. His slight smile revealed a depth of detached compassion. The narrow beak of a nose lent an air of toughness and determination to the long face. His dark blue eyes seemed fierce and unsurrendering.

When the taximan said 'New bullshitter, new religion,' waggling his finger at the placards and then at me, their bullshit substance, I could only laugh. Of course I wasn't a bullshitter. I only felt like one now because I knew myself as the people wielding the placards could not possibly know me.

I was no more (and no less) a bullshitter than anyone else, even those who didn't know the bullshit in themselves, or turned away when they saw it. It was one of those paradoxical questions of degree.

Because I was a bullshitter like everyone else, I was in fact not a bullshitter.

'You must be a bullshitter too,' I said to the taximan.

'Of course. You think I would kill myself to prove I am not a serious person? Would this not prove only that I was very serious about being unserious? And would this not in fact prove that I was actually a fatally serious person after all?'

'The bishop shore wuz serious,' said Mather.

'Not a bullshitter,' said Paw Paw.

'You don't know how deep bullshit can go,' I said, and paid the fare.

I turned to see Libor opening my door and Tomas, behind him, beaming through his bumfluff. For a moment I felt utterly manipulated by them, as though they had been sent from the Buddha-realms to force my weary hand beyond it's strength.

'Why didn't you tell me about this?'

'We not sure how many peepols comink, or if anybody comink.'

'Are you in charge of them?'

'No, Lama. You in charrge.'

'Well then, tell them I want them to go home.'

'I shall tell them.'

What? *I shall tell them?* I was thunderstruck.

'No, no, tell *me*, why are they here?'

'They will stay this night to pray for this world.'

'All night?'

'Yes.'

'What do they want from me?'

'Tell them somethink. Help them.'

I'm bone tired. My brain's aching with the agony of Beelzebub's final antisocial antic. I get out and stand in front of them. Paw Paw and Mather slide off wearily to the hotel. They've had more than enough too. The word *parable* bobs up and comes to rest in my fidgety mind.

All right then; Parable:

There was a world which became infected with the desire for progress. It wasn't that progress was indispensible because the people had everything they needed. But progress was out there for the taking and so, being people, they wanted to lay hold of it for its own sake. It would improve their lives by fulfilling certain needs which they had not yet contemplated. This seemed a good idea.

They invested in a thousand devices and a thousand systems which would make their lives easier and give them access to new things and new experiences. The devices, gadgets, gimcracks, thingamees and the rules, regulations, guidelines and imperatives for managing the devices and themselves and their progressive lifestyles piled up in their world. The easier things became the more complications they brought in their wake. The more objects and instruments at the peoples' disposal, and the more finicky regulations for managing their new lives, the more anxiety and misery they felt. Nevertheless, their anxiety and misery felt like happiness. For every new thing or rule there was a new anxiety, but for every new anxiety there was a new thing to experience. By now, although life was certainly easier and more rewarding, they were working much harder and longer to sustain this life of ease.

Whereas, previously, if you had looked at them from a great distance they would have resembled slowly moving dots like grazing cattle or sheep, they now looked much more like a swarm of bacteria seen through a microscope, busily writhing with destructive and infectious vigour. Only a scientist could bear to look at it without a layman's twinge of nausea.

But of course there were enough scientists in the world by now, as well as a few thousand more leaders of all sorts than had ever been necessary or desirable in the simple past. There were also more gods and more religions for serving them. In short, there was a varied group of leaders, specialists and experts to control and analyse every new thing, rule, decision, activity and anxiety.

The people, by now greatly increased in numbers and wealth, had never been happier. And they were kept reminded by advertising agencies just how happy and privileged they were to live in such a time of marvels, convenience and liberty.

Every new need, as it was fulfilled, created another need and, naturally, in this time of wonders and proficiency, the new need could be met almost as soon as it made itself felt. A little more labour, a little more time, a little more anxiety, and the need was met, together with its set of conditions and regulations, which cost very little, relatively speaking, in this age of the miraculous, an epoch so much more exciting and teeming with possibilities than any age preceding it.

The buddhas and bodhisattvas looked down from the enlightened realms upon the teeming pasta of maggots at their futile but inescapable activities. They shook their heads at the heartlessness of the world. 'What a people!' they said to one another, 'Would it make any difference at all if we went down there and warned them of things to come? Should we bother at all?' They put the question to a vote and decided, by a very small margin, in favour of sending some teachers to try to persuade the earthlings of the error and madness of their ways.

Well, you all know what happened. Some of the teachers were cursed, others laughed at, others put to death for political or just for sporting reasons. Even among those purporting to follow the advice of the teachers, the number of the sincere could be counted on the fingers of one hand with several fingers amputated.

Having established institutions for paying lip service to the holy men and prophets, in order to flatter their own sense of wisdom, the people reverted to the worship of progress; that is, to the frenzied pursuit of ever-increasing orgies of buying and selling, bargains and discounts, and the endless generation of new ideas and new inventions giving rise to a plethora of needs never before conceived.

They fought wars and concluded treaties with neighbouring and remote nations, they deceived and defrauded one another, and they learnt the principles of cut-throat practice, all in order to increase the pace and intensity of buying and selling. The vista of possible needs, of needs yet to be born out of the vacuum, became so vast that there was room for nothing else in all their thinking. If they thought of anything else, of the most fundamental aspects of their humanity, of things like love and peace and community, these notions immediately became entangled in and modified by the prospect of their past, present and future needs. Love became a transaction, peace a bargaining chip, community a pool for mutual exploitation.

Within no time at all their resources were being exhausted. Their lands and oceans could not yield enough food, their mines enough minerals, their rivers and lakes enough water, to continue satisfying their newfangled needs. Their inventions poisoned their atmosphere. But the cycle could not be stopped. If they stopped it now, they must regress. Of all things this *could not be tolerated in a world given over to progress. If progress meant the eventual death of the whole world; still, death must be embraced for progress' sake.*

Then the scent of death arrived. The foundations of their progressive lifestyle strained and then cracked. It was suddenly too late to choose another, simpler way of life, even if they'd wanted to. But this did not make them pause. They made a choice anyway: they chose not to believe what their own eyes were telling them.

The buddhas and bodhisattvas looked down and shook their enlightened heads. What to do? Here was a people so stupid, greedy and unprincipled that the mule was their moral and spiritual superior, never mind the horse. And even the dog does not shit in his own bed. Would descending to instruct them serve any purpose at all? They put the question to the vote again. The result was a unanimous 'no'.

Afterward there was some debate among the enlightened beings, dismayed at the unaccustomed perplexity caused them by their consideration of human behaviour:

'Is there really nothing to be done?'

'We've all agreed on reasoned grounds: it's too late.'

'Yes, it's too late for their material world, but perhaps we can save their minds.'

Socrates was among them. 'As you all know,' he said, 'I was poisoned by those brutes, and long before I drank the cup my mind had already been ennobled. Do you think I could have ennobled it in the brief period of life left to me after the drink had been imbibed? Of course not. I would have been too frightened, too confused, too steeped in habitual ignorance. My whole awareness would have been consumed by the prospect of death and the loss of all my pleasures and even my pains. Now these brutes have poisoned themselves after many generations of continuously darkened thinking. What could anyone say to them to bring them to wisdom before they perish? They've run out of time. Yes, they've destroyed the realm itself which put time at their disposal. It's tragic and terrifying, but they won't listen even now. I, who was considered the wisest man of my day, admit that I have no wisdom to impart to these ... may one still refer to them as "people"? They've had every warning. And, look at them! With the poison coursing* *through their veins, what are they doing? Dragging themselves to work to buy the newest toxins while still paying off their installments on the old. Slaving and carousing. And their leaders rushing to war, devising updated deceits, ignoring the real needs hidden behind the smokescreen of the factitious and the farcical.'*

'There do seem to be some who are ever so slightly aware,' said Siddhartha, 'and although we have voted on reasoned grounds against the futility of coming to their aid, we, as bodhisattvas, should try to find some way to make their inevitable demise more bearable.'

'I agree,' said Jesus, 'although they've made it impossible for me to fulfil my intention to return among them, as there will be no planet to return to.'

'It's the same with me,' said the future Buddha, Maitreya.

'Since they have proved utterly incapable of heeding the counsel of the wise,' said Socrates, 'there is only one possibility left us, don't you agree?'

The other enlightened beings waited patiently while the ugly Greek gazed at them from beneath his beetling brows. Since it was his habit to draw the truth out of his hearers rather than to state it on their behalf, they searched their own minds for the answer. It did not take very long for them to light on it; it was all too obvious.

'Since they won't heed the wise,' said Padmesambhava, 'send them fools instead.'

They didn't applaud this time. There was no laughter. I stood with them, taking it in, barely understanding it. It chilled me to think what the wise were doing in the Best Hotel behind me.

'If there are any fools among you,' I concluded, 'your time has come to shine.'

I took leave of Tomas and Libor. We didn't say much; shook hands. We'd see one another in the morning. I greeted the crowd and someone cried out, 'I am a fool!' Someone else said quite calmly from near the front, 'I have always been a fool.' Then someone shouted, 'Hey, Lama, I am the biggest fool which ever lived!'

At the front desk the dry young man smirked drily at me. 'Sirr, you no longer have to share your room with Mr Banana.'

'Professor Mbana, you mean.'

'Yes.'

'Well, I've changed my mind about that.'

'I am sorry, sirr, but the conference manager has instructed me to inform you that you are no longer a delegatt at this conference. Your accommodation has been cancelled. You may now collect your bags.'

I was taken aback to realize how untaken aback I was. It was as though I felt stung on behalf of someone else called 'sirr.' I merely nodded and turned to go up to the room – and there was Merry, emerging from the crowd outside, coming into the lobby by the glass doors, smiling warmly.

'You've been *what?*'

'Evicted.'

'Yes, it rings a bell. You've been excommunicated. We'll just see about that.'

While she very calmly got the details from the dry young man (I saw him turning brittle as she spoke), I went up to the room. Paw Paw was stretched out in front of the telly, a whisky in his plump right hand. I explained my position. He said, 'No', got to his feet, stuck the Nigerian cap on his head and left the room. I packed my things and went down again.

The dry young man was exsiccated by now. The hotel manager looked petrified.

'Are you a racist?' Paw Paw was shouting, 'Just tell me that!'

'Racist?' asked the incredulous manager.

'You don't want a white man sharing my room? Izi that your point?'

'It is not my decision. You must speak to the conference manager.'

The arse on shoulders arrived in a sanctimonious huff. What was the difficulty this time? He looked down at my packed bags. What had been misunderstood? I'd had fair warning, hadn't I? There was nothing to explain. If the hotel had other rooms available I could check myself in. He couldn't stop me doing that.

'I cannot believe it,' said Paw Paw.

'Excuse me?' asked the startled arse.

'It izi you who are the racist.'

'What?'

'Causing havoc in a blek man's room without evah bothering to consult him. Introducing yowa squabbles into his environment without a by-yowa-leave. Would you do that to a white man? No, nevah!! But because he izi a blek man, what do you care? Why respect a blek man's peace of mind?'

He glared wildly around the lobby, inviting all those gathering about his loud protestations to participate in his representative racial injury.

'But I'm sure you don't understand –' the arse spoke soothingly, quietly, guiltily.

'No! A blek man nevah understands! Even a blek professor is too stupid to understand! No, the poor blek man has to have it explained!'

'It's Mr Fincham we've – er –'

'Excommunicated,' said Merry.

'Yes. It's Mr Fincham, not yourself, Professor Mib – Mibna –'

'Can't pronounce those stupid blek names, heya?'

'– It's Mr Fincham that's been –'

'Excommunicated,' said Merry.

'Look Miss, as a rule we don't excommunicate Buddhists.'

'*Mr Fincham*? Can't you respect hizi title? Because he has lowered himself to share a blek man's room you cannot call him *lama*?'

The rotating eyes bulged from the quivering buttocks, straining to see sense.

'Racist conference!' Paw Paw insisted.

'I won't stand for this. It's too bloody ridiculous.'

'Now you are calling me ridiculous? I am here to represent traditional African religion and you are calling me ridiculous!'

While he went on and on I paid for another room. If the dry one or even the manager had harboured any suspicions of having no more rooms available, they had abandoned them by now. The service was crisp.

I held up my key. French Peter made a subtle gesture of gratitude for my sensible and sporting conduct. With his eyes he invited me to share his baffled scorn for Banana. I saw his loneliness. He was the perpetual manager in his world, never the chairman, and, of course, he was cosmetically handicapped too.

'If a white man had appealed to you as I am doing now,' said Paw Paw, 'you would have been begging Chahli to rejoin the conference.'

'Don't you mean *lama*?' said Father Peter Forbes.

What amazed me about Paw Paw's histrionics was not how wrong he was, but how right, in the face (if that was the word) of the collared posterior's racist bafflement. Banana was just another one of those tribal chaps from Bongoland whose accurate expression of the essential truth of his situation must be tolerated for form's sake, however bizarre it appeared to the developed western mind. In*deed*.

'Thank you, Paw Paw.'

'Bleddy damn racists.' he shook his head, 'I'm going to bed.'

'You're a racist too.'

'Chahli, I know. But you and me, we don't pretend.'

Merry stayed close, a taut smile playing across her impatient lips, her sapphires alight with distaste, as the hotel manager and French Peter cornered me. I noticed that they glanced back rapidly at the lift doors now closing behind Paw Paw.

'You realize, of course, that there's a further problem,' said French Peter.

'Yes?'

'Oh yes, in*deed*. That mob out there, your – disciples.'

'My disciples?'

'They should go home now,' said the manager.

'Disperse,' said Peter.

'On your orders?'

'No, on yours. It's clear that they're your responsibility.'

'They're here of their own accord.'

'No, they're here because of you.'

'Yes. Certainly because of you, sirr.'

'They're here because the world is dying. They're praying for the dying world.'

'The *dying world*,' the puckered orifice announced, 'is *your* idea.'

'My idea?'

'Look, be a sensible chap now, Lama. They have to leave, or else things might turn unpleasant. The hotel management is most upset.'

'I shall have to call poliss.'

'If they were here to applaud this conference you wouldn't be shalling having to do anything. The archbishop and Father Forbes wouldn't want you to. I think these people have a right to mourn the dying world in the presence of this conference.'

'Once again, it seems you want to leave us with no choice. It's up to you.'

'Yes, it's up to me to tell them that the conference intends to call the police.'

'That would not be true. It's the hotel management –'

'In that case it's a matter between the hotel management and myself. I don't see why you should interfere. We'll sort it out between us.'

I could see that the bum was beginning to come apart at the crack. But he was lying to me and he was trying to manipulate a gradually advancing karmic sequence into retreating before the will of his superiors. I felt coolly stubborn with regard to this intention. The manager's anxious irritation was now pleadingly directed at Peter: 'If these peepols are very peacefool? No noise? No bother?'

'No!' the bum exploded, 'Absolutely not!'

'Very well, sirr,' said the manager.

I went outside and called for an interpreter. I explained the dilemma. Everyone seemed confused. No one budged. Libor came up. I told him what had been said inside. He repeated it to the interpreter. The megaphone blahed amateurishly across the uplifted faces of the gathering. There was a collective muttering.

'We can stay,' said Libor, 'It is allowed.'

'I don't think so. It could turn bad.'

'Cannot turn bad.'

'I advise you not to stay.' (The megaphone crackled out this advice. Murmurs and mumbling.)

'They says thank you for advice, Lama.'

'If the police are called, I'll come out. But I must go in now.' (Translation.)

'Not need come out.'

I felt my joints and sinews ache with weariness. The other mind in me wished these tiresome people would just play the game and agree to depart. I looked at its desire and let it go. It wasn't up to the size of these events.

French Peter and the manager had disappeared. I found Merry ordering tea and a cold platter. We sat for a while without speaking. I could tell she was troubled. Her usually brisk and confident shoulders were rounded now with girlish vulnerability; she sat bent slightly forward. I smiled at her and poured out our tea.

'I'm sorry it had to be you, Charlie. I wasn't sorry before, but I am now. And I don't know exactly why.'

'On whose behalf are you apologising?'

She didn't know. It made us both laugh.

'I'm not sorry, Mary, even though I, too, can't understand much of it. I feel like a madman who's stumbled onto the stage, mangled a Steinway and somehow hit all the right notes, the discordant but resonant ones. Now the audience sees me as an accomplished musician, possibly playing Ligeti. So, is the audience to blame?'

'What about the false notes? Bishop Bell? Myself?'

'Did you notice that Forbes didn't even mention Bell? Didn't even try to insinuate that I'd played some sort of role in his suicide? It wasn't an absent-minded slip on his part. He's a man under authority.'

'What are you saying?'

'The big kahuna, *His Grace*, you know; *he* knows why Bell jumped. Only he knows what he said to the subordinate bishop, what means he used to get to him, to stop him from walking this path with us. Know what he and Forbes are saying to themselves right now? *He had fair warning.*'

'Bloody blow me over. How did I miss that one?'

'You're not concentrating on your job, bringing no imagination to it. And tell me this, why do you suddenly see yourself as a false note?'

'I'm feeding all this truth, *this energy of truth*, back into the system, down a zillion optic fibres, up to a satellite which bounces it back to a million TV screens, and on the way it's bound to get twisted and battered out of shape. There are people working to present it to the other people in just the right way. It'll be murdered, I promise you.'

'Is that why you've been hanging back?'

'Yes. On my own I'm just too small a force. You saw all the media clowns out there today, and they're out in front of the hotel right now.'

'All the more reason why you should be out there too.'

'That won't help. I won't be able to change a thing.'

'It's not about your changing things; it's about you changing.'

'That's what's happening to you, isn't it, Charlie?'

'It's what I'm most aware of.'

Then the rabbi came swooning towards us like an overweight bumble-bee. He crashed into a chair, bumped into a table. Merry exhaled a little sigh. Tannenbaum, with that callow insect's knack for reaching its destination smug and intact, sat down bulkily. The index finger of his right hand went up to the yarmulke.

'I tried,' he said, his voice a tired kissingerian croak, 'but I couldn't face it.'

'Would you like some tea? A bit of cheese?'

'If it had gotten out of hand – it did get out of a hand a bit, didn't it? – I would have been too upset. I can't trust myself in such situations – too sensitive.'

'What got out of hand?'

'I saw it on the television, or maybe I was right there in the crowd – that cowboy Mather. Thank God you were there, Lama. If it had been up to me to do something – and of course I would have felt I must.'

'Never mind. Have some tea.'

'Just some bread and cheese. Is it kosher? Probably not. Who knows? It might well be. I have the feeling it is.'

'You saw the people outside the hotel?'

'Yes. How could I not? It's a worry. I'm concerned. Nothing violent should happen. It's my greatest fear: violent actions. I know the conference organisers aren't pleased, not happy at all.'

'They've threatened to call the police. They may be doing so as we speak.'

'Swines, bastards; I know their type, especially the Catholics. They went along with Hitler, you know. Yes, they were right up Mussolini's ass too. And now look what the Pope's up to, won't see the Dalai Lama – slap in the face. Vatican's up the Communist Chinese' asses now. It's shameful.'

'I didn't know about that.'

'Yah. It's on the news, right after your story: *the conference wrecker.*'

'Conference wrecker?'

'Yah. They showed a newspaper headline: *Man who saved plane wrecks conference.*'

'Bugger!' said Merry.

'Yah. Everyone's up somebody else's ass.'

'Whose ass is the conference up then?'

'Who knows? They're probably up so many asses, you couldn't identify them all if they passed by in the nude, and now you're a pain in theirs.'

Then, as Tannenbaum's face began to writhe like a muppet's, I heard the police pull up very loudly outside. We all jumped to our feet. The rabbi had the yarmulke in his hand now. Merry conjured a small tape recorder from her bagful of everything. We hurried out into the cold.

The dicks were shouting curt instructions through their megaphones. The tone was imperative and threatening. Some had snarling dogs on leashes. There was a ripple of disturbance in the crowd as some people began to pack up and move off, grumbling. Most stood their ground, many in attitudes of prayer or meditation. You could feel them waiting for the next move. They saw me approaching and a babble broke out. Libor ran up.

Two dicks strode across to where we stood. Libor, gesturing with his hands, tried to tell them something. The dicks pushed him aside. The more senior ranking of the two, young with a boy's (blond) moustache, tried to square up to me but proved too short to an embarrasing degree. I stooped to eye-level, palms at my chest. While the older, with no tinfoil on his shoulders, looked on sheepishly, the young brat began shrieking up at my face.

'I don't understand Czech,' I said.

'I translett,' said the older, '*Tell thass peepols go now.*'

'No.'

'Yass!'

'No.'

'Yass yass yass!' the youngster screamed, his puerile moustache riding wildly above the upper lip like a furry child on a rocking-horse.

'No.'

He nodded vigorously at me and seemed about to let fly, but the older one stumbled deftly between us, as though by accident. Something was said. The screaming infant pointed his megaphone at the group of dicks behind the crowd and spoke into it. There was some hesitation, then they began to lay into the people.

Libor suddenly flicked an inner switch. I watched him mutate into a belligerent Barishnikov dancing effortlessly into battle. He grabbed the boy with the epaulettes, lifted him above his head and pitched him down hard into the tar of the parking lot. The cop lay still. Then he went for the next and the next.

Wherever a policeman was engaged in arresting, punching, conching or collaring anyone, Libor danced across light-footed as a buffalo and hurled him about. As he danced he shouted, 'The way of the Buddha is non-violent! We should strive to be harmless!' Then a uniform would fly from his hands to hit the earth with a thud. 'I hate violence!' he bawled, 'I hate violent peopols! I hate violent thoughts and violent words and violent hands!' On every fourth beat or so, as he preached his pacifist sermon, he made his point with another thud.

There were not enough cops to corner him. He had dealt with all eight by the time the chief of police arrived to put a stop to the terrible mistake. The boy with the scrambled egg on his shoulders, recently back on his feet, now got egg on his face. I saw the chief (elegant, civilized) waving a sheet of paper at him, and I could hear through all the gibbered Czech the name *Helena Pikardt* and the word *permit*.

Those dicks who had recovered sufficient self-esteem by straightening their uniforms now tried to corner Libor in order to arrest him. I saw the rabbi take Libor by the arm and fend the stunned cops off with big sweeps of his paws. He wagged a finger in the face of one persistently shaking a pair of handcuffs at him. Then he said something in sharp-toned Czech and the cop desisted, shaking his head in a tormenting mixture of anger at being thwarted and relief at not having to deal with Libor again. The rabbi brought Libor across to where I stood with Merry.

'We have city permit for being here,' Libor explained to me.

'Why didn't you tell me earlier?'

'I surely told you, Lama, and we told hotel manninger. He knows.'

'Why didn't you explain to the police?'

'No time, Lama. You saw.'

I knew then that Archbishop Manners and the servile arse were undone. Merry stood beside me with her eyes shut, listening and trembling. She began to cry soundlessly, tears rolling out from her closed lids. I put my arm around her.

The people nursed the fallen dicks, helped them to their feet, brushed off their uniforms. The rabbi went off into the commotion, his head down, his finger on his crown. The chief approached him. They spoke a little and I saw the rabbi take out a passport and some documents. The chief examined them and laughed. He called the boy, showed him the rabbi's passport, and laughed some more. The boy tried to laugh too. The crowd broke out into confused smiles. The rabbi's papers were returned to him. He didn't smile. He said nothing. He trudged slowly back to where I stood with Merry.

The chief made the brat address the people. It needed no translation. It was an apology and a warning not to abuse the terms of the permit arranged by Helena Pikardt. *Yes*, I thought, *she does get things done.*

Rabbi Tannenbaum (Ton-of Bum) searched my face ruefully, but anger lingered in his eyes. For a moment I thought he might take it into his head to attack me, the apparent cause of all the trouble. But he put one of Merry's hands between his shovels and said, 'I'm sorry you had to witness this.' At this she crumpled into his shoulder and cried softly, as though he were her copper father.

The cops were leaving now, the people returning triumphantly to their vigil. Merry emerged from the folds of the rabbi's coat. 'What on God's earth did you tell them?' she asked, her curiosity emerging like a ray of sunshine through the trailing sobs and sighs. The rabbi patted her cheek. 'Nobody should know this,' he warbled, 'but what the heck; if you say I said it, I'll say I didn't. Or if I did say it you heard it wrong. Or if you heard it right you heard it from someone else.'

He huddled the two of us together as though we were curious snot-nosed kids, and he whispered, 'I have some minor diplomatic privileges of a top-secret nature, get it? *Top-secret*, I said. Get it?'

My spirits weren't much lifted by this information. Yet it wasn't more incongruous than most of what had taken place today. What difference, when all was said and done, between the top-secret diplomatic rabbi and public-knowledge undiplomatic me? More than anything, my non-violent mind now yearned to see the archbishop and his uriah-heepish lieutenant flung about by Libor, and then flung about some more by their own unwholesome karma.

(*In spite of myself*, said His Holiness once, revealing the human baggage slung heavily across the shoulders of the living Buddha, *I swat the mosquito on my arm.*)

I walked among the people. Some shook my hand and others embraced me. Libor said, 'You have best bodyguard in the world, Lama, I tink.' God, yes!

I spoke to those who'd been roughed up by the cops. They made light of it. One girl had a gaping gash above one eye. I thought it needed stitching.

I took her into the hotel and pounded martially the bell at the front desk. The dry one appeared, now ashen. 'Get Forbes,' I ordered. In the meantime I dabbed at her eyebrow with a serviette from the tray of gourmet snacks. Then French Peter bounced up on broken springs.

'Get a doctor,' I said.

'Oh dear, oh *dear*. One moment.'

I sat with her in the gorgeous ruby foyer. She might have been eighteen. I thought of Clara and I boiled. We said nothing. I ordered a coffee for her, the most expensive concoction of beans I could extract from the waiter's knowledge of these things, and told him to bill it to Forbes. This wasn't questioned. The hotel was in a state of emergency.

A doctor arrived, bearded and scarved like Pavarotti, and took her to the first-aid room. I went along from sheer insistence on making my primacy felt. He hummed as he worked. He'd been called from a musical soiree, he explained. 'Debussy. So ethereal, so …' He couldn't find the appropriate English word. He pondered. 'Out of tune with reality,' I suggested. This tickled him, and he continued to work with light, impressionist touches. Then he turned her over to me, nicely patched up.

'Please ask her if she would like to be taken home.'

'Can't be done,' she said in a New England accent, 'I live in Boston.'

'Would you like to be taken to your hotel?'

'No. I'll spend the night out there with all the other fools.'

'Fools?'

'Yes, Lama. The world's fools, you know, like you said, or was it the Booder who said it? No, it was Padmesambhava, right?'

'Yes, I think it was.'

I didn't go out again. I found Merry in the unlit corner of the lounge that seemed to have become our place of tryst. We sat without speaking. When she'd recovered, she said, 'I have reports to file. It's been one crazy day.'

I said, 'I'm sorry.'

I felt it too, a sorrow that sat wedged and palpitating like a wounded bird in the centre of my breast.

'I know,' she sighed, 'It's the time of parting. Today you travelled a few light years away from everyone, including me. And there's no catching up with you now, Lama.'

I didn't mention how many light years I felt I'd travelled away from Charlie Fincham. This notion was still too fresh and disturbing.

I was glad to be alone in my own room. From the window I could see the vigil going on by candlelight. The World's Fools. I felt separate from them too. The sense of loneliness panged about inside me. I tried to meditate but my mind was reeling off images of thousands of people walking, the tense and anxious cops, Mather leaping into egotistic action, Libor into his selfless dance, Ton-of Bum disclosing his top-secret self, Beelzebub slipping calmly over the wall of the Charles Bridge and Paw Paw leaping after him, and Merry weeping.

I curled up on the bed in my robes and drew the shawl over my head.

CHAPTER 11

The Third Day In Prague, On Which Facts And Falsehoods Are Skilfully Deployed And A Quiet Dinner Ends With A Bang

It's a night of dreams; dreams and nightmares of floating, flying, falling, sinking, rising. In one I am pursued by a sinister shadow, a thing that wants me drowned. I'm swimming for my life but the thing gains on me as I lose strength; it has me by the hair and is forcing me under and I turn to see what it is and find that I am gaping into my own face. I struggle with all my remaining strength, and I hold the thing underwater until it stops thrashing. I watch it sinking and am appalled.

In another I leap into the Vltava, the wedged bird of loneliness accompanying me in my downward flight. I slice into the cold water and allow myself to sink. I don't want to surface again; I've let go. But there is another down there, searching me out, swimming easily and with grace. He takes me by the arm and slides me upward into the air and light. I search the face of my saviour, and again it's my own.

When I wake up for the last time it's a little before dawn. Outside the people are winding up their vigil. I drench myself in the shower, my thoughts and intuitions full of the sense of water, its power and danger and mystery. My head is clear.

In my meditation there is nothing but the single object before my mental vision: a golden glow of light, a sun through whose centre I pass into the spaciousness of the sky, and remain there. For a long while I sit in this calm and then, materialising in the space before me, I see the face of Precious Teacher. He's wracked with laughter and I'm lifted up into it so that the rest of my sitting is spent howling and cackling until I almost exhaust myself.

Something very funny has certainly happened in the far reaches of the cosmos.

Still in the grip of the afterlaugh I turn on the TV news. It's all there: the lama and the goons appearing from behind the museum,

Helena Pikardt walking up, balancing a pile of invisible books on her head, lifting my hand in hers.

'After the long march to the presidential palace a petition was handed over to a government representative. Dr Pikardt gave a brief speech in which she stressed that the foremost priority of governments today is recognizing the real nature of the global crisis, but the demonstration was not entirely peaceful – *there's Mather's assault on the castle, the fracas with the cops, and there's the lama speaking sedately into Tyrone's face* – the maverick monk, calling himself Lama Charlie – *a very adept curl of the newsreader's upper lip* – who appears here to be calming things down, has in fact been characterized as a conference wrecker –'

Now I'm hooting into my shawl again, wiping my eyes.

'– occasion further marred by the apparent suicide of Bishop Charles Bell, a theologian and anthropologist holding what have been described as quote *unorthodox views* unquote (*no pictures here, no Paw Paw screeching his way down to the misty river*) – also associated with Lama Charlie.'

I don't know how even this can be so hilarious, the memory of Beelzebub scuttling off to his escape from life, religion and *something else*, floating gauchely down to his *death by water*.

'– violent incidents outside the Best Hotel in the evening of the second day of the conference – police called in – assaulted by an unknown man (*not a single shot of Libor tossing people about, but there is Lama Charlie again, looking down bemusedly at the young dick lying at his feet*). A conference spokesperson said it was a pity that one man had marred the dignity and importance of these proceedings by deciding to stage his own quote *farcical sideshow* unquote.'

Or stealing the limelight from theirs.

'The group held an all-night vigil for what they called quote *the dying world* unquote and several members of the group referred to themselves as quote *the world's fools* unquote, apparently derived from a parable in which Lama Charlie – real name Mr Charles Gwillim Fincham, a South African small businessman – made the point that it's up to the fools of the world to tell the truth about the real state of the planet and to act quote *to liberate their minds from the system* unquote.'

I light a fag and settle down for the remainder of the entertainment. They've enticed two experts on remote screens to give their views on the deadbeat lama. Will it be one for and one against?

'And we welcome our two guests, Dr Hazel Green, head of environmental strategies for the Gene-Genie Group, and Professor Martin P. Humbert, former lecturer in religious studies and currently attached to the department of eastern religions at the Chippanoogie University College in South Dakota.'

'Dr Green, Lama Charlie has been described as quote *the man who saved Air France Flight 732 but doesn't want to give the planet the same chance* unquote. Your comments?'

'Well, Conchita, Lama Charlie's way out of line here, not to mention way out of his depth. If I read it right, the only evidence he's given for his point of view is that nothing better can be expected of the human race. I'd say that's a pretty dark view for any religion or religious leader to propagate.'

'Professor Humbert? – er, Professor Humbert – yeah – your views on Lama Charlie? – er, Professor Humbert, can you hear us?'

'Yeah. Thanks for inviting me onta yer show, Concheeter. Yeah, I'd say Charlie's probably suffering from some form of bipolar disorder. Ya know, this kinda disorder can be – what's the word? – *made worse*, yeah, *made worse*, by too much withdrawal from everyday life, by long periods of meditation, fer instance.'

'You're going with *bipolar disorder?*'

'Yeah, yeah, just let me finish. Ya know, we witnessed his very sharp action on board that French airplane. Ya know, the way he just kinda leapt into the fray without a second thought? Now, ya see, that was probably a high moment fer Charlie. He was feelin' on top of the world, ya could say. Now, ya know, if you'd asked him then what he thought of the world's chances of survival, I'll bet he woulda said the world's in great shape.'

'Dr Green, the bipolar hypothesis? How would you rate it?

'Well, frankly Conchita, I'd rate it a zero. Lama Charlie's consistently confident, and he seems at peace with what he's saying and doing, however crazy it might seem to you and me.'

'Professor Humbert?'

'She'd rate it a zero? On what grounds?'

'Well, Conchita, on the grounds I've just given and on the grounds that I'm a qualified clinical psychologist?'

'How come you're working with environmental issues then?'

'I also have degrees in zoology and botany, Professor Humbert.'

'Yeah, I gotta coupla degrees too, and I can tell ya that Charlie's not well, not a well person at all. Ya notice the way he seems outta touch, sorta detached from everything and everyone around him, like he's in his own universe?'

'Dr Green?'

'I'd say he's a threat to his own universe right now.'

'Yeah, that's a very interesting statement coming from Dr Green. I mean, what degree do ya have ta back that one up?'

'Our time's up. Thank you both. Well, bipolar disorder or a monopolar threat to the universe, Lama Charlie's certainly caused disorder at, and remains a threat to, the conference of religions on planetary issues.'

'In other news, the Vatican has retracted its invitation to the Dalai Lama to meet with Pope Benedict XVI. This about turn was made after Chinese diplomats told the Vatican that such a meeting would quote *hurt their feelings* unquote.'

If I were a bipolar case, this would be the high of my life and there'd be no low low enough to compensate. I'm weeping with laughter, drenching my shawl, choking on the smoke I've just inhaled. It's this, just this: *this* is the wonder of life, the key to understanding how mysteriously crackers we are. And if we would only take hold of this potential for lunacy and harness it to love ...

The *hurt feelings* that are really only the arrogance of an oppressive machine (made in China), yet enough to cause the Vicar of Christ to stonewall an old friend of infinite integrity. Deep beneath the surface of this petty tragedy is the joke that stabs me in the funny place. The ridiculous Fuzzer under the weighty white skull-cap convinced of his papal *savoir faire* because he is broad enough to learn his statecraft from Machiavelli.

I take the lift down and go out among the gradually departing World's Fools. At every few steps I inwardly sputter and stagger with the remnants of laughter. I'm hard pressed to keep a sane face on my outermost self. There isn't much to say: thank you, thank you, goodbye and thank you all.

I notice, too, that Charlie's back in town. The lama's gone off somewhere for the time being, or is still resting, perhaps, in Charlie's room.

Back in the hotel I hurry along to the internet centre. The sleepy girl on the dawn beat takes my ten *koruna* and I get online to retrieve my mail. Nervous now. How must my disruptive activities (or those of the lama) be viewed by those who know me best and have not yet met the red-robed buzzard?

Hi dad,

What can I say? I mean to my friends? A monk with an estranged wife and two daughters? The best I can find to tell them is 'that's my father.' They all think you're cool and actually, dad, I think so too. You're doing it for the planet, and I know you mean what you say. You have real courage. Love, Clara. See you soon. Work it out with mom. That's a non sequitur or, no, it's a sine qua non.

Your Lamaship,

Remember when you told me you're a superior person? Well, I've thought about it and I have to tell you I disagree. I could go into a detailed explanation, but what's the use? It won't change your mind. Keep up the (good?) work and don't stress about the warehouse. This is a tight ship. Harvey.

Dear Charlie,

Well done old bean. If you thought the days of the crazy teachers were gone forever, think again. The world's fools. Indeed. But when are you going to raise the really vital question, the one about killing off the two-thirds? Don't you ever take a friend's advice? Waiting on tenterhooks, Paulus.

I confess, daddy, you have me bewildered. Are any of the things I see on television your doing or have they just happened, as always, while you were passing through? I like you in your robes. You actually look respectable. How long will it take for your hair to grow out, or what's left of it? I'm behind you all the way! Kisses, Jessie.

Charlie,

The divorce is on hold. I can't bring myself to get divorced from a man I don't even know. Love, Mona.

Dear Charlie-la,

I'm very enjoying His Holynes teaching here in Canada. In many things it is same as your teaching there in Perg. I see you having many troubles but Im not concerning. I have spoking with His Holynes and Im saying Charlie do continuing to wearing your robes. Lama Yeshe Rinpoche.

Charlie,

Now at last I know why you worship Glen Gould. In your mind it is not Bach that is important at all; it's what one does with Bach that matters to you. Nor does it matter what's done with it, as long as it's different from what's been done before or done by Bach himself. In your own way you are a great original. Ego te saluto, Adam.

I can see the shining thrill in my daughters' eyes; I can hear their supportive giggles as I stumble about this ancient city like a piece of china in a bullshop. I can feel their irresistible love.

How Halfwit must have delighted in telling his friends (all of them swilling beer as they slumped from their chairs, heads almost touching the carpet with the downward pressure of laughter) about the nose-in-red on the box, his boss, the superior person.

How long did Mona's finger hang over the 'L' before she thought, *Okay, the bastard doesn't deserve to hear it, but it's what I really feel anyway, so, Love, Mona?* How many times did she delete it and type it in again? Then, knowing me as no one else can, she made the choice for love again. That's her greatness.

Paulus is one of the world's fools by the accidents of his own karma. His approval is important to me because, unlike me, he dwells in the mental clarity of an almost unbroken happiness. *Well, Paulus, look closely; it's not two-thirds but three.*

I'm not sure I know what Adam thinks he knows. But I know that Precious Teacher knows exactly what he knows. He knows, for instance, that His Holiness sees in me a man fit to wear these robes.

Eh? Nope. That can't be it.

But I leave the computer with a surge of relief which settles down into an unpresuming ease. In the red lounge they're serving coffee and, reluctantly, tea. I jiggle, swirl and squeeze the bags in the pot until something the colour of my customary brew appears.

Merry appears too in our place of tryst. She seems both worn out and nervily excited. The milky skin is stretched tight across her cheekbones, reflecting rather than absorbing, and vaguely repellant. The smile is gleeful, not warm. She's reverted to the journalist persona and the persona is aggrieved.

'I've arranged an opportunity for you to state your case.'

'Oh? But I've already done that.'

'Have you seen what they've done to you on the television news?'

'Yes. But I'm not put out. The World's Fools know better.'

'Oh, dry up, Charlie. They're turning you into a clown.'

'Yes, well … so what?'

'I'll get to the point,' (sigh), 'You have an invitation to go on BLUNTtalk.'

'*The* BLUNTtalk?'

'Yes. They're arriving tomorrow. They like the idea of having you on.'

'Mmm.'

'You can get your message across without secondary distortions.'

'You mean, the bipolar thing?'

'What bipolar thing? No, I mean what's being said about you by the members of this conference. It's all over the BBC.'

'Surely they're not making me out to be a loon too?'

'No. That won't hold up in the long run. They're saying that you're an attention seeker, that your views would have enjoyed consideration by the conference if you'd stuck to procedure, that you chose to make use of the high profile given you by the Air France incident to turn yourself into a cult leader. A common though unfortunate tendency among certain types of religious personality, and so on. A maniac, in other words, and not a mere loon.'

'Next I'll be convincing my flock to commit mass suicide by leaping off the Charles Bridge into the Vltava? I see what you mean. But, as you know, I won't be doing that, however much I might be tempted to. I've played my part. It's over and out now, Merry. Next stop, home.'

'I *want* you to do BLUNTtalk.' (The spoilt little girl laying it on her old copper dad, playing him up against mum's explicit orders.)

'Me being bowled over, bulldozed, bloodnosed and bludgeoned by Devastation Jim? You want that for me? What for? I won't get a word in edgewise anyway.'

'I know some people. I'll ask them to ask him to go easy.'

'You think the BBC hasn't tried and failed?'

'Charlie, they're coming to do one interview. The conference has offered them the archbishop and I've offered them you.'

'I see. You want me in the *circus maximus* with a rhinoceros and a fox?'

'I want them in the arena with a human being.'

'Oh Mary, Mary, is that the real you speaking?'

'I want the world to see you justifying your view.'

'All right. But it's the last thing I'll allow you to ask of me.'

'Agreed.'

'And you have to do something for me in return.'

'Whatever you say.'

'Raise Bishop Bell from the dead. Ask him why he jumped. If you can do that by this evening, I'll take on Jim and the prelate.'

'It's not enough time.'

'It'll have to be. Here's a clue: speak to Paw Paw. Ask him what the bishop said before he died. And, one more thing; last night you said you were sorry it had to be me. Not sorry any more, I take it?'

'You told me to do my job.'

Every word counts and is counted, and the speaker held accountable.

'You say it as though I'm to blame.'

'I was inside your heart and mind, Charlie, drifting there and loving it, and you sent me out to do my job. And you're right. You're doing yours. I must do mine.'

'You're not saying that you felt rejected? Crikey. Is that it?'

'Well, yes, but not by you. That is, not by you before you became this other unknown being. That was just Charlie hesitating about breaking his own rules, again. I could have worked around that, believe me. But this other being; he has no choice. It's not in his power to accept or reject. By his nature he has to work alone, so I must be excluded. You were right. I have my function in all of this, but it's a separate one.'

'Oh Mary –'

'And now my function is to get you on BLUNTtalk.'

'But why? *Why* really?'

'Because I believe in you. I believe what you're saying. I can see it.'

'But don't you also see that it spells the end of all your hopes? You're an environmental journalist, a Gaia-ist. What about all that then?'

'Not the end of my hopes, the end of my fears. From now on I'll be able to work without fear because I know the world can't be saved. I'll have to do what's right for its own sake. If we'd all done that from the beginning we wouldn't be in this end zone now. But being in it doesn't make what's right any less right. Isn't that your dharma?'

'I do love you.'

'Yes. It's the highest expression of mutual understanding and agreement.'

'*Eines in Einem.*'

'Unfortunately.'

We leave our island, she to find Paw Paw and I to send off another emailed newsletter. It's pointless my filling them in on the details of my exploits; they already have them in psychoanalytic form. Instead, I try to explain my motives:

> *I hope you can all understand and accept that I'm doing all this under an inner compulsion. I'm not seeking applause or attention of any kind, not even for my comic antics. I have taken hold of something that has taken hold of me and I must see it through to whatever conclusion it throws up. I hope none of this is an embarrassment to any of you (Harvey excluded). I love you all.*

Back in the hotel foyer I'm by and large ignored by the rest of the delegates, but there are one or two exceptions. In a few cases I'm treated to politely nervous smiles (*does it bite when approached?*), in others to cold shoulders of the demonstrative kind. One man (dementedly Russian, I assume) makes the triple sign of the cross every time he passes me by, looking away studiously as he does so. An American woman with an otherwise altogether sane demeanour launches into song as she hurries by: *Then sings my s-o-u-l my saviour God to th-e-e, how great thou a-r-t how g-r-e-a-t thou a-r-t ...*

An unexpected exception is Mother, who plods up in her blatant German way and treats me to a searching look. I look back passively, allowing her to enter by my eyes. She remains standing after

I sit down. She folds her arms at me.

'You have surprised me, und not in ein completely bad way.'

'I hope that's a good thing.'

'I will tell you what I sink. I believe zis konference will have no practical value whatever. It is only ein cesspool of academic ideas. All words und no actions. When I see you on ze television, I sink zat you at least are doing somesink, no matter I do not know what ze heck it is. You are inspiring ze people to do somesink as well, again I do not know what. I hope it is somesink more than only protestink in ze streets.'

'I hope so too.'

'If you are doing a good thing, I hope ze good lord will bless you.'

'Thank you.'

'Und I will tell you zat I am disappointed zat ze Holy Fuzzer has decided not to invite ze Dalai Lama to ze Vatikan; disappointed in ze Holy Fuzzer, I mean. Such an impoliteness cannot be chustified.'

'I don't think *impoliteness* is quite the word.'

'Zat is not for me to say. I can say, however, zat I am surprised to notice zat ze same impoliteness is not being practised towards ze Chinese in zis hotel.'

'I haven't seen any Chinese at the conference.'

'No. Zey arrived while you were making ein rumpus at ze castle, und Gott knows what else; chumping into ze river und so on.'

'I'm very grieved about Bishop Bell.'

'Ja. Unfortunately suicide is ein mortal sin.'

'I can't disagree with that.'

'Ja, so, goodbye, Lama.'

'Goodbye, Mother, and thank you.'

It hits me. It's not *Bayjee*, It's *Beijing*; it's *Beijing locuta*.

My nose seems to be stretching itself out physically to smell out the Catholic skullduggery. It's throbbing so wildly that tears spring to my eyes. The last thought in Beelzebub's mind apparently had to do with what he perceived to be the *ex cathedra* power of Beijing. Beijing locuta, Beijing has spoken. And now bits and pieces of a self-assembling hunch are tumbling down on me and placing themselves rapidly in a haphazard sort of order.

I call Merry on her cellphone.

'Can't find Mbana anywhere,' she says.

'Never mind Banana. Can you come to my room?'

'What?'

'Yes. A big old bird just told me something. We need to speak privately.'

'You're all over the news, Charlie. There could be talk.'

'I think we might be the ones doing the talking.'

At my door she's peevish for a moment until she reads my troubled face. I've ordered up a pot of tea. She sits by the window while I pour. Her eyes are tired. She kicks off her shoes. I light a cigarette. She frowns.

'I think I know why the bishop jumped.'

'I know that question's important to you but why all this? Your room? Privacy?'

'Paw Paw told me the bishop's last words were something like *bayjee locuta*. It came to me suddenly: *locuta* means something like *having spoken*, you know, the ablative absolute; it's a peculiarity of Latin grammar.'

'Oh for God's sake, Charlie.'

'No, bear with me. When Mother told me –'

'*Mother? Mother who? Mother Mary? Mother Theresa? Mother Earth?*'

'The old German bulldozer. She told me that some Chinese had arrived yesterday while we were out on the town. Then the penny dropped. Of course the bishop hadn't said *bayjee locuta*. It must have been *Beijing locuta*.'

'Beijing has spoken.'

'Well no, it's an ablative absolute, you see.'

'An absolute what exactly?'

'It's a way of using a verbal adjective in the ablative case to indicate *something having happened, by which something else is accomplished*.'

'Charlie, I did French, and I hated it.'

'I'll get right to the point.'

'Ah.'

'I don't suppose you know the Augustinian Catholic insiders' slogan, *Roma locuta, causa finita*, or the slangier version, *casa finita*?'

'The Catholics have Latin slang?'

'Please. *Roma locuta, causa finita* means *Rome having spoken, the case is closed*. You know, Rome, the Pope, the Vatican, the big boss speaks, and that's that. Only, Bell was saying, *Beijing locuta, causa finita*, except, of course, he didn't get the last bit out. He died.'

'Beijing has spoken, case closed?'

'Yes.'.

'Spoken what?'

'You know about the Vatican throwing the Dalai Lama out on his ear?'

'That's rather strongly put.'

'No, no, it isn't. Come on, Mary. Anyway, the Vatican's given His Holiness the shaft, *under Chinese pressure*. Since when has the Pope bowed to Chinese pressure? Something ugly is going on between the Vatican and the Chinese. That's my theory. And I think the bishop knew about it and wanted to expose it and then was prevented, blackmailed perhaps, or reminded that he was in no position to judge the church's morals. So, frustrated, disappointed, unable to speak out, threatened by his own confreres, morally torn, mentally unstable, too – he jumped. That's what I believe. Does it sound crazy? Not to me, it doesn't.'

'Blackmailed? In the Catholic church that can usually mean only one thing. Just as well he jumped then.'

'It may not have been that.'

'His résumé shows that he taught history, I think, at a Catholic boys' school.'

'Yes. Bishop Beelzebub.'

'Not funny, Charlie.'

'But you see my point? What are they up to right now, right here in this hotel? Why are they so upset about my drawing the whole world's attention to these foreordained proceedings? Some American bigshot scientist, name of Hancock, tried to bully me into silence. Looks and talks like Humphrey Bogart.'

'That must be Richard Hancock. Now that's interesting. He's not a scientist exactly. He's an economist. A good Catholic economist. Way up in the *Caritas* organization. You know *Caritas*?'

'It's the Latin for charity, in the sense of compassionate activity.'

'Does it have an ablative absolute?'

'No. It's a noun. Of course, it has an ablative case, but it can't be used –'

'Oh for Pete's sake, Charlie.'

'So Hancock's an economist and a Catholic? What does that tell you? Eh?'

'We need to find out who the Chinese visitors are.'

'Can you do it?'

'If I can get you onto BLUNTtalk I can do anything.'

'Yes, but I'm easy.'

'That's not the point. And, Charlie, believe me, you're not easy.'

I see now, with a tug of disappointment, why my robes have been endorsed at the highest level of the Tibetan cabal. I'm just the political stooge they need in this inconvenient situation. They have an idea of what's going on here. Obviously His Holiness doesn't think his invitation's been rescinded because of a papal double-date. He knows it's a double-cross. And here's convenient Lama Charlie, all dressed-up and nowhere to go, and making one hell of a fuss.

Still, I hope I've been a good de facto monk too.

It isn't long before there's a knock at my door again. Merry enters, effulgent in an aura of superciliousness. I can tell she thinks she's been a very clever girl. I shrug my shoulders questioningly but she only says, 'Wait. It's worth waiting for.' Then she embraces me with effusive happiness. I've been a very clever boy.

Five minutes later there is another knock, shy, discreet. I open the door and in slips the voluminous rabbi, exuding the perspiration of intrigue. He looks around as if to ascertain that we are indeed alone. He seats himself on the bed. The yarmulke comes off, is replaced, twirled about, comes off again. The opaque dark eyes bore into mine.

'I'm putting my career on the line here,' he rasps.

'We promise not to tell if you won't.'

'I trust you, Lama.'

'Just call me Charlie.'

'But can this persuasive journalist be trusted? You know me, a Jewboy to the bone, too trusting, too human. She's lovely, so I think she must be lovely all over, including inside. It's an old Jewish failure of judgement. Take the Germans; we thought they were so straight, so industrious, so practical, intelligent, efficient; the race most like us Jews in every way, just a little less imaginative. Jesus Christ, was that ever a mistake!'

'I am lovely inside,' says Merry.

'I knew it. I just had to hear you say it.'

'I'm *kosher*.'

'She's a real *mensch*.'

'I have a lot of *chutzpah*.'

'Okay, okay, I'm convinced. Oy.'

'You know about the Chinese?'

'It's one of the reasons why I'm at the conference. Mary figured that out for herself. I should never have told you about my diplomatic privileges. A high moment, a human moment. Big mistake. Now you've got a handle on me. I could have you liquidated. You're in more danger than I am.'

'We'll risk it,' says Merry.

'No. The point is, don't risk it. Don't expose me; that's what I'm saying. Or else.'

'All right, we won't risk it.'

'I'm very glad you said that. Relieved like you won't believe. Now I can really open up.'

'The Chinese and the Catholics are conniving at something. Have I put that much together correctly?'

'Sure,' he croaks, 'Only, you don't know what the real deal is, right?'

'Yes.'

'And if I tell you? Will you sit on it?'

'That wouldn't be right. But I'll make sure you won't be implicated in the leak.'

'You will, Lama? How? Will you claim special Buddhist telepathic powers? The third eye? You have the third eye?'

'I think Bishop Bell knew. I'll say he spoke about it before he jumped.'

'You think he knew?'

'I'm sure of it. It's why he jumped, more or less. But I'll test the theory on Manners, see how he reacts.'

'And Hancock,' Merry adds.

'Okay. But know this: Archbishop Manners isn't the top dog here today. There's a cardinal arriving this afternoon. Man in red, like yourself.'

'The one I saw on TV? The Italian, Giovanni Batista?'

'Dammit, you're good, Lama. I could get you a job.'

'I'll talk to Manners. He'll want to speak to me before BLUNTtalk.'

'I could get you a job too, Charlie,' says Merry.

'If I don't get him to give himself away, I'll lay off.'

'You won't sacrifice old Rabbi Tannenbaum, you're sure? You'll honour my semitic open-heartedness? Otherwise you might even get in the way of those shits, the *Mossad*. Know about them?'

'Why are you even willing to share what you know? That's the

question that's more important to me than whether or not I may be
liquified by the *Mossad*.'

'Liquidated.'

'Right.'

'Human kindness and open-heartedness not good enough for
you? Yah, you do have the third eye. Charlie, I'm a holocaust man.
Not a survivor, of course, but a – *survival*. Holocaust is always
lurking around the planet. If it's not the Jews it's someone else; the
Amerindians, the Rwandans, the Bosnians, the Tibetans. You think
I attached myself to your group of beatniks just to follow your line
on the end of the world? Well, yes, there's something in it; I wrote
a book about it myself, you know. No one bought the idea. Bad
timing; another Jewish failure. Looks like they're buying it from
you though. So much for that. No, I joined your fan club because
I'm a holocaust man. I knew this Chinese deal was coming off here.
I saw you weren't buying into this conference *schlepp*. A man of
truth, Lama, even when the truth's against you. I liked that.
Obviously you're for the Tibetans. Those Chinese have murdered
more than a million of them; imprisonment, torture, it still goes
on; you know it all. And now, with this Chinese-Vatican deal
being brokered at the cost of the Tibetans, Dalai Lama thrown
out the church door, and me being a holocaust man, *I'm* for the
Tibetans too.'

'Do you know who these Chinese are? Are they the representatives who'll meet with Batista?' asks Merry, bringing us back
on key.

'Sure I know. I'm Rabbi Tannenbaum. *Tanny Tattle* they call me.
Shouldn't have told you that. These guys are posing as representatives of traditional Chinese religion; shrines to the ancestors, all
that jazz. Actually they're from two government ministries: state
controlled religion and state controlled finance. Yeah. They're here
to tantalize the Catholics with religious freedom and the handing
over of Catholic assets that were seized by the commies in Mao's
day. Now that's what they're offering. You want to know what
they're buying? Vatican blessings; *indulgences* I suppose you could
call them. Silence over the Tibet issue for now. For later, approval
of the Chinese occupation of Tibet, at the right time, when the new
Chinese face gets up on the world's screensavers, the friendly,
happy, charming face, with loads of money in the smile. Tibet's
important to them. That's stating the obvious. There's mineral

wealth, loads of free space for all those Han Chinese billions, the sources of all the important rivers in the region, nuclear bases ... You know all that. Land of plenty. The Vatican's always stood by the Tibetans. Not any more. Not after today.'

'I could have guessed most of that,' I tell him.

'Sure, even without the third eye. But you remember *apartheid*, Lama? It still goes on all over the world and no one cares. What made it immoral in your case was that it was signed into law. That's what's going on here; a signing up. Vatican friendship with the Chinese is being signed into official existence. That's like signing a declaration of enmity against Tibet, and most of the Chinese population too. It's a moral disaster.'

'But why meet here? At this conference?'

'Are you kidding, Lama? This is the Conference of World Religions on Planetary Issues! You think China doesn't qualify as a planetary issue? And, even better, the conference provides the perfect cover. Remember, these Chinese guys are representing their indigenous religions, ostensibly.'

'Will the church get away with it?'

'Oh, Charlie,' moans Merry again, 'Is there anything they haven't gotten away with? They hold the keys to the portals of heaven, the one true church.'

'*Roma locuta* ...'

'*Beijing locuta* ...'

We sit in silence for a while, staring around the room, digesting it all. It's as diabolical as it's somehow very ordinary. It's what you've known all along, that the devil exists. But now you've seen his face where you least expected to find it. He's a very shabby, very mundane, very religious bloke.

'May I ask you,' I enquire, not irrelevantly, 'are you really a rabbi?'

'Are you really a lama, Charlie?'

'I really was one once.'

'Well there's your answer. But tell me this, is the Pope really a Pope? Is the Dalai really a Dalai? I mean, is the one really the vicar of Christ and the other a reborn Buddha?'

'No,' I reply.

'Well then, take comfort in this; whatever you once were and I once was, we're what we are now, and at least we're something real; lama, rabbi or not.'

'So you are a real rabbi.'

'That third eye again. I have to go, Lama.'

'Thank you,' says Merry, 'You're a wonderful person.'

'Not half as wonderful as you. Got me to blow my cover twice. Think hard about all this, Charlie. There may be more to it than even I know, or don't know.'

He goes out, wagging a finger of warning. We don't know whether to smile or weep. Bad day at Black Rock. I can't believe the church, *my church* (ex-Catholic Buddhist that I am and am not), is selling out my beloved Tibetans for a pittance.

'There probably *is* more to it than Agent Tanny knows.'

'*Agent Tanny?* Who said anything about *Agent* Tanny?' she says.

'Just a thought.'

Whatever the more may be, the lesser picture remains simple and awful in itself. The Catholics are in the process of reconciling their faith and morals with an emergent superpower of the most undelicious kind. They're hedging their bets, kowtowing to a tyrant with unscrupulous global ambitions, and methods to match.

Why not? Weren't they the China of their heyday?

'I have to find Mather and Banana,' I tell her.

'Those two ineffectuals? Why?'

'Ineffectuals? Didn't you see them jump into the Vltava?'

'Yes. Yes. You're right. But *why?*'

'I told you. They heard everything the bishop said before he died.'

'Yes. They heard him say *bayjee* something or other.'

'They'll have heard his complete last words when I'm done with them.'

'I see,' she slowly nods.

'Can't pretend I was the one who heard them, can I? I was up on the bridge.'

'Are you a special agent too, Lama?'

'I don't know about *special*. But I'm definitely an agent of sorts.'

'You've said it exactly. That's what I feel too.'

'I'm off to find them then.'

'Mather's in with workgroup three. I couldn't find Mbana.'

'You didn't know where to look.'

I find gesticulating Paw Paw down in the cellar bar, a cosy dark hideout of the speakeasy kind. He's chatting up a curvy German tourist, young but not black enough to be his granddaughter. He's rolling along nicely. She's enthralled by his *mystique d'Afrique*. He's at his professorial best, holding forth on the ten reasons why Oliver Tambo was a greater general than Julius Caesar and a more important historical figure all round than, say, Charlemagne. He's cultivated, fascinating, charming and rather pissed.

It's hard to unwedge him, so I decide to dislodge her instead. I tell her, in German, that he's due to give a keynote address in three minutes. His wife and children are waiting in the auditorium. *Schluss.*

'*Er sagte mir, er sei unverheiratet.*'

'*Ich spreche Ihnen an als Buddhistischer Lama. Er muss sofort mitkommen.*'

'*Tscha. Solch ein dreckiger Idiot!*'

'*Genau.*'

She leaves without finishing her beer. He sighs and shakes his head at me.

'Why aren't you with your workgroup?'

'Chahli, I'm no longah partaking of this bleddy damn racist conference.'

'Fair enough. But I need to speak urgently with you and Mather.'

'You need me now, Lama? Now you want to share my room?'

'Yes.'

'You chase away my gel, nice German gel, and now you need me?'

'Paw Paw, I need you more than she does.'

By the time I'm back in the lobby he's behind me, a little stumbly, a little zigzaggy. I keep going to the door marked 'W/G 3' and open it with a bold authority. It's not Cunliffe who meets my eyes but a shoulder-padded female exec. I nod curtly at her and wave Mather up and out.

Back in my room I begin the briefing. Paw Paw's at my mini bar. Perhaps it's for the best, given the sober part he has to play. Mather's still belligerent, but controlled; a hostile contemplative waiting for his chance. Beelzebub, the good man, has perished under the system and Tyrone is angry with sorrow.

'You're not a Catholic, are you, Dr Mather?'

'Not a Christian, Lama. Leastways not one o' *them* Christians.'

'But the bishop really effected something; in you, I mean?'

'Yeah, that's ride. He sure showed me somethin'. But it was

somethin' human, ya know, not somethin' magical. Sheeyit, he musta suffered among them goddamn Catholics.'

'Celibate priests,' says Paw Paw, 'No chance to be a man. It izi sinful.'

I explain what's on my mind, what I suspect from the few clues dropped on the television news, from the arrival of the Chinese delegates and the cardinal, and from my reconstruction of Beelzebub's cryptic *bayjee locuta*. Do they agree that I might be onto something? Or am I reading it from a biased viewpoint? I convey my tentative theory about the bishop's suicide, leaving out the boys' school aspect. Might I be confused about all this? How do they see it?

'It has a sorta Catholic ring about it, don't it? *Jesuitty*. Know what I mean?'

'I could be horribly mistaken.'

'But we must find out,' Paw Paw says with an unexpected boozy gravity.

'Yeah, we gotta know fer sure. Bishop Bell was a good man. Those Tybeetans don't need no more raw deals neither.'

'It's about them I'm most concerned.'

'What izi the best way to do this thing?' Paw Paw slurs.

'Confrontation,' I say, 'Lay it on the table for Archbishop Manners. Be inventive. Use verbiage and cheek. Get him riled and confused enough to react with bluster, to give himself away.'

'Play up the hunch,' says Mather.

'It may be more than a hunch.'

I prime them on the appropriate motives and angles, and set their performance on course. Mather reacts instinctively to his outraged sense of injustice. I see his eyes harden, the lips compressed and the chin firmed up above his craning neck. Paw Paw is pensively angry, holding something down within himself. Through the mists of his inebriation I can see it's authentic.

We go down to the front desk, where the dry one is by now quite chary of me, and wary of Banana. He stands at a sort of indifferent attention, his expressionless eyes resting on mine as I instruct him to summon French Peter Forbes.

'The racist priest,' Paw Paw adds for colour, with a brief informative nod.

Father Forbes takes his time. Making people wait humiliates them. It breaks their rebellious spirit. We sit down to wait in the foyer. When he arrives at last, he makes no apology, only treats us to his version of a devastating look which changes tack by stages to one growing increasingly devastated as we outline our request.

'I don't know whether the archbishop will be much interested in those matters just at the moment. He is extraordinarily busy right now.'

'Do you know that I'll be on BLUNTtalk with him tomorrow? Does *he* know? He may want to be prepared for some of the questions I intend to put to him. It wouldn't be fair to spring them on him then, would it?'

'Bishop Bell said some pretty darn incriminatin' thaings,' lies Mather.

'Just before he died.' Paw Paw adds dramatically. 'Do people lie when they are staring into the face of death?'

'That's not my area of expertise,' the sibilant orifice hisses, 'but I shall speak to the archbishop at once. I shall convey what you've said, Lama.'

'And we shall wait here,' grunts Paw Paw, 'while you convey.'

As it turns out, the archbishop will make time for us. We're invited up to a mock baroque suite and ushered into sinuous velvet armchairs. From a room off to the right we can hear Manners speaking on the phone in a remote official tone. Then he makes a prelate's dignified entrance, self-possessed and a trifle haughty, but humbly aggrieved in spite of all that.

'So it is you again, *Lama?*'

'Yes, *Your Grace*, and Professor Mbana and Dr Mather.'

No one seems inclined to shake hands.

'The *world's fools* have their share of academics too?'

'Yeah, we have all sorts,' says Mather, 'Had us a Catholic bishop too, till yesterday afternoon.'

We all sit down again. The archbishop lights a cigarette. Since he's not offering, I light up one of my own. There's a gloom settling in among the tastelessly ornate furnishings. It's the depression that accompanies knowing you're about to be lied to.

'As you gentlemen all know, I'm very pressed for time. I believe you wanted to speak to me about the sad incident involving Bishop Bell.'

'Yes,' says Paw Paw, 'about hizi suicide and also about everything he said before he died. We think you should know about that. We think everybody should know.'

'We are not at all convinced that it was suicide,' Manners asserts, opening his arms with a sermonizing flourish. 'One can't speak of simple suicide in the case of those who are mentally … unbalanced.'

'He sure was balanced when he gave me his wisdom,' Mather protests.

'Gave you his wisdom?' Manners inquires with a faint smirk of distaste.

'Sure. The kinda wisdom that comes sudden-like before you die. If I could believe in your God (which, honest to God, I cain't), I'd say God was with him.'

'Oh, I'm quite sure that God was with him.'

'So,' Paw Paw asks, 'if God wazi with him, how could he be unbalanced?'

A philosophical perplexity glints for a second in the archbishop's eye.

'I was told that he said something to you before he died,' he drawls, deciding not to waste time on philosophy and Paw Paw both, 'something that caused all of you – and *you in particular, Lama* – some distress, or did it only intrigue you? What was it the bishop said?'

'*Beijing locuta*,' says Mather.

'*Beijing locuta*?' He sniffs at the words as though they were a dying penitent with poor personal hygiene.

'Yeah. But not *causa finita*. No sir, "*Beijing Locuta, Roma finita*" is what he said. Mighty strange thaing to say, I tellya'

'Beijing hazi spoken, Rome izi finished,' Paw Paw translates with a jabbing finger.

'Yeah, and that warn't the whole of it neither.'

'Yes,' the archbishop muses absently, 'very intriguing indeed. But it *does* sound rather unbalanced. What *was* the whole of it?'

'Well, he didn't have a whole lotta time to say what he needed to say, but I guess the gist of it was that the church had betrayed the principle of justice fer the principle of money. Yeah, that's ride. And that it had betrayed him too, threatened him with some kinda exposure if he talked about this ecclesiastical sellout. Kinda blackmailed him, I'd say he meant.'

'Justice betrayed for money? A bishop blackmailed? By whom? And how did he think the church was betraying justice, and for whose money? And on what basis could he be blackmailed? Do you see my point? Very unbalanced.'

'Yeah, tilting over dangerously on the side o' death.'

'Damn games!' Paw Paw explodes, 'He said it very clearly, from a very clear mind. He said the Tibetan people have been betrayed for Chinese money. And now you can see for yowaself that the Dalai Lama hazi been excluded from yowa circle of friends. It izi everywheh, on the teevee. So we know that, in that regard at least, the bishop wazi not unbalanced. What he spoke, we saw aftawards on the world news.'

'Then it's clear that the church has nothing to hide. As you say, it's on the world news. Of course, I've seen it myself.'

'What you have to hide are the detailed reasons behind this cheap betrayal,' I offer.

'And what might those be, do *you* think, *Lama*?'

'Whatever the Communist Chinese have promised you in payment.'

'You don't believe it may have more to do with protecting the lives and wellbeing of the courageous Catholics within mainland China? That we might have thought it wise to come to an arrangement with their government out of concern for our own Christian flock?'

'I know that'll be your line, but of course it doesn't stand up under scrutiny. The Chinese wouldn't want to persecute Catholics in China now. The Chinese regime is making big money in the West. Doesn't make good business sense to put the Catholics down. Besides, the church openly supported the Tibetans during the time when persecution of Catholics was just as openly practised in China. It wasn't considered ethical then to sell out one group of oppressed people at the expense of another. No, I have good reasons for believing that this is a far more cynical exercise. And these reasons are based on information obtained at the highest levels.'

'You deal with the highest levels, *Lama*?'

'Oh yes. Directly and indirectly.'

'May I ask what you've been told, directly and, er, *indirectly*?'

'Pointless, *Your Grace*. You'd only deny it.'

'Will you be raising this matter on BLUNTtalk tomorrow?'

'I may ask some questions about it. And they'll be asked in the context of my views on the demise of the planet. You already know about those.'

'Yes, naturally I do. I think those unbalanced too, I must confess.'

'I think you yowaself must be unbalanced,' Paw Paw opines with a dismal glare. 'That izi why everything appears unbalanced to yowaself.'

'Tell me if this is unbalanced, *Your Grace*: your economist, Richard Hancock, is signing an assets deal with the Chinese as we speak, and the whole process is being assented to and monitored for final agreement by Cardinal Batista.'

'That's bloody outrageous!' hollers Manners, but it's an implosive yell.

'We agree,' says Mather, 'That's why we're takin' it to the noos.'

'It won't stand up to examination.'

'Maybe not, Yer Grace. But it'll stand up on its own feet alride.'

'Everyone knows that the Chinese delegates are representatives of traditional Chinese religion,' Manners insists. 'They are here in a strictly religious capacity.'

'My high level sources don't agree,' I misinform him again, 'but I'd be glad to hear Hancock's side of the story.'

He rises testily (and shakily, if that were visible) and moves across to the phone. A moment later he's speaking stridently to the economist. It seems Hancock has been mistaken in his estimate of the confidentiality of this enterprise. The churchman's brusque attitude makes it clear that the PhD money-man is only a civil servant in the Vatican's pay.

We don't wait half as long as we did for Bumface Forbes. Hancock's on fire with the rage of sudden calamity. There's murder in the eyes of the *Caritas* man as Manners explains the tenor of our interview.

'Just who the hell are you lot anyway?' he fires at us. 'Why the hell should we speak to you at all?'

'Who the hell we are ain't what's important ride now,' Mather rattles back. 'It's who the hell you are's what we'd like to know.'

'Dr Hancock represents *Caritas*, our social justice organization.'

'The one that's selling out the Tybeetan people, that ride?'

'Or are we to assume that Dr Hancock's meeting with the Chinese delegates to discuss social justice in the context of Chinese religion?' I throw in.

'You can damn well assume whatever you want,' bawls Hancock.

'Then I'll assume that you're working out a financial deal in exchange for dropping all support for the Tibetans. After all, you're a renowned financial buff, just the man for a tricky job like this.'

'Supposing all that were true, which it isn't, why the hell should the church continue to support the Tibetans anyway? What the hell have they ever done for us? Hardly a single Catholic among them, hardly a Christian for that matter.'

'Dr Hancock ...' the archbishop reaches over soothingly.

'I told you before, Charlie, you don't know the trouble you're causing. You're getting right under my skin here. You can go out there and say whatever you want. All I'm willing to tell you is that we're acting in good faith in the interests of our Catholic brethren in China.'

'And signing a document betraying everyone else.'

'Who said anything about a document?' he shrieks at me.

'Chahli says it,' Paw Paw shouts back, 'because he knows!'

'If there were a document, which there isn't, how the hell would you know about it?'

'If there were not a document, which there is, you wouldn't ask that question.'

'Well, you just go on guessing, Charlie, and we'll just go on proving to the world that your guesses can't be substantiated.'

'Shouldn't that be *transubstantiated*?'

'You *are* unbalanced,' Manners asserts, this time with real conviction.

At this Paw Paw leaps up and flings his Nigerian *fila* to the floor.

'You people are the worst of the worst!' he rages. 'You think I don't know why Bishop Bell died? He knew all about this skullduggery and you blekmailed him! Yes, I know! I am a Xhosa from Transkei. We Xhosas are a tight community, just like yowaselves. We guard our information just as you guard yowas. The bishop worked among my people a long time ago, when he wazi still a parish priest, and we know what you have done to him. We all know that he wazi in love with a Xhosa woman and that there izi a son; his son. That young man, that coloured boy, wazi raised in yowa orphanages. And he izi now a priest in one of yowa blek parishes, a priest in yowa hands. To keep those hands from destroying that priest, the bishop had to die. You are quite right in saying that it wazi not suicide. No. It wazi murder! And I am not guessing. I knew what wazi on his mind when he gave his blessing and comfort to this man Mather. He wazi thinking of his son. I jumped down into that rivah to save him for his son, but I failed. Now he izi dead. You fools who think you are serving God with yowa penises tied in a knot! At least he wazi a real man!'

We all sit numbed. Paw Paw looks around at all of us, his eyes full of fathomless disgust. Then he retrieves his hat and leaves the room, shaking off the archbishop who attempts to hold him back.

'I guess *he* ain't guessin',' Mather eventually mutters, breaking the long ten seconds of pensive shock.

'This is a total shambles!' Hancock exclaims, glaring at his boss.

'Please, Dr Hancock,' breathes the archbishop coldly, 'nothing has changed.'

'Damn ride,' says Mather.

'Thank you for your time, *Your Grace.*'

'I hope you will act wisely, *Lama.*'

'I hope that you will do the same, *Your Grace.*'

'Oh I shall, I shall.'

'You shall, shall you? The worst of it is that you're signing a treaty of cooperation with a billion-strong termitary whose combined productive instinct will play the biggest part, after the Americans, in tearing the planet to shreds. And you're doing it *at this conference.*'

'You know nothing,' Bogart Hancock insists. 'The World's Fools! Jesus!'

Back in the foyer I stare at Paw Paw. His eyes tell a long winding story of institutional victimization. Now he is stuck. His carved face is wooden. There is the wildness in his glare of an animal trapped between *fire and fire* (to be redeemed by neither).

'That was quite a revelation, Paw Paw.'

'But it izi a revelation which you must keep to yowaself.'

'I'm sorry, Paw Paw.'

'No need for sorry, Chahli. We did our job. We got him riled.'

'I'd be riled too, if I weren't so exhausted.'

'What now?' asks Mather, still ready to rumble.

'Will you do it, Tyrone? I'm just not up to it today.'

'Sure, I been on teevee many times. I'll do it alride, boy.'

Merry appears, a sensuously quivering question mark. I fill her in. I tell her that Mather will speak to the media. She shakes her head vigorously, frowning at me, but I look away. It's true that I'm tired, but that's not why I'm suddenly media-shy. It's Mather, not I, who was anointed by Beelzebub.

'Hell of a conference,' says hangdog Paw Paw. 'I'm going to the bar.'

'I suppose you're the lama, Lama,' says Merry. 'It's your call.'

'Mather's the one for this job.'

'You're the one with the third eye.'

'My third eye tells me that we need a break. Hang on, it's telling me something else – yes, yes, it's telling me to invite you to supper in a nice little – can't quite make it out – yes, a nice little *inexpensive* restaurant in the old square.'

'I'll just get Dr Mather introduced to the gang.'

'Meet me at the front desk at seven.'

I realize now that I haven't eaten all day. I go up to my room to take a shower. There's a palpable ache at my heart-centre, a sense of being wounded by something sharp and quick, a smart arrow that has left its tip of depleted uranium behind. Of course it's Charlie, not Lama Charlie, that's been wounded. I don't think the lama was present at that vicious little conference with His Grace.

Is this what it's all about? Charlie and the lama working together? Dirty Harry and the Buddha agreeing to disagree in order to get the job done? Oy. Boy. It's like living yer life, innit?

Should I discard the robes and climb into my jeans? I want to go out as a normal joe, an unencumbered tourist taking in the splendour of Prague-the-lovely, street by street. But I can't wriggle out of the settled weight of devolved responsibility. I can't discard the lama until it's lifted.

Downstairs she's waiting, beautiful and vulnerable again. Her strength, like her carapace of duty, is easier lost than sustained. But she's smiling for my sake and her eyes are full of inviting warmth.

Is she playing the role of Mara in all this? The temptress? The devil? The siren drawing me down into the sea-change of illusion?

Charlie doesn't seem to think so. But Charlie's more than a little smitten.

We clatter and judder in the tube train to the central station. Around us the glum Czech commuters are packed in tight, some hidden behind their newspapers, some looking blankly out at the day that's been. They become animated with curiosity as we board; nods, waves, smiles and titters of greeting. Room is made for us on one of the seats. I take up my *mala* beads and recite soundlesly: *om mani peme hung.* They won't interrupt a monk at prayer, I hope.

Merry is squeezed up against me, her soft body pressing ever so slightly, so gingerly, against mine. I'm shot through by an innocent thrill, like that of an adolescent in a naively compromising situation. I can enjoy this contact with the essence of woman without wanting more. I must not want more.

But I know that keeping my distance makes her sad, and I care. So I drop the beads into my lap and talk about the days of the Holy Roman Empire and the chivalrous medieval kings who made this mysterious city their seat and citadel. It may not be history we both want right now, but history will have to do.

Some people are photographing us on their all-in-one cellphones and one young man even seems to be making a video. Perhaps they're surprised to see the lama out with a gal. I just smile at them and press my palms together. But I can see now how right I was to stick to the robes. It's not just that the whole world's looking on breathlessly. There's Mona too.

The restaurant juts out into the square, a raised platform enclosed by wooden railings and covered by a canvas roof. Among the tables the tall gas burners keep the patrons warm. It's homely and (alas) romantic.

I'm recognized immediately. A table is set for us with much civilized fuss. I play it like the Dalai Lama: smiles, bows, palms together, laughter when it gets too much. And I feel very happy. Through me they are honoring their highest instincts.

Although the steak calls out at me from the menu I select a vegetable stew and I refrain from lighting up a smoke. Merry has her grilled veg with a light Auslese. I stick to water.

'World's fools,' says the waiter serving us. 'Maybe I will becoming one too.'

'Why?' asks Merry.

'Like court jester, no? Fools must speak the troot. That is good, I think.'

'What is the truth?'

'Everything which the world leaders are not telling us?'

Over our meal we speak about anything at all to distract us from what's still to be done. She supplies me with nostalgic, funny glimpses of her childhood holidays at Margate, her intellectual struggle in a family of functionaries, her early ambition to become a cop like her father. I tell her about my training as a monk, the frustrations of life in a monastery in India, the bizarre events and people. I remember how good it was to be young and impressionable. How easy it was to imbibe uncritically whatever nonsense made you feel at peace and at one with the turbulence of life.

'But you gave it up for love of a woman.'

'Yes, I did.'

'Any regrets?'

'Yes. But I'd have had regrets too, if I'd stayed a monk.'

'Just can't be all the things we want to be, can we?'

'No. But we must be all the things we have to be.'

Afterwards we decide to stroll through the lesser lanes of the new town, some straight, some winding crookedly into unexpected finales of architectural charm. We peer through lit-up windows at the sparkling glass and crystalware, examine the offbeat furry fashions and hear the Czech versions of 70's rock spilling from little nooky coffee-shops.

We are bending forward to get a closer look at a set of shimmering champagne glasses, intricately cut, poised like fragile musical notes in a delicate score of glass, when I hear a sound like a dart softly piercing a cork board, and Merry drops suddenly beside me, blood streaming from her temple and onto the sidewalk. The dazzling shop-window cracks and falls apart all over us.

I turn around and scream at a man running away into darkness.

CHAPTER 12

The Fourth Day In Prague, On Which The Lama Is Dewormed Of Untruth While The Global Remainder Abide Infected

Doubtless the bullet was meant for me. Our heads, only centimetres apart as we admired the intricate craftsmanship of the glasses, must have moved fractionally this way or that while we chuckled with pleasure; moved at exactly the moment when the trigger was squeezed with the sights fixed on my shoplit cranium.

I shouted with shock and inert dread until a crowd tumbled out from the nearby bar. Merry lay very still. I sat down and put her head in my lap. Some men took off their jackets and wrapped them gently around her for warmth. I put a finger to her neck and could feel a strong pulse. I dabbed at the wound with my zen-shawl and saw that it was a deep blood-filled furrow, as though her temple had been gouged by a smooth metal talon.

My heart was drumming and thundering with blank desperation. I carefully turned her lolling head and felt through her hair and down her nape for any further wounds. There were none. Someone was calling a doctor, someone else the police, when her eyes opened on the strange and agitated scene. She looked out mildly, like a child just waking up.

I went along in the ambulance, holding her hand. I prayed to the Buddhas of the ten directions and to every enlightened energy in all the realms, praying first for Merry and then for myself; for her, that she should survive intact, and for myself, that I would not be carried away by the violent rage storming behind my eyes. And by this dangerous falling, falling …

At the hospital she was taken to the emergency room. Within a few minutes, I was once again surrounded by a group of overexcited dicks. The one closest to my face was the same little boy whom pacifist Libor had bounced off the tarmac of the hotel parking lot. He was professional or embarrassed enough to pretend not to recognize me and I extended the same courtesy to him (with an inner Charlie-chuckle-of-unlamalike-loathing).

When I'd explained everything and made another sworn statement they left. A skinny doctor (probably the only Woody Allen
look-alike in the Czech Republic) assured me with a pessimistic
frown that Merry was doing fine. She'd been treated for shock and
was currently asleep under sedation. The wound was superficial.
But he would prefer to keep her overnight. He seemed very uncertain but also rascally behind the thick lenses of his glasses. What
would the lama like to do?

He'd like to sit at her bedside.

I slowly digested this latest violent outrage while I watched her
sleep. It couldn't be a simple (or even a complex) quantum karmic
cock-up. What then? The Catholic Church sticking a Jesuit hitman
on lama-me? The Richelieuesque Archbishop Manners? Bogart
Hancock the duplicitous tough guy? Cardinal Batista the sanctimonious go-between? No, it had to be the Chinese, surely.

Maybe they hadn't intended to kill me, only to scrape my skull
in warning, the skull that had bent down to the window a mere
moment before the admonition could touch it with shock and pain.
For a lingering second I found relief in this idea. But no again: they
weren't that subtle. A nation that feeds live goats to its zoo-bound
lions for public amusement wouldn't bother with reproachful
niceties.

Then it all penetrated inwards to the concentrated drop of light
at the centre of my whirling brain: this crude pact between Beijing
and the Vatican must be only a small but pivotal part of something
much bigger. Otherwise they'd just have laughed me off.

I stood appalled, as before a warning: the suddenly illuminated
realization that I was intended to be the thoroughly dead warning
to all others intending to mess with this sinopapal thing.

I went out and down the corridor to find a spot where I could
light up. As I emerged from the door of Merry's ward two outsize
heavyweights in shiny suits nodded grimly at each other and tagged
along close behind me. Lama-minders, courtesy of the Czech
state.

Why not? This is the only country in the world that hoists the
Tibetan flag on March 10th, the day of the Lhasa uprising when the
Chinese opened fire on scattering, yelping monks and nuns in
the streets below the phantasmagoric Potala.

I went out into the night air, my guards staying close, casting about themselves with apparently casual intentness. It was cold with a slight misty drizzle. I kept my face averted as the tears rolled down my cheeks and chin.

What a fucked up world. (When has it ever been any better etc.? Short answer: at any other time in its fucked up history.)

I addressed the less gargantuan of the two who seemed to have retained sufficient humanity to allow himself gnarled attempts at smiling as I spoke. Yes, the state had put them on my case. To protect me from whom? The smile twisted in concert with an amused frown. Was I kidding? No, I wasn't kidding. Did they have any idea who was trying to blast me into my next stint in Samsara? They did not. But a man had been arrested. Chinese? They couldn't say.

Were they in any way given to understand that part of their assignment was to protect me from myself?

This enquiry was thought amusing enough to bear translation for the benefit of the really big giant. Haw haw ho ho ho. Yes, they thought that might be part of their brief.

How long would they be on my case? Until I went through the airport departure gates the day after tomorrow.

So I stood there smoking one fag after another, growing damper and calmer in the enveloping fumes.

When I went back Merry still lay blissfully drugged. I toyed with my *mala* beads as I entered the high court:

'What brings you into the August Presence this time, *Lama* Fincham?'

'Global skullduggery, M'lud.'

'Ah, yes. One contends with that *ad nauseam*. In my profession one is even called upon, from time to time, to play one's part in it. But, please, would you care to be more specific. There are so many instances.'

'Yes, M'lud; the Chinese have bought out the Vatican.'

'Are you about to enter upon the same old tedious Tibetan complaint?'

'Only in the context of its global meaning.'

'And what are the charges against the defendant? I take it this geriatric fellow in white *is* the defendant?'

'Yes, M'lud. The Pope is charged with abuse of his *ex cathedra* privileges.'

'And how do you plead, Pope?'

'Ja, zis is ein very complicated matter. First of all, ze *ex cathedra* privilege has only to do mit mein pronouncements on matters of faith und morals.'

'Indeed, but my question to you now is: how do you plead?'

'Not guilty, surely. I am ze representative of Gott Almighty.'

'Lama Fincham?'

'I must contend that, when the Holy Father *acts* on matters of faith and morals, he sets *ex cathedra* precedents which are much more influential than mere pronouncements. In this case the Holy Father has acted contrary to every Christian precept, thus giving license to all Christendom (since the Roman church claims to be the one true church) to do the same. In entering into a compact with Beijing, he has made the *de facto* pronouncement that might is right, no matter how vicious and destructive that might might be.'

'I see. And, in your opinion, Lama Fincham, how vicious might this might be?'

'In a word, M'lud, *terracidally* vicious. Yes, the Holy Father has entered into an alliance with a terracidal regime, in the process marginalizing the non-violent six million Tibetans whose country is currently under illegal and oppressive occupation by this same regime. Not to mention the billions of oppressed Chinese inside China.'

'Your response, Pope? Please stand up when you address this court.'

'Mein response is really very simple und to ze point: I am ein very much higher authority zan zis ridiculous court. I am, *in der Tat*, ze Vicar of Christ. Whatever I declare is bound in ze heavens und loosed on ze earth. Zerfore I also refuse to stand up in zis worldly courtroom. You speak only for ze chudiciary, but I speak for Gott.'

'I see. God has declared himself in favour of the Chinese regime then?'

'Gott is ein great und holy mysterium. He is not required to state his position or to divulge his mysterious reasons.'

'Has he informed you of these at least?'

'I cannot question zese sings. Mein chob is only to do what is best for ze Church.'

'I suppose there isn't much hope of asking him to take the stand then?'

'In a word, no.'

'Lama Fincham?'

'If God has chosen for the Chinese, it's just as well the Tibetans are Buddhists.'

'Pope?'

'If zey had chosen to be Catholic, Gott might have chosen differently, assuming of course zat Gott has chosen for ze Chinese government.'

'But the Chinese – are they Catholic?'

'A small fraction are. But a small fraction is ein big chunk in a country of one billion people. Und Gott might well have chosen for zis big chunk.'

'Lama Fincham?'

'I understand there are financial benefits for which God has chosen as well.'

'Pope?'

'Gott always chooses what is best for His Church.'

Very seldom, in the great crises of the world, has the church chosen for the good and the right if the good and the right were also the weak and unprofitable. This did not matter in ages past, because the church had never been other than a compound buffoon of the bureaucratic kind, cruel, tyrannical, unrepentant beyond measure. And the poor breathless multitudes could still look forward to the time when their God might finally touch it with grace.

But it matters now, as the world dies around us. We can forgive the young all their vices, even the most heartbreaking, because they are both beautiful and ignorant. And there is still time for sobering up after the hangover. But vice in the aged, crookedness in the face of death, is a blow to the heart that leaves it lame.

'Are you afraid now, Chully?'

'I suppose I am. Not sure what I'm really afraid of, Rinpoche.'

'You scared of so many things. That is how it feeling when you seeing clearly into the all truth, good and bad. So many things to making you afraid. But, truly, you only needing to afraid of yourself. Nobody else can failing you.'

'I don't know if I can walk this road.'

'Heh heh … nobody is sure, but only fear can stopping you now.'

'My biggest fear is that I'll try to fight them on their own

terms.'

'Heh heh heh … if you will doing that, then very for certain you will losing, Chully. That is for sure as I am sitting here upon the crown of your head. But you hava some small wisdom. Let go your anger. You can let it go. Then fear is also gone.'

The truth is I'm not afraid for myself. The sense of my own significance in any sense now seems utterly senseless. There is only what lies ahead of me, and its value is as uncertain as everything that lies behind. It's this uncertainty that rouses the terror.

I plunge into *now*. Its waters are clear, cool and liberating, refreshing my mind for the encounter with the next moment only. All the moments that have been are useless dregs. From them I have salvaged insight and foresight, experience and warning. Good. But they have no authentic call this situation.

The clock says two ayem. Merry begins to stir. I want her to see my face as she opens her eyes. She wakes, confused. I smile down at her and take her hand. Then, as she gathers coherence, I outline all that has happened.

'They want to kill you now?'

'Yes. They've paid me that tribute.'

'We need to get out of here.'

'You have to stay until morning.'

'It *is* morning.'

I call the doctor. He fiddles through his examination and shrugs. He frowns through his thick spectacles. She's fine. He instructs a nurse to re-dress the wound. The curtain round the bed is drawn while Merry puts on her clothes. I wait at the door.

She comes out looking groggy. Before we go out I prepare her for the state-sponsored heavies. She just nods once with a tired, pained expression in her eyes.

'Screw them all,' she says brokenly. 'They deserve to lose their planet.'

I want to call a taxi but the two heavies wag their jowlish heads in tandem, the one a bulldog, the other a pitbull terrier, their stumpy tails stiffened with curiosity over this other animal, red, bald, beaked. They'd bite me if I weren't so strange. But they snarl kindly at Merry who took the bullet for this other thing.

They lead us to their vehicle, a shiny black skoda with a smell of brand-newness pervading the interior. We drive to the Best Hotel in silence. The city lights shine down on the deserted streets waiting for morning in dead solemnity.

My heart leaps and sinks and my eyes shut of their own accord as we turn into the hotel parking lot. There is a press of people milling and shoving, shouting and gesticulating with disastrous uproar. Yells. Catcalls. Curses. The World's Fools have returned, ignited by anger. The hotel is under siege.

Cops all over the place, their vehicles flashing lights, blue, red and white. The media are spread out in clusters, picked out in the hard, alternating colours of the police lights, feasting with professional fastidiousness on this eruption. I close my eyes again. It takes an act of will to force them open.

I look across at Merry's grim face. The fun's gone out of everything now. Lama Charlie was only supposed to stir the pot, not bring it to the boil and the boiling over. There were to be dangerous words and rebellious ideas, not wounds. Above all, not wounds to herself received on his behalf. Especially not the wound of stubborn withdrawal. Why should she take a bullet for a man who belongs to something and someone else?

'Well, there are your bloody fools, Charlie,' she says bitterly. 'And don't they just look the part.'

'Do you hold me responsible for this too?'

'Insofar as you've allowed a rabble cult to develop, yes.'

'I'm sorry you got hurt for me.'

'No, you're not.'

I want to get out but the rear doors have been rigged not to open from the inside. I'm a protected prisoner. I glance at the pitbull. I'm exasperated. He's on the phone, reporting and receiving instructions. What to do with the recidivist Buddhist and the helpless journalist?

I think I can see the dilemma. The Czechs are violently anti-red, especially the Chinese hue with its history of blood-spattered cultural revolution. Yep, the Czechs hate the commies, but they're also sunk to the neck in the bogs of Catholicism. And here's Lama Charlie declaring that the institution of their god and tradition is, as the rabbi might put it, crawling up the Chinks' chink.

The pitbull tells me we're to be taken straight to our rooms, for our own protection. Merry doesn't protest but I decide to make a fuss. These people are here because of me. I have to speak to them, quiet them down. The police will quiet them down, I'm curtly told. The bulldog drives slowly up to the glass foyer doors, one of which has recently been smashed.

As I'm bundled out I see Koomaraswami, white cotton clad, shining like Shiva, speaking to the crowd. So, he's taken the burden upon himself. As they catch a glimpse of Charlie being hustled into the hotel they erupt with cheers and chants of 'Lama! Lama!' I look over at the swami. He presses his palms together and yells, 'No prrblem, Lama! Nutting to worry about! All calm now, I'm vrry much hoping!'

So there was violence. This has been a revolt, not another vigil. Merry's right: I have started a new rabble cult, and its first political instinct is to attack all who disagree with its tenets.

The pitbull leads her away. She doesn't turn around or say one word to me. After a wait of some minutes I go along with the bulldog. The night-staff at the front desk look on shyly. None of them can tell whether I'm a celebrity or a miscreant. I'm taken up in the lift, propelled to a door, ushered through it, and it's closed behind me.

It's not my room. It's a sprawling suite. My things are neatly arranged in the luscious bedroom. I allow myself to be silently mystified and go through to the five-star living room.

Deafeningly alone.

It's almost four and still dark outside. I can hear the crowd's complaints reverberating against the walls and windows and on the deaf ears of the Roman and Chinese conspirators. I turn on the TV news.

They're broadcasting live from outside the Best Hotel:

'This conference of religion on planetary issues has turned into a fiasco, Jerry. At least, that's what the people out here are saying. Dr Tyrone Mather's report on the link-up between the Vatican and Beijing has got the World's Fools wild with anger. And now, with the attempted assassination of Lama Charlie, things have really got out of hand. The police are out in force. The crowd's only just been brought under control. The question they want answered is: who fired the shot that was meant for the lama. That's all for now. It's back to you in Atlanna, Jerry.'

'Thanks, Tom. Well there ya have it. Crowds under the banner of the World's Fools, an organization that's sprung up overnight under the nominal leadership of Lama Charlie, are protesting, sometimes violently, outside the Best Hotel in Prague, the Czech Republic, and elsewhere around the world. Let's go live now to St. Peter's Square in Rome, Italy –'

A travelling shot of the papal palace with its vacant balcony, and then a downward sweep across thousands of demonstrators holding up banners, placards and torches. Focus is pulled on a large placard held up by four wild-eyed youths. It has three doctored photos: the pope wearing a Chinese Liberation Army cap with its red star, Mao crowned with the triple tiara and the Dalai Lama smiling serenely at them both. '*The End of Decency at the End of the World*' reads the legend.

Many placards read simply, '*Beijing Locuta, Roma Finita.*'

I'm taken on a satellite tour to some of the cities where the World's Fools are hard at their folly. Berlin, Brussels, Paris, London, Washington. It seems they're particularly foolish in Warsaw, Budapest and Vilnius, those towns that have tasted the policies of experimental governance across the bloody spectrum from over-man fascism to sub-human sovietism.

'We'll return shortly to listen in again on what Dr Tyrone Mather had to say earlier today,' newsman Tom smoothly advertises. 'But first we'll take a commercial break. Some more footage of the failed attempt to slay Lama Charlie, too, all here on your favorite noos channel. Stay with us.'

The ads. A rampantly exploitative oil company with a Dutch flair for public relations shows us its caring side, its concern for nature and the wellbeing of the universe. That's why we should buy its petroleum products, cadged amid the brutalities of the Nigerian oilfields.

Then we float through the Disneyworld of Dubai Airport. We step off the aircraft into a wonderland of exotic plants, *objets d'art*, and beautiful dames. They're gliding up escalators to an unknown airport paradise. Everyone's smiling, apparently doped on *soma*.

Yah. It's the *brave new world* of come-and-get-it-if-you-got-it-to-get-it-with.

And fuckya if you don't.

Music. Logo. Cut. Pan in on the Best Hotel. There's Tyrone, craning his neck, ogling the cameras.

'Now I can tell ya'll, without a shadder o' doubt, that our Catholic brethren have done sold them poor Tybeetans out. Yeah, sold em out fer dirty money and a political deal with the communist Chinese regime. More than that, it's a signed agreement, a long-term thaing. That's why Bishop Charles Bell jumped to his death in the river. He cuddn't take the shame of it all. I know cuz I jumped in to rescue him and I heard him say, "Beijing has spoken, Rome is finished", and I noo what he meant, too. But don't take my word fer it. You do what yer paid to do, go sniff it out, it'll come to the surface alride. And I jest wanna say, as one o' the World's Fools, that it's exactly this kinda dealin' that makes it clear to us that this world cain't hope to be saved. We're sunk in too many dirty deals and there's no extricatin' ourselves now. The tragedy is that the Christian church, the highest representative of western morality, is demonstratin' to us, once again, just exactly what the real nature of that morality is. Yeah, we're all dead in the water already, just like poor Bishop Bell.'

After some more verbal fuzz there's a short video clip (cellphone generated) of Merry's head resting in my lap as I sit dumbfounded, dabbing at the wound with my zen-shawl, at a loss for first-aid technique.

I stare at the screen as the story flows on and on, until the words fuse into a stream of meaningless sound.

It's been quite a night. Haven't experienced this kind of thing since the day Mona pulled her papa's shotgun on me one weekend on the farm. But it wasn't loaded on that occasion, as we discovered when she pulled the trigger. Click.

I doze off in the comfy armchair.

My fragmented dreams appear as if projected onto mirror-shards. There's Merry bleeding and muttering, 'And screw you too, and screw you too, and screw you too.' The faces of Manners and Hancock appear, but Hancock's dressed up in the prelate's garb. There's Koomaraswami crying out: 'Pleez, no more violence, it doesn't vork!' Then Precious Teacher looms close to my face. '*You hava split the fruit, Chully, and hava finding the worm of the untruth inside. But, how can you killing it?*'

I'm woken by the faraway ringing of the telephone which is suddenly close and loud as I take my bearings. I let it ring a little longer as I drift to fuller consciousness, shaking off the dream-guests. I lift the handset with befuddled anxiety.

'Mister Fincham, sirr?' (It's the dry one.)

'Yes.' (groan.)

'Call from South Africa.' (Heartleap of joy!)

'Put it through.'

Crackle and scratch.

'Hello, Charlie? Charles, can you hear me?'

'Mona! God, it's so great to hear your voice! I was just thinking about you – about the great times we had on the farm!'

'Who's the fricking blonde lying in your lap?'

I'm struggling with tears. My throat's constricted. I want to go home.

'Don't take time to think about it, Charles. Just tell me who she is.'

'Oh God, Mona, I love you so much!'

'Who's the fricking blonde?'

'She's a journalist and a friend. She got shot. It should've been me.'

'What were you doing out on the fricking town with a fricking blonde journalist in the middle of the fricking night?'

'I had a bad day. I needed a break and some company.'

'So you picked up the fricking blonde. Jesus, Charlie! In your robes, too! Now you're becoming a monk again? A monk with a fricking blond on his lap? What the hell's going on? What the hell am I supposed to think? What the hell is my fricking family supposed to think? I'm telling them I've dropped the divorce and they see you on teevee with this fricking blonde chick! We're confused, *capisci*? On the one hand, how do I stay married to a monk? On the other, how do I stay married to a monk who's fooling around with a fricking dumb blonde?'

'Are you being serious, Mona?'

'And what do you think the girls think?'

'You're serious.'

'Of course I'm fricking serious!'

'The blonde's only a friend. No, not a friend, a colleague. A blonde colleague, Mona. The monk will permanently disrobe when I leave Prague.'

'It's one thing to make fools of your family at home. Now you want to make fools of us all on fricking CNN too?'

'I'm very, very tired, Mona.'

'You think you're the only one who's tired? Typical! Charlie's tired, so the whole fricking world must have a siesta!'

'Mona, I love you.'

'You've got a lot of explaining to do when you get back.'

'But you know the truth already. You know it, Mona.'

'What do I know? Only what I see on CNN. You'll have to explain it all to the girls, to papa, and to everyone else too. And you'll have to explain to papa why you're going after the fricking Roman Catholic Church! Going after the fricking pope himself, for Christ's sake! How do you think papa's taking that? I don't want them thinking I'm a fool, too. One of your fricking *worldly fools*.'

'I need your help, Mona.'

'You need my help? Now you're in a big mess and people want to kill you! Now you want my help, you stupid little boy? What help?'

'I've split the fruit and found the worm of untruth inside it. *How do I kill it?*'

'This is the help you want?'

'Yes.'

'How to kill a fricking worm?'

'Yes.'

'Buddhists don't kill worms. Is this a riddle?'

'I'm speaking figuratively, Mona: *the worm of untruth in the split frui*t.'

'You think I'm a dumbo? That I don't know what you're saying?'

'All right. How do you kill it?'

'You kill it in your fricking self, Lama.'

'You're the only one who really knows my mind.'

'Well you just get that blonde bitch off what's left of it.'

'Will you be at the airport when I get back?'

'I'll be there. We'll all be there. Just shape up.'

My taut nerves collapse and dissolve in a fresh downpour of tears. They are raining down on the ugly, parched desert of my life with its sour fruit. I see my nothingness. I feel the writhing worm drowning and a glow rising in its place around the miniscule seed, the heart of my heart.

On the TV news things are taking a startling turn: '– where police have revealed the identity of Lama Charlie's would-be assassin – twenty-two year old man, known only as Gabik G., is a member of a radical environmental group – the organization has a record of violent activism – previous death-threats – according to a hospital spokesman, Gabik.G. has been under long-term treatment for schizophrenia ...'

Not bipolar disorder this time?

I study Gabik's face. Nothing there to indicate either madness or murder. Might have been a waiter at the restaurant last night, a congenial young man working his way through college or the *conservatoire*. It's bewildering, the assassin's warm smile, as though the photograph was taken by a close friend or a lover. It hangs there, pasted on the screen, the picture of youthful *sans souci*.

What makes Gabik want to kill me? That I am preaching the inevitable destruction of the same environment which he is striving, in his schizophrenic way, to preserve? If that's the case, how many more Gabiks are lying in wait?

I take refuge under the shower.

The telephone's ringing again as I stumble out swathed in clinging steam. It's the rabbi this time; *Tanny Tattlebaum*.

'I'm asking you, Lama, as your friend and as a rabbi,' he croaks, 'do you believe a single word of it?'

'Yes. I believe he tried to kill me.'

'No, no, not that! The *meshugga* environmentalist *spiel*; d'you believe that?'

'It's what the police have told the media.'

'Of course, of course. They've told the media what they know. How could they tell them what they don't know?'

'I see, I think.'

'I'm speaking only from my Jewish instinct and my rabbinical wisdom.'

'I understand, I hope.'

'I hope you do. But let's say you don't. Jewish history is full of betrayals and cover-ups. I'm drawing analogies as a rabbi and only as a rabbi, and even as a rabbi I won't go on record. But who was really behind the crucifixion of Yashua? The Sanhedrin, or the Romans, or the crazy mob; let's say the *schizophrenic people*, on the streets? You want the answer? It was the Romans, Charlie, and the Sanhedrin. I don't say the Sanhedrin was wrong. That I won't say. But neither the Romans nor the Sanhedrin were willing to take the can. That's my drift, speaking historically, as a rabbi. Again I say, Lama, they let the *schizophrenic mob* take the blame. That's all I have to say.'

I clamber back into my superhero garb: shemdap-skirt, dhonka-jerkin, zen-shawl, red socks, sandals. I'm trembling. It isn't fear. It's a new intensity of disembowelling disappointment, the kind that shocks you into a perspective on reality so bizarrely coloured with conspiracy it resembles an hallucination.

So then the real questions are: What did they offer Gabik to take the fall? And, was the offer made by the Chinese or the Catholics, or both? No, the catholic eunuchs wouldn't have the balls, would they? Even so, they must know what the rabbi knows.

I'm thinking how dearly I'd like to speak with patsy Gabik when there's a knock at the door and the bulldog opens it to reveal the swami, waiting in an Indian flap of confusion behind the tough-guy's bristly bulk. I nod my assent. Koomaraswami enters. The door is pulled shut behind him.

'They won't let me bring my laptop inside,' he muses, passively perplexed.

'Is there a bomb concealed in it?'

'In a way, yes.'

'Let's get it then.'

I stick my snout down close to the bulldog's forehead and growl at him. He may be big, but I am taller and very important in my way. Let him maul me if his brief goes that far. But it obviously doesn't. He hands me the laptop with a shake of his jowls, as though reluctantly parting with a repossessed bone.

The swami, sitting down at the desk, attacks the keyboard with rapid ease. After a minute he calls me over, points at the screen, says nothing, smiles, shakes his turbaned head, cringes with delight.

It's the official website of the World's Fools. It has all the gim-cracks in place: *Home, Who We Are, Press Releases, Join Us Now, Subscribe, Contact Us*. At the top of the page is an image of Lama Charlie in severe mood. Someone has caught him in profile as he stares out with grim intensity at the dying world. It strikes me how very guru-ish he seems, and the convex dark blue eye and hooked nose heighten the Brahminic effect. The aura of sorrow emanating from the total countenance takes me by surprise. Does this man have anything to do with the Charlie I know and – love?

'Look,' says Koomaraswami, 'Alrrdy over one hundrrd-tirty tousand-membrrs.'

'Whose work is this?'

'Your work, Lama.'

'But, who set this up? Who's running this thing?'

'We don't need to speak about that. Prrhaps it's anonnmous.'

'You?'

'Well, India is the holy land of cumputerr know-how.'

'But is this a good idea?'

'Good idea? This is not the only vebsite. Sevrrl others too. But this is the official one; the one which rrprrsents your authentic dharma.'

'If you say so, Swamiji. God help me.' (There *he* is again.)

'This is bigrr than I thought, Lama. This is rlly big.'

'Can you put out a message from me right now?'

'Oh yes, oh yes. Nutting could be simpler.'

'Say I'm fine, I'm not angry, I'm full of peaceful thoughts, I love everybody, I forgive the shooter, I don't want violent demonstrations.'

'Vrry good, vrry good.'

He types again, pauses, embellishes it with some Bombaybombast. I see the words assembling themselves onscreen: 'Violence belongs to the system from which we fools are distancing ourselves with ever-increasing inner enlightenment. The sign of our positive fool-ishness is that we deal only with the truth as we sincerely see it and that noble truth has no need of negative means of propagation. It will realize itself because it is what it is, which is simply truth. In wisdom and compassion we discover all our necessary tools.'

'Who's with the crowd outside?'

'Tomas and Libor, and you won't believe who else!'

'I'll believe it.'

'Mbana and Doctrr Tyrone and … you won't believe this!'

'I'll believe it too.'

'Doctrr Helena.'

'Helena Pikardt?'

'She's a World's Fool too, I believe.'

'Somehow I don't think so.'

'Nevrrthless, she's there.'

'Would you ask her to come and see me?'

'Are you being held captive by these vrry large gentlemen?'

'I'm not sure. Helena may know.'

'Then I'm going out to gettar right avay.'

Morning twilight tarnishes the windows. The one-hundred-and-thirty-thousand World's Fools scattered across the globe weigh heav-ily on my ragged emotions. Like them, I am also set against the end of decency at the end of the world, but I haven't wanted a legion to com-mand. It is tedious, even nauseating, to think how easily people huddle up around a cause. Why can't they all just stand together but alone, cleanly, singly, unbendingly? Why this need for the eternal leader, the drawn face staring out across the adulating hordes?

And for what larger purpose is this sino-catholic deal the small end of the wedge?

I meditate awhile, shrugging off the deadweight of responsibility, resting in solitary spaciousness. But my mind loses luminosity, fades to a buzzing drowse. I'm jerked out of it by another loud knock.

'Helena.'

'Lama.'

'Thank you for coming.'

'I am known to all those people,' she waves her hand at the window, 'I have some standing with them. But it was difficult last night. They were demanding to see the cardinal and the Chinese delegates. I had to persuade them to desist. Some threw bricks at the hotel lobby. There were rumours, you know, that you had been shot. It was only when they saw you arrive that they calmed down completely.'

'What do I mean to them? What do they expect of me?'

'You've started a politico-environmentalist movement, of course.'

'Have I? Others tell me I've started a new religion.'

'That too, and that's the most dangerous aspect to control.'

'I don't want to control anything. I didn't bring this thing into being.'

'No?'

'Not deliberately.'

'Everyone who speaks an unpopular truth brings something into being, Lama. Ask me. Then, when you've risked your life for it, the cause redoubles in intensity. Whereas you had followers before, you now have devoted acolytes, and that places you in even greater danger. That is how a non-conformist movement propels and multiplies itself, driven forward by the lethal reactions of the establishment.'

'You think the shooting was a political reaction? You don't believe the lone schizophrene potty environmentalist assassin theory?'

'Your bodyguards have been supplied by the president himself, even though the assassin has been arrested. So what do you think the president believes?'

'But why would someone want to kill me over this Chinese-

Vatican deal? I mean, unless it's actually a crucial part of a much more elaborate scheme.'

'I don't doubt it is. But more than that I cannot say.'

'Because you don't know?'

'No, because I don't know *for sure*, which is the same thing.'

'No it isn't.'

'Anyway, It's not something I would care to speculate about.'

'Why not? Are you afraid of what you suspect, or perhaps you approve of it?'

'Of course I don't approve of the marginalization of Tibet.'

'You speak like a politician.'

'Yes. Unlike you, I am not at liberty to flail about. I work against the system, but I am obliged to carry out my tasks from within it.'

'I don't criticize you for that. You're probably more courageous than the fool who rushes in where statesmen fear to tread.'

'I have a long task ahead of me and I intend to live to do as much as possible.'

'You think I may not?'

'That depends on what your enemies judge most expedient. As a politician, I try to avoid making enemies. It's not always possible, but at least I am perceived as someone who can be compromised with, although I can't be bought.'

'I must appear to you as something of a sot then.'

'Not at all. I envy you your foolishness.'

'It's not the Chinese tried to kill me, is it?'

'Only Gabik G. could say with certainty who it was.'

The Roman establishment and the Sanhedrin. That's what the rabbi said. Crikey Godalmighty blow me down. What a dunce you are, Lama!

For a long while we look at each other in helpless silence. I'm surprised again by the charming inner frailty enfolded in her outward strength, the spontaneous tenderness warming her unyielding green eyes. I wonder, does she know how much the superior she is of us two? Or is it part of her peculiar power that she wouldn't know how to think in those terms?

'Am I being protected or held in custody?'

'Both. But so far as your being held in custody goes, you are expected to view it as a courtesy. Just look at your prison environment. They know you will be leaving tomorrow, when the conference ends. If you were contemplating extending your visit, for tourist reasons perhaps, I should say you would not be allowed to stay.'

'Banned from Prague, my favourite town.'

'Banned from the Czech Republic, I should think. And from a number of other countries too. Not officially, of course. But visas will be refused for all sorts of reasons.'

She gets up and leans forward to shake my hand, smiling ruefully. I don't want her to leave, taking with her this mystique of the *Ur*-Goddess. To be suddenly deprived of it is to feel lost, abandoned, *motherless*.

'Thank you for remaining with the crowd last night.'

'The World's Fools. Yes. They will disperse now.'

'And for coming to speak to me.'

'I had intended to see you one last time.'

'I'm very glad we met.'

'Goodbye, Lama Charlie.'

It's the distance she keeps that makes her seem so deceptively close. She makes a brief polite exchange with the bulldog, a perfunctory pat on the head. He wags his stubby tail. Then the door closes on her flowing white cotton dress.

Floored again, with my thoughts strongly diverted towards Bishop Beelzebub. Was he, after all, mistaken in the finer details of his reasons? If he had known what I now know, would he have jumped anyway, or perhaps jumped with a greater load of despair? Or would he have been consoled to know that Beijing was the object and not the culprit of the ruse?

I go through to the suavely appointed bedroom and curl up. Sleep falls down on me like a sudden eclipse, blotting out my confused thoughts of Beelzebub, Helena, Merry …

I can sense the assassin skulking at the dark end of the alley. Grabbing hold of Merry, I try to drag us both away from the entrance, but we're leaden. The bullet slices into the centre of her forehead, in the place of the wisdom eye. She sinks down and crumples on the floor. The second shot is fired and I feel a touch of intense heat between my eyes. I know I am dying. The gunman approaches, slinking like the Nosferatu vampire in fragments of a walk. It is myself. Looking dispassionately down at me, myself asks, 'How can you kill the worm of untruth?' I lie there, paralysed. Myself shakes his head forlornly. 'You put it in the light,' he says.

I'm woken around nine by the rattling and chinking of the break-fast trolley. It's laden with all the first class stuff. Nothing seems too good for the lama under suite-arrest; there are both coffee and tea. I tremble as I stir up my brew.

By the third cup I've come awake. I dial the front desk and ask for Merry's room.

'Hello, it's me.'

'I can't speak now, Charlie.'

'Have you managed to sleep at all?'

'Why are you calling me?'

'Are you being held hostage in a suite as well?'

'What do you want, Charlie?'

'All right, all right. I want to know what to do about BLUNTtalk.'

'Oh – that …'

'Yes, that. The *that* that you insisted I go on today.'

'I don't know – just wait – or something – I'm sure they'll find you.'

'How's your head?'

'Please, I need to pack now.'

'No. Tell me what's going on.'

'I have to pack. Please go now.'

'You have to pack? Are you leaving just like that? What's going on?'

'Nothing. Another commitment's come up. Bye, Charlie.'

I'm puzzled and hurt. She's dropped the phone on me, which has always been Mona's prerogative. Is she concussed? I have to get to her.

The bulldog's gone, replaced by his change of shift, a diminutive, dapper man with a crooked nose and sharp green eyes. The black outsize pupils are those of a B-grader demoniac. Taken all together, he might be constituted from the same gene pool as Vladimir Putin (or the feline Conradian Ricardo), but in his case they've scraped the bottom of the barrel. He answers to the name of Vaclav, like a zillion other Czechs.

It turns out he speaks German. While I explain my intended mission he stares at my abdomen, rather like Halfwit. He weighs things up, also Harvey-like, until I want to shake him by the shoulders.

'Screw it man!' I bellow, 'I'll just bugger off and find her myself!' And I think: 'You can fucking well shoot me too, if you like!'

He takes hold of my forearm with a grunt signifying, I imagine, withered patience, and frowns out a smile. He turns about and beckons me along behind him to the door of the room next to mine. He nods at it with a trace of uppity amusement, and knocks.

When she opens the door and sees me, an irked and then a *really irked* expression crosses her brow and veils her eyes. She groans (a heartfelt groan-wail) and moans, 'Oh no, not now.' I'm left staggering under this unexpected intensity of rejection, can't find an appropriate response.

'Chased away your bodyguard too?' is all I can think of.

'He left early this morning. Obviously you're the one who needs protecting. I'm just the one who takes the bullet.'

'What are you saying? What's happened here?'

'I've already told you I don't want to speak to you. Please ...'

'Please nothing. You owe me an explanation.'

'Yes, everyone owes you something. But I owe you nothing, *Lama* (sizzling irony) You're the one who owes me in this little partnership.'

'Explain and I'll go away, if that's what you really want.'

'It is. But I'm too exhausted to go into this now.'

'Explain briefly then.'

'You're so damned insistent. The truth must out. Lama Charlie's the man of truth, blah blah. Well here's your brief truth about us. Briefly, I feel as though you're the one who shot me in the head.'

'Grazed your temple you mean.'

'It's obviously a feeling not reasonable enough for Charlie the man of reason. But it's an insistent and very credible intuition. It's as though you meant all along that I should be shot. That's why you ducked just in that split second.'

'I wanted *you* to be *shot*?'

'You wanted me to get hurt in some way. You want to hurt everyone.'

'I want *what*?'

'You concoct the danger but it only touches those around you.'

'You – you need a doctor.'

'You invited me out to dinner,' she sobs and breaks down, 'and this was the result. I wanted to be with you but you got me – shot. It was our last opportunity.'

I try to put my arms around her but she forcefully resists my nearness. Vaclav gapes, dumber than dumbfounded. This is no everyday

Czech soapie. She pushes me away and returns to her packing, her shoulders sagging brokenly as she bends over the suitcases.

'I'm sorry. I really am. But I must plead not guilty,' I stammer, amazed with pain.

'Please,' she pleads back at me, 'just leave now.'

I leave the room with Vaclav at my heels. I'm shaking like a spurned adolescent and I realize with a trickle of terror that I have indeed been leading her on, and not inadvertently. She's right. Mona was right too: there was a blonde in my lap.

Back in the suite I sit and sit, growing number, watching the sewer of Charlie's self-deceptions fomenting. She knew all along what was intended to happen after the charming stroll through the nightlights of Prague. And as for me, I only pretended not to know, in order to be taken unawares, guiltlessly.

I wish now I had been shot.

The worm of untruth coils and uncoils itself in my belly. It's obvious that I need a thorough lavage, a momentous spiritual puke. *Kill it in yourself. Put it in the light.*

'You sitting, sitting, very long time, Chully.'

'Stuck.'

'You can feeling it, this worm of the untruth, moving, biting, turning over inside.'

'Yes.'

'Very disgusting, no?'

'Very.'

'That is why you not wanting to looking at this horrible thing. Too disgusting.'

'Yes.'

'But how you will seeing it if you won't looking, Chully?'

I look. I see the worm in the split fruit of myself. It's a sickening hue of fleshy pink, wrinkled, slimy and sinuous. As it sees me seeing it, it raises its many heads, some furious at being exposed in the dark comfortable intestines, some screeching in agony. One laughs maliciously.

I look, gaze, stare, no longer feeling anything. I've seen it. It's seen me. It's seen me seeing it. As I look on, the heads begin one by one to lower themselves in babyish self-pitying shame. They peek up at me.

I am rent apart by their mawkish expressions, by their cute attempts at beguiling me. I am laughing so loudly, roaring and bellowing, that tears fly from my eyes and snot from my nose. I can't stay in my chair. For all its slick design and ergonomic comfort, it can't hold this rippling and shaking creature in its frame. I fall out of it, rolling on the carpet, grabbing at the plush red pile to prevent myself from floating up to the ceiling.

The possibility of death by laughter now begins to occur to me but I can't stop myself. I want to cry out for help but laughter thunders over the attempt. It rocks the very thoughts of death that arise as I howl and gasp without recourse. Then I find myself engulfed in a blaze of hilarity that leaves me semi-conscious.

When I'm finally able to roll over on my back, still helplessly rocked by intermittent gusts, it seems to me that I've tasted the essence of my mortality.

Vaclav is looking down at me, panic inscribed in his featherweight pugilist's face. It sets me off again so that I can't get to my feet. I can tell that he's sniffing at me, trying to nose a whiff of whatever I've been drinking or smoking. He's looking around at the mini-bar but there are no bottles, no glasses, nothing. His obvious dismay pumps the laughter up again as I crawl about on my knees, desperately searching for something by which to drag myself up. I try to wave him away.

'*Chully!*'

The dignified summons is even funnier than Vaclav's mystified gape. Perhaps this is a nightmare, all of it, starting with Merry's mad rebuff. This thought, too, is extremely funny. I'm laughing, crawling, waving and drooling all at once.

'*Look again, Chully. Worm is gone now.*'

It's true, the viscerous creature of untruth is nowhere to be seen. Contemplating this simple fact, I begin to sober up and clutch my way back into the chair. The relentless hilarity hasn't let go of me though; it's pent up behind a very insubstantial wall. Every move Vaclav makes almost brings it down. I wave him out of the room.

I daren't switch on the telly. One daft word, one stupidly serious newsreader's mug, is bound to let the pealing bats out of the ticklish cave. I'm too afraid even to meditate. Anything may happen in that realm.

Appallingly enough, the phone now rings.

'Hello, *Lama Charlie* speaking – yah hah hah haha.'

'Dad?'

'Clara! – hee hee hee.'

'Is everything ok?'

'Yes my darling girl – haha – someone tried to kill me – yee hee hee – but couldn't – heh heh heh – manage it – yaahk aahk aahk.'

'And that strikes you as funny?'

'Funny? – yaahk yek heeahk – in a way – yek yeek – yes!'

'I love you, dad.'

The guileless concern riding in her tremulous voice breaks the curse. I dry my eyes on the zen-shawl, turn away to guffaw one last time, rub my twitching nose.

Still, it's a struggle.

'Thank you, Clara. No need to worry about me. I'm being looked after, I think. Are you all well?'

'It's not about us right now, is it?'

'You've been following all the goings-on?'

'Glued to the screen.'

'Yes?'

'Yes. It's like a family cricket sit-in. Mom, Jessie, Adam, Mauro, grandpa, all waiting for the next curved ball. You've started some major shit, dad. I mean, *the World's Fools?*'

'Where are you?'

'We're all at home. We'll all be at the airport tomorrow.'

'I miss you.'

'Who's the blonde?'

'Oy, forget about the blonde. She's just doing her job.'

'I hate to ask what kind of job.'

'Good Lord, Clara! She's an investigative journalist. She exposes things.'

'You don't say. And, grandpa says to leave the Catholics out of it.'

'No chance of that, I'm afraid.'

'I know. Can't blame you there.'

'Have you joined the World's Fools?'

'Of course not! Don't forget, I know Lama Charlie up close.'

'Good for you.'

'I have to tell you something else.'

'Sounds ominous. Go ahead.'

'Some journalists caught up with mom and uncle Mauro.'

'Is that right?'

'Yes. Mom couldn't resist her fifteen minutes, you know.'

'And Mauro?'

'Yes. We've been watching it. You know how they put it on over and over again.'

'I'll take a look.'

'I hope you like it.' (suppressed gurgle and giggle.)

'I see.'

'Ok, dad. So you're still alive at least. That's good. See you tomorrow.'

'I love you.'

'... too. Bye dad.'

It isn't very long before the revealing personal interview is screened as an aside to the ongoing global saga of Lama Charlie and the World's Fools. My heart flutters and dips as Mona and Mauron appear. She's freshly made-up, beautiful as a well-preserved Roman *matrona*. He looks like a *mafioso* with his wide, over-confident tie, outsize cufflinks and heavy dark blue chin.

They've invited the chic reporter right into our apartment. She's an English professional and bound to be thoroughly outdone by Mona in the Italian pizzazz department. So *that's* Lama Charlie's wife, and the other one (the *capo*): that's the brother-in-law.

'Mona, how come Lama Charlie has a wife?'

'Because he married me.'

'What I mean is, aren't these monks supposed to be celibate?'

'Well, he was celibate and then we got married. Now he's celibate for a while in Prague, I hope, and then ... Anyway, that doesn't change what he is deep down.'

'What is he, deep down?'

'Deep down he hates stupidity, including his own stupidity. He thinks I'm stupid, but I'm not. He thinks Mauro's stupid – everybody's stupid – for him it's the human condition.'

'Yes,' Mauron interjects, 'He's honest. Too honest. Stupid honest. It freaks people out. Nobody likes being seen as stupid, especially by a stupid person.'

'So it seems.'

'I think,' muses Mona, 'that he hates stupidity because he's mostly so very stupid himself. But somehow stupidity suits him. It works for him. It's his *modo operando* or whatever. It keeps him moving forward, quite quickly, rushing off to do the next stupid thing. That's how he grows. I've always thought of Charlie as a big stupid man trapped in a clever little boy's brain, if you know what I mean.'

'Naïve?'

'No, just stupid. But we love him that way, mostly.'

'Yes,' adds Mauron, 'We have to love him. *He's family.* He hasn't made it easy for us, that's true. I mean, he's a Catholic who spat at the church to become a Buddhist. We always hoped he'd find his way back, and we still hope so, and maybe he will. In the meantime, why does he want to attack his one true spiritual mother? Does that make sense to you? That's stupid again. So we worry about him. And now some idiot tries to kill him.'

'Charlie was born to rub people up the wrong way. He can't help it.'

'Yes,' says Mauron. 'And most people don't like it.'

'I don't think you're getting my point,' Mona sighs. 'Of course people don't like it. They don't understand his stupidity. He's like a little boy that says things about his parents in front of the guests or when the priest comes round for dinner. The things are true and the parents don't like it. But is that a reason not to say them? I mean, who's really the stupid one in a situation like that? Think about it.'

The price of notoriety. I bow my head wearily, or perhaps it's so heavy with unpleasant surprises that it just drops under its own weight. But this does not prevent the next surprise from happening almost as soon as my chin touches my chest.

It starts with Vaclav's version of a discreet knock (three resounding blows). The door is opened to reveal the bum on shoulders with a broad smile pulled disconcertingly across itself. It looks uncomfortable.

'May I?'

He may and does come in, peering about with approval expressed in a series of little bobs of the buttocks. He's clearly excited.

'You'll be interviewed here,' he informs me.

'You mean BLUNTtalk?'

'*Of course.*'

'How are you involved, Father Forbes?'

'How in*deed*? In preparing the stage, so to speak, for *His Eminence.*'

'Has *His Grace* been promoted?'

'Very humorous, *Lama.* But no; *His Grace* has been recalled to Rome. You'll be interviewed together with *His Eminence.*'

'Giovanni Batista?'

'That is correct.'

'Well, suppose I don't want you all pottering around in my room?'

'That would be very ungracious of you, *Lama*. This *room*, as you call it, has been provided for you at the expense of both church and state, and on *His Eminence's* gracious advice. *His Eminence* felt that you might need something rather more comfortable after the unpleasant experience of last night.'

'Small recompense, I'd say.'

'*Recompense*? You're hard to understand, *Lama*.'

'Just call me Charlie if calling me *lama* costs you such an effort of emphasis.'

'Well, *Lama*, we don't really know what you are, so we're not taking any chances. Some say you're a businessman, others that you're a disrobed monk, others that you're a married man with two daughters, and now there's even the odd theory that you're some sort of Peter Pan who just won't grow up.'

'You saw Mona on TV.'

'Yes. And the other one, the concerned Catholic. *His Eminence* was pleased to note the Italian connection. He's Italian himself, you know. And of course we now know that you're a Catholic as well as a Buddhist. It's all quite confusing.'

'I have a dispensation from the Dalai Lama to wear these robes, so there's no need to be confused about *lama*. Please convey that much to *His Eminence*. And as for any other confusions, they'll all be cleared up for you on BLUNTtalk, *Father*. Odd that, isn't it? I'm a lama with two kids and you're a father without any.'

'Again, very humorous. Now you'll have to excuse me; I must prepare for the interview. In fact, the idea was that you might proceed to lunch while I tidy up and rearrange things here. But please be back by ten-to-two.'

Vaclav shadows me down to the dining hall where a discreet crescendo of whispering voices occurs as I enter. I look around for Merry but she's not there. But Paw Paw Banana gets up at the far end and calls out, 'Lama Chahli! Over here!' Even from this distance it's clear that he's sozzled. The swami and Mather rise and wave as well.

It's not just the enemies, it's the friends one makes.

'This is Vaclav, the newest member of the World's Fools.'

'Looks like vool Vooladmir put Putin,' stammers Paw Paw.

'That would make him the one-hundrrd-tirty-tousand-seven-hundred-sixty-seventh membrr,' the swami rejoices, 'and the tree-tousand-four-hundrrd-and-tird Czech membrr spessifcly.'

'And a real big welcome to you, sir!' hollers Mather, craning his neck.

I don't have the goodness of heart to reveal the joke. So Vaclav is treated to a thoroughgoing exposition of the constitution, aims and methods of the World's Fools while tucking into the tangy selection of local processed meats, and understanding considerably less than nothing at all.

But it's an eye-opener for me as I take in Koomaraswami's elegant overview of the movement I'm reputed to have initiated, and for which Merry has very nearly lost her life and has actually lost her faith in me.

I also notice that it's a movement based exactly on the principles of Mohandas K. Ghandi, the Mahatma, for the liberation of India from the forerunner of the Empire of the New World. Are they powerful enough to set the whole world free?

'It's *satyagraha*,' I say.

'Oh vrry definitely yes,' Koomaraswami agrees.

'Then I can't be blamed.'

'Oh, nobiddy's blaming you at all, Lama.'

'That's ride. We know who's to blame, boy. It's all them non-World's Fools, just like it was *ers* before we became fools. Whaddya say, Vaclav?'

'*Sehr schmackhaft*,' replies my bodyguard, ripping into a sausage.

'What izi he saying, Chahli?'

'He says it's completely smack-on.'

Paw Paw ponders this while propelling himself, by means of another gulp of Jack Daniels, onwards to the next dimension.

'I hope you'll all join me for a little farewell gathering in suite eighteen this evening,' says I.

'Be glad to, boyo!!' (What else has Beelzebub bequeathed to Tyrone?)

'So vrry sad, these farewells, but the movement will indubitably go on.'

'Powah to the people!' very inebriate Paw Paw bellows, lifting a clenched revolutionary fist. 'Viva Lama Chahli viva! Down with British racism! Down with the Catholics! Down with the Chinese! Down with America!'

In usquebae veritas, I reflect, as the one-hundred-and-fifty-two embarrassed non-racist diners endorse Paw Paw's outburst by studiously raising no outward objections.

A ripple of polite laughter, expressing God-knows-what deep-seated anger or terror or self-abasement or incorrect correctness, wafts along the tables.

He studies their awkward tolerance with a wicked gleam of humour, looks wryly across at me, and shakes his head.

'You're a born bullshitter, Paw Paw.'

'You're my born friend and brother, Chahli.'

By ten-to-two the suite has been metamorphosed into a TV studio with angled lighting, sound equipment, cameras, make-up department and several crisp individuals fluttering about with clipboards in their busy hands.

I'm led to the bathroom by a jaunty homosexual who proceeds to dust me down and to fiddle about with my visage in a number of deft and ticklish ways. I can tell he's not much taken with my jagged physique. But he says, 'You have a wonderful aura, Lama,' and, 'Don't let that nasty bugger Jim get the better of you.'

The first thing I see through my wonderful aura as I emerge from the bathroom is the corpulent cardinal, beaming, gesticulating and chuckling. He's emanating benedictions from the vast mental catacombs of his primate self-righteousness.

'Ah, Lama Charrli,' he expostulates, agleam with obese cordiality.

'*Your Eminence.*'

'I know your bigga boss, the Dalai Lama, very well!'

'It's a pity *your* big boss doesn't want to know him anymore.'

'The world is nowadays so complicated, and there is so leetle time for meeting all the people in it. How nice it would be to know them all.'

Devastation Jim is ushered in by three fussing assistants. The unshaken centre of attention, his presence is intended to be felt in his air of absent *sang-froid*. His diaphanous blue eyes look disinterestedly into mine as he shakes my hand cursorily. Cardinal Batista is given the same limp treatment before we're all shuffled into our respective seats under the harsh studio lights.

He nods at the cameras, introduces the primate and the lama, and charges out of himself with a sudden howl:

'Lama Charlie, small-time entrepreneur, happily married man, or so we presume – you've recently been publicly decribed by your wife as a little boy – Who or what are you really!?'

'Your worst nightmare, Jim.'

'Well your theories and pronouncements on the planet can certainly be described as nightmarish!' he rasps. 'Or, as *some* would have it, stupid!'

'That's not what I mean.'

'Oh? Isn't it? Tell the perishing world what you mean then!' he bawls.

'I mean that I'm the messenger who brings the straightforward facts. No point arguing with me. I'm only reporting what I've been told. I have no further mandate. You'll have to bully His Eminence instead.'

Desperately muffled titters from the crew. His Eminence suddenly much less jovial. Where's the fun without the rules? Jim's supposed to scream and you're supposed to work your way tactfully through the minefield of abuse, to emerge either triumphant (though battered), having partially made your point, or to slump down in silence and abject disgrace.

'But I repeat,' he explodes, 'who are what are you, straightforward messenger aside!? What am I looking at here!?'

'I'm what you see, a lama.'

'A *lama* with very dicey antecedents and extremely curious ideas!' he thunders.

'No; it's the lama who's curious, not the ideas, and my curiosity didn't light only on ideas but on simple facts, as I've already said.'

'Cardinal Batista, are you aware of these simple facts!?' he wails.

'Si, but I would be inclined to see them neither as simple nor as facts.'

'Complicated speculations then!?' he trumpets.

'Si. Exactemente.'

'No. These are facts relayed to me by the Buddha Maitreya himself, the Future Buddha who was to come, but won't come because there'll be no planet to come to.'

The crew look uncomfortable now, their smiles a little stricken.

'And these are your facts?' Batista gently intones, looking me over with real concern.

'Is it a fact that the Pope is the Vicar of Christ?'

'That is our traditional belief, yessa.'

'And is it a fact that Christ exists, having been resurrected from the dead?'

'Mosta certainly.'

'Well I'm the vicar of the Buddha Maitreya who also certainly exists.'

'And what *facts* has Maitreya conveyed to you!?' Jim booms, casting sidelong glances at the security man.

'First, the fact that the planet will be unliveable in five to ten more decades. Second, the factual reasons for its decline. And third, an example right here at this conference of the kind of insanity perpetrated globally by those who are its foremost destroyers.'

'Mosta interesting.'

'I can hear global laughter right now!' screeches Jim.

'That's right. I can hear it too. It's one of the signs of the times.'

'It might also be a sign that something really lunatic is being put over on the world!' he rumbles. 'The World's Fools, for example?'

'Please, letta the lama go on. It is fascinating in its way,' Batista coaxes.

This is right up his street: the fruitcake lama about to reveal the Vatican's misdemeanours as imparted by the Buddha Maitreya. Devastation Jim has a doubtful look, a *wild surmise* growing wilder by the second, in his see-through eyes. Some of the crew are frozen, some are emitting curious coughs of amused contempt. None of them know quite what they are dealing with and how rabid it may yet become.

'We're all holding our breath for Maitreya's simple facts!' snorts Jim.

'The chief cause of our planet's ruin will be the globalization of the American law of the jungle ...'

'Law of the *jungle*!?' bellows Jim. 'You mean free enterprise?'

His Eminence sits back with a tolerant smile.

'No, I mean dog-eat-dog under American rule.'

'So it's the naughty Americans again, is it?' he froths testily and yet somehow sympathetically.

'Yes. You see, the mad urgency to attain the global empire by any and all means won't permit the necessary pauses needed ...'

'Global Empires!' Jim flails and thrashes. 'So Maitreya's a conspiracy theorist, is he!?'

His Eminence can't but erupt into obese laughter.

'... to radically alter the destructive aspects of the present world system. It's our only real problem, but the urge to power won't permit it to be solved. The intention is to run the world at any cost, even if it means bringing it to ruin.'

'Very alarmist,' opines the cardinal calmly, beating Jim to it, 'A piece of popular fiction, in facta.'

'Nowadays most of the really frightening facts look like fiction. Yet we see the expansion of this empire being achieved on all fronts and by a variety of means: the centralization of resources, even resources as basic as food ...'

His Eminence casts his eyes to the heavens from whence he hath his help.

'There's a centralization of the entire economy, ranging from vital medicines to the mind-altering shite we watch on television ...'

His Eminence apparently doesn't hear this bit.

'... and centralization of military and nuclear power, so that most countries today can be attacked by America at will. And America is on the attack. Whether or not the planet must be sacrificed doesn't seem to matter.'

'Please, allow me to comment,' His Eminence wheedles at this point. 'We were notta in favour of the invasion of Iraq. But we have to acknowledge that the Americans had certain reasons for that war, whether we agree with those or notta. To say, however, that there is an imperialist agenda is simply ridiculous. Such an agenda would notta be tolerated in the post-modern world.'

'Such an agenda wouldn't be tolerated if there were anyone strong enough to stop it. The only real threat to the empire is China, and the Americans are working very hard on that problem, and with catholic help, I may add.'

'Preposteroso! You will excuse me, Lama, if I say that this statement seems to me quite lunatic! This is notta the way to proceed!'

His Eminence's face grows rounder and redder. Jim's happy again. Things are going along at a smashing pace. I'm clearly nuts and the cardinal's puffily insulted. Can Batista be pushed over the edge? All that's needed now is a suave suggestion to lower the debate into the furnace of the hell-realms.

'Is the lama's statement really all that preposterous, Your Eminence!?' Jim blazes. 'Didn't the Vatican cooperate with the Americans to bring the Soviet Union to a fall!? It's common knowledge now that Pope John-Paul worked closely with the CIA! Jesuit priests were used as spies, Catholics in the eastern bloc were incited to rebel. There were all sorts of unholy shenannigans!'

'*Unholy?* It seems to me that you are the unholy one, insinuating such nonsense! We had a Christian responsibility in Russia, just as we have in China now. That is why we are at this time working so hard to improve our relations with the Chinese.'

'At the expense of the Tibetan people, according to Charlie!' Jim rages.

'At the espensa of the Tibetan people? Whatta rotta! Have you never heard of diplomacy? We must proceed delicately, for the sake of the Tibetans especially.'

'By delicately shafting the Dalai Lama.' says I.

'The reasons for that have nothing to do with China.'

'No,' says I. 'They have to do with America.'

'What canna you possibly be implying?'

'That you need to pretend to be playing along with the Chinese. You want them to welcome you into their territory.'

'Of course we want that! We want to be able to minister to our Catholic brothers and sisters! Is that so strange?'

'What you really want is to be America's eyes and ears in China, an espionage network and a destabilizing force.'

'Dear Lord Jesus Christa! You are certainly *matto*! *Pazzo*! Mad as a dogga! I won't standa for this, Jim! You cannotta broadcast such rubbish!'

'That's why the Americans were so displeased by my exposure of your meetings with the Chinese delegates—'

'Holy Mother of God!'

'—that they tried to have me killed, possibly without your knowledge.'

'Possibly without – *possibly without*!—'

Words fail His Eminence. For several seconds together they fail Jim too. Then, gathering up his stunned kundalini, he twists in his seat and snarls at me:

'On what evidence are you basing these ludicrous allegations?'

'I believe what the Buddha Maitreya has told me.'

Batista raises both hands in languid despair and shakes his fat head. He starts removing the tangle of recording equipment from around his neck and ears and gets to his feet. Jim silently watches him. The crew scratch themselves.

'Enough,' mutters His Eminence with a smile of disbelief. 'You will understand that I cannotta continue to participate in such a vaudeville of a farce.'

Jim rises to soothe the holy man's righteous indignation. The cardinal pats his hand paternally and leaves the room with a series of humble bows to the trembling crew. While I disentangle myself he shoots me a glance from the door. It communicates a blend of loathing so tangible that I recoil as from a slap.

'Shut it down,' says Jim to the crew. 'We can't air this.'

When the studio paraphernalia have all been hauled out he dismisses his attendants and is left alone with me.

'You were right about one thing,' he laments. 'You are my worst nightmare.'

'I only regret that this fiasco won't be broadcast.'

'Believe me, so do I, but I'm not allowed to broadcast messages on contemporary issues from the Buddha Maitreya to his vicar.'

'It's a great pity.'

'I'd like to ask you though, how reliable are Maitreya's sources?'

'He gets it straight from the horse's mouth.'

'Your death would have been a loss, Charlie. Be careful.'

'Is that why you won't put me on air?'

'No. Self-preservation's my game. I'd be laughed at. For me that'd be worse than being shot by an environmental sociopath. Besides, I guarantee you that everything you've said in this room is being fed to the networks as we speak. Every little sod that's just disappeared through that door will be on the phone by now, feeding you to those dogs you mentioned. You've no idea, Charlie, no idea.'

'Maybe not.'

'There is one more thing perplexes me. By giving away the American game, aren't you damaging the Tibetan cause? If what you say is true – and I of course don't believe a word of it – wouldn't it have been in the Tibetan interest to have kept it under your hat? It really seems as if you were on the Chinese side.'

'America and China are two sides of the same coin, Jim. If neither gives a shit about the planet, why should either give a fart about Tibet?'

'I wish I'd said that.'

Devastation Jim ain't kiddin'. Half an hour later, when I'm alone again (Vaclav-at-the-door excepted) and waiting to be thrown out of the grand suite by His Eminence, the story breaks on TV.

The talking head is a greying wall-eyed fella with an American flag tattooed on his soul. Beside him sits Miss Himachal Pradesh 2004, drinking in the American dream and giving the subtlest intimations of outraged head-shakes as he reports:

'And just in from Prague in the Czech Republic; Lama Charlie has accused the US government of hiring the hitman who tried but failed to assassinate him after a dinner date with a female friend. The woman, British journalist Mary Grimes, was slightly injured when the bullet grazed her left temple. Asked to provide evidence for his claim, Charlie cited – wait for it – the Booder Maitreya as his sole informant. Maitreya, in Boodist mythology, is the Booder-to-come, the Future Booder, who, says the self-styled lama, won't be coming after all. Why? Because there won't be a planet to return to, according to Charlie.'

Miss Himachal Pradesh can't suppress a smile. No; actually she's trying to duck beneath the desk and laugh out loud. George, the talking head, exhibits a facial control perfected through long experience of having to read with a deadpan expression the reams of delicious drivel and farce surprising him daily from the screen-prompt. With him the ticklings of hilarious bewilderment are all crammed into several nuances in the detached impartiality of his voice.

'To talk about Lama Charlie's allegations we have in our Washington studios former CIA Assistant Director of Public Relations, Mr Don Gonzales. What should we make of Charlie's claims, Don?'

'In a word, George, nothing.'

'You're telling me categorically that the CIA were not involved?'

'I'm telling you the CIA wouldn't stoop to involve itself with a man like Charlie. The guy's a stand-up comic and his act's in real bad taste. The only people who'd benefit from his death would be the Tibetans themselves, but I don't believe they'd use assassins. More likely they'd just put him into permanent deep meditation or something. This guy just can't be taken seriously.'

'Someone took him seriously enough to try to kill him, Don.'

'Yeah, a fellow loon, George; an unbalanced radical environmentalist.'

'According to Lama Charlie the US intends to use the Catholic Church to quote *spy on and destabilize* unquote the Chinese government. Any comments?'

'George, why would the US wanna use the Catholics to do a job that we're more than capable of doing for ourselves?'

'Charlie seems to think the church institution would provide the perfect cover.'

'Yeah, George. The way we do it is, we have the Catholics convert all the top leaders of the People's Republic of China and then we bug the confessionals. Then, George, if we find that one of the leaders has been plotting against the United States we instruct the Pope to excommunicate him. Works like crazy.'

'All right – ha ha ha ha ha ha – Thanks for coming on the show, Don.'

'Haw haw haw – my pleasure, George – haw haw haw …'

How are the British coping? I switch channels:

'—and from a somewhat embattled Conference of World Religions on Planetary Issues in Prague comes this piece of news, just in. The South African small-businessman popularly known as "Lama Charlie" who last night survived an attempt on his life, has claimed that the assassin known only as Gabik G. was hired by the Americans.

'US officials have reacted strongly to the lama's allegations, labelling him an attention-seeker and an irresponsible maverick with an obviously anti-American and anti-Catholic agenda. Charlie also claims that the Americans and the Vatican have established a partnership of convenience for the purpose of carrying out acts of espionage in China. So far there has been no response from Chinese officials. The Vatican has so far also declined to comment.

'And now in today's top story, British milkmen in the Greater London area are on strike for a third consecutive day …'

Then the sublime piece of news breaks on American TV about twenty minutes later. George and Miss Himachal Pradesh are ecstatically announcing that:

'Gabik G. has told police in Prague, the Czech Republic, that he was acting on his own and that his target was in fact British environmental and ecological reporter Mary Grimes. According to Gabik, a member of the ultra-radical underground environmental group "Enviro-KGB", Grimes has in the past written articles criticizing the group's radical tactics, especially their philosophy that violence was an acceptable method for achieving their aims. Gabik's view, said a spokesman for the team that interrogated him, is that Grimes is part of a media fifth column used by establishment institutions to play down their environmentally destructive policies and activities.'

I feel as though I'm drifting off to a nebulous and jittery sphere as yet unvisited by any other human mind. My hands and knees are shaking violently. My nose is vibrating like a clapper on a buzzer-bell. There's a cold steel clamp squeezing at my temples. My stomach lurches and heaves, rippling and knotting up the writhing large intestines. My heart is apparently trying to punch its way out through my chest. My lungs have ceased functioning altogether.

The ostentatious suite is now too busy and too vulgar, too full of furniture and gimmicks which threaten me with their multitudinity. It's too much of too many kinds crammed into a very small area. I feel overwhelmed, startled by each object as I look around, and crushed by the floor, walls and ceiling of the steadily shrinking living room. I make for the door, moving like a jelly escaping with wobbly difficulty from an over-ornate bowl.

When I come round I find myself laid out on the triple-size double bed. Vaclav and the rabbi are peering down at me. The former's pupils have all but entirely displaced his irises as he stares down vampirically at his troublesome charge. The latter is clucking.

'Goddamn it Charlie – shouldn't be saying that. Jesus Christ, you had me scared shitless. Thought some demented bastard finally got to you. Any number of possible ways; neurotoxins, slow-acting, one-of-a-million dirty chemical cocktails – who knows what! Thought it might have been Vladimir Putin over here. Bumped him around a bit. Jesus, Lama, he almost pulled a gun on me! What might have happened next? Who knows? I might have wound up dead too. Not that *you're* actually dead, yet.'

'Severe panic attack,' I whisper weakly.

'Under attack from every side, huh? It's in my face but I don't believe my eyes. A Buddhist monk blown over by a panic attack? You forgot to meditate, son? To switch on the third eye? You guys are supposed to be so calm it's an effort to elicit a knee-jerk reaction. What brought it on?'

I get up gingerly and repeat the story about Merry being the hitman's intended target. The rabbi has a laughter attack, pressing down on his yarmulke in case he guffaws it off his head. We go through to the living room and Vaclav goes out to take up his position as doorman.

'What brings you here, Rabbi?'

'Had a mystical feeling you might be under attack by panic. No, I came for several reasons. To wind things up you might say. Make sure you don't get lost in this jungle of perverted misinformation. Why? you might ask; why's Tanny taking such an interest in keeping me on the level? Because you don't deserve the shit they're going to pour all over you, Lama. At least, you don't deserve to be fooled by it.'

'Are you finally going to tell me who you are?'

'Haven't I told you, Charlie? I'm a minor diplomat of sorts, get jerked around all over the planet to report on things. Religion's my specialty though; I mean, the political side of religion. Religions, believe it or not, are an almighty danger in the modern world. Never was a time when they weren't. If you can sell someone religion, you can sell them anything, a kalashnikov, a homemade bomb, even an atomic device, see my point?'

'The CIA's religious department?'

'Between you and me, yes, something like that. But forget about the CIA. The CIA are a bunch of dilettante bunglers. Shouldn't have said that. Look, all you need to know is that I'm on your side. You're clean, no nonsense, you tell it like it is. Besides being a minor diplomat I'm a person too, a good Jewish person. I like the way you persevere, some might say *stupidly*, but you're the real thing. Now me, I don't suck up to any particular agenda. I'm employed by governments, *plural*. I'm up no-one-in-particular's ass. I have a green card and a lot of other cards besides. My job's to get at the truth behind the truth, just like you. The people I report to want the truth because there are wheels within the system's wheels, and very often, *very often*, the big wheels don't know what the smaller wheels are getting up to. That's why there have to be a lot of different fingers on the Big Red Button. Believe me, if it were up to the small wheels, the big bang would have happened a second time by now. Know why? Because the small wheels generally don't see the bigger picture, they just see the red button under their noses and it tempts the hell out of them. So let's just assume that some medium size wheel sent an instruction to a small wheel to pay a really insignificantly small nutcase scumbag wheel to shoot you, Lama, in the head. Was this done with the big wheel's consent or even tacit approval? If not, my job's to inform the big wheel so the medium size wheel gets it in the neck and the small wheel goes back to filing petty cash slips and the scumbag takes the full punishment of the law. Am I making sense? Once I get started! You mind if I help myself to a drink? I'm allowed a drink, nothing against it in the rabbinical law.'

I judder across to the mini-bar, my head still feeling weirdly elongated towards Nirvana. He watches me prepare the two drinks, whisky for him and a stiff brandy for myself. I throw mine back with a shudder and a sense of Buddhist remorse, but I need rapid restoration even at the cost of clarity.

'So it was, after all, myself that was to be shot in the head.'

'Slow down, Charlie. Yes, you were the target. Forget about the slop they're pouring out on the news. Damn typical clever: the killer freak had Mary in his sights, so it must be the freak operating out of his own *meshugga* top storey. After all, why would any government agency want Mary killed? And it leaves the maverick lama looking like – well – a *fool*. And the Americans can say, *Yeah, we told you he was a dangerous crackpot all along.*'

'But you know better.'

'It took me a while – not as sharp as I used to be. Like you, my first inclination was to stick it on the Chinese. But then I got to thinking all the obvious thoughts. For one thing, no Czech will work for a communist regime. Had the commies up their asses far too deep for far too long. So I did a bit of checking up, Charlie, and I can tell you this is a fact as certain as the holocaust – some say the holocaust never happened, can you get your head around that? – revisionist pricks. Charlie, the order from the medium sized wheel was that you should be frightened off, wounded at most. But I can tell you also that the order from the top had a sharper ring of finality. In this case the medium sized wheel took a different line, more compassionate, or just less dangerous for himself.'

'But the hired idiot wounded Mary instead.'

'Gabik's a born loser, what can I say?'

'And my life's still under threat.'

'Not after all this. Just too risky now. No need for any more panic attacks.'

'Mary's left the conference. It's clear she blames me for something.'

'Oh, *that*. I had to have a talk with her too, remind her to stay on my good side. She seemed pretty cut up. Scared stiff. Main thing is, her bosses have ordered her off your case. Not for her safety. Why should they care about that? Journalists are ten a penny. They gave her the line that you'd eventually take her down with you, know what I mean? She's bound to come out looking like a media fool if she associates herself with a public fool like your-self, not to mention the *World's Fools*. And if she comes out looking like a fool, it taints her company, and her bosses ... you follow? Her career's more important to her than you are, Lama. Who can blame or judge? She's a respected journalist. You're a shooting star.'

'I see.' (Rejection at an even shallower level.)

'It's good that you see. I've been helpful to you too, and my career's important to me as well, you follow? Tit for tat, Charlie. As far as you're concerned, you and I never discussed anything other than the degree of difference between the Buddhist and Judaic religious ethic, or whether and in what form God exists, or whatever.'

'Of course. Tomorrow this'll all be over anyway.'

'Over but not out. You've started a long and controversial conversation.'

'When do you leave?'

'I hang around here for another week or so to pick up various loose ends, including Gabik. But I didn't tell you that.'

'We're having a goodbye bash up here this evening.'

'No can do. This is it. Glad to have known you.'

He finishes his drink, lifts his bulk off the sofa, shakes my hand. I press my palms together from the heart. I've never been trusted this way before. His generous assessment of my character (and my sanity) have gone a long way to bringing about a deep acceptance of whatever obstacles I may have to face next.

I'm also left devastated by the lengths to which the establish-ment, in the name of the system which is its mother, father, sister and brother, will go to protect itself. It is quite Byzantine in its fanaticism. For how many decades now has heterodoxy again been punishable by imprisonment, torture, ostracism, and death?

Not that I'm suddenly struck down by the abstract fact of its tyranny. That's all old hat. It's in the having tasted it in its rawest form: the deviousness, heart-corruption, systematized malice, slight regard.

And now, Mary (because, really, *Merry* is no more) being com-pelled to come in. Yes, she may have felt, somewhere about the surface, that the lama had let her down and *turned her down*, but in the area of undeniable insight she must have known better. From the outset she was, after all, aware of his weaknesses and his rash impulsiveness. She must have known that she could finally have persuaded him to turn again, else she would not have taken the risk of so blatant an invitation; not she.

What actually injured her, I must suppose, was that I turned out to be a real fool after all. The metaphorical bullet that clawed her temple was my refusal to establish myself as a force credible enough to be used for her own elevation, that she could show off as her *find*. But the find turned out to be only what it had always been, a knot of self-doubt disguised beneath an impossible demand for objective honesty. The man who was born to be found out, and to be content in that matrix.

Not that she saw all this for herself. It took someone unattached to the phenomenon, unthrilled by the ride, to point out to her what the world would say, and was already saying, about the buzzard in red and yellow. For her, I now realize, acting outside the system meant living at its exciting periphery, but not utterly beyond its security. It was Helena Pikardt she should have betted on and elab-orated for her own ends, and not the friend of such outsiders as Paw Paw, Tyrone and Koomaraswami.

I walk over to the window and look out across the steepled city. It's spread out tiredly in the hazy evening air, waiting for the sudden surge of night to light it up with a new round of buzzing, self-destructive life.

All tending towards death, my death.

Withdrawing to the bedroom, I slowly disrobe – donkha, zen, shemdap. I fold them with habitual tenderness, the more poignant for knowing that it's all finally over. I've been the monk I always knew I should have been. Now it's done and I can cast it off, not for the sake of this or that adventure in being human, but because the monk has actually lived and died.

Worthily, I hope.

And, *crazily*, at least in the eyes of that composite demon into whose ugly truth I have bludgeoned my way, and managed – by the infallible operation of cause and effect – to hit a nerve.

I'm satisfied.

Pulling on my jeans and an old striped shirt, I feel as though I'm entering on a new and foreign life, in which I may well feel *lost and at home, but not unhappy.*

Then the goons arrive.

Paw Paw's whizzing ahead on the nebulous plateau beyond inebriation. He shakes my hand as though we're meeting for the first time. Perhaps it's the sudden absence of the robes. He takes in the ritzy suite, looks into my face, recognizes me as the unlikely occupant, and begins to weep like a bereaved mother.

Tyrone, ignoring the obvious element of alcoholic remorse, puts an arm around his shoulder and pats, pats, consolingly. I'm reminded of the episode with Beelzebub. The warmth in Mather's eyes and the fatherly patience in his voice are quite disconcerting, like seeing a childhood friend suddenly all grown up.

Koomaraswami embraces me.

'It's all still going along vrry vell,' he assures me. 'Quite swimmingly, relly.'

'Yes. It's your responsibility now. As you see, I've disrobed.'

'I know, Lama.'

'You know?'

'Oh yes, oh yes. You're not wearing your robes – ha ha ha. But seerrsly, I know that you've fulfilled your role. It has been quite a lead role too, if I may grope for a hollywoodism. You must go home now. But I've only just found my home, you see. Among one-hundrrd-forrty-nine-tousand fools.'

'Not growing less then? In spite of the lunatic lama?'

'Oh no, quite the contrary. As one fellow writes – we have a huge inbox now – he writes: *If the choice is between Maitreya and the leaders of the world, it's Maitreya I'll believe every time.*'

'I believe Maitreya too!' wails Paw Paw while Tyrone pats.

'Pity Maitreya won't be coming back, least not this time.'

'But he *has* come back,' says Koomaraswami impatiently. 'Or do you seerrsly believe that a global rrbellion of fools was something thought up by a mere ordinrry person, a mere bluddy anybody?'

'I believe Maitreya,' Paw Paw repeats, 'because he spoke to me. He told me all about the bishop's Xhosa wife and his son, the priest.'

I am reeling.

'You made all that up, Paw Paw?'

'No, Chahli. Maitreya told me.'

'My God, Paw Paw ...'

'Yes. But at least I did not relay Maitreya's information to the world at large.'

'Then why did the bishop jump?'

'Yeah, Charlie, why?' Mather wonders. 'All we heard were those weird last syllables, ya know, *bayjee* or *beejee lokooter* or something. We'll never know what he was really trying to say.'

While I sag inwardly under the shifting weight of fact and hallucination Paw Paw bursts into tears again. The pain and urgency of the past three days dissolve like the mist on the Vltava. Everything is suddenly thrown back into a sealed-off past, as if all these events and mindstates have been part of some lonely dream.

Paw Paw eventually dries up and the three goons fall to debating. It's outlandish, raucous, rent by laughter. Most of what they're asserting and refining doesn't make clear sense, even to me. They've taken it to a higher plane altogether, where a disrobed monk, apostate, can't follow. An intimation of sadness rises in me as I see them soar.

CHAPTER 13

In Which The Eternal Cycle Returns To
The Point Of Departure

After Vaclav had escorted me to the airport and all the way to the departure gate I was, figuratively speaking, on my own again. My life, at least, was no longer at risk because a hundred TV analysts had ensured the world at large that I was oppressed by several forms of socially disruptive dementia.

I was not literally alone. The flight back to South Africa, with a stopover in Paris – I wasn't allowed to pop in on the city of lights – was crammed, and no one had invited me up to business class. I had Paw Paw for company, but the intimacy was all in the snoring and gasping that erupted from the seat beside mine as the crudely chiselled academic slept off his cumulative hangover.

We arrived in the early evening. As I came through the gate a happy screech went up from Jessie who scrambled across to hug and kiss me while Adam loitered nearby with his hands embarrassedly stuck in his pockets.

Then I ran the gauntlet of guileless love (Clara), unquenchable suspicion (Papa Italo), pretence at familial acceptance (Mauro), and the renewed bonds of volatile conjugal friendship that had made up most of the sense of my life.

'Thank God you didn't pitch up in those robes,' cried Mona, pecking up at my cheek, 'and your hair's beginning to grow back. Look at him papa! He looks like Ben Kingsley playing Gandhi!'

'Telly Savalas,' muttered Italo who knew neither the Mahatma nor Sir Ben. 'But at least Savalas had style.'

'Charlie's got style too, papa. He just needs a hair-style.'

'And hair,' said Mauro.

But Clara said, 'Daddy doesn't need style.'

Outside, along the paved expanse of the drop-off zone, were gathered a troupe of media monkeys and a stampede of the South African World's Fools. No longer insulated by my robes, I was at a loss how to react to either. I was at a loss to know, also, what had become of the lama. I poked around inside my mind only to come face to face in every corner with the well-known Mr Charles Fincham, tired, bedraggled and defensively anxious.

So I smiled, waved briefly and resumed pushing my luggage trolley with gathering speed. Perhaps they would guess at my exhaustion or suddenly see through me or respect my nuclear family reunion and simply let me go.

But I was ambushed by cynicism from the troupe and worship from the stampede. To the media I said nothing, Mauro helping me by physically fending off the cameras and microphones. I thought at one point he might stoop to using his fists again. The idea didn't rouse my aversion.

It was clear that the Fools, on the other hand, considered themselves – however much I yearned to disown them – the offspring of my vision. So I allowed them to batter me with shouts of acclamation and a good number of protest chants and songs. Then I told them that they must look in future to Koomaraswami for leadership.

'Who's he?' someone attired in masochist neo-gothic wanted to know.

'The Indian bloke on the website,' I called out over the gathered heads.

'What's a bloke?'

'A very high-ranking guru.'

Paw Paw now came through the exit doors, stepping gingerly among the demons of his hangover. Seeing the gathered crowd, he tottered up with an air of familiarity, perhaps believing he might still be in Prague. The black kids in the group, recognizing him from the footage taken in the parking lot of the Best Hotel, cheered with gusto, as though they were about to be liberated all over again.

It seemed an auspicious situation into which I determined to read as much karmic significance as possible. Lifting up his arm as Helena had raised mine in Wenceslas Square, I introduced him as the leader of the World's Fools in sub-Saharan Africa. He accepted the appointment with a gracious attitude of entitlement. And incorrigible Paw Paw, taking heart, opened his maw to begin roaring out a provocative impromptu speech on the state of the dying planet.

'Can we get the hell out of here now?' Mauro pleaded. I greeted the raucous assembly, palms together, nose red and twitching, and left them to their gesticulating messiah.

Mauro drove us to the apartment, Papa Italo beside him arguing over the best route to take, the dubious quality of his driving skills and whether the traffic lights were red, amber or green. Sitting in the backseat with Mona, I closed my eyes and felt her hand reach out for mine.

Once home, I was pressed to relate the entire odyssey, my mythological part in it and, of course, *myself*. It was hard going, involving the need for delicate omissions, reticent understatement and even blatant fiction, all in the service of higher truth.

In the evening Precious Teacher arrived for supper, a small homecoming surprise arranged by Mona. We all sat for a while in silence, adjusting and reconfirming our interrelatedness. Then Teacher laughed out loud, infecting us all. When the commotion had settled down he inquired simply, 'So, Chully, you hava enjoying the conference?'

'There were some daunting moments.'

'That is very much usual in such busy and intense situations. So many ideas and activities in such small time.'

'True.'

'I think you hava done a very good job.'

'Not from the Catholic point of view,' said Italo.

'Dumb thing to do,' Mauro opined, 'going for the Americans like that.'

'Oh fuck the Americans,' said Clara, staring him down, amazing us all.

'I hope that's not your view on the Catholics too,' Papa Italo gasped.

'No, Poppa, it isn't. I have a different, more *contumelious* view on them.'

'I'm glad to hear that. They make mistakes. They're human. But they're ours.'

Adam bit down hard on his bunched up napkin.

'It's the planet that matters,' said Jessie.

'It's how you live on the planet that matters,' said Mona, 'otherwise there's no point in having a planet.'

'And for popularizing that integral truth,' Adam grimaced, 'we're indebted to Lama Charlie and the World's Fools. Let's hope they're all wrong in their prognosis.'

'That is your only hope,' said Precious Teacher. 'And that is very for certain.'

Later, in the glowing darkness of the bedroom, I lay beside Mona.
'Charles?'
'Yes.'
'Everything has to change now.'
'I know.'
'Of course *you* know. Now I have to know.'
'You'll know. It's all there inside you. Just don't be afraid.'
'Mmmm ... Charles?'
'Yes.'
'What happened with the blonde?'
'You mean the journalist?'
'Yes, Charles, the fricking blonde journalist Mary Grimes.'
'Well, nothing *happened*. She buzzed off, you know. Got cold
feet. It seems she wasn't prepared to risk her career by being associ-
ated any longer with the dubious character you sketched on televi-
sion. Gave me up as a bad job, saw through me, wanted me
scratched off her résumé – I don't know.'
'That your theory?'
'Yes, along with the fact that she wasn't pleased at taking a bullet
on my behalf'
'She didn't tell you then?'
'Tell me what?'
'That I called her up.'
'*You called her up*? When?'
'Yesterday, to the Best Hotel.'
'You called her up in Prague? For God's sake! *Why*?'
'You have the fricking bumption to ask *why*?'
'You mean *gumption*? Well, I have the bumption to ask why
because I want to know what you had in mind, *this time*.'
'I wanted to tell her some things, Charles, about us. About me.
About you. I think I got through very clearly. What's the word? –
penetrated? Yes, I think it penetrated.'
'I really don't know what to say. Blimey! God! No, I just
don't know.'
'Just say *thank you*, Charlie; say *thank you for caring enough*.'
I am silenced and touched by irritation, and happy that my own
world of love and meaning has been re-established, whether by
love, luck, or sheer *bumption*. I know how sorely I have always
needed this safe place of the heart and mind where Charlie dwells
at ease.

I'm done with the lama. I want to be human. I want to share my life.

My last thoughts while being pulled gently down into the twilight of sleep are of the robes I've left behind in the glitzy suite of the Best Hotel. Into whose hands, I wonder, will they fall? And to what purpose?

Acknowledgments

The four concluding lines of *The Hollow Men* are taken from T.S. Eliot's poem in *The Complete Poems and Plays of T. S. Eliot*, 1969, Faber & Faber, London. The lines from Rabelais are taken from *Gargantua & Pantagruel, transl. J.M. Cohen*, 1955, Penguin Classics, Harmondsworth.

The lines from *Verses Written After an Ecstacy of High Exaltation* are taken from Roy Campbell's translation in *St John Of The Cross: Poems*, 1960, Penguin Classics, Harmondsworth. The sub-headings in Ch. 5 are paraphrased from James Martin, *The Meaning of the 21st Century*, 2006, Transworld Publishers, London.

Lightning Source UK Ltd.
Milton Keynes UK
20 May 2010

154434UK00001B/17/P